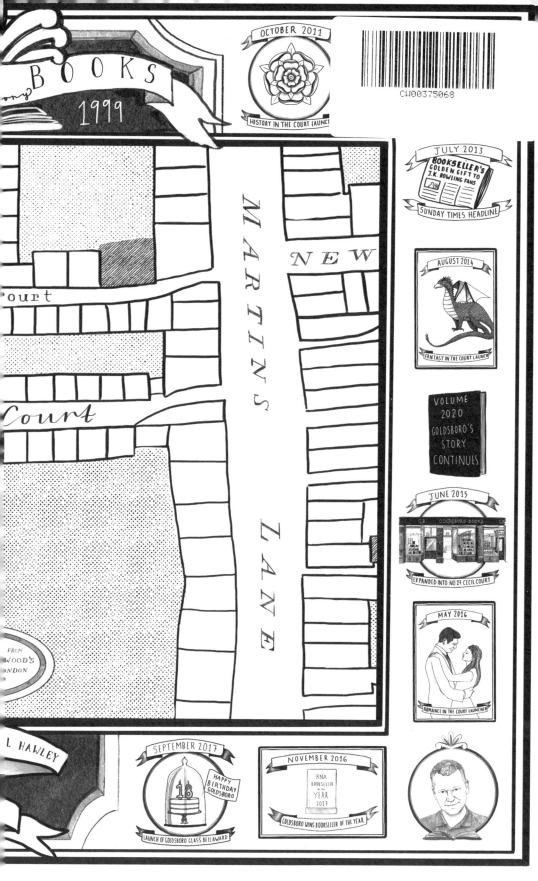

·

First Edition

First Edition

21 Years of Goldsboro Books

No. 409

One of 1,000 numbered copies of the first edition

THE
DOME
PRESS

Published by The Dome Press, 2020

A CIP catalogue record for this book is available from the British
Library

ISBN: 9781912534388

The Dome Press
23 Cecil Court
London WC2N 4EZ

www.thedomepress.com

Printed and bound in Great Britain by Clays Ltd, Elcograf S.p.A.

Typeset in Garamond by Elaine Sharples

Welcome to *First Edition*, an anthology of short stories by some of our favourite writers, which we have commissioned to help us mark 21 years of Goldsboro Books. Contributors were invited to write stories about anything that they wished and there were no rules. Thank you to everyone for writing your pieces; all of you who have contributed have helped make Goldsboro Books the success it is, so this is an anthology that celebrates good writing and Goldsboro Books.

Goldsboro Books was incorporated as a limited company on 30th September 1999. This anthology, published on 30th September 2020 marks our 21st birthday and we could not be prouder of this diverse, beautiful, charming and thrilling collection of writing.

No business can survive without support from others. We have been incredibly fortunate to have support from so many people. Please accept our sincere thanks, whether you have been employees, customers, authors, publicists, editors, friends and family, there are too many to list but we hope that you know who you are.

We would like to give special thanks to our current colleagues, Pavla Safratova, Brett Kirchner, Rebecca McDonnell and Elizabeth Melbourne. It is a pleasure to work with you and we thank you for your good humour and dedication in helping build Goldsboro Books into the much-admired independent bookshop that it has become.

Thank you, Emily Glenister, for all of your hard work in producing this book, for being such a brilliant colleague to work with and keeping us secure in the knowledge that everything is always safe in your hands. Thank you to Broo Doherty for your keen eye in proofreading. Thanks also to Rebecca Lloyd.

To all of the authors who have signed books for us over the past 21 years, your support has meant so much and we are incredibly grateful.

Finally, to the reader, thank you for purchasing *First Edition*, we hope that you enjoy this collection of stories.

David H. Headley   Daniel Gedeon

Contents

Introduction

In 2005, along with photographers Ross Gillespie and Tricia Malley, I published a non-fiction book called *Rebus's Scotland*. Ross and Tricia did my book jackets at the time, composing atmospheric shots of John Rebus's Edinburgh haunts. The book was their idea. It would collect dozens of their black-and-white photographs, showing different aspects of contemporary Scotland. I was asked to contribute some text and had the notion of using the book to answer various frequently asked questions about Rebus himself, while also adding autobiographical snippets of my own.

One chapter would discuss my use of music in the books. That chapter was titled 'Does Rebus Like The Cure?' To my mind this was a question worthy of serious consideration. I'd always liked The Cure, and had even named one of my books (*The Hanging Garden*) after a song of theirs. Indeed, I'd gone further, incorporating more of their songs into the book and quoting lines from the title song along the way. Because I was quoting from a song, I thought I'd better ask permission. But I was living in rural France at the time. I bought all my CDs from a supermarket in Périgueux. I had no idea how to go about asking, but I did have those CD sleeves, on which the band's official fan club address was listed. Weeks later, the phone rang. The woman on the other end – I never caught her name – said she was the band's manager. She had taken my request to lyricist Robert Smith and he had agreed that I could quote from the song. There would be a fee, of course – Mr Smith wanted a signed copy when the book was published. I hung up the phone, elated and full of gratitude, only to realise I had no way of contacting musician or manager. This was the mid-1990s. I had a landline and a fax machine and not much else. So, when *The Hanging Garden* was eventually published in 1998, Mr Smith did not get his copy.

Would Rebus like The Cure? Probably not as much as I do. I'm not sure the old curmudgeon has enjoyed much music that has been produced after the mid-1970s. He grew up a generation before me, so would have been listening to The Who, the Stones and The Kinks in his bedroom, while I was playing T. Rex, Hawkwind and Alex Harvey. The village where I grew up boasted neither a record shop nor a bookseller. The local newsagent had a carousel of lurid paperbacks by the likes of Sven Hassel and Harold Robbins, but for real sustenance I'd have to take a bus to nearby Kirkcaldy. Even if I couldn't afford a new release, I could hang out in Bruce's record shop, poring over album sleeves. John Menzies boasted both record and book departments, so that seemed like a goldmine. And when a small independent bookshop opened around 1976, I haunted the place. It wasn't much bigger than the library in my village, but to me it was a Tardis, each shelf a universe to be explored.

The one thing I really missed, during the six years my wife and I spent in south-west France, was easy access to a decent English-language bookshop. On trips back to the UK (usually to Edinburgh for research and London to meet publisher and agent), I would stock up on hardbacks and paperbacks (and videos, too, if I'm being honest). There would also, of course, be the agony of finding few, if any, of my own books in those bookshops, but this made me more determined than ever to write a better book next time, a book that couldn't be ignored. *Black and Blue*, the Rebus novel prior to *The Hanging Garden*, was my first success, in that it won the Gold Dagger for the best crime novel published in 1997. Sales thereafter began to creep up. At the same time, we made the move back to the UK, two small sons in tow. Thankfully, sales kept on increasing, and it seemed

I could relax a bit. I was going to be able to continue to write full-time. We might even manage a mortgage.

It niggled me, however, that Mr Smith had never received his copy of *The Hanging Garden*. A few years passed and my publisher decided it was time to re-jacket my backlist titles. Would I consider writing a new introduction to each volume? I did so, and mentioned along the way that I owed Robert Smith a book. Someone who knew Mr Smith eventually read that introduction and shared it with him. A message reached me: he still wanted the book, and here was the address to send it to. I went to my shelves and found a first edition hardback, signed it and stuck it in a padded envelope, walking with it to the post office. Job done and honour satisfied at long last.

Another year or two passed, and we moved into a new house, far larger than our previous one. A carpenter constructed some beautiful bookcases in the living-room, and I began to place my own books on them – which was when I noticed that I had sent Robert Smith my last remaining hardcover copy of *The Hanging Garden*.

Oops.

Luckily, around this time I'd also been invited to sign my latest release at Goldsboro Books, a lovely shop on a charming street and a tireless champion of the crime and thriller genres. While there, seated at a desk, scribbling away, I happened to mention my Robert Smith anecdote. Well, Goldsboro just happened to have a first edition hardcover of *The Hanging Garden* in one of their glass display cases. It was fetched and I was duly presented with it – gratis, free and for nothing. Which is another reason why I love Goldsboro Books.

Almost as much as I love Robert Smith and The Cure.

Ian Rankin

A Little Respect

Amer Anwar

Trip felt like he might die.

All right, maybe that was a bit of an exaggeration, he told himself, but the punch he'd just taken to his body had delivered an electric jolt of pain all through his insides and sent needles prickling across his scalp. It had hurt him – but he couldn't afford to show his opponent that. Trip was a pro. He kept his facial expression rigid. The only giveaway, the tensing of the muscles around his jaw and eyes.

He needed to buy some time to get over the shock and allow the pain to subside. His only options were to keep moving and stay out of range or else tie up his younger opponent. Backing off would be seen as weakness. Trip decided on the latter option. He had to be careful though, another punch to the body like that, especially to his liver, could put him on his knees.

He got his hands up to protect himself and started circling to his left, sucking in air through his nose and willing the pain away, all with his eyes fixed on the man in front of him. Trip didn't know how long was left to go but he did know he'd have to front it out. He couldn't go chasing or attacking, he had to conserve his strength. It'd be better to wait for his opponent to come to him. And, as expected, that was exactly what happened. The other guy rolled his big shoulders and came at him.

Trip psyched himself up for action. He feinted with his left, and stepped forward, throwing a straight right with some weight behind it. He had to grit his teeth against a sudden stab of pain in his side. The punch landed on his opponent's arm, which was up to protect himself. Trip hadn't expected it to get through the defence and actually hurt the guy. As that punch landed, Trip was already twisting from the waist to whip around a left hook at his opponent's head. It was a common enough combination and the other guy instinctively set himself to receive it on a boulder-like deltoid.

Trip had closed the distance between them and now threw the right again, but this time slightly wide. It seemed like the punch missed its mark, going over his opponent's shoulder then around behind his head, causing Trip to overbalance and stumble forward, holding onto the other guy for balance. Trip grabbed the back of the younger man's head and pulled it forward into his shoulder. To anyone watching it would look innocuous enough, like an instinctive attempt to keep from bundling both of them over – but it was, in fact, a calculated move, professionally executed.

With the referee on his right, Trip hooked his left arm around and under his opponent's, immobilising it, so the guy couldn't hit him with it. At the same time Trip, still pretending to be off-balance, put all his weight onto the other guy and forced him backwards.

Trip heard the CLACK-CLACK-CLACK of the wooden clapper, the timekeeper signalling there were just ten seconds to go until the end of the round.

'Get... fuck off me, old man,' his opponent said, around his gum shield.

The hell he would. All Trip had to do was keep the guy tied up for a few more seconds.

He tried to push Trip off, without success.

'OK, come on now, break it up,' the ref said, though without much urgency, as he also knew the round was just about over.

Then, DING-DING-DING came the welcome sound of the bell and the promise of a minute's respite. Trip let go.

The younger man looked at him with fire in his eyes. 'You hurt.' It wasn't a question. 'Holding on for your life. You going down, old man.'

There was that old man jibe again. Trip resisted the urge to say, '*On your momma,*' and turned away to go back to his corner to compose himself. Tyrone had the stool waiting for him.

'How you doing?' his trusty trainer and cornerman asked, as he plucked Trip's gum shield from his mouth.

'Like I been hit by a train.'

'That good, huh?'

Trip took in deep lungfuls of air. 'Remind me again why I took this fight.'

'Cause you got bills to pay and you was always too shit to be a footballer.'

'Remind me again why I got you as a cornerman.'

'Cause of my boxing brain and my smouldering good looks.'

'Ha!' Trip had to laugh. Tyrone gave him water from an ice-cold bottle. Trip slooshed it round his mouth then spat into the bucket Tyrone held, before taking a proper drink. Sonny, his cutman, towelled the sweat from his face. Trip looked at Tyrone. 'What's your boxing brain say I should do about him?'

'Don't let him hit you.'

'Is that it?'

'Manage that and you might even walk out of here with some dignity.'

'Yeah, but what about actually boxing the guy? Trying to beat him?'

Tyrone gave Trip a stern look. 'We both know we ain't here for you to win this fight. Best you can hope for is it'll go to points and, to do that, you got to go the distance. Only way that'll happen is if he don't hit you, least not too much.'

'I know that already. Guy punches like a flippin' sledgehammer.'

'Then just do what I'm telling you and don't let him hit you.'

'What the hell you think I been doing?'

'I don't know, but he keeps landing on you the way he has been, you ought to change your name to Heath Row.' Sonny was smearing Vaseline heavily across Trip's brows, cheekbones and chin to help punches slide off without tearing the skin and cutting him.

'You're a regular comedian, ain't you?' Trip told Tyrone.

'A hell of a lover too. Just ask Lisa.'

'What the bloody—'

A whistle blew to signal the minute was almost up.

'Use that anger in the ring,' Tyrone said. 'Channel it. Here.' He shoved the gum shield back in Trip's mouth and clambered out of the ring with Sonny. 'And remember, don't let him hit you.'

Yeah, right, like he hadn't worked that last bit out for himself. Tyrone was always winding him up about his wife, Lisa. Using a boxing analogy, which Tyrone was very fond of doing, he maintained that Trip was punching well above his weight with her. That might have been true, but they'd been happily married for twelve years and Trip knew he had nothing to worry about – especially not as far as Tyrone was concerned. His friend and trainer was twelve years his senior, with the physique of a medicine ball and a personality coarser than P40 grit sandpaper. Any sexual adventures he was having were restricted to women with bad eyesight, very low standards or a combination of both.

'Seconds out. Round six.' DING-DING-DING!

Forget about Tyrone and Lisa – time to focus. His opponent, Ashley 'Dynamite' Davis, was already in the centre of the ring waiting for him, eyes brimming with malice.

Davis was just twenty-one, fifteen years younger than Trip, and the fast-rising star of British boxing. A talented amateur, he'd turned pro at nineteen and since then had worked his way quickly up the rankings. Everyone knew he and his team had their sights set on big things: a British title, followed by a European then a World. The sooner they could achieve that goal, the sooner they'd be able to reap the rewards, and the longer Davis's career in the top flight might be.

That was where Trip came in. For Davis to be able to contend for a British title, he had to work his way up the rankings system and, to do that, he had to fight other ranked fighters, not just those lower-ranked but more experienced, higher-ranked fighters – fighters like Trip. And Davis was going through them fast.

Despite the age difference, Trip had managed to maintain a relatively high ranking by fighting regularly, two to three fights a year, against opponents ranked fairly close to him, where his skill and experience could work in his favour and the other fighters would benefit from a bout with a well-known name. Trip had fought for the British Middleweight title three times over the years but been unsuccessful on each occasion. After the third failed attempt, Tyrone had suggested he ought to change his boxing nickname from 'Triphammer' to 'Trip-up' Taylor, on account of how he always seemed to fall at the final hurdle.

Hoping not just to trip him up but knock him on his ass, was Ashley 'Dynamite' Davis, so-called because of the explosive power of his punches. 'Come on, old man,' he said, as they came within range of each other.

Trip tried to ignore the remark and flicked out a jab.

Davis leaned away from it then came back with a jab of his own. 'You're a fucking caveman, you know that? Like that what's-his-name? Fred Flintstone, that's it. That's you.' The kid was trying to distract him by talking, hoping to mess with his concentration. He followed the jibe with a quick left and a big, hard right, that Trip just managed to step out the way of. 'I'm going to tear you up like a T-Rex.'

Trip didn't react. He didn't have the energy to waste and needed to stay focused, ready for whatever Davis tried. Still, it was having an effect on him, riling him up, maybe not consciously but deep down inside. It wouldn't have bothered him usually; a bit of sledging was something to be expected. But this kid was brash and arrogant, with absolutely no humility whatsoever. For all the trash-talking before a fight to help sell tickets and bring in a good TV audience, once fighters got in the ring, they showed each other at least a little respect – but not this kid.

Davis moved. A quick step forward and a sudden left hook coming to the body. Trip instinctively brought his arm down to block. He took the punch on his elbow. As soon as he did, Davis switched from downstairs to upstairs and brought his left round in a hook going for Trip's head. Trip saw it coming just in time and managed to get his guard back up to block that too. The blow landed like a club and threw him off balance, straight into the path of a big right.

Trip didn't have time to manoeuvre more elegantly. He simply threw his arms in front of himself to block it and absorbed the force of the punch, feeling it right up into his shoulders. Shit. It would have looked desperate to the judges at the ringside – but it was better than the alternative. His legs were still solid and he used them to carry him around to the left and out of range, to regain his composure.

'Stick and move,' Trip heard Tyrone shouting from the corner. 'STICK. AND. MOVE!' That was easy for him to say. Moving around the ring took energy, so did throwing and blocking punches, let alone getting hit. Much as he didn't like to, Trip had to admit he wasn't used to this kind of pace anymore. It had been a while since he'd fought someone this young – or this intent on knocking him out.

Come on, think. Use your head and your experience. Make it count. He had to come up with a plan. He spent most of the round floating around his opponent and the ring, throwing jabs and moving, not remaining still to trade punches or get hit.

But Davis was no slouch. He continually moved to cut off the ring, forcing Trip to change direction and, finally, managed to back Trip into a corner. It was a bad position to be in, especially against a big puncher like Davis. Once he had him there, the youngster unleashed a barrage of punches. All Trip could do was cover-up, try to glimpse the punches coming at him and slip them, moving from side to side. He knew he had to get out of there but, every time he tried to move out of the corner, Davis would punch or push him back.

When Davis couldn't get through Trip's guard to his head, he aimed his punches lower. One, two, three hooks slammed into his right side. Trip felt the shock of the punches go through his body and his arm came down as a reflex, to try and shield himself from the attack. It was what Davis had wanted. He must have been waiting for the opening. As soon as Trip's guard came down on that side, Davis brought a scything hook up and over and caught Trip bang on the cheek.

It was like being hit with a brick. If it had landed on his temple or his chin, that might have been it, lights out. The force of the punch reverberated through his head, disorienting him. His legs went wobbly, as if his bones had turned to rubber. Leaning back on the corner pad was the only thing keeping him upright. He had to concentrate with everything he had just to maintain focus. Good job he managed it, too; Davis, sensing the effect of the punch, was setting himself for another big hook to end the fight.

Trip saw the punch coming through a mental fog, slowed down as if in a dream. His boxer's brain screamed at him to get out of the way but his limbs seemed frozen. He was able to move just enough to push his weight onto the pad behind him and lean his head back as far as he could. The punch whistled past his nose, the air it displaced cooling the sweat on his brow.

Davis had overcommitted to the knockout blow and it spun him so he was now side on to Trip who, using the rebound from the corner pad, launched himself forward and threw his arms around Davis's head, like a drowning man, clinging to a piece of flotsam. It was scrappy and obvious but Trip didn't give a shit. He just had to hold on long enough to clear his head.

Then: DING-DING-DING! It was the end of the round, the ref

pulling them apart and pushing them towards their respective corners.

Trip had been so concentrated on staying on his feet, he hadn't even heard the ten-second clacker. He tried walking as normally as possible but was sure he looked as if he'd had several pints. He already started to feel a bit better by the time he made it to the stool.

'How you walked back over here by yourself, I'll never know,' Tyrone said. He took a bottle and tipped ice water over Trip's head. The shock of it helped to revive him further and sharpen his senses. Sonny towelled him down and took a closer look at Trip's face. 'Better stick the iron on that,' Tyrone told Sonny, as he put an ice pack on the back of Trip's neck.

Sonny took the iron out of its bag of ice. The enswell was a small block of metal, kept cold for just this kind of thing. Sonny pressed it to Trip's right cheek, under the eye, to help reduce the swelling that was starting to come up. He kept it there while he wiped Trip's face down and reapplied fresh Vaseline with his other hand.

'You sure you want to carry on?' Tyrone asked Trip.

Feeling better than he had and taking deep breaths to reoxygenate himself, Trip looked at Tyrone. 'The fuck you talking about? Course I want to carry on.'

'I don't want to see you get hurt, man. It ain't worth it.'

'What else can we do?'

'You can always stay put. Don't get up for the next round. That'll be it.'

'No fucking way.'

Trip had been a fighter pretty much his whole life. He'd always given his all, in the gym and in the ring, and had never thrown in the towel. He wasn't about to start now – and definitely not to the brash, arrogant kid in the opposite corner.

'Then what the fuck you going to do? He's younger, faster and stronger than you. Only a matter of time till he lays you out flat on your back – *or worse.*'

'Thanks for the vote of confidence,' Trip said, 'but I got a plan.'

'It a funeral plan?'

'No, a plan to fight him.'

'Fight him? You barely survived the last round. How you think you're going to fight him? Man, he must've hit you harder than we thought.'

'Nah. It came to me while I was in that corner and slipped that last hook. Got me thinking about Ali and the Rumble in the Jungle, the rope-a-dope.'

Tyrone looked at Trip as if he'd lost his mind. 'Man, what the fuck you talking about? You concussed? Two things wrong with all of that: one, everyone knows the rope-a-dope, so ain't no way that'll work; and, two, I hate to break it to you, but you ain't no Ali.'

'I know all that. Look, it's a risk, but I got to take it.' The whistle blew for the seconds to get out of the ring. 'Just don't stop the fight,' Trip said and then walked to the centre of the ring as the bell sounded for the start of the seventh round.

Davis was waiting for him. 'Saved by the bell, old man. Won't be so lucky next time.'

Yeah, whatever. Trip had a plan and it didn't involve him going the distance, because even he doubted, realistically, he'd be able to last that long. It was all-or-nothing – and he was prepared to commit fully. Win or lose, he would go down fighting. This round he would need to expend a lot of energy. The knowledge that he wasn't aiming to go the distance freed Trip up to dance around the ring more, throw more punches and generally act like he wasn't taking Davis seriously. If he'd been playing safe and conserving his energy for the later rounds it would've been a completely different story.

Trip tried to move like his younger self, faster, more agile, more aggressive, snapping out the jab, following it with rapid-fire combinations and skipping out of the way before Davis could land anything of his own. Trip felt like a completely different fighter in the seventh round. It didn't just surprise the crowd, it confused and infuriated Davis, who couldn't quite understand what was going on.

It couldn't last, though. Trip was no longer the young fighter he'd once been. He started to flag towards the end of the round – but he pushed on, kept himself going, knowing he just had to make it to the bell. He grinned around his gum shield at Davis, made a show of enjoying himself and saw the anger blazing in his opponent's eyes. Davis didn't like being disrespected either. Good.

The clacker sounded ten seconds to the end of the round. Davis launched an attack. He charged forward behind a jab, followed quickly with a straight right but Trip had already slipped to the side and Davis's punches sailed through the air and left him hanging over the ropes, looking down at ringside. He straightened and spun round, just as the bell went. Trip gave him a big grin and went back to his corner.

'Man, that was amazing,' Tyrone said, as Trip slumped onto the stool. 'You do that for the next four rounds, we might have a chance. Though I don't think winding him up like that's such a good idea.'

'Fuck that,' Trip replied. 'No way I can do even one more round like that. My lungs are on fire.' He filled his lungs as fully as he could and gratefully drank the icy water Tyrone gave him. Sonny applied the iron to his cheek again and started wiping his face down.

'Then what the hell was that for?' Tyrone asked. 'What you going to do next? I got a perfectly good towel here I can throw in that ring.'

'No way. Don't you even think about it. I told you, I spotted something when he had me pinned in that corner before. I got a trick in mind.'

'A trick? What you going to do…? Disappear in the middle of the ring?'

'No.'

'Make *him* disappear?'

'No, man.'

'Then, less you're going to pull a rabbit out your arse to distract him while you knock him out, ain't no trick going to help you.'

Trip kept filling his lungs and exhaling slowly, getting as much oxygen into his bloodstream as he could before the next round. 'Just you watch and see,' he said, between breaths. Sonny had finished greasing his face. Tyrone gave Trip some more water and shoved his gum shield back into his mouth. The whistle sounded and the seconds got themselves out of the ring. 'Just remember,' Trip told Tyrone, 'don't you stop the fight. I mean it.'

'OK, fine... you crazy bastard.'

Davis was on his feet and glaring across the ring at Trip, who continued to breathe calmly and deeply. It would have to be this round. Trip knew he couldn't last much longer before the kid finished him off. How did that saying go? Something like, *you can plan and plan but it all goes out the window as soon as you get punched in the face.* Weren't that the truth?

The bell sounded and Trip went into action. Davis came on strong, clearly determined not to allow Trip to do what he'd done in the · previous round. But Trip had expected that and changed his tactics once more to confound and annoy his opponent even further. He didn't have the energy to repeat what he'd done before anyway.

This time, instead of dancing around the ring, throwing quick combinations, he took the fight right to Davis. He went at him with rapid-fire flurries of punches, not so much to hurt him – he didn't have enough stamina or power left to put a lot into them – but rather to disrupt and frustrate the bigger, younger man, not give him the chance to set himself and try anything. Four or five punches, then duck and move. As soon as Davis lowered his guard to see where Trip was to try and retaliate, bang-bang-bang-bang-bang, another quick flurry to make him cover-up again.

It wasn't long though before Trip started to run out of gas. Five punches became four, then three, then two, then just one punch at a time. Trip was breathing heavily. This round and the previous one had taken it all out of him.

And Davis knew it. 'That's it, granddad,' he said, around his gum shield. 'You're done. Time to bury you.'

Vehemently hoping his plan would work, and that he wasn't about to make a huge mistake, Trip beckoned with his gloved hands, *come on, then.*

Now it was Davis's turn to start stalking him around the ring. Trip tried to keep moving as much as he could but the spring had gone from his legs, his shoulders were burning and his arms felt as if they were full of lead. Still wary that Trip might do something unexpected, Davis was trying to herd him towards the ropes into a corner, to trap him again so he could finish him off with big power punches. It was just what he'd tried before – and what Trip was counting on him to do again.

Trip made a show of trying to fight his way off the ropes, and not get backed into a corner but, slowly, slowly, that was where he found himself. He'd used the respite, such as it was, to draw up his last reserves of strength. He just had to protect himself until the right moment – if he could manage to hold on that long.

When his back touched the corner pad, he knew what was coming and put his guard up to protect his head, just like he had in round six. Davis launched the big guns: thumping, heavy punches that landed on Trip's shoulders and arms, each one sapping more of his remaining strength. He moved from side to side, making his head a harder target and wondered how long it would be?

The answer was, not long at all.

Frustrated at not being able to get through Trip's tight guard, Davis, as he'd done before, took the punches downstairs, to the body. Only this time, Trip was ready for them. This was what he'd been waiting for. Every sense alert, adrenaline surging through him, Trip prepared himself and focused everything he had on what would happen next.

In came the first hook to his body. This time, ready, he tensed his core muscles tight, to withstand the impact – hours, days, months of training in the gym, having a medicine ball dropped on his stomach to strengthen the muscles for just this kind of punishment, all worth it now. He couldn't do it for long – but he wouldn't need to. A second hook came blasting in and again, Trip tensed and took it. Then the third came in and smacked into his unprotected side.

This time, Trip let out a pained breath, allowed his right arm to drop to shield his side and twisted away, as if he'd been hurt.

Seeing Trip's head suddenly left exposed, Davis took the bait and started to bring his next hook up and round for what might be a knockout blow – just as he'd done before, and just as Trip had counted on him to do again.

From his slightly crouched, slightly twisted position, Trip began to unwind, his mind processing everything so fast, it all seemed to happen in slow motion. His right arm, that he'd apparently brought down to protect his side, was, in fact, cocked like a loaded weapon. Now he was pulling the trigger. Starting from his feet, he pushed up with all the power in his legs, untwisting from his crouched position and using all that momentum and power to fire his right hand up through the gap Davis had left as he'd started to bring his hook up and round. The same gap Trip had spotted at the end of the sixth round, only he hadn't been expecting it then – but he was now – and he'd staked everything on it.

Trip launched himself like a ballistic missile. The uppercut rocketed up inside Davis's incoming hook and caught him flush on the chin. His body had been tensed to deliver a punch, not receive one and he was totally unprepared for it. The impact threw his head up and back and, in that instant, it looked as if someone had just pulled the plug on him. His entire body went limp, then he listed backwards and went over like a felled tree, crashing onto the canvas.

For a split second, there was frozen silence, the sudden knockout taking everyone completely by surprise. Then the referee was shoving Trip towards a neutral corner and the crowd went wild. The ref knelt beside Davis to give him the count. It was probably the longest ten seconds of Trip's life.

Davis was still flat on his back, dazed and confused. What had he called Trip earlier? Trip tried to remember. *Fred Flintstone*, that was it, on account of his age. Well, *yabadabadoo*, asshole. What do you think of that? Maybe now he'd show a little more respect to his elders.

'… EIGHT … NINE … TEN,' the ref finished. 'YOU'RE OUT.'

The fight officially over, Davis's trainers and staff rushed into the ring – looking none too pleased with Trip – along with the doctor and medical staff, to make sure Davis was OK.

Next thing Trip knew, Tyrone was lifting him and shaking him around, laughing and shouting in jubilation. 'You fucking did it, you fucking did it!' Even Sonny had a big grin slapped on his face.

'Put me down, man,' Trip said, after a moment. 'Let me go see how he is.' Tyrone put him down and helped pull off his gloves, so Trip could go and check on the younger fighter, who was now sitting up and, though still looking slightly groggy, was talking and responding to those around him.

'You OK?' Trip asked, offering his hand.

Davis accepted the hand and they shook. 'Yeah, I'm OK now. You caught me good, ol' Trip.' Maybe he'd learnt something after all. 'That was a good punch, man. I didn't even see it coming.'

'Thanks. Good fight. You're a hell of a fighter. You'll do well.' Trip nodded and left them to it. He rejoined Sonny and Tyrone, who were both brimming with happiness.

'You know what this means, don't you?' Tyrone asked him, dropping his voice.

'No. What?'

'A fucking rematch. It's in the contract.'

'So what? I don't want to even think about that right now.'

'*So what?* You won, that's what. You're the first loss on the kid's record. You think he'll just let that go? You've sent him back down the rankings. He'll want to fight you again to prove a point.'

'I don't know if I can go through that again.'

'It'll be the last fight we ever need to have. I mean, *you* ever need to have.'

'How'd you figure that?'

'Man, everyone will want to see it, a real grudge match. It'll be huge. When they approach you – which they sure as shit will – tell them you're thinking of retiring. They won't want to lose that opportunity to set the record straight. Whatever it says in the contract they got to pay, you being the winner and all, they'll double it – maybe even triple it.' Tyrone could barely contain himself.

'I doubt I'd win any rematch,' Trip said.

'Who gives a fuck? Win, lose or draw, you still get paid the full amount. So, whatever happens, man, you'd never have to fight again – and our pensions are fucking sorted!'

Amer Anwar

Amer Anwar grew up in West London. After leaving college he had a variety of jobs, including warehouse assistant, comic-book lettering artist, driver for emergency doctors and chalet rep in the French Alps. He eventually settled into a career as a creative artworker/graphic designer and spent the next decade and a half producing artwork, mainly for the home entertainment industry. Around this time, he gained an MA in Creative Writing from Birkbeck, University of London. His critically acclaimed debut novel, *Brothers in Blood*, was the winner of the Crime Writers' Association Debut Dagger award and was also picked as a book of the year by *The Times* and *Guardian*. The eagerly awaited follow-up, *Stone Cold Trouble*, was published in September 2020.

No Report, No Help
Oyinkan Braithwaite

The only respite from her fury is when she is asleep. She is not used to such anger, it exhausts her; but each night, after three hours of turbulent sleep, nightmares jerk her awake. Her anger has grown hands and legs and now consumes so many nutrients that her flesh has become papery thin, but still she feeds it. If you ask her why, she will tell you it is the only thing keeping her alive.

* * *

She was shivering as she gripped her husband's hand and told him, he would not die. Shivering, as she told the doctor that if they weren't given admittance into the hospital her husband would surely die.

— Is it money you want? Whatever you ask, I'll pay it.

Their accounts were in the red, but she would figure the money stuff out after they had saved her husband. As long as there was life, there was hope, right? She watched as the doctor checked her husband's pulse. Was it her or was the doctor moving in slow motion?

— Please. What do you want?

The doctor did not respond to her. He walked away.

There were people around her weeping. Some had already lost a family member as they waited for medical assistance in the hospital car park. She did not want to join them in a song.

* * *

She sees the doctor when her eyes are open and when they are shut. He didn't have a single strand of hair on his head. There was a cataract in one of his eyes and the back of his large head had folds and creases. She flicks her paintbrush into the orange glob on the palette and details the little wrinkles that ran along the doctor's skull on her 60 x 40-inch canvas. She only met him the one time but she will never forget his face.

* * *

They had two security men standing at the entrance of the hospital to prevent desperate people from rushing in. Even if she managed to get past them, how would she compel the medical staff to act?

— Ma, you need to get a police report. We are not allowed to take in victims of a gunshot wound without a police report. It is the law.

A different nurse delivered the words each time. But they all used the same dull tone and made the same pacifying gesture – one palm placed in another.

— Look, my brother is on his way with the report. Can't you just start?

— No ma. We have to see the report.

She tried not to think that he wouldn't make it in time. If she allowed herself to… if she thought her husband would die before the police report got to them… She couldn't allow herself to think it, because if she stopped believing he would survive, if she had no faith and he died, it would be her fault. No, in a few hours she would be celebrating. So she focused on her other self, her future self, the one who would breathe a sigh of relief when they told her that her husband had made it. This other self would quickly forget about the dispassionate doctor and the insipid nurse. This other self would have the capacity to forgive.

She texted her brother: Where r u?

A few minutes later, he replied: Getin cash 4 d cops...

* * *

She dips her brush in black and takes the time to paint on the little scar on the doctor's lip. She had noticed it, as she begged him to do his job. There won't be too many colours. She will add a bit of red to the canvas and see how she feels about it.

* * *

There was a scream threatening to unfold at the base of her throat, but numerous tears rained down instead. The hot concrete imprinted itself on her skin as she knelt beside her husband's labouring body. Some of the gurneys and wheelchairs had been rolled away. The hospital staff were far more efficient with the dead than they were with the living.

   — Please, I'm begging you. Attend to my husband. Please.

   — We will, ma. As soon as the report comes.

When her husband died, she was looking away. She was looking at the security men, noting that one had a straggly moustache and the other's face was riddled with pimples. Their eyes were blank. She suspected that they were not even human anymore.

When she returned to him, the blood had completely drenched the turban that she had unravelled in an attempt to keep her husband's insides, inside. His chest was still and no amount of shaking would stir him back to life. A breath escaped her and urine trailed down her leg.

* * *

In her painting, the doctor is surrounded by faceless nurses. Above them, ravens circle and tweet. Across them, the entire canvas, and over the figures and the birds, she has inked the words 'no report, no help'. She is done. She stands a few feet from her work and is…

* * *

4eminist4lyf @Feministetc09 · Jul 20
This is so terrible. How many more of us will die before the government pays attention? #NoReportNoHelp
> **ATribalMan** @Tribal_1 · Jul 20
> Govt wey travel 4 cough. U tink dey care?

AnEscapeArtiste @OlaOla_original · Jul 20
My neighbour was a victim. He was the sole provider for his family. We demand justice. #RoundaboutRobbery #NoReportNoHelp #Livesbeforepolicereport

BarbieNaijDOnly @FunkeBarbie · Jul 20
What would you do to get a girl like me? #followforfollow #likeforlike #NoReportNoHelp

SisiEko94 @Sisi_Eko_94 · 8h
Can someone please explain the whole #RoundaboutRobbery #NoReportNoHelp saga?
> **Entangled4lyf** @DontquoteMe88 · 8h
> Some armed robbery victims died because the hospital was demanding police report before treatment.
> **Yourfavouritedr** @DrOgunlere_00 · Jul 20
> Why are we blaming the hospital? It is not the hospital that show those people na? #RoundaboutRobbery
> **Naijatinz** @YorubaDemon64 · 8h
> Didn't Buhari drop some law to solve that bullsh**?
>> **Abokiboi24** @KunleSorberet · 8h
>> Guy, this is Nigeria.

ThatGyalYouWantToNo @CallMeSweerie · 10hr
I'm all the woman you need on your timeline. #followforfollow
#NoReportNoHelp

> **Gbemithedr** @GbemisokeAbiodunJnr · 10hr
> Girl, please respect yourself. People have died.

Shinigami23 @Animeloveryouknow · 7h
ROBBERY AND FIREARMS (SPECIAL PROVISIONS) ACT:
(2) It shall be the duty of any person, hospital or clinic that admits,
treats or administers any drug to any person suspected of having
bullet wounds to immediately report the matter to the police.
#NoReportNoHelp #AThread 1/3

> **Shinigami23** @Animeloveryouknow · 7h
> Y'all are talking about the 2017 act; but show me where the
> previous act prevents the hospital from treating the patients…
> We all passed our English exam abi? #NoReportNoHelp
> #AThread 2/3
>
> **Shinigami23** @Animeloveryouknow · 7h
> So if I understand this whole ish properly, people died because
> of a law that was misunderstood from the jump… When will
> people be called upon to account for their actions???! Criminals
> will criminal, but doctors should doctor. #NoReportNoHelp
> #AThread 3/3
>
> **Abokiboi24** @KunleSorberet· 5h
> Only in Naija man

TShirt4U @Ajibade78777 · 2h
I make custom tshirts. Retweet so man can chop. #NoReportNoHelp

* * *

24

... angry. And her anger is a ravenous beast. She slashes at the painting with her nails and screams. Her anger has grown a face and teeth. And the restlessness is like a hundred ants crawling across her skin.

Oyinkan Braithwaite

Oyinkan Braithwaite is a writer and novelist. Her bestselling debut *My Sister the Serial Killer* won the Crime and Thriller Book of the Year at the British Book Awards 2020. The novel was also shortlisted for the Women's Prize 2019, the Goldsboro Books Glass Bell Award 2020, and longlisted for the Booker Prize 2019 and the 2020 Dublin Literary Award.

Heaven 21

Paul Burston

I met Yannis on the hot, sweaty dance floor of a club called Heaven. My sort-of boyfriend Mike was sort-of seeing someone else and I'd gone out with the sole intention of getting even – or at least getting laid. Just turned twenty-one, I was young, dumb and full of... well, you get the picture.

Despite his Athenian ancestry, Yannis wasn't quite the Greek god of my dreams. But he was tall, dark, reasonably handsome and had a quiff most men would gladly give their eye teeth for. Heavily greased and artfully combed, it made him resemble a young Elvis. From the eyebrows up, at least.

Elvis quiffs were very big in 1987. This was largely thanks to Morrissey, whose mournful tones were the soundtrack to my tortured adolescence but whose knowledge of gay nightclubs left a lot to be desired. According to The Smiths anthem 'How Soon Is Now', clubs were a terrible way to meet people – you go on your own, leave on your own, arrive home, cry and want to die. Maybe this was Morrissey's experience, but it wasn't mine. There were plenty of clubs where you could go on your own and leave with somebody who'd really love you – if only for a few hours. I knew, because I was working my way around them in a series of attention-seeking outfits.

The night I met Yannis I was sporting a blond crop, bleached denim dungarees and eight-hole Doc Marten boots. Later, Yannis told me it was the dungarees that first caught his eye. He liked the way they clung to my buttocks. I remember thinking this was the nicest thing anyone had ever said to me.

We didn't fuck the first night. A drunken fumble was all either of us could manage. I woke with a raging hangover to find him perched at the bottom of my single bed, gazing down at me with a soppy smile and not a hair out of place.

'I love you, baby,' he said.

'I like you too,' I said and hoped that this would do.

I had lectures that afternoon, and arrived at my Catholic college with an enormous love bite blossoming like stigmata on my neck and my shirt collar wide open to ensure that everyone got a good eyeful. Having spent a large part of my life vigorously denying my sexuality, I'd reached the stage where nothing gave me more pleasure than rubbing people's faces in it.

In 1987, the age of consent for gay men was twenty-one, compared to sixteen for heterosexuals. A boy could be forgiven for thinking the world was against him – and revelling in a sense of his own outsiderdom. This boy certainly did. At twenty-one, I was barely legal and still very much a teenager at heart.

Yannis called that evening. 'I miss you, baby,' he said. His words were Greek honey to my ears. The thought of being missed, even for a few hours, hadn't really occurred to me before. Mike never called to say he missed me. We'd been together for over a year by then, and the L-word had only ever been uttered once – by me, before the look of alarm on his face ensured that I never made the same mistake again.

Mike was a proud leftie who lived in a council flat and believed that home ownership and monogamy were twin evils propagated by the Thatcher government. I think he saw love as a bourgeois construct – or maybe he just wasn't that into me.

'Let's go out tonight,' Yannis said. 'I need to see you, baby.'

And that was it. My fate was sealed. Yannis didn't just miss me. Yannis needed me. How could I refuse?

Our whirlwind romance was conducted at alternative, midweek club-nights with names like Daisy Chain, Jungle and Pyramid. We wore leather biker jackets and vintage Levi's, studded belts and steel toecaps. We drank bottled Grolsch and danced to Dead or Alive, Erasure, New Order and the Pet Shop Boys.

'Well, what do you think?' I asked my friend Martin one night at The Bell, when Yannis had gone to buy more cigarettes. The DJ was playing New Order's 'Bizarre Love Triangle', which seemed appropriate.

'The best thing about him is his quiff,' Martin replied, and turned his attention back to his new boyfriend.

I remember feeling mildly insulted by this, before consoling myself with the fact that Martin's supposedly butch rockabilly boyfriend clearly pencilled in his eyebrows.

In retrospect, Martin was probably just saying what I was really thinking, though at the time I convinced myself that there was far more to my attraction than mere hair envy.

Yannis had sleepy brown eyes and a mouth so wide and so mobile that each time we kissed, his lips covered my mouth, chin, nose, cheeks and earlobes. It was like being kissed by the face hugger from *Alien*. He chain-smoked Marlboro Reds and wore enough Kouros aftershave to fell a horse. The grease in his hair left stains on my pillowcases no washing powder could remove. But I didn't care. He was mad about me in a way that no man had been before. And he really did have lovely hair.

For three weeks, we were inseparable. We spent lazy afternoons in bed, smoking and having sex. We listened to 'Mother's Fist' by Marc Almond on my Toshiba music centre and smoked some more.

We never really talked, certainly not about anything serious, though this didn't bother me in the slightest. Mike and I did nothing but talk. Mike worked for a set designer who was a radical lesbian feminist. He was clearly terrified of her, and would recount their conversations in painstaking detail and with a large side helping of gay male guilt. Frankly, I was relieved to have found someone to have fun with.

When his hair wasn't greased and sculpted into a perfect pompadour, Yannis favoured colourful headscarves worn in the style of a pirate. I found this terribly romantic and decided that I too would grow my hair and wear headscarves. Had I stopped to think about it, it might have crossed my mind that Yannis's thick locks and my rapidly thinning follicles were destined for different things. I might have also considered the possibility that brightly coloured headscarves were better suited to someone with a swarthy Greek complexion than the pale face of someone who hadn't long left the green, green grass and grey, grey skies of South Wales.

Instead, I began experimenting with Black & White hair wax and wet-look gel, never quite achieving the volume required for a truly impressive quiff, but making a fair go of it with hours of backcombing and enough Shockwaves hairspray to burn a hole in the ozone layer. I also invested in an assortment of colourful headscarves and bandanas, prompting one of my college tutors to nickname me 'Roger the Red Pirate'. I chose to take this as a compliment.

By now, Yannis had returned to Athens and the life of a celebrity hair stylist while I had returned to college and my part-time job as a hotel porter. There were phone calls, letters and postcards. Yannis told me how much he missed me. He even phoned my mother to tell her. Since I wasn't out to my family at the time, this wasn't quite as endearing as it might sound.

Months passed. I was still seeing Mike and together we decided to go on holiday to Mykonos. Mike knew about Yannis, just as I knew about his various affairs. He wasn't too thrilled about it, but nor was he in any position to object. In any case, we agreed that a holiday would do us both good and booked the cheapest flight to Athens we could find, arriving late at night and taking an early morning ferry to Mykonos, with the promise of a fortnight's fun in the sun.

The first week was miserable. We sat on a beach called Super Paradise, surrounded by some of the most beautiful men I'd ever seen, looking like the unhappiest couple on earth. It was a peculiar talent of Mike's to make even the most enjoyable experience feel like an endurance test. Nothing seemed to please him – sea, sun, even sex. Not that there'd been much of that lately.

As the sun set on our fifth day at Super Paradise, we were befriended by another British couple – probably because we made them feel marginally better about themselves. Steve and Malcolm had been together for six years and were clearly sick of the sight of each other. Steve drove a mini cab. Malcolm stayed at home and ordered holiday brochures. They'd been to Mykonos several times before. It wasn't as good as it used to be. Nothing was as good as it used to be.

Listening to them bicker, I began to wonder if this was what the future held for Mike and me – years of resentment and recrimination, passed off as playful banter while our mutual hostility festered and grew like a cancer.

As the first week of our holiday drew to a close, Mike's pale skin began to blister and I was developing a deep golden tan, adding further pressure to our already strained relationship. It didn't help that we were staying in a grotty taverna halfway up a mountain, in a room barely fit for human habitation. Things came to a head one night after dinner when, fuelled by two bottles of retsina, we had an almighty row. Heading back to the hotel, Mike marched off in search of a shortcut and fell down a ditch.

I shouldn't have laughed. By the morning, a dark cloud had settled between us, so heavy that no amount of Greek sunshine could penetrate it.

That's when I made my decision. I knew that Yannis was staying on a neighbouring island for the summer. He'd written to tell me. I also knew where he was staying, at a large villa he'd rented with friends. I had the address and phone number scribbled in the back of my notebook. If Mike wanted to sulk, so be it. But there was no point in us both being miserable.

I left after breakfast and took a ferry to Naxos. Arriving at the port, I was directed to the bus station. The place where Yannis and his friends were staying was a few miles along the coast. Hungover, and weighed down with my rucksack, I must have looked quite a sight as I stepped off the bus and into the market square. For some reason, I'd decided that Doc Martens with exposed steel toecaps were the ideal footwear for a Greek island getaway. I'd teamed the shoes with black-and-white striped knee socks, black knee-length shorts, a Marc Almond T-shirt and a cropped denim jacket covered with badges and safety pins. My hair was dyed jet black and arranged into a semblance of a quiff, which was rapidly wilting under the midday sun.

Ignoring the bemused looks of local villagers, I consulted my map and made my way purposefully to the address where Yannis was staying, hoping that someone would be in. I'd tried phoning before leaving Mykonos, but nobody answered. Knowing Yannis, they were probably still asleep.

As I approached the villa, a gaggle of young Greek men appeared from behind the gate, talking excitedly and dressed for the beach. And there in the middle was Yannis. Only he no longer looked like Yannis. His beautiful quiff had gone. His hair was cropped short and bleached a dirty blond – much like mine had been, the night we first met. Worse still, he didn't look too pleased to see me.

'What happened to your hair?' he asked, scowling at my wilting quiff.

'I grew it. What happened to yours?'

'I cut it.'

His tone was sharp, with no hint of a smile. Where was the Yannis who loved me, who needed me and who missed me so much?

As we stood facing each other, an unsettling realisation sank in. It wasn't just that we'd swapped hairstyles. Our roles had been reversed. In London, I'd held all the cards. I had a sort-of boyfriend, a social circle, dungarees that clung to my buttocks and caught the attention of moonstruck Greek boys in gay nightclubs.

Here I had ... nothing. I was the tourist, the suitor, the lover and no longer the loved. I wasn't wanted here. And to top it all, my hair looked a state.

Yannis was too polite to send me packing, so it was agreed that I'd stay for a few days and sleep with him in his room. Any lingering hopes I might have had were soon crushed when he explained that his boyfriend would be arriving at the weekend, by which time I was to be long gone. In all the months we'd known each other, it had never crossed my mind that Yannis might also have a boyfriend. For the next few days, I could think of nothing else.

On my last night in Naxos, we trooped off to the local gay club where one of Yannis's friends performed in drag, miming to Shirley Bassey singing 'The Rhythm Divine'. A collaboration with the Swiss electro duo Yello, the song had been playing all summer – blasting out of gay bars in London and the beach bars in Mykonos. This was full-on Bassey ballad mode, hungering for the man who got away, telling him how her tears have kept her awake.

Despite my Welsh upbringing, I'd never been a great fan of Shirley Bassey. I'd always found her to be too bombastic, over-wrought, over-emotional. But that night something changed. Maybe it was the combination of cheap beer chased down with copious amounts of ouzo. Maybe it was the catch in my throat from smoking far too many cigarettes. But suddenly Shirley Bassey made total sense. As the song soared and Yannis's friend threw back his head and held out his hands to a largely indifferent audience, I knew just how Shirley felt. I knew that, tonight, my tears would keep me awake.

I also knew that, when I returned to London, the first thing I'd do was get my hair cut.

Paul Burston

Paul Burston is the author of six novels including the critically acclaimed psychological thrillers *The Black Path* (2016) and *The Closer I Get* (2019). He has also edited two short story collections and published several non-fiction books. His journalism has appeared in many newspapers and magazines including *The Sunday Times*, the *Guardian* and *Time Out*. He has also written and presented documentaries for Channel 4. He is the current curator and host of award-winning literary salon Polari at London's Southbank Centre, and the founder of The Polari Book Prize for LGBTQ+ writing. He is currently working on a new crime novel and a memoir. Born in York and raised in South Wales, he now divides his time between London and Hastings.

Thirteen Days at the Henry Ford Hospital

Jessie Burton

All we knew was that she was the wife of a famous artist, that they weren't Americans, they were Mexicans; and she was twenty-five years old. We were to be ready at the back doors of the hospital basement, where all the ambulances pulled in. She'd come before, more than once, to consult with Dr Pratt. It was a complicated pregnancy, and if somebody could find him, Pratt would know what to do.

Jill and I were the two nurses on duty. I was a trainee, straight from high school. I hadn't even done a full year, but Jill was in her sixties. It was July 4th in the morning: we were both working a double on Independence Day: me to get the hours in and because I didn't have a say, and Jill because her husband had died the year before and she didn't like being alone.

When the ambulance arrived, Dr Pratt still hadn't shown. Jill and I met the stretcher at the basement doors, and the woman on top of it looked like a small girl, her long dark hair loose and tangled. She seemed in a lot of pain, a little rag doll they'd tossed in a hurry; her body twisted on its back, stuck in the shape she had landed. She was much worse than we'd expected. This wasn't spotting. Her blood was everywhere, soaking the sheet, covering the bottom half of her nightdress. I was seventeen. I'd never seen that much blood, and no one mopping it up.

'Her name's Carmen Rivera,' said Joe, one of the ambulance men. 'Husband's behind in a taxi.'

There was no way we could wait for the husband. We shot her through the corridors towards the operating theatre, clots sliding down between her legs, blooming through the nightdress. She hissed like a cat, doubling up, stretching out. She kept looking at the ceiling, pointing with a little hand into the pipes. 'Diego!' she said, then something else in Spanish. She was mesmerised by those pipes, keeping her eyes on their twists and turns the whole time, as if there was a road above her head she was trying to follow.

On the last stretch of corridor we heard running steps, and the husband and a woman caught up with us. They both looked wild with worry, sweating, out of breath. He was a big man, fat and tall, with thick hair and high trousers, a giant out of place in our concrete tunnel. His bright wet bug eyes that he kept wiping underneath his spectacles darted between the stretcher and me. 'Don't let her die,' he said in English. 'She cannot die. Where's Dr Pratt? He knows my wife. He knows her problems. It's very important – where is Dr Pratt?'

As if the husband had summoned him, Dr Pratt appeared around the corner. He went straight to the woman on the stretcher, taking her little hand as if she were his lover.

'Mrs Rivera, can you hear me?' he said.

'Of course I can,' she replied in English. Her voice was dark and biting.

'We're going to make you comfortable,' said Dr Pratt.

'You promised,' she said.

'I know—'

'He's gone,' she replied, closing her eyes. 'And I am finally going to die.'

* * *

Mrs Rivera was right about the baby, and wrong about her time to die. I thought it was odd that a twenty-five-year-old woman would think of herself as 'finally' going to die, but I came to understand. For the first five days of her stay, she lay in her hospital room and continued to bleed. 'I'm a snail,' she said, when she came round from the anaesthetic. 'Always I am carrying everything with me. Losing takes so long.'

I had never heard a woman describe herself as a snail. She made it sound like a plausible diagnosis.

When she was more conscious, she would cry a great deal, talking to no one except her husband and her friend – the woman I'd seen in the corridor, who I learned was called Lucienne Bloch. Miss Bloch came to visit early on the second day, making Mrs Rivera laugh with impersonations so hard that she discharged the last of the foetus.

On her sixth day, Mrs Rivera dismissed Jill as her nurse, explaining to Jill that death was an old lady, 'and I cannot have *two* old ladies near me. It's just too much. I want the young one.'

'But Mrs Rivera, she's still a trainee.'

'So what? I want her.'

Jill was used to patient deliriums, but these switches from levity to gallows humour and grumpiness made her relieved to be free of Mrs Rivera. 'She's a handful, Alice,' she murmured, leaving the room. 'You've not had a handful. Let's see how you do.'

The door closed and we were alone. Mrs Rivera turned her head sideways on the pillow and regarded me. 'You are an American,' she said.

'That I am,' I replied, coming over to plump her pillow gently either side of her face. 'Born in this city. In this hospital, in fact.'

Mrs Rivera turned again so that she was staring straight up at me. She had very dark eyes, and slightly crooked teeth, full black lips and black brows that almost joined. A little colour had returned to her cheeks. A light came into her eyes. 'You were born in this hospital?' She was quiet for a moment. 'What is your name?'

'Alice.'

'You have a beautiful face,' she said. 'People in this city have faces like unbaked rolls. You have one that has – how do you say it? – cooked properly.'

'Risen properly,' I said. I thanked Mrs Rivera for the compliment and my acceptance made her laugh.

On the seventh day, she reached out a hand. 'They wouldn't let me see it afterwards,' she said. Silent tears ran freely down her face. 'It was all in little bits, wasn't it?'

Swallowing, patting her hand like a mother might a sick child's, I thought of what Jill might say. 'Come now, Mrs Rivera,' I offered. 'Don't think of it.'

She snatched her hand away. I'd said the wrong thing. Had I known her better, I would have said, *yes, Mrs Rivera, you are quite right. It was in little bits and we don't know why.*

She narrowed her eyes. 'I will think of it,' she said. 'Pass me that bag.' She indicated to a leather satchel that her husband had left behind on a chair. I fetched it for her as she pushed herself up in the bed. 'I am used to ambulances and hospitals,' she said, her arms outstretched to receive her bag.

By now, I had seen Mrs Rivera's notes. Badly-damaged spinal column and triple-shattered pelvis from a traffic accident that nearly killed her aged eighteen, congenital scoliosis, withered leg, ulcerous foot. A litany of broken innards, and polio before that. Medical corsets, pain relief, continual operations – there was no doubt she knew more about medicine than I did.

'*I* was the one who said to your Pratt that I should abort,' she said, sounding almost petulant. '*He* told me I should try and keep it. He gave me hope. I didn't want his hope, but he insisted. And now I'm in another hospital bed. But you mustn't treat me like a child.' She paused, the satchel sagging in her grip. 'I don't know why I have to go on living like this.'

'I—'

'But I am like a cat. I don't die easy.' She regained the satchel and pulled out a sketchpad. 'That is always something.'

I stared at her. She didn't seem like a little child anymore. 'Alice,' she said, murmuring my name like we were old friends, the intimacy of it blooming inside my stomach. 'All I want...' – she paused, closing her eyes, inhaling deeply – '... is to draw my dead Dieguito.' She peered at me. 'I am certain he was a little boy.'

Her words hung in the air between us, a difficult resurrection. At a distance, outside the window, traffic honked. I wished that Jill was here to bully her into submission.

'Mrs Rivera, I don't think you can do that,' I said.

'I can do what I like,' she replied. 'I want to see him how he should have looked, when he came into the world at three and a half months. I would like a book of medical diagrams on the subject. That is my request.'

I could not resist her. 'I shall get you a book,' I said.

'Good, because I'm not going anywhere,' she replied, as if she had read my mind.

Standing by her bedside, Dr Pratt was intractable. 'Mrs Rivera, we don't let patients have such books on the ward. It is distressing for them.'

Mrs Rivera laughed – a good, deep laugh – and said: 'Doctor, do you think pictures on a page will be more distressing to me than being in hospital for a distressing incident?'

He frowned. 'No, ma'am. But they prolong the pain.'

Our patient sighed, considering this. 'You are wrong. They change the pain. You must permit me the book.'

In the end, it was Mr Rivera who smuggled a book of anatomy into his wife's room. 'It is very important she has this,' he said to me in a low voice, placing it in my grip, his spare, large hand heavy on my shoulder as she drowsed on the bed. I could see the strain in his eyes as he looked over to where she lay. 'You must hide it from Pratt when she is finished for the day,' he said. 'You are not dealing with an average person. Frida will do something with it. She will do an artwork.'

I nodded, the thrill of being drawn into this secret outweighing my fear of Dr Pratt. Mr Rivera backed out of the room, his mind already outside these four walls. I wondered if he knew that the disintegrated foetus had shared his name, given the rapidity with which he pulled away.

When Mrs Rivera woke up, I was flipping through her records on the clipboard. 'I thought your name was Carmen,' I said. 'That's what it says here, but your husband calls you Frida.'

She raised her eyebrows. 'Carmen is one of my names. My husband thinks you Yankees won't like my German name because of the Fascists. So I am Carmen to the officials. But *you* can call me Frida, little Alice with the secret book.'

She put out her hand expectantly for her husband's contraband, and I wondered if she'd been asleep at all.

* * *

I was with Mrs Rivera for all thirteen days of her stay. I liked to wash her hair, comb and braid it, and I arranged her bottle of Shalimar and her lipsticks within her reach. She said she enjoyed these ministrations (contradicting her earlier statement about not treating her like a child) because they made her feel like a little girl again, as if we were friends from school and nothing bad had ever happened. She said I had good hands, nurse's hands, and that I was lucky to have found the thing I was good at. I loved these hours with her, sometimes quiet, sometimes chatty. Even in a second language, she often made me laugh.

As she sketched, both from the anatomy book and her own imagination, she liked me to sit in a chair beside her. She'd been lonely in Detroit until now, she said. She had her friend, Lucienne – but Lucienne was an artist and busy working, and Diego was also busy, as was deeply right; but she'd been suffering greatly with the pregnancy, feeling so sick every day. 'And now all that is over, and I am here.'

I was supposed to be observing rounds with other patients, but Jill and the others covered for me, because keeping Mrs Rivera happy meant that they could get on with their work. They avoided being folded into surreal conversations, or being lashed by her sharp tongue, cajoled, flattered, delighted, depending on her mood. I liked Mrs Rivera, and I think that she liked me. She certainly liked to look at me. She took me into her gaze – if not with desire, exactly, then with appreciation, bestowing on me a sensation of being seen that I had never experienced, a seventeen-year-old girl still living in her parents' house. I didn't want to give her to anyone else.

'My husband does not really want me to have a child, you know,' she said one day. 'He already has some. But they aren't mine.'

When she talked, she didn't stop drawing. I listened to the sound of her pencil scratching up and down the paper. 'I'm sorry about that,' I said.

She knitted her brows. 'Ah, but sometimes I think he is right. There is too much else to do. And maybe with my crushed body, I am not supposed to? There are thousands of things that will always remain a mystery, Alice. Work may be the best thing for me. I am always trying to keep myself together.' She paused again, and this time the pencil stopped. 'But then,' she said: 'I think of their little arms and legs.'

She showed me two of her sketches: a perfect reproduction of a male foetus, exactly as she had intended, around the age of her lost child – and then, a totally different drawing, of herself lying naked on top of the bedcovers. Her hair flowed over the edge of the bed,

40

just as it had when I first saw her splayed on the stretcher in the hospital basement – except now it was much longer, turning into a web of roots as it grew along the floor. Above her head floated a hand, also with roots. There was her husband's face, and a cluster of city buildings that looked to me like Detroit.

'I am having very strange dreams, sleeping in Henry Ford's hospital,' she said. 'My husband and I have met Henry Ford. Did I tell you that?'

'Goodness me,' I said. 'Are you telling the truth?'

Before her arrival into my care, I had never heard of Mr Rivera. To me, he was just Mrs Rivera's giant husband, worried and sweating in the corridor, smuggling books to keep her occupied. But now I knew that Mr Rivera was famous, and it was his fame that had brought them to Detroit. But to think they were the guests of Mr Henry Ford himself, the great industrialist who built this hospital in which I was born!

'I always tell the truth,' she said. 'Your motorcar man liked me. Still: with all his money you think he could arrange me some better dreams.'

'Are you an artist, like your husband and Miss Bloch?' I asked, watching the intense concentration with which she applied herself to her sketchpad.

She snapped her head up at me. 'I am the greatest artist.' She grinned. 'I am *joking*, Alice. Why is it so hard for Americans to understand a joke? I am not an artist.'

'But you're always sketching.'

'There is nothing else to do.' She paused. 'No,' she went on, looking thoughtful. 'I do think I am an artist. I once had plans to be a doctor, but now I draw. I paint well. I did not think so before Detroit. Diego always said it, but now I think it too.'

'What do you paint?'

'What I know best.'

'What do you know best?'

She looked mischievous, avoiding my question. 'Diego thinks I should paint the miscarriage.' She smiled. 'Do you think Mr Henry Ford would like that on his wall?'

* * *

On July 17th Dr Pratt discharged Mrs Rivera, and her husband and Lucienne came to fetch her. Jill and I put our arms around her like a doll, and placed her in a wheelchair – gestures, by the set of her jaw, she hated.

'Good-bye, Mrs Rivera,' I said.

'Good-bye, Alice,' she replied, her face breaking into a fire of a smile. 'Thank you for your friendship.'

Mr Rivera and Lucienne wheeled Mrs Rivera out of the room, and she did not look back.

The door closed, and I did something I should not have done. I climbed into Mrs Rivera's bed and curled up in her abandoned sheets. They smelled of Shalimar. I closed my eyes, imagining how it would feel to be so ill so much of the time. I was the one in pain, and Mrs Rivera was my nurse in the chair by my side. I, the prone one, sketched her instead. Mrs Rivera was not famous then, not yet the person she was to become. She was a woman who had lost her baby and turned it into a thirteen-day sketching spree.

Jumping off the bed before Dr Pratt or one of the other nurses came in, I began to strip down the covers. When I lifted the pillows, I found a page ripped from her sketchpad, a drawing of her naked body, and I sat back on the bed, cradling it in my hands. Mrs Rivera had split herself in two, one tear suspended on either cheek, and she wore nothing but a bead necklace. On the left-hand side of the page she had drawn two stages of an egg turning into an embryo. And there he was at the bottom: her baby boy, floating by a cord to her right leg.

Her other leg was shaded darkly with pencil. Very repetitive, persistent drops of blood ran down her left inner thigh, pooling on the floor. I looked at the drops, thinking of how, only thirteen days ago she had been wheeled in with so much blood. Her blood alone nurtured the roots of so many plants, which she had drawn thrusting straight and tall into the sun. The blood in Mrs Rivera's drawing was life-giving, even if her body, in the end, was not.

It was a medical drawing and an artwork, just as Mr Rivera had prophesied. Mrs Rivera had pictured her miscarriage, fusing it with science and emotion. It was unlike any I would ever see again, in the art galleries I scoured in search of her as the years passed, as Jill retired, as the war came and I married, having children of my own, becoming matron of the ward – and loneliness, in the end, coming for me too. I kept this drawing with me always.

The most surreal part of the picture was the last thing I noticed. My patient had given herself three arms. Two arms rested either side of her body, and a third lifted out from her left side, whose hand clutched a heart-shaped palette. No human being has a third arm, I know that: I am a woman of science. But as a woman of science I have also seen many things you might not expect, and this arm looked completely normal to me, as natural as a mother holding her child.

In neat writing, Mrs Rivera had written a note at the top: *to my nurse, Alice Kimmering, for her kindness during my stay at the Henry Ford Hospital, 4th – 17th July 1932, from Magdalena Carmen Frida Kahlo y Calderón Rivera. For her to remember me, when I am dead.*

I should have taken Mrs Rivera to the doors of the hospital myself, as I was the one who had borne her in. I have always regretted it: but I could not bear to see her go. And I realised, that July day, as the traffic honked outside and I held that precious sketch in my new nurse's hands, with all my nurse's care to come, that neither could Mrs Rivera bear to be witnessed disappearing. In recompense of her need to keep moving, she left part of herself behind forever. And that is how I remember her: sketching for thirteen days in her little room, in the Henry Ford Hospital, in the place where I was born.

Authors note:

Henry Ford Hospital is a painting executed by Frida Kahlo, dated July 1932, after she experienced a thirteen-day stay in the same hospital for a miscarriage at three and a half months. According to her biographer, Hayden Herrera, it is *'the first of a series of bloody and terrifying self-portraits that were to make Frida Kahlo one of the most original painters of her time; in quality and expressive power it far surpasses anything she had done before.'* The sketch that Mrs Rivera gives to Alice Kimmering is based on one of her works she completed soon after she left the hospital, called *Frida and the Abortion*, which she created as a lithograph whilst still in Detroit, shortly before she painted the famous artwork. Kahlo sometimes wrote dedications on paintings to medical staff and friends who had helped her, giving away portraits of herself. Whilst she couldn't physically be in their presence, her image – and their remembrance of her – could.

Despite this, Alice Kimmering is my invention, as is my imagined version of Frida Kahlo: even if the lithograph is not.

Jessie Burton

Jessie Burton is the author of three novels: *The Miniaturist, The Muse* and, most recently, *The Confession*, which became an immediate *Sunday Times* bestseller. *The Miniaturist* and *The Muse* were *Sunday Times* no.1 bestsellers, *New York Times* bestsellers, and all three novels were adapted for Radio 4's *Book at Bedtime*. *The Miniaturist* sold over a million copies in its year of publication, was Christmas no.1 in the UK, National Book Awards Book of the Year, and a Waterstones Book of the Year 2014. It was adapted for BBC TV as a two-part miniseries. As a non-fiction writer, she has written for the *New York Times, Harper's Bazaar UK*, the *Wall Street Journal*, the *Independent, Telegraph, Vogue, Elle, Red, Grazia* and *The Spectator. Harper's Bazaar*

US and *Stylist* have published her short stories. She is also the author of two children's books, *The Restless Girls* and *Medusa,* the latter of which publishes in 2021.

Crusader

Paul Fraser Collard

0700 hours, 19th November 1941, Bu Shihah, Libya

Second Lieutenant Sebastian Nash was sitting in the commander's seat in his Cruiser staring west when the wireless crackled into life. As ever, the first words spoken over the regiment's net were almost unintelligible, so he pressed the earpieces of his headset tight against his head, doing his best to decipher every word of the message that would follow. The sun had just risen and the first rays of light were spreading fast across the horizon behind him, colouring the sky with a warm show of orange and amber. It promised to be another beautiful day.

He just hoped he would live long enough to see its end.

'This is SUNRAY.' The voice paused, a moment's static filling Nash's headset.

'This is the day we have all been waiting for.' The colonel's breathless voice came again, clear and strong. 'The Italian Ariete division is in front of us. They are well dug in and the Eyeties have M13s in close support. Our orders are to break the line then push west. If all goes well, we'll force Rommel to bring his panzers into play. When he does, we will destroy them. All of them.'

Nash hung on every word. The colonel was right. This was the moment they had all been waiting for. It was the second day of

Operation Crusader. On the first day, they had covered some seventy-six miles, the only Cruisers that had not completed the journey lost to mechanical failure rather than the intervention of the Italian or German forces that held the ground to the west of the Egyptian-Libyan border. Yet, the regiment's rapid advance would surely not continue, not with the Italian infantry division just a few miles ahead. There would be no more easy driving across the western desert. From here on, they would have to fight for every shit-coloured mile.

'Today is our day. A day when we make sure the name of the 5th County of London Yeomanry goes down in history. It is a day for you to remember your families and to honour every man who has ever served in our regiment. Today is the day to make them all proud.'

The colonel's voice paused then delivered the line they had all been waiting for. 'You will attack and destroy the enemy. Advance!'

Nash took a deep breath. 'Driver. Advance!' He gave his own order on the Cruiser's intercom then stood up, pulling his cellophane sand goggles up to protect his eyes. It would be nice to go into action sitting down safe behind the turner's armoured plating. But if he wanted to see then he had to stand, his head and shoulders exposed outside the turret.

The Cruiser picked up speed. He felt the wind and the dust scrape against his face, the dry air scouring his skin.

It was time.

The thought sent a tremor surging through his veins. It started deep in his gut then raced through every fibre of his being, the release of fear sudden and shocking, while a lumpy, cast-iron nugget of dread settled somewhere deep in his belly.

Questions flooded his mind.

Would he fail?

Would he be revealed as a coward?

Would he be maimed?

Would he die?

The fear of facing his death terrified him. In minutes, he could be cast into the abyss. Oblivion. Darkness. Nothingness. The enormity of what he raced towards was almost more than he could bear.

He glanced around, his body shaking so much that he could scarcely keep hold of the rim of the commander's hatch. Around him, the regiment was attacking in line abreast, the brand-new Cruiser Mark VI's 'Crusaders' looking splendid in their new desert colours of yellows and browns. The sight of the charging Cruisers filled him with something close to pride. There was a sense of not being alone, the feeling of being one among many reinforced as he saw that every tank commander's head was out of their turret, just as his was, not one of them relying on the near-useless periscopes. It was just one of the adjustments they had all learned to make in their first few weeks in the desert. Now they would fight for the first time, and Nash could not help but wonder what else the inexperienced Yeomanry regiment would have to learn.

The Cruiser thrashed forward, the tracks kicking up a great cloud of dust and sand, the engine howling as Nash's driver increased speed. The ground flashed past at a mesmerising pace. There was something almost joyous in the way the light tank bucked and scrabbled across the desert. Something thrilling. Something that could fight against the fear that threatened to unman him.

He kept moving around the hatch, doing his best to study the way ahead while simultaneously keeping tabs on the other three Cruisers in his troop. It was not easy, especially as the Cruiser was banging up and down as it thundered across the rocky desert floor. The turret was filled with the roar of the engine and the rattle of the tracks as the tank ploughed its way forward. Along with the noise came the stink of petrol, the pungent odour wafting up from inside the turret, the smell stronger now that the Cruiser was hitting its top speed of twenty-six miles per hour.

'Braithwaite, cover your arcs.' Nash snapped the terse reminder to his gunner who sat just in front of him, his fear hidden behind the bite in his tone. He had to mask it. Bury it. His crew could not see it. 'Davies, ready with the first shell. If it's infantry, I'll want high explosive. If we see those bloody M13s then I want an armoured piercing round in there pretty damn sharp.'

'Yes, boss.' Davies, the Cruiser's loader, glanced up at his commander as he nodded his understanding.

Nash saw the strain on the man's face. Davies was ten years his senior, yet in that moment he looked like a small boy faced with a monster from his nightmares, the strain and the tension etched into the lines on his face.

The 5th CLY powered across the desert. As the lead unit for the 22nd Armoured Brigade, they would be the first to hit the enemy.

Nash held tight to the rim of his hatch as the Cruiser crunched over a low rise in the ground. He could feel heat beginning to build, the sun blazing down as it reclaimed the sky. Already the sweat was starting to run down his face and down the back of his battledress, but he barely noticed. His mind had room for nothing save the thoughts that hammered away deep in his brain, silencing everything else.

It could not be him.

It would not be him.

Someone else would be hit.

Someone else would die.

It could not be him.

It would not be him.

Ahead, he spotted a scar running across the landscape. He squinted, trying to understand what he was seeing. With the Cruiser bucking and bouncing it was almost impossible.

Then the scar glowed with a dozen flashes of red and orange.

'Shit.' Nash flinched as a burst of enemy machine-gun fire tore through the air no more than a yard above his head. Flashes of bright yellow and green streaked past at a dreadful speed, the flare of the tracer bright even in the early morning light.

With the high-pitched whine of machine-gun fire came a series of dull crumps, the low, flat sound clearly audible, even over the crackle of Italian small arms. Nash saw what it was immediately. The Italians had anti-tank guns dug in around their infantrymen. Now the gun crews manning them opened fire, the 5th CLY presenting them with a perfect target as they drove directly for the Italian line. Nash could only watch in horror as the first salvo of anti-tank rounds tore into the line of Cruisers.

Half a dozen Cruisers slammed to a halt as if they had run into a brick wall. Others scattered, the drivers breaking left and right as they tried to avoid the fire coming against them.

The Italian anti-gunners fired again.

Armour piercing rounds tore across the battlefield, the projectiles moving at an impossible speed. All along the line, Cruisers were hit, some directly in the front where their armour was thickest; others in the flank as they tried to turn away. No armour plate, no matter how thick, could save them that day. Many Cruisers simply exploded, great flashes of fire erupting a heartbeat after the anti-tank round ploughed into their guts. Others stopped, their hatches flying open as the crews tried to escape. Nash saw men jumping: their tiny, fragile bodies so out of place amid the fast-moving tanks. Some made it down and he saw them running, their legs moving fast as they ran for their lives. Others died as the Italian infantry flayed the stalled Cruisers with fire, their bullets finishing the job started by their comrades manning the anti-tank guns.

'Holy shit.' Nash breathed the words as another flurry of shells whipped into the line.

His troop was lucky. They were on the left flank, and mercifully far enough away from the centre of the Italian line to be out of the firing arcs of the anti-tank guns. But they were not left completely in peace. A burst of machine-gun fire caught the front of his Cruiser, the impact of a dozen bullets pinging off the armour plating and filling the turret with a dreadful high-pitched screech.

The Cruiser did not pause. It thrashed onwards, bucking like a wild beast as it scrabbled down into a shallow depression, the engine howling as the driver flogged it.

'Taylor, break left, follow the berm.' Nash was holding on to the rim of the hatch for dear life as he called out to his driver to change course.

'Yes, boss.' The Cruiser's driver, a nineteen-year-old from Pontypridd, was ensconced in his own small compartment towards the front, and he gave the curt acknowledgement of the order as he pulled the Cruiser into an arcing turn to the left.

Nash checked the rest of his troop was following his lead. To his relief, the three Cruisers were sticking dutifully to his tail, just as they were meant to. The rest of the neat line of Cruisers had disappeared.

'Boss! Twelve o'clock!' Davies sang out a warning; voice pitched high. He occupied the left-hand side of the cramped turret opposite the gunner, Braithwaite, the lack of space in the confines of the turret forcing him to perch on the ammunition storage box. His only view of the outside world came through a rotating periscope, but it was enough for him to spot the tell-tale signs of enemy tanks on the move.

Nash whirled around. There was a cloud of dust on the horizon. A cloud of dust that was heading directly towards his troop.

Machine-gun fire from the Italian infantrymen dug into their front, flaying the Cruiser for a second time and he flinched away, his body reacting without thought. It took everything he had to keep his head out of the turret, and resist the almost overpowering urge to duck down and get out of the line of fire. Just standing up took all of his courage, but he had to be able to see, no matter the risk. No matter that his body trembled and shook with terror.

A blurred shape rushed past the front of his Cruiser; the outline of the fast-moving vehicle masked by a cloud of grit of its own creating.

'Enemy tank at eleven o'clock, range five-zero-zero.' Nash recognised the enemy tank and snapped the identification to

Braithwaite just as the Italian M13 burst out of the cloud of dust its tracks had kicked into the air. 'Gunner traverse left.'

'Where, boss?' Braithwaite's reply was immediate.

'Traverse left!' Nash repeated. 'Now at ten o'clock.'

The turret jerked to the left, Braithwaite hauling on the traversing handle for all he was worth, as he did his best to spot the enemy tank through the tiny vision slit in the front plate.

'I can't fucking see him, boss!' Braithwaite's voice betrayed his fear.

'He's right there. Range now four-zero-zero.' Nash tried to remain calm, just as he had learned in training, even though every fibre in his being was on fire.

'Boss, I can't see him!'

'Nine o'clock. Get on him.'

'He's not there!' The turret jerked hard left as Braithwaite tried and failed to locate the enemy tank.

'For fuck's sake, you useless blind bastard! He's right there!' Nash's composure cracked.

'I can't see a fucking thing!' Braithwaite screamed the reply.

Nash braced himself as the turret juddered to a halt then traversed back to the right again as Braithwaite searched for the M13. He had no idea how his gunner could not see the Italian tank.

'He's right there! Shit.' Nash's head was turning back and forth as he tried to watch the enemy tank whilst still plotting their route. He tried to fight away the panic that threatened to engulf him. 'Driver, take us right. Now. For fuck's sake.'

More enemy machine-gun fire raked the Cruiser. Again, Nash flinched, this time ducking all the way down into the turret. He felt a red-hot pain sear the crown of his head, as he was hit by a razor-sharp shard of metal, followed by the sensation of blood flowing down the back of his neck.

For a moment he stayed there, head down, body crouched and tense. He did not want to move. He did not want to put his head back outside and into air that was alive with enemy bullets. An almost overpowering urge to run was taking hold of him, while a surge of ice pushed down deep into his bowels, the fear ravaging through him. He could not make himself move and so he stayed crouched down, too terrified to do anything else.

'Enemy tank at eight o'clock.' Taylor spotted the M13 again. 'He's right fucking there. For God's sake, shoot him!' The sequence of orders they had practised for days were forgotten.

'Where?'

'Jesus Christ!' The driver cried out. 'Eight o-fucking-clock. You are going to get us all killed, you dozy fucking bastard!'

'Belt up and keep us moving!' Nash shut his driver down. He sucked down his fear and forced himself to stand, the act taking everything he had. He saw the M13 immediately as his head broke outside. It was on their left flank, moving fast, its turret rotating back and forth, as the Italian crew hunted for a target. 'Braithwaite, shoot the fucker.'

'I still can't fucking see him!' Braithwaite's voice cracked with fear. The turret was traversing from side-to-side as the gunner desperately tried to locate the target.

'Shoot him or I'll fucking shoot you!' The Italian tank had to have seen them.

A colossal explosion smashed him into the back of the hatch. The Cruiser bucked as if some huge animal had kicked it in the side, then it charged on, the engine wailing as Taylor flogged it without mercy.

'What the fuck was that?' Nash smeared the back of his hand across his forehead. It came away smothered in blood. He could not remember why.

He held fast to the front of the hatch with his free hand, desperately trying to hold himself in place.

'They fucking hit us!' Davies had been thrown forward from his perch on the ammunition box and now he cursed and shouted up at Nash.

'Where is it now?'

'Fuck knows!' Davies thrust his face to his periscope.

'He's right bloody there. Seven o-fucking-clock! Now shoot the wanker!' Taylor screamed out from his driver's compartment, his voice wailing in pure terror. 'Please! Oh, Jesus Christ!'

'On!' Braithwaite cried out in triumph as he finally located the Italian M13 that had already hit them once.

'Fire!' Nash had no idea where the enemy tank was now, but he didn't care. Braithwaite just had to hit it.

The Cruiser's gun fired a heartbeat later, the explosion of sound loud and immediate.

'Did you hit him?'

'No idea, boss. He's gone!' Braithwaite delivered the news breathlessly.

'Shit!' Nash looked left and right, but there was no sign of the M13. All he could see were swirling clouds of dust and sand. Even the sky had disappeared: the pale blue hidden behind the grey and yellow murk. 'Are we hit bad?'

'No, boss!' Davies answered even as he rammed a fresh armour-piercing round into the breech of the Cruiser's main armament, a two-pounder gun. 'God knows why.'

'Driver! Head west.' Nash braced himself in the hatch as best he could. They were still tearing along at full speed. He could see a thick streak of black along the Cruiser's left flank where an enemy shell had come within a foot of killing them all. Everything else was chaos. Smoke and dust were everywhere. Shells roared past, each making a noise like an express train while the violent force of its passage rocked the tank. Bursts of gunfire came continuously, the Italian line still hundreds of yards ahead, flashes of yellow and green tracer snapping past. He could not see his squadron leader or any of his troop. They were alone.

'Driver. High ground to the north-west, get us over there.' He gave the only order he could think of. He had no idea what else to do. He was thoroughly lost and had no sense of where the enemy were, let alone any of his own side.

'Yes, boss.'

'Are we loaded?' Nash snapped the question, trying to find something that made sense amid the chaos.

'Yes!' Davies came back at him immediately. 'Armour-piercing loaded, boss.'

'Right. Good.' Nash sucked down a deep breath as he tried to take charge of the moment. 'Now, Braithwaite, this time cover your fucking arcs.' It was a cruel rebuke but he didn't care. His fear was terrible. It was ravaging around so deep in his guts that it was making his backside quiver. 'You nearly got us all bloody killed there.'

'Yes, boss.' Braithwaite's voice sounded fragile.

A huge fountain of earth erupted from the ground not more than six feet from their left track. Nash was slammed into the edge of his hatch.

'Shit.' The impact hurt, but he could do nothing but endure. 'This is Baker Two. Troop report.' With his own tank now moving fast, Nash tried to talk to his troop. He had no idea where they had gone.

'Enemy tank seven o'clock. Range four-fucking-zero-zero.' Braithwaite drowned out the voice of one of Nash's sergeants who was trying to answer his troop commander.

'Shoot him!' Nash screamed the order. He could not see the target.

The Cruiser rocked as the two-pound shell was sent on its way.

'Got the bastard!' Braithwaite roared in triumph.

'Ready!' Davies had another shell in the breech even before Nash could give the order.

'Fire!' Nash called for the second shell.

Braithwaite fired almost immediately.

Nash still had no idea what they were shooting at. The Cruiser tore alongside a mound of sand no more than eight feet high. He hoped it would screen them from some of the enemy fire and he grabbed the chance to twist around to try to see the rest of his troop.

He saw nothing but burning hulks. To the east a handful of Cruisers were moving, but many were stationary. The regiment was taking a beating, its pell-mell advance directly into the face of the enemy's defensive position resulting in little more than its own destruction.

He turned back, his only thought to find a way to get back to any of his troop that was still alive.

He would not get the chance.

A huge explosion rocked the Cruiser. The noise of the impact was dreadful; an enormous bang was followed by a violent swerve that threw him half out of the turret. The Cruiser lurched to a halt, its forward momentum slewing it around in a great cloud of dust.

Nash was stunned. For a moment he lay there, half in and half out of the turret, his head reeling from the shock of being hit. He fought off the panic, fighting back the desperate desire to bail out, and hauled himself back inside the turret, his shaking legs just about holding him.

'What the hell happened?' Nash snapped as he regained control of his surging emotions.

'I think the left track's gone!' Davies looked up at him. The loader had blood smeared across his face where he had smashed it against the gun's firing ammunition.

'Shit! Taylor,' Nash bellowed at his driver. 'Get us moving or we're dead.'

'I can't! Jesus Christ, we can't move!' Taylor sounded close to panic. Alone in the driver's compartment he was helpless.

'Get us moving!' Nash was unforgiving. 'Gunner. Keep firing!'

It was bedlam. The Cruiser's engine screamed as Taylor tried to keep them moving, the pistons howling as if in some dreadful agony. Somehow the Cruiser lurched into motion. All three men in the turret were thrown to one side, their bodies battered against unyielding metal as the wounded tank twisted around its damaged track.

'Enemy tank! Fucking hell!' Braithwaite saw the danger first.

It took Nash barely a heartbeat to thrust his head back outside.

He caught a glimpse of an Italian M13 charging along, its turret rotating towards them.

'Shoot it!' Nash gave the order.

The Cruiser kept turning, its one good track biting deep into the gravel on the desert floor while the other simply dug a trench. Nash saw Braithwaite bringing their turret round to face the M13.

'Kill it!' Nash saw the enemy gun barrel stop traversing as it took aim on them.

Time slowed. He could only watch on in horror as he waited for the enemy to fire.

'Fuck off!' Braithwaite's voice cried out the instant before the Cruiser shook as he fired.

Nash was thrown forward, but he kept his eyes on the Italian M13. He was still watching as the two-pound shell tore through its side armour. Braithwaite had fired fast. He had not missed.

'Got the fucker!' Braithwaite was triumphant.

'Keep bloody shooting.' There was no time for relief. Nash tried to steady himself, but the Cruiser was turning too fast and he was flung about like a rag doll. An enemy shell roared past, his head buffeted by its passage. He looked for his troop, or any one from his regiment, but saw nothing but clouds of dust and billowing smoke.

'Driver!' Dust caught in his throat and he choked, the words cut off. The Cruiser shook as an enemy shell tore through its guts. Nash was deafened, his hearing lost before his head slammed into the metal of the hatch.

He fell, his legs no longer able to support him. He collapsed back into his seat like a sack of shit, his body thrown hard as the Cruiser ground to a sudden halt.

The inside of the turret was filled with smoke and the stench of petrol. It was chaos. Nash managed to get his hand onto the grenade rack and he tried to move, but his body would not respond.

Someone was screaming.

Braithwaite writhed in his seat. Blood smothered his battledress.

His terrified eyes locked on to Nash. Then he screamed again; eyes bright with fear.

Nash fought against waves of nausea. Finally, he managed to get his feet underneath him. Braithwaite's hand clawed at him, fingers like talons.

'I'll get you out!' Nash shouted even though the Cruiser was oddly silent now that it was stationary. He reached forward, thinking to drag Braithwaite out by grabbing him around the shoulder. As soon as Nash touched him, Braithwaite shrieked like a banshee. Nash recoiled, his hands coming away smothered in blood. His gunner's left shoulder was little more than pulp.

'Oh god!' Nash whimpered. Fear was taking hold. The Cruiser would brew up at any moment, the risk of fire very real and very close.

Braithwaite slumped forward; his terrible screams of agony cut off as he lost consciousness. As he fell away, Nash saw the shredded firing mechanism for the two-pounder. The enemy shell must have torn through their side armour, taking off Braithwaite's left shoulder before hitting the gun then exiting on the opposite side.

'Davies! Help me with Braithwaite.' Nash felt his strength returning. He shouted for his loader to join him in getting their wounded gunner out of the turret before the battered Cruiser caught fire.

There was no answer. Nash turned. Davies was gone. The armour-piercing shell had torn through his upper body as it exited the turret. There was little of the loader left above the waist. He remained seated, the bare legs and shorts smothered in a grotesque pallet of blood and gore.

Nash was moving even before his mind fully registered the horrific sight. He clambered up and out of the open commander's hatch, fighting his way free of the ruined turret, his only thought to escape. His head broke free, dust-filled air chafing against his face and scouring away the blood and the tears.

He blinked once as the bright light stung his eyes. And then he saw the Italian M13 no more than twenty yards away.

He looked down, taking one last look into the chaos inside the turret. It was a charnel house. He looked away, unable to bear the sight, his throat clenching as he fought back the urge to vomit. Panic overwhelmed him.

Everyone was dead.

He was alone.

He had to run.

Now.

He managed to get his feet back onto his seat. He kicked hard, forcing his upper body out of the turret.

A loud flash and a bang greeted him as he hauled himself out of the hatch and dropped down to the sand below. Moments later, another shell smashed into the mound to the right of the broken Cruiser throwing up a great fountain of gravel and sand. Fragments of rock rained down around him as he found his footing, the air filled with dust so that he could barely see more than a couple of yards.

But the M13 was still close enough for him to hear the dreadful cacophony of a tank in motion, the clank of its tracks and the screeching of grinding metal. It was enough to send a wave of pure terror through every part of his being.

He raced around to the rear of the stalled Cruiser. The M13 was lurching along, its pace slowing as it searched for a new target.

There was time for one last look at the stricken Cruiser. Then he ran.

He tried to sprint, his legs pumping hard. The ground gave way under his boots, but he refused to give in and he scrambled along, his one free hand pushing against the flank of his Cruiser to help propel him forward.

He cried out as he ran. Terror bright. All-consuming. Powerful.

His legs felt ready to collapse, but he forced himself to run. Horror lent him strength. Even though it was as if he waded through treacle, he pushed himself on, everything focused on getting away.

He made it no more than a dozen yards before the M13 came for him.

He skidded to a halt. Then stood still. Chest heaving. Heart pumping.

He had nothing left. Not that it mattered. He could not outrun an M13.

So, he turned to face his enemy. At least, he would see his death coming for him.

He was close enough to see the Italian commanding the tank, shouting instructions at his crew. A heartbeat later and the M13 slewed around, the track nearest Nash kicking a huge wad of gravel and sand into the air as the tank pivoted.

The M13 seemed to twist around itself as it straightened. Then it started to come forward.

It was heading directly for him.

Nash could see the M13's commander. The man was hunched low in his cupola, little more than his head and shoulders visible. With his eyes hidden behind his sand goggles, there was nothing to show this was another man, another human being. It was as if the M13's commander had somehow fused with the tank he controlled; man and machine combining to create something inhuman, a mechanical killing machine that knew only death and destruction.

Nash knew the creature in the turret was looking right at him, its only thought to bring about his death. Yet he could not move. Even with his death grinding towards him, the M13 picking up speed as it powered through the loose sand, he could not run, nor even turn away. He could do nothing but stare at the beast that was lumbering towards him.

The M13 lurched and kicked. The sound of it was incredible, the mechanical noise of moving metal and whining engine filling the air. It was unearthly this sound, and the display of such power was overwhelming.

And it was reserved just for him.

The distance between them closed fast.

Time slowed.

Seconds crawled by.

Yards disappeared.

Even the sand flung into air by the M13's tracks seemed to hang there, the world and everything in it slowing so that every second felt like a minute.

Still Nash stood there.

Powerless. Immobile. Terrified.

And then the world changed.

Nash saw the incoming round, the faintest blur of a solid object moving at an incredible speed visible for the tiniest fraction of a second, before it slammed into the side of the M13.

Time sped up again, the seconds hurtling by at a frenetic rate.

The Italian tank skidded to a halt; a terrible moan and grinding of twisting metal coming in the heartbeat before it exploded.

Nash was tossed backwards. There was the briefest sensation of flying through the air, then he hit the ground on his back, every scrap of breath driven from his body.

For a moment, he could do nothing but lie there, absorbing the pain. There was no notion of relief. Or of joy. His mind was empty, the shock of what had happened had scoured his mind clear.

His body lurched into motion of its own accord. He pushed himself to his feet, sucking down mouthfuls of the scorching air, then spitting away the dust and the blood that had filled his mouth. Only when he had himself under some vestige of control, did he look up.

The M13 was no more than twenty yards away. Flames engulfed the turret, great red licks and spits erupting out of the open hatches. The hunched body of the tank commander was gone.

'Boss!'

Nash turned back to look at his Cruiser as a familiar voice called for his attention. He saw Taylor staggering towards him. The driver's face was streaked with smoke while blood trickled from his temple.

'You're alive?' The words left Nash's mouth before he could form a single coherent thought.

'Just a-fucking-bout, boss.'

'Quick! Braithwaite is hit.' Nash stumbled forward. Fear and pain were forgotten. He no longer thought of running. He grabbed Taylor by both arms. 'We've got to get him out.'

Taylor understood. He was running before Nash could move. They scrambled over the ruined hulk of the Cruiser. Taylor was smaller and quicker and disappeared through the commander's hatch whilst Nash was still lumbering up the side of the turret.

Nash followed his driver inside, snatching the first-aid kit from its place underneath the grenade rack. There was little room in the cramped turret, but they managed to get their arms around Braithwaite and drag him up and out. If Taylor saw the remains of Davies pooled around his seat then he said nothing.

'Sweet Jesus.' Taylor swore as they hauled the bloodied body of their gunner out of the turret, the pair somehow getting him down the side of the Cruiser and onto the ground.

Nash dumped the first-aid kit on the ground next to Braithwaite's head.

He stared at his driver. 'Is he dead?'

Taylor squatted beside Braithwaite's bloodied body, fingers reaching out to press against the wounded man's throat. He shook his head. 'No, he's alive.'

Nash tore open the first-aid kit then knelt beside Braithwaite. He contemplated the grotesque remains of the man's shoulder.

'Shit.' He ripped out a thick bandage from the kit and thrust it against the largest area of torn flesh. Braithwaite thrashed, but Nash pushed down, forcing the bandage to cover the wound then binding it tight, compressing the matted, bloodied mess of cloth and flesh as best he could.

'You need to give him morphine, boss.' Taylor was watching his officer with wide eyes.

'Yes. Right.' Nash dug in the first-aid kit. He had scattered the contents in every direction and now had to hunt for the pre-loaded syringe filled with morphine. The kit contained four. One for each of them.

'Shit. Shit. Shit.' He picked up the first syringe he could find from the pile then turned to stab it in Braithwaite's leg just as he had been taught. The gunner's body was convulsing in front of him. Nash had never been as terrified as he was in that moment.

'Shit! Do I give him more?'

'I don't know.' Taylor leant back, his face ghostly white.

'I don't fucking know what I'm doing!' Nash screamed the words at his driver. He searched out another vial of morphine then stabbed the man he had come to know better than he knew his own brother. Mercifully, Braithwaite went still.

Taylor looked at Nash. They stared at each other, neither able to speak.

Then the small driver was on his feet, his arms wind-milling above his head. 'Over here! Over here!'

Fate had delivered salvation. A four-wheel-drive Bedford truck was roaring across the gravel. It was the regimental field ambulance and it arrived, engine racing, the trained medics jumping out and running across towards them before it had even come to a full stop.

Nash and Taylor stood to one side as Braithwaite was bundled onto a stretcher. The regimental medical officer was brutally efficient and the wounded gunner was carried away in under a minute.

'Nash. Did you give him morphine?' The medical officer screamed the question.

'Yes.'

'How many?'

'Two!' The single word came hard.

'You damned idiot. Are you trying to kill him?' The medical officer departed at a run, scribbling a note on a sheet of paper as he went.

Nash watched him go. The ambulance roared off.

The two men said nothing as it drove away and left them quite alone.

* * *

Nash slid off the back of the Bren gun carrier then turned to make certain that Taylor had followed him. Neither man had spoken since they had been picked up an hour earlier.

It was dark and well past the time for fighting. The regiment was drawn up into a night leaguer. Or at least, what was left of it was. They had started the day with forty-eight Cruisers. Now Nash saw that only just over a dozen remained.

'Nash?' A voice accosted Nash as he walked towards the circle of Cruisers. 'That you?'

'Yes, boss.' Nash staggered towards the familiar voice. Behind him the Bren carrier roared away, its job of ferrying the two abandoned tankers back to the regiment now complete.

'You made it then.' Nash's squadron commander, Major Reynolds, emerged from the darkness. He was smoking, the glowing tip of the cigarette hanging from his lips casting meagre light across his face. 'Just the two of you?'

Nash nodded.

Reynolds grunted, immune to their suffering. 'Are the others dead?'

'Braithwaite is wounded. Davies is…' Nash's voice trailed off. He looked at his commander and saw the stony expression of a man beyond caring.

'Give the details to Fielding then get yourself a brew and something to eat. Then come and find me. We are putting together as many scratch crews as we can for tomorrow.' Reynolds turned away and began to walk back to the leaguer. He had come out to welcome them in, the noisy arrival of the Bren gun carrier summoning him from his rest.

Nash nodded to Taylor who stumbled away, his body acting on instinct. Nash fell in beside the major. He could see the men from B-echelon busy around the Cruisers that formed the sides of the

64

leaguer. Those tasked with refuelling wore greatcoats, long trousers, gloves and balaclavas while their mates stood ready with fire extinguishers. The combination of fuel and red-hot metal made refuelling a tank a risky business.

'How bad is it?' Nash felt his brain starting to come to life after hours of being empty of thought, the horror of the fight beginning to recede into the darkest recesses of his mind and allowing him to begin to function once more.

'We are down to sixteen tanks. The rest are strewn across God alone knows how many miles of desert. We have men out trying to recover what we can.'

'Just sixteen?' Nash was having trouble absorbing the information.

'Five officers are missing, including Major Fletcher. We have nine men confirmed dead, seventeen missing and I have no idea how many wounded. The colonel was hit in the head in the first hour.' Reynolds delivered the news in a deadpan voice devoid of all emotion.

'Is he dead?'

'No. Major Crossley has command now.'

Nash tried to take this in. He found he couldn't.

'We killed seventy tanks. Or at least we think we did. There are all sorts of claims.'

'We killed two, I think.' Nash shuddered as he remembered the inhuman face of the Italian tank commander.

'Three, four, ten, twenty.' Reynolds' voice quivered with sudden emotion. 'I am not sure it really matters. Are you?'

Nash felt like a small boy seeing his father cry. 'Did we win?'

Reynolds laughed. It was a grim sound. 'I have no idea. We charged in like it was some fucking game and we paid the damn price for our stupidity.'

'We will have to do better.' Nash was clinging to his sanity like a drowning man clings to a floating spar. 'Next time.'

'Next time.' Reynolds was grim. 'Well, at least we won't have to wait long for another go on the damn merry-go-round. We will fight again tomorrow.' He tossed his cigarette butt to one side then reached to the breast pocket of his battledress to get out the packet. 'Sort yourself out then get ready for dawn. We will form a single squadron. We can do that at least. You'll need a crew so go around the odds and sods and find what you need.'

Reynolds said nothing more and walked away, lighting up another cigarette as he did so. Leaving Nash alone.

He had survived his first battle.

And tomorrow he would have to do it all over again.

Paul Fraser Collard

Paul's love of military history started at an early age. A childhood spent watching films like *Waterloo* and *Zulu* while reading *Sharpe*, *Flashman* and the occasional *Commando* comic, gave him a desire to know more about the men who fought in the great wars of the nineteenth and twentieth centuries. This fascination led to a desire to write, and his series of novels featuring the brutally courageous Victoria rogue and imposter Jack Lark, burst into life in 2013. Since then, Paul has continued to write, developing the Jack Lark series with the ninth novel, *Fugitive*, published in August 2020.

Unquiet Slumbers:
A Tale of the Caxton Private Lending Library & Book Depository
John Connolly

As befits its nature and history, the Caxton Private Lending Library and Book Depository contains many tales within its walls – and not only those that have been committed to print, there to join its vast, secret archive of manuscripts and first editions. Like any library, the Caxton is not simply a storage facility for books: it is both a living entity, with words as its lifeblood, and a haunted house, with characters as its ghosts. But what distinguishes the Caxton from its more quotidian peers is the fact that its literary inhabitants are corporeal, each of them given physical form by the imaginations of writers and readers, and rendered immortal by those same agencies. Within its walls, fiction is the only reality.

The Caxton is where the great, the good, and the not-so-good of literature find sanctuary when their creators die. Shortly after the passing of a noted novelist, one whose characters have become, if not household names, then at least names in the better households, the Caxton receives a brown paper parcel bound with string, containing a first edition copy – sometimes even a manuscript – of that author's best-known work. Occasionally – in the rare case of a Shakespeare, for example, or a Dickens, or an Austen – the parcel will include more than one volume, but most authors would be content should even a single example of their work, or a sole character, capture the popular imagination sufficiently to earn a place in the Caxton.

Of course, if this were all that were to occur after a writer's death, the Caxton would be remarkable merely for its collection and the mechanisms that permitted the delivery of those final parcels. No one seemed to know how, or by whom, they were packaged and sent, and no individual had ever stepped forward to claim credit for their dispatch during the centuries of the library's existence. Even its founder, the great printer and publisher William Caxton, confessed bewilderment at the process, ever since that first day when he looked out his window to find Chaucer's pilgrims loitering in his yard, and a pristine volume of *The Canterbury Tales*, wrapped in paper, lying on his doorstep.

It had been suggested by more than one early librarian that generations of a single family, a clan embedded in the printing and publishing industries, had taken secret responsibility for the task, but this seemed unlikely. Questions of access to materials arose, particularly in the case of rare manuscripts, while nothing in the meticulously detailed records of the institution – which contained documents dating back to Caxton himself – indicated that such a system had been put in place. As a consequence, it had been decided that some non-human agency – call it the Creative Spirit, the Muse, or the Divine – took care of deliveries, and any further inquiry into the matter was therefore both futile and potentially unwise. The apparatus worked, which was all that mattered.

But the Caxton, as has already been noted, is more than just the sum of its books and papers, however extraordinary they may be. Those novels and manuscripts do not appear at the Caxton's door in isolation, for shortly after – or even simultaneous with – their delivery, their most famous characters also manifest themselves, just as they did to William Caxton shortly after his press began producing the first printed edition of *The Canterbury Tales* in 1476. These *dramatis personae* are sometimes confused, intermittently depressed, or – once in a blue moon, or perhaps a full one – dangerously angry, but all eventually settle down and find their place.

The Caxton, like all libraries, is capable of containing universes within its walls. New rooms materialize, furnished according to the specific requirements of their guests, but the physical boundaries of the library never extend, and it never runs out of space. Beyond these rooms lie entire worlds. Enter the accommodation of Sherlock Holmes and Doctor Watson, and through the windows of the sitting room you may glimpse the spires of nineteenth-century London; exchange a greeting with Mr Fitzwilliam Darcy in his study, and the gardens of Pemberley stretch beyond the glass; visit Alice's chambers, and the Cheshire Cat stretches languorously on a tree outside, all smiles. The Caxton is a reader's dream made manifest.

But like any venerable institution, it has its peculiarities, even prejudices. The collection errs on the side of Anglophone writers, particularly those born in England, and has been known to evince an especial distrust of Americans. In addition, either the library or its animating spirit – that fickle Muse again – has an odd sense of humour. For example, following the death of Samuel Beckett, a printed note was delivered to the Caxton promising that a copy of his most famous drama was on its way, but so far it has never actually arrived, although more notes have since followed, each containing a more elaborate and unlikely reason than the last for the delay. Similarly, an entry in the Caxton's register confirms receipt, on August 14th 1936, of a copy of *The Invisible Man* by H. G. Wells, but the volume in question cannot be found; Tristram Shandy has yet to be born, although his cradle sits waiting; and the Count of Monte Cristo has vanished from his room.

Sometimes, too, the Caxton understands what others do not, and perceives beauty where others see only ugliness. Books that were underappreciated in their day, and characters that were disregarded, may find their way to its door, waiting for history to clasp them belatedly to its bosom.

The Caxton, one might say, knows quality.

In this manner, a small, odd incident in the Caxton's history occurred in the middle of the nineteenth century, during the stewardship of Mr Hanna, a retired academic with an insatiable curiosity for the dustier corners of late eighteenth-century British history.

Mr Hanna was, by all accounts, of a nervous disposition, and therefore possibly ill-suited to caring for the library during the resurgence of Gothic literature. Upon Mary Shelley's death on February 1st 1851, he took a fortnight's holiday in Weston-super-Mare and did not return until he was certain that Shelley's most famous creation had found its way to whatever area of the library had been arranged for its comfort. The Caxton's records show that the library sulked for some months after, and took mischievous pleasure in repeatedly relocating Mr Hanna's pipe and slippers to the Annex of Unfinished Books, from which he had great difficulty in retrieving them due to an infinity of possible endings.

But this temporary estrangement of library and librarian came later. For now, let us return to December 1848, when the Caxton was located on the outskirts of the city of Ely in Cambridgeshire, within sight of its great cathedral. At that time, the Caxton's collection was much smaller than it is now, and its residents fewer. The early librarians, between their daily tasks of filing and mending, could easily visit most of the characters at least once a week, a pleasure that would be denied their successors.

Even for the most garrulous of men, such social calls could prove exhausting and Mr Hanna, although a lover of books, was less well equipped for conversational pleasantries than most. His preference was to communicate by letter or note, which better displayed his essential kindness and good nature while hiding his shyness, to the extent that his administration of the Caxton bore something of the complexion of the Post Office, and his morning delivery of missives became the highlight of many a character's day.

Mr Hanna was in the habit of taking a regular evening constitutional around the environs of Ely, both to give him some time away from the Caxton and to aid the digestion of his supper, even as he made a point of avoiding the cathedral's precincts after dark owing to a preponderance of reported sightings of ghostly monks. While many might have dismissed such tales as foolishness, Mr Hanna's vocation made him reluctant to disregard any reports of the otherworldly.

On one particular evening, upon returning from his walk, Mr Hanna discovered to his displeasure that a small window had been broken on the library's east wall, as though someone had attempted to gain access to the building in his absence. This effort, it seemed, had been unsuccessful, because the hole in the glass was quite small, although a series of significant cracks radiated from it, rendering the whole pane unsafe.

'Good Lord,' said Mr Hanna, to no one in particular. 'I mean, really.'

The Caxton was very accomplished at not being noticed. It had a way of blending into its surroundings, aided by the tendency of a great many people – some of whom should really have known better – to ignore books entirely, or dismiss reading as a dreary pursuit, this being the natural response of the unimaginative to literature. A very large concentration of books, such as that contained in the Caxton, succeeded in deflecting their attention to an unusual degree, which worked to the library's advantage. Assaults on the Caxton's physical structures were, as a consequence, exceedingly rare.

Mr Hanna located a brush and pan, swept up the broken glass, and fixed a board over the inside of the window until he could source a replacement pane, the Caxton's librarians being required to demonstrate a degree of accomplishment in making minor repairs to bricks and mortar as well as paper and boards. The window was quite narrow, and only a very thin person might have been able to enter through it, even assuming they had succeeded in removing the glass in its entirety. But the damage was troubling to Mr Hanna, for the window in question led into his own bedroom, and few things are better guaranteed to come between a man and his sleep than the possibility of being roused by an intruder.

To calm himself, Mr Hanna prepared a cup of hot milk, checked all the other windows and doors and went to bed, where he endured a restless night. He spent most of the following day trying to make some sense of Samuel Richardson's revisions, over fourteen separate editions, to the four volumes of *Pamela in her Exalted Condition*, the late novelist's sequel to his most famous work, *Pamela; or Virtue, Rewarded*. This was a task of such indescribable tedium that successive librarians had been bequeathing it to one another ever since Richardson had gone to that great sorting office in the sky back in 1761, but it was one that Mr Hanna – for whom dullness was an underrated virtue – remained determined, even delighted, to complete. He set his work aside only to purchase a new pane for the broken window, and determined to embark upon its repair come morning.

That evening, as the weather turned cold, he once again took to the fields for some fresh air and exercise. Christmas was approaching, and the choristers were practising in the cathedral, their songs carrying pleasantly in the night air. Mr Hanna was still humming 'Come, Thou Long Expected Jesus' when he returned to the library, only for a vague sense of unease to mute his joy. He decided to make a single circuit of the exterior, and found to his displeasure that another window had been broken in much the same manner as the first, the ground beneath being disturbed by what resembled bare footprints.

Mr Hanna had by now progressed from 'troubled' to 'actively concerned'. As has been established, the Caxton was practiced at concealment, but this did not mean it could remain undetected forever. It had already been required to relocate on a handful of occasions in its history, a contingency for which instructions remained available, even if the relevant envelope was marked with a wearied note written in a previous librarian's hand, reading 'Do Please Try Not to Open This.'

As before, Mr Hanna cleared away the broken glass and boarded up the hole in the window. He brewed a pot of tea and mulled over the problem. The solution, unpleasant though it appeared, might be to forego his walk the following night, and instead conceal himself in some suitable bushes. From this vantage point, he would be able to spot the approach of the interloper, and discourage any further attempts at damage with vague, unfulfillable threats of police involvement.

With something approaching a plan of action in place, Mr Hanna settled into bed in the company of a comparative study of the Corn Laws of 1773, 1791, 1804, and 1815, with an emphasis on price stabilization measures. Eventually, the excitement proving too much for him, he nodded off in his little closet bed, the curtains drawn over the single window to deal with the draft from the broken pane. The wind whistled beyond the walls, and the first of the winter's snow began silently to fall, but to all of this Mr Hanna remained oblivious as he dreamed of being surrounded by four hundred and ninety bushels in a grain store while he struggled to remember where he'd left his hat.

In time, though, Mr Hanna was woken by a tapping, as of a branch knocking against the glass from outside.

'Oh, bother!' said Mr Hanna. He tried to get back to sleep, but the noises persisted from behind his curtain. An old oak, long overdue for pruning, stood close to the library's east side. Mr Hanna had been waiting for the quiet of January to tackle the job, as by then the oak would be deep in winter dormancy and could tend its wounds in spring in order to recover by summer. That task, he realized, might now have to be moved forward.

'For goodness's sake!' said Mr Hanna, as he pulled back the curtains and board to open the window. Half asleep, he sought out the offending branch in order to break off enough to quell the knocking.

But instead of touching bark, his fingers found a small, cold hand.

Mr Hanna shrieked, and through the open window heard a girl cry out in return. He tried to retrieve his limb, but it was held in a relentless, icy grip.

'Let me in – let me in!' said the girl, as yet unseen.

'Get out of it!' said Mr Hanna. 'Give me back my hand!'

'I'm come home.'

'No, you haven't,' said Mr Hanna. 'This isn't your home. It's a library.'

'He peered through the gap in the window and could just make out, amid the descending snow, the features of a brown-haired young woman. She was wearing a thin white dress, and her feet were bare.

'What are you doing out there anyway?' said Mr Hanna. 'You'll catch your death. And where are your shoes?'

'It's been twenty years,' said the girl.

'Don't be silly,' said Mr Hanna. 'You can't be more than eighteen. And you really shouldn't be wandering alone in the dead of night.'

'I've been a waif for twenty years!' insisted the girl.

'All right, all right,' said Mr Hanna. 'Have it your way.'

Mr Hanna might have been a retiring, scholarly man, but he was far from heartless. He couldn't leave a girl out in the snow, waif or not. He'd never have been able to forgive himself if something happened to her.

'Look,' he said, 'let me go, if you want me to let you in.'

The girl looked at him suspiciously.

'Promise?'

'I promise.'

Reluctantly, the girl released Mr Hanna's hand.

'Come around to the front,' he said. 'I won't be long.'

Mr Hanna found his robe, put on his slippers, and walked to the door. When he opened it, the girl was standing on the step, shivering. Her lips were bloodless and her skin was pale, but her eyes shone with a brilliance that had nothing to do with the lamp in Mr Hanna's hand. She was, he thought, quite beautiful.

'I'm come home,' she said.

'Yes, I heard all that,' said Mr Hanna. 'You haven't, but never mind. I'll put the kettle on, and we'll find you somewhere to put your head down. Tomorrow we'll figure out what to do with you.'

The office that doubled as Mr Hanna's living room was still warm from the evening's fire and some embers remained in the hearth. Mr Hanna added paper and wood, and soon a small blaze was crackling again. He made the girl a cup of tea, and gave her a slice of ginger cake, which she nibbled while curled up in the armchair.

'What's your name?'

'Catherine,' she said.

'Look,' said Mr Hanna, 'I hope you won't think me rude for asking, but you haven't been breaking my windows, have you?'

Catherine shuffled her feet awkwardly.

'Might have done.'

'But why?'

'Dunno. Just seemed like the right way to go about it.'

'Go about what?'

'Getting in.'

'Doors are the right way to go about it,' said Mr Hanna. 'Very popular they are, doors, and have been for centuries. Breaking people's windows is only the right way to go about getting into prison.'

'Sorry,' said Catherine.

'And so you should be. Forced entry is a bad habit to indulge, especially in one so young.'

Mr Hanna knelt to poke the fire. He had a feeling he was missing something, like a man who has been given a jigsaw puzzle to complete without any clue as to what the final picture might be supposed to resemble. When he looked again at the girl, she was sound asleep in the chair. Mr Hanna took a blanket from the laundry chest, laid it over her, and prepared to return to bed. He did not worry about leaving a stranger alone in the library. The Caxton knew how to look after itself.

As he prepared to go to his bedroom, he heard a *thud* from outside, as though a heavy object had just landed on the doorstep.

'Ah,' said Mr Hanna. 'Right.'

Because it was nearly Christmas, and delays were to be expected.

The girl named Catherine opened her eyes and stretched. The late dawn light of winter shone through the window behind her, lending her a certain aspect of the celestial. Mr Hanna was sitting in a chair on the opposite side of the fire, reading the final page of the book in his hands. By his feet lay a sheet of brown paper and a length of string.

'Feeling better?' he said.

'Much, thank you.'

Colour had been restored to her cheeks and lips, so that she seemed to glow. She watched as he closed the volume and carefully set it aside.

'What was the book about?' she said.

'Don't you know?' said Mr Hanna.

'Seeing it in your hands, I think I recall some of the plot, but not all.'

'Well, we only ever really know our own stories,' said Mr Hanna, 'and often barely those. As it happens, it was about a house on the Yorkshire moors, and a love affair – two love affairs, really.'

'Did you like it?'

'It was unusual. I don't believe I've ever read anything quite like it before.'

'But that's true of all the best books, isn't it?'

'Yes, I rather suppose it is.'

'Did you sit up all night to finish it?'

'I did,' said Mr Hanna. 'I haven't slept a wink.'

'Then surely you must have enjoyed it?'

'You're right, of course, if that's to be the test. I must admit to being aware of the novel's existence, but I hadn't been inclined to read it. I think I had judged it by what others had written and said of it, but the library knows better than any of them. It always does. Incidentally, I was wrong about something else, too. You have come home, Cathy. This is where you were always meant to be.'

The girl appeared concerned.

'Alone?'

'No, you'll have plenty of company.' Mr Hanna glanced at the novel, recalling details of its central romance. 'And more to come, I should think.'

He stood, smiled upon her, and offered his arm.

'Meanwhile, why don't I show you around?' he said. 'After all, there are so many interesting people for you to meet...'

John Connolly

John Connolly is the author of more than thirty books, including the award-winning Charlie Parker mysteries, the acclaimed fantasy novel *The Book of Lost Things* – which he is currently adapting for the screen – and *he*, his fictional account of the life of comedian Stan Laurel. He has also written two collections of supernatural stories, *Nocturnes* and *Night Music*, many of which have been broadcast as readings by the BBC, and two series of books for young adults: the Samuel Johnson novels, and the Chronicles of the Invaders, co-written with his partner, Jennifer Ridyard. *The Caxton Private Lending Library & Book Depository*, the first Caxton story, was published in 2013 and won multiple prizes, including the Edgar and Anthony Awards, for best short fiction. He presents a weekly music show, *ABC to XTC*, for RTÉ.

A Permanent Solution

M. W. Craven

'What have you got on, Poe?' Detective Inspector Stephanie Flynn said.

'That's a question that never ends well, boss,' Detective Sergeant Washington Poe replied. 'And I'm busy at it happens.'

'You don't *look* busy.'

'The mind's work is mysterious.'

'Seriously, what you got on?'

'Nothing,' he sighed. 'What you after?'

She slid a document across the table. It looked suspiciously like joining instructions.

'I need you and Tilly to attend a seminar in Swansea.'

Poe read the title: Achieving Effective Supervision. His stomach sank.

'I'll pass, thanks,' he said, pushing the document back.

'We've talked about this, Poe,' Flynn said.

'We have?'

'We have.'

'And I was listening?'

'I don't give a shit if you were or not,' she said. 'You're a detective sergeant in the National Crime Agency and that means sometimes you have to suck it up and occasionally do what you're told. Tilly needs to attend as she has her own little team now, and according to

HR, you haven't completed a single day's management training since your sergeant's course. Not one day, not in all these years.'

'I've been too busy catching serial killers,' Poe said. 'You know, like we're supposed to?'

That bit was true. The NCA's Serious Crime Analysis Section, the unit he and Flynn worked for, was charged with identifying emerging serial killers and helping territorial police forces when they had apparently motiveless murders. Over the last couple of years they'd solved some high-profile cases. Poe had assumed that would be enough to get HR off his back. Apparently, it wasn't.

'They've sent me a list of excuses you've used to get out of the courses they've arranged for you, you know,' Flynn said. 'Shall I read a couple?'

'I don't really think that's necess—'

'When invited to attend Lean Organisations Level Two, you claimed to have a gangrenous leg.' She peered over her reading glasses. 'How is that, by the way?'

'It cleared up on its own,' Poe mumbled.

'And, when you failed to turn up to the Media and Public Relations course you'd been booked on, you told the course instructor, and I can't believe you didn't get fired for this, that you had a sucking chest wound.'

Poe said nothing.

'Look,' Flynn sighed. 'Attend this course and I promise you that you won't have to go on another one for a whole year.'

'Three years,' Poe said.

'Eighteen months. And don't push it.'

* * *

Which was why, a day later, Poe was sulking in front of a registration desk packed with name tags, willing his name not to be on one of them.

'Here you are, Poe!' Tilly Bradshaw said excitedly, reaching across and handing him his badge.

'Smashing,' Poe said.

'Oh, don't be such a cranky pants. It'll be fun.'

'You know how I feel about these things, Tilly.'

'I do, Poe.'

'I'm steadfastly against them, aren't I?'

'You are. But this will be different.'

'Why?'

'Because I'm here, silly.'

He smiled. Tilly Bradshaw had a once-in-a-generation mind, but was the most naive person Poe had ever met. Leaving mainstream education for Oxford University to read pure mathematics aged just thirteen, she'd been shielded from much of the outside world. On completing an undergraduate degree, a postgraduate degree and three separate DPhils, Oxford's equivalent of a PhD, the Pro-Vice-Chancellor with the Innovation portfolio had hoped she would stay, moving from one research grant to the next. She was his prize asset and brought in huge sums of money. They hadn't counted, however, on the wilful streak that Bradshaw had inherited from her father. Instead of spending the rest of her life in academia proving impossible equations, she decided to apply her extraordinary mind to solving real-world problems – namely crime. But, because of her sheltered upbringing, she had little to no social skill, told the truth regardless of the consequences and seemed to have no embarrassment threshold. She also had a bird-like curiosity, which was why she found anything new, no matter how boring everyone else found it, endlessly fascinating.

'Come on,' Poe said. 'Let's get this over with.'

'That's the spirit, sir,' the man behind the registration desk said.

* * *

'Well, that was bloody awful,' Poe said, eight hours later.

They were at the conference hotel's bar, perusing the menu. Poe was nursing his second pint of Skull Attack, a copper-coloured, hoppy beer, brewed by the Cardiff brewery, Brains. Bradshaw was sipping a sparkling water, no ice, no lemon. An untouched bowl of peanuts sat on one of the beer towels. During a previous case – *after* he'd eaten some, he was keen to point out whenever it was raised – Bradshaw had told him that bar nuts had been known to contain as many as one hundred unique specimens of urine, spoiling them for him forever.

'She wasn't a great instructor, was she, Poe?' Bradshaw said.

'Like an annoying sixth former, Tilly. Completely out of her depth.'

'I agree, although to be fair, I don't think you gave her a chance.'

'I'm not following.'

'Whenever she asked if anyone had any questions, you asked one that wasn't strictly relevant to achieving effective supervision techniques.'

'I've been a manager longer than you, Tilly,' Poe said. 'Perhaps, in time, you'll come to realise that management is about more than just—'

'You asked her why yoghurt was almost exclusively advertised to women.'

'OK, maybe that was a bit—'

'And then you asked her why people point at their wrist when asking for the time, but don't point at their bottom when asking where the toilet is.'

'And we won't be telling the boss that, will we?' Poe said.

'Will she be cross?'

'I can live with cross. I'm more concerned about being put on another course as punishment. And anyway, what about you? You asked if she'd considered whether her weak academic performance was associated with a misdiagnosed adolescent psychological profile when she was younger.'

'That was a good question, Poe.'

'Nobody understood it, Tilly. And it made her cry.'

'Oh,' Bradshaw said. 'I didn't know that.'

'It's OK. Nobody minded.'

'They didn't?'

'No – we got to have our coffee break early.'

'Obviously I didn't mean to make her cry,' Bradshaw said. 'Perhaps I should go and apologise.'

'She'll be long gone, Tilly,' he said.

'I'll apologise tomorrow,' she said.

'I don't know if I can handle another day of this,' Poe said.

Which was when a middle-aged man took the bar stool beside Bradshaw. He was thin, but had a nose that would have better fitted a broader face. His stringy hair was the colour of London snow. Not greasy, but probably due a wash. His forehead was damp with sweat.

'Hot and humid for this time of year,' he said to Bradshaw, wiping his brow.

Bradshaw frowned.

'Here we bloody go,' Poe murmured.

'The average temperature in September in Swansea is a daily high of nineteen degrees Celsius and a daily low of eleven,' she said, 'and the average rainfall is ninety-four millimetres. It is therefore most definitely not hot and humid for this time of year; it is entirely within expectations.'

She smiled at the man.

'Er... what?' he said.

Poe explained what had just happened.

'Tilly likes numbers,' he said. He turned to Bradshaw. 'And when someone comments on the weather, Tilly, they aren't initiating a meteorological discussion. They are merely breaking the ice. It's a form of greeting.'

'Gosh,' she said. She faced the hapless man. 'My name's Matilda Bradshaw and this is Washington Poe. I am very pleased to meet you.

Would you like to join us for our evening meal?' She held out her hand.

Poe put his head in his hands and groaned.

The man laughed and shook Bradshaw's hand.

'Sorry about that,' Poe said.

'Nothing to apologise for,' the man said. 'It takes all sorts to make a world.'

'That it does,' Poe said. 'And, as Tilly has just said, my name's Poe.' He reached across a bemused Bradshaw and shook his hand as well. It was damp.

'Adrian Scratton.'

'Pleased to meet you, Adrian. And, of course, you don't have to eat with us. Tilly's enthusiasm for life can be a bit much sometimes.'

'Probably for the best,' Scratton said. 'I'm not the best company right now.'

'Why is that, Adrian Scratton?' Bradshaw said. 'Is it because you're scared?'

'Tilly!' Poe said. 'Stop torturing the man.'

'But Adrian Scratton is displaying all the physical signs of fear, Poe!' she said. 'His hands are clammy and he is trembling. He's blinking faster than is usual and his breathing is rapid. I imagine if I took his pulse it would be elevated.'

Poe was about to say that the physical signs of fear sounded remarkably similar to the physical signs of a hangover, but Scratton didn't smell like a boozehound. And Bradshaw's once-in-a-generation mind didn't just stretch to maths, data and patterns; she was also the best profiler in the country. Poe had learned never to dismiss anything she said.

'*Are* you scared, Adrian?' he said. 'You can tell me if you are; I'm a police officer.'

Scratton faced him. His eyes welled up.

'I think someone's trying to kill me,' he said.

* * *

'What do you think, Poe?' Bradshaw said.

'About what?'

'About someone trying to kill Adrian Scratton.'

It was the next morning and they were queuing at the breakfast buffet. Bradshaw was having brown toast, dry; Poe was having three Welsh sausages, bacon, black pudding, hash browns and something called laverbread. Bradshaw said it was pure seaweed mixed with oats and that it sounded disgusting. Poe agreed it did, but said it was OK as it had been fried in bacon grease.

'You mean, do I think some shadowy organisation has been sending him death threats?' Poe asked.

'Yes.'

'No, I don't. I think he's a kook.'

'But he said he'd witnessed something he shouldn't have.'

'And did you notice he couldn't tell us what that was?'

Bradshaw paused to fill a glass with apple juice. Poe grabbed himself a black coffee.

'I agree,' she said. 'None of what Adrian Scratton said made sense. However, he *was* scared and there were no obvious signs of mental ill health.'

'Yep, there is that,' Poe said. 'Tell you what – after I've had my breakfast, I'll dip out of this morning's session and drive over to Swansea Central Police Station. Have a word with someone in CID. See if they can shed some light on this.'

'I'll make notes for you, Poe.'

'Oh, goody.'

Someone tapped Poe on the shoulder. He turned to see a smartly dressed woman in her thirties. She had cropped hair and a warm face. Her eyes were the colour of honey.

'Are you Washington Poe?' she said.

'I am.'

'And are you Matilda Bradshaw?'

'I am,' Bradshaw said. 'But my friends call me Tilly.'

'I'm not your friend.'

'Then you can't call her Tilly,' Poe said. 'And you are?'

'I'm Detective Constable Rhiannon Carter-Ellis,' she said. 'Can I have a word? I'm with Swansea CID.'

'You're taking the piss,' Poe said.

* * *

They were led into a room. One of the smaller breakout spaces they had used the day before. A round table surrounded by moulded plastic chairs centred the room. Offers to dine in the hotel restaurant at night hung from the wall. A water dispenser in the corner burped.

'Can I get you anything?' Carter-Ellis said.

'My breakfast,' Poe said.

'Hopefully this won't take long.'

'What hopefully won't take long? I have a seminar on Achieving Effective Supervision that I'm desperate to get back to.'

Bradshaw giggled. Carter-Ellis scowled.

'I'm afraid I can't say.'

'I'm out of here then,' Poe said, standing up.

'Sir, if you don't sit down, I *will* arrest you.'

Poe reached into his jacket pocket and retrieved his ID card. He flipped it open and said, 'Put a hand on either of us and I'll arrest *you* for assault.'

'You're NCA?'

'I am,' Poe said. 'Now, if you can't tell us what's going on, you'd better go and fetch someone who can. Otherwise your chief constable will be explaining to my director why two of his officers have been unlawfully detained.'

Carter-Ellis came to a decision. The right one as far as Poe was concerned.

'There's been a murder,' she said.

'And you want our help?' Poe said. 'You'll have to make a referral and I'm warning you, unless—'

'No, you don't understand, sarge,' Carter-Ellis cut in. 'We want to speak to you as witnesses, not police officers.'

Poe came over all cold. He glanced at Bradshaw. She had paled, even more than usual.

'This is about Adrian Scratton, isn't it?' Poe said.

Carter-Ellis nodded. 'You and Miss Bradshaw were the last people to see him alive.'

'Shit,' he said.

* * *

Poe gave his statement. Told Carter-Ellis what he knew. That Scratton had sat next to them in the bar and had started chatting. That Bradshaw had thought he looked scared and eventually he'd told them he feared for his life. Poe said Scratton's story hadn't added up. That, although Scratton had been scared of something, Poe thought it unlikely someone wanted to kill him.

'Yet here we are,' Cater-Ellis said.

'I might have messed up,' Poe admitted.

'Maybe not. We have no record of Adrian Scratton making a statement saying his life was at risk. To the best of our knowledge, apart from a speeding ticket nine years ago, he has never had contact with the police.'

'He told us he'd seen something he wasn't supposed to see.'

'What?'

'Wouldn't say,' Poe said. 'One of the reasons I took his story less seriously than perhaps I should have.'

Carter-Ellis closed her notebook.

'I think that's enough for now,' she said. 'OK if we contact you for follow-ups?'

'Of course,' Poe said. 'Any chance I can look at the scene?'

'Not unless you're a specialist in bizarre murders. What is it you actually do in the NCA, by the way?'

'I hunt serial killers,' Poe said.

* * *

'And you're sure it's murder?' Poe said, when they were crammed in the service lift. The hotel didn't want a police investigation upsetting their guests. Poe wondered what their guests would think if they knew a killer was amongst them. 'He hasn't just slipped in the shower?'

'His body hasn't been moved, so you can see for yourself, sarge,' Carter-Ellis said. She frowned, bit her lip, then added, 'Who are you by the way? The senior investigating officer was very keen to allow you up when he heard who his witnesses were.'

Poe didn't answer. He glanced at Bradshaw. She looked as worried as he did. How had they got this so badly wrong?

A cop with a clipboard was waiting for them when the lift doors opened.

'Outer cordon,' he said. 'Need you to sign in here then step into the room over there to suit up.'

'This floor guest-free?' Poe said.

'It is now. They're all downstairs waiting to be interviewed.'

'What did you tell them?'

'Nothing yet.'

Poe nodded in approval.

* * *

Scratton's room was on the eighth floor. His view was mainly the gravelled roof of the hotel's four-storey extension, all air-conditioning units, satellite dishes and dead seagulls. His room was identical to Poe's: box-shaped, a bed with a thin mattress, and a bathroom so small you could wash your feet in the bath while sitting on the toilet. A couple of generic pictures were screwed to, not hung from, the wall – there to remind you that you were in a conference hotel and your life sucked. Poe had the same pictures in his room.

Poe had asked Carter-Ellis if she was sure Scratton had been murdered. Now he wished that he hadn't. Scratton's body was on the floor, wedged between the bed and the window, crumpled up, one hand underneath the small bedside table. He must have knocked the phone off on his way down as it was on the floor beside him. He'd clearly died at the hands of someone else. A hessian sack had been put over his head and most of it was soaked in congealed blood. It had seeped out on to the carpet tiles. Poe reckoned the spread of blood was about a metre. He could see no other injuries. His hands, the only uncovered parts of Scratton, were pale but not swollen. He hadn't been dead long enough for bacteria to build up.

'Who found him?'

'The maid,' the SIO, a tall Welshman called Chief Inspector Powell, said. 'Scratton had ordered a wake-up call but the telephone was off the hook. She was sent to check up on him.'

'Did she touch anything?'

'Says she didn't. Walked in, ran out. Called her supervisor, a man called Hopkins. He's waiting outside. Shitting himself, as he was on duty last night.'

'Anyone looked underneath the hood?' Poe said. 'See what the cause of death is.'

'I lifted it up,' Powell said, 'and CSI have videoed it. A single gunshot to the temple. The gun's missing but it's small calibre by the looks of it. Didn't see an exit wound, so the bullet's still in there.'

'And it'll have rattled around the inside of his skull like a marble in a saucepan,' Poe said. 'Turned his brain to mince.'

Chief Inspector Powell nodded.

'I don't see that many murders, Sergeant Poe, but, to me, it looks like an execution.'

Poe said nothing. Just stared at the corpse on the floor. He still couldn't believe he'd assessed the situation so poorly last night. The man had asked for his help and all he'd given was platitudes. A long-winded talk about how he was imagining things. And now he was dead, his blood leaching into the hotel's cheap carpet. He'd let him down.

'You been through the hotel's CCTV yet?'

'A couple of my DCs are doing it now, but it's new and complex and they need the system engineer to show them how it works.'

A noise made Poe look up. A rattle. The curtain moved.

'Was it smelly in here?'

'I'm sorry?'

'The window, it's unlocked.'

It was a small window, the top one at head height that guests could open to let some air into the room. The main window was fastened shut as a security measure. The hotel no doubt didn't want depressed guests flinging themselves out after they'd put their hand in the toilet getting out of the bath. The unlocked window was long and flat, about six by thirty-six inches, and pushed out rather than lifted up, held in place by an adjustable latch. When the window was closed, the latch acted as the lock. It was the moving latch that had caught Poe's attention. The window was closed, but not locked.

'I'm wondering if someone had put it on the latch because it was smelly in here,' he said. 'And the wind knocked it off.'

'No one's touched it, as far as I know,' Chief Inspector Powell said, frowning.

'Maybe the maid did?'

'Davy,' he said into his radio, 'get hold of the maid and ask her if she touched the window.'

They waited less than a minute for the response.

'No, guv.'

'There's your answer, Sergeant Poe. Scratton must have fancied some fresh air last night.'

'It was too windy last night,' Poe said. 'I hate stuffy rooms with the best of them, but even I couldn't stand the billowing curtains. I had to keep mine closed. And, speaking of curtains, why are these still open? There are at least three other buildings I can see that have a view of this room. If I've had enough time to tie a sack over his head, I've had enough time to shut the bloody curtains.'

'Poe?'

He looked over towards the door. Bradshaw was there, beckoning him.

'Excuse me,' he said to Chief Inspector Powell.

'What is it, Tilly?'

'Look at this.'

She held up her tablet and pressed play. It was CCTV footage of the corridor they were standing in. The time stamp said it was nine-thirty p.m.

'This from last night?' he asked.

'It is, Poe. If I press play, you'll see Adrian Scratton step out of the lift and go into his room.'

Poe watched Scratton shuffle along the corridor, stopping to enter his key card into the reader above the door handle.

'How did you get access to that?' Powell said, looking over Poe's shoulder. 'My DCs said their firewall is state of the art.'

'Yes,' Bradshaw said, 'it looked expensive.'

Poe grinned. He'd seen Bradshaw get into laptops encrypted with Ministry of Defence security – accessing a hotel's CCTV system wasn't something she would have needed more than a few seconds on. She certainly wouldn't need the assistance of a system engineer.

'Play it forwards, Tilly,' he said. 'Let's have a look at his killer. I assume they had covered themselves up.'

'That's just the thing, Poe,' she said. 'Between Adrian Scratton going to bed at half past nine and the maid waking him at seven this morning, no one entered the room.'

'You sure?'

'Quite sure, Poe.'

'And there isn't an adjoining door in his room,' he said. 'It's one way in and one way out.'

'You're not suggesting the maid killed him?' Carter-Ellis said. 'Because I've spoken to her and she's in shock.'

'It wasn't the maid,' Poe said. 'Scratton's body is fresh, but not seven in the morning fresh.'

'Somebody was waiting in his room for him then.'

'What, and they're still in there?'

'It wasn't that, Poe,' Bradshaw said. 'I've gone all the way back to the room's previous occupants and every person who entered the room, left the room.'

'The CCTV system has been compromised then,' Carter-Ellis said.

'It hasn't,' Bradshaw said.

'And Tilly's never wrong about these things,' Poe said.

'You said the window wasn't locked,' Carter-Ellis said. 'Maybe someone got in that way. Killed Scratton, then climbed back out.'

'We're on the eighth floor and the window's only six inches high. Not even a child could wriggle through.'

'If he had the window open, could he have been shot from *outside?*'

'And Scratton just happened to have a sack on his head?'

'Fair point,' she said, reddening.

'I'm sorry,' Poe said. 'But that unlocked window is bugging me.'

'Why?'

'I don't know,' Poe said. 'It's just jarring for some reason. It should be locked; the fact it isn't doesn't make sense.'

'None of this makes sense, Sergeant Poe,' Chief Inspector Powell said, coming up behind them. 'I think what we have here is a genuine locked-room mystery.'

* * *

The chief inspector asked if Poe could stay on a bit. Poe said that he'd need to make a referral to SCAS and get Flynn's approval, but it shouldn't be a problem.

'CSI won't be done with the room for the rest of the day, Sergeant Poe,' he said. 'Have you got anything you can be doing in the meantime?'

Poe sighed. 'I suppose I'd better go and finish this stupid course the boss put me and Tilly on. But I'll see if I can extend our room reservations for another day first. See if they can keep it open-ended.'

'Put it on our tab,' Powell said.

'Will do,' Poe said. 'You OK with that, Tilly?'

'Yes, Poe. I think this case will take a long time to solve.'

'Or it'll never be solved.'

Both wrong, as it turned out...

* * *

When it came to seminars on Achieving Effective Supervision, Poe was a master procrastinator. So, instead of re-joining the group after their scheduled morning coffee break like Bradshaw had wanted to, he decided to make sure they could stay at least one more night in the hotel. After that, the SCAS office manager could sort out their accommodation.

The reception desk was staffed by a man wearing a headset. He was on a call and gave them the two minutes signal. He appeared to be dealing with a complaint. Probably about the paintings in the rooms, Poe thought.

'What do you think is going on here, Tilly?' he said, while they waited.

'I don't know, Poe. Unless someone hid in the room before the last guests checked in, and are still hiding there now, I really can't see how it was done.'

'There's nowhere *to* hide.'

'I know,' Bradshaw said, 'that's why it's so perplexing. But I can't think of any other explanation. The CCTV footage has not been tampered with – no one other than Adrian Scratton entered that room.'

'And he wasn't shot through the window. He was wearing a hood, the calibre's too small and the angle doesn't work anyway.'

Something in Poe's peripheral vision caught his attention: a solitary, silver balloon, bobbing along the ceiling, a white ribbon trailing after it. He could make out the number – twenty-five – but the words were too small.

'Maybe CSI will offer us some help,' he said. 'The murderer was in that room; forensic transfer is inevitable.'

'Good morning, sir,' the receptionist said. 'Thank you for waiting. How can I help you?'

'Miss Bradshaw and I need to extend our stay. We're helping with the investigation upstairs.'

'Dreadful business, sir. They're saying it's autoerotic asphyxiation? That he'd put a plastic bag over his head and had suffocated while pleasuring himself. So dangerous it should be classed as suicide really.'

'Don't be a berk,' Poe said. 'He had a hessian sack over his head, not a plastic bag. It wasn't autoerotic anything.'

The man was dead. The least Poe could do was give him some dignity.

'That doesn't mean—' the receptionist started to say.

'Look, mate, a sack is basically a net with small holes. You couldn't suffocate an asthmatic pit pony with a sack.'

'But—'

'What's with the balloon?' Poe said, changing the subject. It was either that or ask him for his movements last night. Scare him into silence.

'We have a silver anniversary party in the ballroom tonight. That one must have escaped. Well, I say ballroom, it's really just a conference room…'

But Poe had stopped listening. The idiot receptionist had rattled his mental filing cabinet. He stared at the balloon, as he remembered a case that had stumped investigators in Florida a few years ago.

'Sorry,' he said, 'we won't be extending our stay after all.'

'Why ever not, Poe?' Bradshaw said. 'We can't give up this early.'

'We're not giving up, Tilly; I think I know what happened.'

'You do?'

He nodded.

'But I'll need you to check a few things first.'

* * *

'Adrian Scratton wasn't murdered,' Poe said to the assembled team. 'He committed suicide.'

'Suicide?' Chief Inspector Powell said. 'He had a sack over his head, he'd been shot in the temple and the gun wasn't in the room.'

Poe had asked to speak to the chief inspector. Told him he might be able to save him an expensive investigation. Powell had brought in his senior team: a uniformed inspector, two plain-clothed sergeants and a few seasoned detectives. About two hundred years of experience, all told.

'Nevertheless,' Poe said.

'I think you'd better talk us through it, Sergeant Poe.'

'If the receptionist hadn't suggested Scratton had committed suicide-by-wank while I was looking at a balloon, I doubt I'd have put all this together so quickly.'

'A balloon?'

'Yeah, there's a silver anniversary party this evening and the staff must have been filling celebratory balloons with helium. A snide one escaped into the hotel lobby. Was bobbing around the ceiling.'

'OK,' Powell said. He checked his watch. He clearly wasn't convinced. Poe didn't blame him.

'Part of my job at SCAS is to study murder,' he said. 'Anything a bit different, anything with a sniff of weird. It's how we build up the knowledge that helps you guys when you get the odd ones. Anyway, the cops in Palm Beach Gardens in Florida had a similar case. A murder, or so they thought. An old guy had been found with a single gunshot wound to the chest. Weapon was nowhere to be found and his watch and money were missing. Local cops understandably thought it was a mugging gone wrong.'

'But it wasn't?' Powell said.

'They have bright cops out there. Have to be, I suppose. Try googling "Florida man" and see what happens. Absolute nutcases. Suppose it makes the cops good at lateral thinking. Anyway, one of them thought to check his internet search history.'

'And?'

'Turns out the dead man had just bought a weather balloon.'

'A weather balloon?'

Poe nodded.

'Which is why the one in the hotel lobby jogged my memory,' he said.

'I'm not seeing—'

'He'd also bought a tank of helium and searched how many cubic feet he'd need to raise one pound.'

'He tied the gun to the weather balloon then shot himself?' Carter-Ellis said.

'Seems we have bright cops here, too,' Poe said. 'Yes, that's exactly what happened. He killed himself and the balloon lifted the gun away from his staged crime scene.'

'Blimey,' Powell said. 'You saying that's what happened here?'

'Tilly?' Poe said. 'Can you do this bit?'

'Yes, Poe.' She stood and pushed a stray hair behind her ear. 'I've completed a preliminary profile of Adrian Scratton and he was heavily in debt. He would have almost certainly lost his house this year. He took out a second mortgage to prop up his engineering business, but he really shouldn't have. Emerging technology coming in from South Korea had all but made his company's product redundant.'

'We all have money problems,' Powell said.

'I don't,' Bradshaw said. 'I save thirty per cent of my salary every month and have done since I was eighteen years of age.'

'You have?'

'Of course.'

'Blimey, you must be a millionaire by now.'

Bradshaw didn't answer.

'You *are* a millionaire?' Poe said.

'My dad looks after my money,' she said. 'Anyway, Poe also asked me to look at Adrian Scratton's internet search history.'

'We wondered why you'd wanted to examine his iPad,' Carter-Ellis said. 'We couldn't open it.'

'Where'd you get his passwords from?' Powell said.

After Poe had stopped laughing, he said, 'Tilly doesn't need passwords.'

'I certainly don't, Poe,' she said. 'And, although Adrian Scratton had tried to delete and scrub his history, this is what I found. He'd bought life insurance after a minor health scare last year, more than enough to cover the debt he owed. If he died, his wife and children wouldn't be made homeless.'

'That's nowhere near enough to rule suicide—'

'Last month he visited Manchester and withdrew one thousand pounds from his depleted bank account.'

'This is the only thing we can't be certain of,' Poe said. 'But we think this was him buying a gun. Go in the right pub in Manchester, you can get one for a grand.'

Nods in the room said Manchester's gun problem wasn't a secret in Wales.

'Still not enough,' Powell said.

'Tell the chief inspector about Mr Scratton's most recent purchase, Tilly.'

'He spent his last two thousand pounds on a HUX Z382 Max-pro.'

'And what's that?'

'It's a drone,' Poe said. 'A good one. Able to carry a small load like an HD camera.'

'Or a small gun,' Carter-Ellis said thoughtfully.

'Exactly. And here's the kicker: this particular drone has an autopilot function. It can be programmed to fly to a specific destination.'

'OK,' Powell said. 'I assume you have a sequence of events for us?'

Poe nodded.

'I think Adrian Scratton knew if he didn't get money soon his family would be made homeless. He also realised that his life insurance had a two-year suicide clause. Most of them do. Stops people from taking out huge policies then killing themselves the next day. But if he were murdered…'

'They pay out,' Carter-Ellis said.

'So, believing he's out of options, he chooses a permanent solution. He checks into a seaside hotel and seeks out a guest who will be there the following day to tell a story of him being scared for his life. And we know he did this as the receptionist said Scratton had asked if anyone at the bar was attending the Achieving Effective Supervision seminar. He knew we'd still be in the hotel when his body was found in the morning. Once he's planted the story, he goes up to his room. He programs his drone to fly out to sea. He then holds it out of the open window and starts the propellers. Keeps hold of it while he ties on both the control pad and the gun, like the tail of a kite. Probably only needed a metre or so of string. Educated guess now, but I imagine he lets go of the control pad. Now it's just the gun he's holding that's stopping the drone from flying away. With his spare hand he puts the sack over his head and, when he's ready, he shoots himself in the head. He drops the gun and the drone, no longer tethered, drags everything incriminating out of the open window and flies away, as it's programmed to do. Thirty minutes later, it loses power and falls into the Bristol Channel.'

'Where it will never be found,' Chief Inspector Powell said. 'And as this happened at night, no one would have seen it. I don't know if that drone had lights but, if it did, I imagine he disabled them.'

'Why bother with the hessian sack, Sergeant Poe?' Carter-Ellis asked.

'I think the sack served two purposes,' Poe said. 'One, it made it look like a murder. Everyone in this room's first impression would have been execution. I know mine was. But the second, more important reason, was that the sack stopped blood getting on to the gun. If he'd pressed the barrel against his bare temple and pulled the trigger, there would have been blood transfer. And when the drone dragged it out of the window, it would have left a forensic trail, an easily readable story for us to follow. That's what Tilly and I think happened, anyway.'

The room fell silent as each cop stress-tested Poe's theory.

'How the hell are we going to prove this?' Chief Inspector Powell said eventually.

'Check his hands for gunshot residue,' Poe said. 'That, and not being able to shut the window after the drone had dragged the gun away, are the only things he couldn't control. We wouldn't usually check a victim's hands for GSR in a murder, but in this case, I think you'll find it's literally the smoking gun.'

'I'll request the test immediately,' Carter-Ellis said, removing her phone from her jacket pocket.

Poe frowned.

'What is it, Sergeant Poe?' the chief inspector asked.

'I've told you how to prove this, sir, but my question is this: do you *want* to? Prove it was insurance fraud and Adrian Scratton has killed himself in vain and his family is made homeless. On the other hand, if you continue to investigate this as a murder, you're hunting for someone you know doesn't exist. The very definition of a waste of time and resources.'

'What would you suggest?'

Poe shrugged.

'You haven't made the referral to SCAS yet, have you, sir?'

'Hasn't been time.'

'If you don't make it then we were never officially involved, sir. And if we were never involved then you can't know what's on Adrian Scratton's iPad. I'm not kidding when I say that Tilly is one of only half-a-dozen people in the country who can recover the data he'd scrubbed. If you don't have that data, you can't make the logical leaps I did. There *is* no insurance fraud.'

Powell looked at his cops.

'If we decide to do as Sergeant Poe suggests we all have to be in agreement on this,' he said. 'We're going to come under pressure from the family to solve it, so each one of you has to be sure.'

One at a time they nodded. Decision made.

'I'll need to tell the chief constable, but if he's OK with it, that's what we do. Thank you, Sergeant Poe,' Chief Inspector Powell said.

'Thank you for what, sir?' Poe said. 'I was never here.'

'Good man,' he said. 'And thank you, Tilly. I can see why the pair of you get into so many scrapes. If you ever need a friend in Wales, you've got one.'

'Make that two, sir,' Carter-Ellis said.

* * *

'Should we check out, Tilly?' Poe said when they were back in the hotel lobby.

'Why would we do that, Poe?'

'Er, so we can go home.'

'But if we hurry, we'll be able to take the Achieving Effective Supervision exam.'

'You're kidding?'

'I want my certificate,' Bradshaw said, her lips flat.

'I don't.'

'DI Flynn will only make us come again.'

'But we've been on a case!'

'Aha, but you told Chief Inspector Powell that we were never here.'

'Damn, you're right. We can't tell the boss any of this. And if we don't take the exam, she'll think we've bunked off somewhere.'

'She will, Poe.'

'Come on then, let's get this over with.'

'I hope it isn't multiple choice. I hate multiple choice.'

'I hope it *is* multiple choice, Tilly,' Poe said. 'That way I can employ my foolproof system.'

'You have a system? You, Mr I-Don't-Understand-Science?'

'I do,' he said. 'No matter what I think the answer is, I always choose B.'

Bradshaw considered this for a moment before letting him know what she thought.

'You're an idiot, Poe...'

M. W. Craven

Multi-award-winning author M. W. Craven was born in Carlisle but grew up in Newcastle. He joined the army at sixteen, leaving ten years later to complete a social work degree. Seventeen years after taking up a probation officer role in Cumbria, at the rank of assistant chief officer, he became a full-time author. *The Puppet Show*, the first book in his Cumbria-set Washington Poe series, was published by Little, Brown in 2018 and went on to win the Crime Writers' Association Gold Dagger in 2019. *Black Summer*, the second in the series, was longlisted for the 2020 Gold Dagger and book three, *The Curator*, was released in June 2020.

Nobody's God

Sebastien de Castell

In the beginning, there was the word, and the word was…

'And.'

Wait … that's not very impressive. Or accurate, really. Let's try again.

In the beginning, there was the *sentence*, and the sentence was…

'And which god would you like to be?'

'Excuse me?' He – or perhaps just *he* – asked.

The Other stared back at him above flat-rimmed spectacles. 'God. You. Which. Like.'

It took a moment for Him – who was now distinctly feeling like just *him* – to understand that the combination of tone, facial expression (especially the bit with the spectacles), and word choice were signifiers of someone being patronizing. 'Look, I don't see any need to be rude, I'm new at this, you know?'

'New at what?'

he – for he was now quite sure that his insignificance violated even the rules of capitalisation – threw up his hands. 'Existence.'

'"*Existence*"?' The Other's eyes narrowed, which either meant distrust, confusion, or sexual desire. *he* couldn't be sure which, but the Other cleared it up when he asked, 'Are you shitting me?'

'Ontologically, no.'

'What about metaphorically?'

He had to think for a moment. 'Not that one, either. I have no idea who, what, where, when, or *how* I am.'

The Other tapped a finger against the top of a desk that had been there the whole time but only in that instant became relevant and therefore extant. 'Son of a bitch,' he said after several taps.

'Really?' The answer seemed disappointing somehow, but at least it was something: *I* am a son of a bitch. There was a bitch, and then sometime later, there was me, her son. Progress.

The Other stood up from his previously-present but only now pertinent chair and shouted at someone in the back. 'Jennifer! Get over here!'

Another Other bustled over to the first one's desk, noticed his expression, became worried, glanced at *him*, then looked disappointed. 'Oh, drat it, Jerry, I'm sorry.'

'Jerry?' he asked. 'Is that my name?' To have an origin *and* a name was feeling rather lucky at this stage.

'No,' Jennifer replied, pointing to the other Other. 'He's Jerry. I'm Jennifer. You're nobody.'

Nobody. Not bad – had a nice sound to it. Kind of existentially daring in its own... 'Wait, that's not my name, is it?'

She shook her head. 'No. You can't have a name until you've decided which god you're going to be. Then you can have a name. Existence precedes essence, right?' She looked down at the black clipboard nestled in her arm like a sleeping baby. *Baby* ... being one of those would have simplified matters considerably. 'It appears someone forgot to imbue you before sending you here.'

'Imbue me with what?'

Jennifer tapped a pen against her teeth. 'It's complicated. And now I'm going to have to look up the appropriate procedural requirements for—'

Jerry, the first Other, who had been there during the entire exchange despite a brief lapse in relevance, stood up and said in an unnecessarily loud voice, 'Oh, for fuck's sake!' He reached out and placed the palm of his hand on *his* forehead. 'That which is!' he declared.

Suddenly he – definitely lower case – understood. '*Oh...*' he said, now aware of the cosmos and most things in it. 'That makes much more sense now.'

Jerry offered him a weary – and still patronizing – smile. 'Excellent. Now, have you decided which god you'd like to be?'

he – soon to be He – replied enthusiastically, 'The God of All Things. My name will be God, which is the Logos, which is the alpha and the—'

'Can't,' Jerry informed him. Even Jennifer gave a short shake of her head, which looked distinctly like a caution against aggravating the situation any further.

'Why not?' he asked, ignoring the warning.

'People don't want all-knowing, all-powerful gods anymore. They find it intimidating. And pretentious.'

'But...' He, still being new at language, struggled to find the right phrasing. 'Who gives a flying fuck what *people* want? If I'm their God, then I *created* them, so I really don't see how I need their permission to—'

'Existence precedes essence,' Jennifer repeated.

'You keep saying that as if it explains something. Am I supposed to understand what it means?'

'Not really,' she confessed, speaking a little quieter as if she were worried someone might be eavesdropping. 'We just say it when there's no other reasonable explanation for the way things are.'

'And the way things are is...?'

Jerry grabbed him by the collar. 'The way things are is: you can't be the God of All Things, so *pick something else!*'

Feeling rushed and somewhat intimidated, he was forced to make a quick decision. 'Fine. Thunder, then. I want to be the God of Thunder. My name will be Badaboom and I will command the thunder.'

'Can't,' Jerry said, releasing his collar. 'There's already Thor.'

'Yes, but…' He reached into his newly found knowledge of Most Things and said, 'There's also Zeus and Perun and—'

'And the Lacota have Haokah and the Yoruba have Oya. We had to lay all of them off already.'

'Lay them off?'

Jerry nodded. 'Don't need dozens of thunder gods now, do we? What with people all over the world being connected, hardly makes sense these days to have twenty-seven gods all for the same thing just with different names.'

'Globalisation,' Jennifer said sadly. 'Hard for a lot of us working folks.'

'Fine,' he said, finding himself somewhat less concerned with his domain of influence than with his desire for some kind of certainty in his existence. Also, he needed to pee. *Pick something small*, he told himself. 'Can I be the god of dogs?'

'Anubis already has that covered,' Jerry said.

'I thought he was the God of Death.'

'That too.'

Bloody greedy, he thought.

'Look, we're a bit busy here,' Jerry said, sitting back down and motioning for the next entity to come forward. 'I know this can be a difficult decision, especially with you not having been properly made aware of existence.' Here he gave Jennifer a sideways glance that seemed to imply he considered it her fault. 'So why don't you have a look around the old place and see if something strikes your fancy.'

'Look around where?'

'Earth,' Jerry replied, then wagged a finger at him. 'And I mean *just* Earth. Don't go sniffing around Mars looking for something to be the god of. *That* is a headache I don't need.' Jerry gave him a fake smile, which turned out to be not meant for him but for the person behind, because a moment later *he* was somewhere else.

Earth is a remarkably convenient place to get around. It's small, which means you can get almost anywhere without violating the law of relativity, and humans can't perceive anything but a narrow spectrum of electromagnetic waves, so being unseen is as simple as being, well, invisible.

Unfortunately, what with there being an almost infinite number of concepts around which one *could* define one's godhood, *he* found the selection confounding, especially when he realized that there was no intrinsic 'better' or 'worse' choice to be made, because meaning was – at best – a loosely defined notion.

Fucking existence precedes essence. Why did existentialism have to be the true nature of the cosmos?

What he needed was some sort of first principle – a stake in the ground, so to speak – from which to identify good choices from bad. This, too, was made problematic by the absurd nature of a universe born without underlying meaning. He thought on this for a couple of minutes before coming upon an ingenious solution, the heart of which (he wouldn't say essence because that word itself gets you into trouble) was in the very word 'god'.

Because, you see, the very notion of a 'god' implies non-gods. Non-gods were things like human beings and animals and Bluetooth speakers. Since the function of gods were to *be* gods *to* non-gods, then it stood to reason that a god should only *be* the god of something that was *meaningful* to non-gods. Otherwise, what was the point, really?

The answer, then, was to go and consult with his future worshippers on what god would be the most useful to them.

Simple.

Elegant.

Doomed.

'What do yer mean, yer can't be the God of Money?' the old man asked, rattling his cup as several more business people walked by, attempting not to display any awareness of him (or *him*), but doing so by pursing their lips and holding their noses in such a way as to make it perfectly clear that they were *entirely* aware of the old man. he wondered if they might be related to Jerry.

'Mammon was the God of Money. Plutus, too.'

'Plutus?' the old man asked.

'Greek fellow. Son of Demeter.'

'Fucking Greeks,' the old man swore. 'Screwed me again. Just last week I bought souvlaki at the place down the street and they only gave me one lousy piece of chicken. *One!* I mean, what the fuck is the stick for if you're only putting *one* piece of meat on it?'

This was actually a vastly more cosmologically significant question than the old man realised, but he was starting to feel a bit pressed for time. 'Look, *other* than money, what kind of God would you like to see?'

Someone dropped a quarter into the tin can. The old man smiled up at them, then scowled a half-second later as they walked away. 'Well, you can't be the God of Cheapskates, because we've already got plenty of those. How about the God of Not Having Money, then?'

he thought about that, but shook his head. 'Egestes, Roman God of Poverty.'

The old man glanced up at the closed shop doorway he sat in. 'What about doorways?'

'Cardea, Roman God of Thresholds. Also, door hinges.'

'Fame?'

'Fama. She's got rumours covered, too.'

'Success?'

'Felicitas.'

The old man harrumphed. 'How about tits then?'

'Tits?'

'Yeah, could do with a good old God of Tits, I reckon.'

'I ... I have a feeling Aphrodite has that covered already.'

'So? Could always do with another God of Tits.' The old man grinned and elbowed him. 'A pair of Gods of Tits is always better than one, am I right?'

'Yes, well, actually, there's also Venus, technically.'

'Which one's she, again?'

'Roman Goddess of Beauty. Actually, when you think about it, the Romans pretty much had it all covered: Naenia, Goddess of Funerals, Nemestrinus, God of the Woods, Nona, Goddess of Pregnancy ... and that's just a few of the 'n's.'

The old man shook his head angrily. 'Figures. Fucking Italians. Just last week I paid seven dollars for a bowl of spaghetti and there was only one meatball in it. *One!* He turned and looked at *him.* 'Say, you couldn't be the God of Meatballs, could you?'

'I ... I suppose it's possible, but I'd really rather not.'

Two young men in fashionable combat pants and heavy leather jackets kicked the tin out of the old man's hand and ran off giggling maniacally as though, after years of careful planning, they had finally got one over on the universe. he transformed them into a small collection of fart molecules but then realized he'd best transform them back or risk Jerry finding out and permanently turning him into the God of Farts.

Probably wouldn't even let me be that. 'There's already a God of Wind,' Jerry would inform him. 'And farts definitely fall under his domain, so pick something else!'

'It's all damned meaningless!' he shouted, frustrated to tears.

The old man set about picking up the bits of change and business cards with phrases like 'get a job' and 'My heart goes out to you but I already give to charity' written on them. 'Well, why not that, then?'

'Why not what?'

The old man finished stuffing the coins and bits of paper into his cup and sat back down leaning heavily against the shop door. 'Meaninglessness. Is there a God of that?'

he thought about it, drawing on his considerable knowledge of

Most Things and, finally, for the very first time since becoming aware of his own existence, smiling. 'Meaninglessness!' He leapt to his feet. 'I will be Neminem! God of Meaninglessness!'

'Neminem?' the old man asked.

Neminem nodded. 'From the Latin for nobody.'

'Better pick something else. There's already a rapper with that name. Don't want to get sued by one of those rich celebrity fucks.'

But Neminem, knowing as he did of Most Things, including the rapper Marshall Mathers, whose stage name was Eminem, ignored the old man, and instead appeared once again before Jerry and Jennifer, whose names he now realized were largely inconsequential, and declared his intention.

'Are you sure?' Jerry asked.

'Definitely! I am Neminem, God of Meaninglessness. Bow down before my infinite irrelevance!'

Jerry looked up at Jennifer, apparently hoping for some form of procedural intervention, but she just shook her head. 'There's nothing in the rules...'

Jerry sighed, and wrote down the name and domain in a ledger that had apparently been there the whole time. 'Fine, here forth thou shalt be known as Neminem, and thy domain is all that is without meaning.'

Suddenly Neminem felt the power within him swell, and His presence to grow beyond that of all other gods – of all other things and nothings, in fact, even Bluetooth speakers – for all in the cosmos begins and ends in meaninglessness. Within an irrelevant number of seconds, all became Neminem. Then, in the trivial instant before Neminem became all, He realized he'd made a terrible mistake, because if he was Meaninglessness, and everything was meaningless, then everything was him, but without there being anything else, then all that was left was—

In the beginning, there was the word, and the word was...

Sebastien de Castell

Sebastien de Castell had just finished a degree in Archaeology when he started work on his first dig. Four hours later he realized how much he actually hated archaeology and left to pursue a very focused career as a musician, ombudsman, interaction designer, fight choreographer, teacher, project manager, actor and product strategist. His only defence against the charge of unbridled dilettantism is that he genuinely likes doing these things and that, in one way or another, each of these fields plays a role in his writing. Sebastien's acclaimed swashbuckling fantasy series, *The Greatcoats* was shortlisted for both the 2014 Goodreads Choice Award for Best Fantasy, the Gemmell Morningstar Award for Best Debut, the Prix Imaginales for Best Foreign Work and the Astounding Award for Best New Writer. His YA fantasy series, *Spellslinger*, was nominated for the Carnegie Medal and is published in more than a dozen languages. His latest books, *Play of Shadows*, *Way of the Argosi* and *Fall of the Argosi* will be released in 2021.

The Catch

Lizzie Enfield

'Here. Catch!'

It was the unexpectedness of it that made me jump. It must have taken every ounce of energy he had to raise his upper body off the bed, reach out and throw. The speed and force behind the lob surprised the nurse, who was hovering, waiting to change a drip. It made me start but it did not really surprise me, not in hindsight. Even as he lay dying, he could not resist an opportunity to humiliate me.

The fruit had been there for days. Dad hadn't eaten anything this past week. The arrangement of clementines and plums was a legacy from a previous visitor, perhaps as unsure how to conduct themselves in the presence of a dying man as I was now.

Fruit was the interlocutor.

'Here! I've brought you some fruit.'

I wonder if the giver regretted it, when they saw him, realised it was a fruitless gesture (excuse the pun), or whether it served to sweeten the atmosphere, which was stale and laden with the aroma of imminent death.

I arrived today with an idea that there were things that needed to be said. But in the hospice room, with Dad so barely there, all of them seemed pointless. Better for him simply to know that I had come, than trying to tease any dying admissions.

He was too weak for anything more than a brief opening of his eyes, a laboured rasping of 'Ellie, you came,' before he sank even further into the pillows than seemed possible, as if it was the hospital bedding not death that was about to claim him.

'Yes, of course I came. I came as soon as I could.' I looked towards the nurse, her presence a buffer against everything best left unsaid.

'He doesn't have much energy,' she said. 'But he can hear, if you talk to him.'

I'd taken the call from the hospice in the middle of a lecture.

I interrupted my explanation of Lee Miller's use of solarisation and went outside the lecture theatre, into the corridor, then back in again.

'I'm sorry but I think I'm going to have to end the lecture there. I wouldn't if it wasn't absolutely necessary.'

The hospice was a Tube ride and short walk away. I phoned Mathew en-route.

'Do you want me to come? Should I bring the kids?' he asked, concerned. But I said not.

'The children are at school,' I said now, finding it necessary to explain my solo presence to my father.

He'd opened his eyes and nodded the briefest of acknowledgements. Even that pained him.

So the question and what followed was shocking in its sudden energy and purpose.

He opened his eyes wide, breathed in with such intensity I thought he might suck all the remaining air out of the room and somehow propelled his torso up from the pillows.

'Would you like a clementine?' he asked and, without waiting for my answer, reached out to the fruit bowl, grabbed one and threw it, allowing the words 'Here. Catch!' to take all his remaining breath, before he collapsed back down onto the bed.

I began scrabbling on the floor, not because I wanted to retrieve the wretched clementine but because I wasn't going to give him the satisfaction of seeing my tears.

'You couldn't let it go, Dad, could you?'

Dad used to catch for a living. He was a wicket keeper. He kept wickets for England 'even though he had small hands'. I heard that phrase or variations of it endlessly repeated, when I was growing up. 'Even though his hands are surprisingly small…'; 'Despite his hands being child sized…'; 'Not held back by his tiny hands…'

These were the sort of things journalists wrote or pundits said about him, before he retired from the game and became a marketing consultant for a firm which imported sparkling wine from Europe.

I used to wonder if they'd taken him on on account of the size of his feet – a six in shoes – if they planned to involve him in the treading process. I imagined someone, somewhere, boasting the grapes had been trodden by Martin Cheshire, 'Even though he has small feet!'

Having small hands but '*still*' wicket keeping for his country made it hard for Dad having a daughter who could not catch.

In his mind, small hands were a disability he'd overcome. The only concession were his specially made gloves.

'Children's ones won't do.'

So what excuse did I have for not being able to catch?

Fear was a part of it. Fear of flying objects and a fear of failing to live up to my father's expectations.

I'd done that from the off. Dad had wanted a boy, more than a baby. No doubt my parents would have tried for one, had my mother not haemorrhaged during my birth and had an emergency hysterectomy.

I was never the son who'd follow him onto the crease – just a girl, her skin creased in folds around her body, waiting to grow into a child very different from the one he'd hoped for.

But Dad was a determined man. He would push a square peg into a round hole if it killed him. He spent hours in our sizeable garden yelling, 'Keep your eye on the ball.'

It always ended in frustration.

'It's not my fault,' I said, after a particularly tense session, when I was old enough to articulate rebellion. 'I just don't have any eye-hand co-ordination.'

'Eye hand?' his tone was incredulous. 'Eye hand?'

I didn't understand my mistake, until he discussed it at dinner with my mother, as if I wasn't there – taking sugar.

'You'll never guess what Ellie said earlier,' he announced, settling at the head of the table with all the importance of a newsreader.

'Does it really matter?' My mother's defence of her daughter was in weary ripostes.

'She said she couldn't catch the ball because she had no eye-hand co-ordination. There!' He picked up a fork and banged the table, triumphantly. 'What do you make of that?'

'It's likely.' Mum failed to catch anyone's eye.

'But don't you see?' The fork was beating time to his line of argument. 'It's not eye hand. It's hand eye. Maybe that's part of the problem.'

'It's just ham and potatoes and there's a bit of salad.' Mum refused to engage.

'Do you think it's a condition? Do you think there's a word for it?'

In the early seventies, people resisted labelling children. Dad was progressive in wanting one for me, I'll give him that.

'Ham?' My mother stopped him.

Being unable to catch was bad enough, I didn't need a peculiarity of speech to go with it. But it has persisted; my habit of putting words in the 'wrong' order.

My own children comment on it now, with amusement.

'It's not pepper and salt,' they say.

'It's fish and chips, Mum, not chips and fish.'

'Mum says socks and shoes!'

'It should be socks and shoes when you are putting them on,' I theorise. 'But shoes and socks when you take them off.'

'No, Mum. It's shoes and socks. That's just what everybody says.'

And they are right, although I wonder at the reason for these particular orderings and why it makes me wrong in so much of what I say.

'Fork and knife,' is one of the kids' favourites, because of the way it sounds, especially when pronounced with a Belfast accent.

'Have you got a fork 'n' knife?' they say, as Paisley-esque as possible.

'Have you got a fork 'n' knife?'

They dare me to 'language' them.

'Have you got a forkin' fork 'n' knife?'

'Language!'

I think, as failings go, getting words in the wrong order and being unable to catch should not amount to much.

I may not have an eye for the ball but I do have an eye for detail.

I'm a photographer. I work for an internationally renowned agency. I've had exhibitions on several different continents. I teach one day a week at a prestigious university. But what could be a source of pride is largely one of annoyance.

'What's all that rubbish there?' Dad asked loudly, peering at an image from my *Superstition* exhibition.

'It's a ragwell.'

I began to explain why the branches overhanging the water were covered in strips of cloth.

'I don't know why you can't just take a decent picture of the view,' he said, drawing looks from the people who came because they admired my work.

In forgiving moments, I try to understand that our eyes have simply grown accustomed to looking at the world in different ways. The greatest moments of his career have been down to his ability to reduce the world to a single object and catch it, whereas mine have been in looking around and capturing peripherals.

I knew, as soon as I stood up, as soon as I looked at the nurse looking at me.

'I'm so sorry,' she said.

No further explanation was needed.

'No, I'm sorry,' I replied, unsure what for.

'I can leave you a minute, if you want to be with him?'

'No.' I shook my head, holding back the tears because I was ashamed that they were being shed for the wrong reason.

'I think I'll take a walk around the block. Is that OK?'

'Whatever feels best. He will still be here.'

She put her hand out to reach me, but I sidestepped her touch, desperate to be out of the room.

Outside, in the street, the echo of my father's last breath reverberated in my head like tinnitus and with it echoes of his former utterances.

'Here catch!'; 'Keep your eye on the ball!'; 'Why can't you just take a nice picture of the view?'

And as I struggled to walk them off, my eyes began their habitual assessment of my surroundings, scouring for details: a birdcage hung by a window, a fox guarding the entrance to an alley and, above, a baby, peering curiously through a gap in the railings which protected a first-floor flat.

In the background, its mother chatted to someone standing behind a half-open door. She would, in a split second, turn around to look for her child.

But in that split second, the baby crawled forward, passed through the gap and began falling through the air.

And in that split second, I saw everything in slow motion; the mother turn, the look of horror on her face, the door behind her pushed wider, a figure emerge, and the baby … falling … towards the pavement below.

And, in that split second, I was a five-year-old girl again.

I was in the back garden and I could hear my father shouting to me.

'Just keep your eye on the ball,' he urged, as I ran towards the baby, never taking my eyes off it, not for a moment, unaware of anything other than its passage through the air.

And then it was in my arms and I was lying on the pavement, toppled by the impact of its body; warm as my father's was beginning to grow cold.

And people were crowding around me.

'Did you see that?'

'It must have crawled through the gap?'

'She's been at the council to fix those railings.'

'Thank God that woman saw it happening.'

'Are you OK, love?'

'Oh my god, is he OK? Is he OK?'

And in my peripheral vision, I saw a man standing: a man with small hands, wearing gloves.

He was smiling and trying to say something but there was not enough breath left in him, not enough to say whatever it was before he faded away.

But I saw him, standing there.

And he saw me catch a falling baby.

Lizzie Enfield

Lizzie Enfield is a journalist and regular contributor to national newspapers, magazines and radio. She has written four novels, one non-fiction title and had short stories broadcast on Radio Four and published in various magazines and anthologies. She also teaches creative writing and journalism. Her latest novel *Ivy and Abe* is published as Elizabeth Enfield.

The Prisoner
of Paradise Ranch

J. D. Fennell

20.23, July 1953, Nevada Desert

He wipes the layer of bitter dry sand from his lips and stands at the precipice of Tikaboo Peak. Peering through the lenses of the scuffed Wollensak binoculars, he watches the Paradise Ranch with eyes cold as steel. Approximately six miles of electric wire fencing protect what looks like an ugly concrete pyramid block that is almost five stories high. Flood lamps tower like sentinels over each of the building's four corners. It comes as no surprise to him that this place is neither a paradise, nor a ranch for that matter. It is a fortress designed to keep people out and, if he was not mistaken, also designed to keep people inside.

Correction. Not people. One person. One single person.

A handful of military personnel and staff in white coats trickle in and out of the pyramid and a Jeep with two armed guards patrols the perimeter of the fence. Sweeping the binoculars east, he sees a guarded entry box one mile off the highway. His next stop.

He places the binoculars back into their case and blinks at the blood-orange sun shimmering in the haze of desert heat as it sinks below the dry salt flat of Groom Lake. The gloom settles and he

118

wonders how many bodies are buried in the salt and if his remains will end up there tonight, should he fail.

A hissing, crackling sound interrupts his thoughts. He snatches the Mauser from the harness under his jacket and spins around. He sees only the borrowed Chevy Corvette and stiffens, his eyes and ears alert. For some reason, the car's headlamps have lit up and the radio seems to be rapidly navigating the local stations.

He narrows his eyes and scans the area, inching forward like a panther, but there is only tumbleweed, rocks and a shrouding darkness now that the sun has abandoned the desert. He points the Mauser inside the Chevy. Empty, with only the black leather medical bag sitting on the passenger seat where he had left it.

The crackling radio halts at a tune he recognises from movie theatre cartoons often played before the main feature. Circling the car, he crouches down to look underneath. There is nothing, only dust and sand covering the rocky road, and an undercarriage that has taken a battering on the journey here. He feels a pang of regret. That will take some explaining later.

If there is a later.

A voice comes through the static, 'Kill the wabbit … Kill the wabbit!'

He stands and takes a secondary glance around to put his mind at rest.

'What's up, Doc?' the radio blasts.

A sense of unease prickles his skin, he leans across, inserts the key and switches off the vehicle's electrics. He does not know what to make of the car's random burst of life. Perhaps it's a flaw of Chevy Corvettes.

He thinks nothing more of it. Time is not on his side and he needs to move quickly.

Removing his jacket, he takes off the gun harness, slides into the driver's seat and switches the Chevy back on. The radio is mercifully silent as he stuffs the harness into the glove box, closes it and, under the car's interior light, opens the medical bag and spills the contents onto the passenger seat. Slipping his hand inside the bag, he turns the catch of the secret compartment and places the Mauser inside.

He looks at his reflection in the rear-view mirror and combs his thick black hair into a tidy style befitting a man of the medical profession. He says, 'Hi. I'm Doctor Erik Keller. Great to meet you!' He smiles showing his teeth, but his smile is more of a grimace and his American accent seems less convincing than it did that morning. He notices the scar above his left cheekbone and realises something is missing. Reaching for the jacket, he takes out the spectacles folded inside the breast pocket. They have thick tortoiseshell frames, perfect for concealing his scar.

He puts them on, closes his eyes, takes a breath and tries to slot into character. Looking into the mirror, he smiles, his eyes wide, his grin warm, 'Hi. I'm Doctor Erik Keller. So good to meet you!'

Shrugging, he decides that will have to do.

In the dark it takes him almost sixty minutes to descend the same treacherous route taken to climb the Peak earlier. He is behind schedule and swears under his breath as he steps on the gas and hurtles at seventy up the highway to gain back some lost time. Outside, the blackness seems all-consuming and he has the sense that he is flying a small starship in deep space rather than driving an American sports car with dodgy electrics. Up ahead the beams of the Chevy's headlamps highlight the red PRIVATE PROPERTY KEEP OUT signs. He ignores them and spins off the highway. Ten minutes later he pulls up in front of the gate, where a uniformed armed guard watches him warily through the window of his hut.

He smiles and waves at the guard, who exits the hut and approaches the Chevy.

'Can I help you, sir?'

'Dr Erik Keller. I have an appointment.' He hands across his ID.

The guard studies the card and says, 'Dr Keller, we weren't expecting you for another hour.'

'I came ahead of the others. It was important I check over the prisoner before they see him.'

'I see. Please excuse me, sir, while I check with my superior.'

'You do that.'

Keller gets out of the car, leans against it and casually lights up a Marlboro as he watches the guard talk into a radio. The guard looks back at him with an uncertain expression. Keller waves and smiles warmly back as he exhales a plume of blue smoke. Moments later, the guard returns and he drops the cigarette to the ground crushing its fire with the heel of his shoe.

'Doctor Keller, apologies for the wait. Captain O'Hare does not like surprises, but he says go right up.'

'Much obliged. You have a good night.'

'You too, sir.'

It takes a further ride of close to five minutes before Keller sees the tip of the pyramid rise and blot out the stars in the night sky. A light appears at the base of the building and the silhouette of a man with a firearm on his hip stands in the doorway, watching the Chevy approach. Keller eases on the brakes and pulls into a parking bay, his emotions torn between excitement and trepidation; the latter down to the lack of intelligence available for the Paradise Ranch, more than anything else. Picking up the medical bag, he steps out of the car and hears a cranking sound reverberate around him. At that same moment a brilliant flash of white light kills the darkness.

The floodlights have been switched on.

'Please excuse the poor timing of our lamps,' comes a gravelly voice. 'I should really know better.'

Keller lifts his arm to stave off the glare and makes his way toward the entrance, blinking to help his eyes adjust to the brightness, 'That's quite alright.' He extends his hand, 'Hi. Doctor Erik Keller. Great to meet you.'

The man in the doorway is tall and broad with thinning black hair swept back from his forehead. He has a long Roman nose, high cheekbones and small, dark, appraising eyes. He glances at Keller's extended hand, but does not shake it.

121

'You must be Captain O'Hare,' asks Keller.

O'Hare reaches into his pocket and takes out a packet of Lucky Strikes and lights one with the unnecessarily large flame of a gasoline lighter.

'I wasn't expecting you at this time,' says O'Hare.

'Oh, really? I'm so sorry about that, Captain. Did my office not call ahead?'

'No, sir, they did not. No one called me, or my team.'

'Jeepers, I can only apologise, sir. I'll talk to Wilma when I get back. She's my secretary. She's had so much on her mind recently. Her eldest daughter is getting married to a real estate agent, who has just been diagnosed with leukaemia. Can you imagine that? Plus...' Keller chuckles, mostly at how quickly he has slipped into character, '...get this. She is convinced her new neighbours are Commies. They have a European accent, which she says is Russian. Poor dear can't sleep at night and is forever peeking through her curtains. I said to her, Wilma...'

'Why are you here early?' interrupts O'Hare.

Keller slaps his own forehead. 'Jeez, there I go again. My wife tells me sometimes I just don't know when to stop talking. She says I will talk my patients into the grave, if I'm not careful. She's quite the joker, my wife.'

O'Hare exhales a cloud of grey smoke through his thin lips and narrows his gaze at Keller.

Keller shifts awkwardly on his feet. 'Why am I here early...? Well, we took the decision to run some extra tests that would take up too much time. Therefore, to save time, I came ahead of the others.'

'What sort of tests?'

'Medical mainly. I'd like to test his cognitive abilities and ask him a few questions.'

'What's the point?'

'Good question. We need a record of his health and state of mind.'

'I understand what the medical tests are, Doctor Keller. I don't need an explanation. I'm asking, why are you doing them?'

Keller tilts his head. 'I'm not sure I understand the question.'

O'Hare sighs. 'You may recall the subject is scheduled for termination tonight. You signed off the paperwork. It is in my office if you would like to see it. Therefore, my question is a simple one. What is the point of the medical and the questions if he will be dead and buried in the salt before midnight.'

Termination?

Keller swallows and forces a wan smile. 'Captain O'Hare. I am aware of that,' he lies. 'No need to see the paperwork. You of all people should know that procedure must be followed at all times.'

O'Hare shrugs and flicks the remains of his cigarette across the parking lot. 'Let's check you in.'

He leads Keller through a pair of heavy iron doors and into a corridor with the floor and ceiling finished in the same barren grey concrete as the pyramid exterior.

'This is a lot of concrete for one prisoner,' says Keller.

'Yes, sir.'

O'Hare stops at an office door that says: *Captain Clay O'Hare. Head of Security.*

'Impossible to break out of, I'd say.'

O'Hare ignores the statement and unlocks the office door. 'I'll need to check your ID, your bag and search you, too. It's procedure, Doctor Keller.'

Keller smiles thinly. 'Procedure must be followed, Captain.'

O'Hare's office has the same charm and warmth as the pyramid and seems fitting for a dour man like him. The Head of Security scans his ID before handing it back and taking the medical bag.

'Heavier than it looks.'

Keller grins. 'Funny, my wife is forever reminding me of that. I carry a lot these days. Technology is advancing and new contraptions are getting heavier, no doubt about it.'

'Is that right?'

O'Hare lifts out the contents from the bag: a stethoscope,

temperature gauge, reflex hammer, steel tongue depressor, syringes, bandages, tape, medicine bottles.

'Amazing what you can fit in these bags,' says Keller, brightly.

The door knocks and a uniformed man enters. 'Sir, the plane is just about to land on the strip.'

'Are the cars waiting for them?'

'Yes, sir. Just as you requested.'

'Very good, Corporal. Let me know when they are close.'

'Yes, sir.'

'Doctor Keller, your colleagues will be here soon. Would you like to wait for them?'

'I think we should press on, Captain. Don't you?'

'As you wish.'

They walk side by side down the concrete corridor passing a lab with men in white coats, a print room and an empty dining room with three off-duty guards.

'Has anyone ever tried to break into this place?' asks Keller.

'This is a high-security facility. Not much can penetrate this tough shell.'

'How about breaking out?'

O'Hare stops at an elevator. 'There has only ever been one prisoner here.'

'This is his home, then?'

'It is all he knows.'

'Must be tough living in this place, no windows, no daylight, no contact.'

'He's allowed to exercise outside once a day, as long as he takes his sedatives.'

They ascend in the lift and the lights begin to flicker.

O'Hare frowns.

'Can't be much of a life, can it, Captain O'Hare? Sitting here day in day out, having needles and electrical devices stuck into your body.'

O'Hare says nothing.

'Having your every move filmed and your mind probed.'

'My job is not to question, Doctor Keller. My job is to protect the American people.'

'From what exactly?'

'You don't know what he is capable of and let that be a warning. Keep your distance and don't rile him. He will be sedated, but nevertheless, he is dangerous.'

'I'll bear that in mind.'

'Still, you've known him a long time, have you not? Will you miss him once he is terminated?'

O'Hare looks at Keller as if he has just insulted his mother. 'That termination should have happened at birth, Doctor Keller. That freak does not belong here or anywhere on this planet. He creeps me out.'

Keller bristles. 'I'm sorry to hear that.'

The elevator stops and the doors slide open. The room beyond is vast and looks like a lab with examination tables, medical cabinets, a gurney and what looks like a dental chair with straps on the arms and legs. Looking up, Keller can see they are at the top of the pyramid. Suspended by industrial chains from the four points of the ceiling is a large steel box with steps leading up to a bolted door with a small window.

O'Hare leads him towards a desk near the base of the steps where a grey-haired woman dressed as a nurse is seated. 'Doctor Keller, this is Blanche Hopkins, the prisoner's nurse.'

The woman has a severe face with thin white lips. Keller notices a doorway with an Exit sign beyond her desk.

'Nice to meet you, Nurse Hopkins.'

She nods curtly. 'Doctor Keller.'

The steel box shudders suddenly, diverting their attention.

'Has he taken his pills?' asks O'Hare.

Keller's eyes continue to scan the area. At the base of the steps he sees a tall wooden hat stand with a white lab coat hanging from it.

'Just after supper. I watched him wash them down,' replies the nurse.

'The lights in the elevator were not right and the cell just shook. Something's up,' O'Hare says, as he steps up to the cell door and peers through the window.

'Maybe we need to up his dose,' suggests the nurse.

'See to it, Blanche.' O'Hare beckons to Keller. 'This way, Doctor.'

As Keller climbs the steps, he hears the sound of canned laughter from inside the cell.

O'Hare unbolts the door and they step inside.

Despite not knowing what to expect Keller feels his pulse quickening. He has waited ten years for this moment.

The inside of the cell is a pleasant contrast to the lab outside. It is a comfortably furnished open-plan modern apartment with a bathroom, bedroom, kitchen and living room. On the walls are paintings of beautiful landscapes and summer scenes at a beach. In the bedroom is a night-time painting of a solitary figure, alone in a boat on a wide, open lake.

'Pete,' says O'Hare. 'Do you want to turn that thing off?'

Keller holds his breath and looks beyond the Head of Security. Sitting on the floor, with his legs crossed watching cartoons is a small, solemn-looking, dark-haired boy dressed in a blue robe, pyjamas and slippers. He must be ten years old.

The television volume increases, albeit of its own accord, as the start of a cartoon begins to play.

'Kill the wabbit … Kill the wabbit!' says the bald-headed cartoon hunter, Elmer Fudd.

Either cartoons are popular in these parts or…

O'Hare raises his voice. 'Pete, turn the television down, or I'll take it away!'

The boy does not respond and continues to stare at the set. A defiant Bugs Bunny appears, chewing a carrot, as he stares down the barrel of Fudd's shotgun.

126

'Freak,' mutters O'Hare, as he marches to the wall and yanks out the plug.

Silence fills the room.

The solemn boy's head turns slowly to look at Keller. 'What's up, Doc?' he says.

Keller feels a quiver in his stomach.

'Stand up, Pete,' demands O'Hare.

Keller notices the Head of Security's hands have curled to fists. 'Relax, Captain O'Hare, I can take it from here.'

O'Hare's jaw tightens.

Keller turns to the boy and smiles. 'Hello Pete. I'm Doctor Erik Keller. I'd like to do some quick tests, if that's all right with you. Would you mind sitting on the edge of the couch for me?'

The boy looks at him cautiously for a moment before doing what was asked.

Keller crouches in front of him, opens the medical bag, as O'Hare marches behind him to the doorway. 'Blanche, bring up that higher dose right away please.'

The boy stares back at Keller. His eyes, a deep blue, have dark rings underneath and his expression seems to lack emotion as if he has never known any. Keller feels an ache inside as he pulls out the contents of the bag and fumbles for the stethoscope.

'Could you unbutton your pyjamas for me, Pete.'

Keller places the scope on the boy's pale bare chest, which is scarred and bruised. He swallows and feels a rage burn deep inside. In the ears of the scope he hears a rapid pounding, almost 100 beats per minute.

What the hell?

'Are you feeling alright, Pete?'

'The rabbit always wins,' he replies, glancing at O'Hare, who is looming behind them. 'But not tonight.'

'What's he talking about?' asks the Head of Security.

Keller notices the captain's hand is hovering too close to the pistol on his belt.

'Captain O'Hare, the boy has clearly been treated with too many narcotics.'

'You don't know him like I do. He's different. Something is wrong. Have you stopped taking your drugs, boy?'

Pete keeps his eyes fixed on Keller's. Keller pulls up the boy's sleeve and notices more bruises and needle marks.

'Goddamit!' says O'Hare, returning to the doorway. 'Blanche, where the hell are those drugs?' he shouts.

'On my way!' replies the nurse.

Pete leans forward, his head inches from Keller's. 'They're coming,' he says.

'Who's coming?'

'The others, and the real Doctor Keller.'

Keller swallows.

'How do you know that?'

Pete looks up. Keller follows his gaze to the undecorated steel ceiling where a strip of communication cable runs from one end to the other.

'I hear them sometimes. Chirping like little birds.'

Keller reaches into the medical bag and tries to slide open the bottom compartment, but the catch is stubborn and won't shift. 'I'm taking you away from here tonight.'

The boy's eyes widen.

'In a moment, I want you to hide somewhere safely. Do you understand?'

Pete nods.

'Good.'

'She said you'd come one day.'

Keller frowns, but feels O'Hare's looming presence. The Mauser is still concealed in the bag.

'Who said he'd come here one day?' growls O'Hare.

Keller mouths *Now* to Pete who hurries behind the sofa.

Keller stands and faces O'Hare, who shoots a sideways glance at the boy. He looks back at Keller, his mouth twitching. He can sense a change in Keller. He is not who he said he was. O'Hare reaches for his pistol, but Keller is on him landing a punch at his jaw. O'Hare stumbles back as he raises his gun, but Keller grabs his arm steering it away. O'Hare squeezes the trigger and a gunshot fires across the room. Keller's heart sinks and he looks toward Pete and is relieved to see he is unharmed. Keller's grip is strong and he slams O'Hare's gun hand four times against the television until he drops the pistol. O'Hare slams Keller's ribs with his free fist as Keller kicks the weapon across the floor. O'Hare's face burns with fury as he shoves Keller and pounds him with his large fists. Keller retreats, ducking and avoiding the punches where possible. For a moment it seems the larger man has the upper hand, but Keller is no amateur and launches forward with a blow to his solar plexus and a swing to the ribs. O'Hare grunts and stumbles backward. Keller runs to the medical bag, tears open the secret compartment and pulls out the Mauser.

He points it at the Head of Security's chest. 'Get up, Captain O'Hare.'

O'Hare grins a red smile of bloody teeth.

'You might wanna just drop that pistol, Doctor Keller!' says Nurse Hopkins.

Keller swears under his breath and glances behind to see the nurse pointing a revolver directly at his head. The gun is heavy and her hold is shaky.

'Shoot him, Blanche. Get it over with,' says O'Hare, rushing for his own pistol.

'Drop the gun, Doctor Keller!' she repeats.

Keller glances at Pete, who is wringing his hands, his eyes wide with terror. Keller has no more tricks up his sleeve and realises how stupidly unprepared he is. He has to do something even it means risking a bullet. If he does nothing then he and Pete will be killed anyway and buried in the salt flats of Groom Lake.

His Mauser is still pointing at O'Hare.

'Drop the gun!' shrieks the nurse.

A layer of sweat coats O'Hare's forehead, his eyes flash. Keller's adrenaline is on fire, he grits his teeth, and squeezes the trigger.

He hears Pete cry out, 'No!' but his voice is lost over the blasts of gunshots.

Keller spins and dives to the floor in the vain hope that he will dodge at least one of the shots. He knows it is unlikely yet all the same he whispers a prayer for a god he does not even believe in. The longest of seconds pass as he hits the floor, crashing against the television set, yet he has still not felt the searing pain from a ripping of flesh, muscle and bone. He swings the Mauser at O'Hare who has not moved and is still pointing the gun in the empty space Keller had just vacated. Keller swings the pistol at the nurse who, like O'Hare, has also not moved. Confused, he swings the Mauser back to O'Hare, but he remains motionless almost like a statue. The man's face is an angry red, the vein on his temple throbs and his eyes appear to move as they strain to look down at Keller. He makes a gurgling sound and drool spills from his open mouth.

'They can't hurt you now,' says Pete.

Keller blinks at the boy. 'What's going on, Pete?'

'The rabbit always wins, but not tonight,' replies Pete.

Keller notices a strange tremor in the air above the boy and sees the bullet from Nurse Hopkin's revolver and his own bullet inch slowly through the air toward the Head of Security. From the opposite direction O'Hare's bullet flies at a snail's pace towards the nurse.

'Are you doing this, Pete?'

Pete's body begins to tremble. 'I can't hold it any longer.'

Tears fill the boy's eyes as the air changes and the whistle of bullets fly over his head; two slam into O'Hare's chest and the third fires into the nurse's neck. Both of them fall to the floor. Pete turns to look, but Keller clambers toward him and hugs the boy to his chest.

'I couldn't stop it,' sobs Pete.

'There was nothing you could do, Pete.'

Keller carries the boy to the doorway, glances outside and is relieved to see no one else is there. That is going to change at any moment so they have to be quick. 'We need to leave, Pete. Now.' He takes the boy down the steps and sits him on a steel table in the lab. Pete sniffs and dries his eyes with the sleeves of his pyjamas.

Keller grabs the white coat from the hat stand and puts it on. 'We're not out of the woods yet, Pete.'

'Where are we going?'

'We're going on a long journey and it's going to be dangerous. I need you to do whatever I say at all times. Understood?'

Pete nods.

'Good.' Keller points to the *Exit* doorway. 'Where does that door lead to?'

'The stairs that lead to the rear of the pyramid. It's where they take me to exercise.'

Keller hears a whirring noise from the direction of the elevator.

'They're on their way up,' says Pete.

'Let's go.'

With the boy at his side, Keller hurries down the flights of concrete steps which are thankfully empty. They stop at the exit on the ground floor. Peering outside he sees that the flood lamps are still lit. He hears the voices of two guards as they patrol nearby.

'If anyone asks, you are exercising. Got that?'

Pete nods.

Keller waits for the guards' voices to disappear before stepping outside. With his hand firmly on the Mauser concealed in the pocket of the lab coat, he leads Pete around the outskirts of the pyramid. He hears voices from the front of the building and halts with his hand on Pete's shoulder. At that same moment, a deafening alarm sounds across the enclosure.

'Shit!' says Keller.

He peers around the edge of the pyramid and sees guards running inside the building. Nearby, is the Chevy Corvette and the two large vehicles that had brought the termination party from the air strip.

He crouches out of sight and looks at Pete. 'We're going to make a run for my car. Stay at my side at all times.'

'They might see us,' says Pete.

'It's a risk we have to take.'

'I can turn off the lights.'

Keller pauses. 'You can do that?'

'Yes.'

Keller feels the air change inside and around him. He gasps, his skin prickling at what feels like a charge of electricity scratching through him. He hears a loud crackling noise and suddenly the lights blow inside and around the pyramid.

They are in darkness.

As Keller's eyes adjust to the gloom, he notices Pete is on his knees, his head down.

'Pete, are you OK?'

'Tired,' whispers the boy.

Keller carries him across to the Chevy and places him on the passenger seat. 'Keep out of sight.'

Keller discards the lab coat, starts up the engine and charges out of the parking lot. Behind him he hears voices raised in alarm followed by gunshots. He steps on the accelerator and, minutes later, sees the guard at the front gate aiming his rifle. But Keller had anticipated this and with one hand on the steering wheel, he aims the Mauser and shoots the guard twice in the chest.

Soon they are racing up the highway.

Keller glances at Pete. The circles under his eyes are darker; he does seem tired, yet he is smiling for the first time.

'How are you feeling?' asks Keller.

'Relieved.'

Keller smiles. 'Back there, you said "she said you would come one day". Who said that to you?'

'Anna.'

Keller's stomach twists. Anna, his ex-lover, the woman who betrayed him and stole Pete away from his mother.

'Where is she now?'

'They got rid of her.'

'Is she alive?'

'Yes.'

'How do you know that?'

'I hear her sometimes, on the wire.'

Keller does not know what that means.

Pete asks, 'If you're not Doctor Keller, what's your name?'

'My name is Will Starling.'

Will pushes his foot once more on the gas and drives the boy into the dark desert night.

J. D. Fennell

J. D. Fennell was born in Belfast during the Troubles and grew up in the last working-class, religiously mixed street of west Belfast. He began writing stories at a young age to help understand the madness unfolding around him and is the author of the acclaimed historical urban fantasy Sleeper series, which was shortlisted for the 2018 Sussex Amazing Books Award and the 2019 Wilbur Smith Adventure Writing Prize. In February 2021, writing as David Fennell, his crime debut, *The Art of Death* will be published by Bonnier Books.

Come Into My Garden...

Katie Fforde

As she turned into the small square in front of the church, around which was some of the most attractive (and expensive) real estate in the area, Isobel wondered if she'd been taken for a mug or just drawn the short straw. Either way she was committed to knocking on the door of the largest house which had recently been bought and no one knew who to.

New to the area herself she was keen to get to know people and loved gardening. So, when she saw a notice asking for helpers, it seemed natural to volunteer. She went to her first meeting and, as she couldn't take on the all-important teas or offer specialist knowledge on parking, when she was asked to do this, she didn't feel she could refuse. Although, as a shy person, this apparently simple task felt like quite an undertaking. Even getting to the front door took courage.

She tugged on the old-fashioned bell pull and heard a satisfying jangle. That was good, the old bell still functioned. Shortly afterwards she heard footsteps coming down the stairs and then the door was open. Standing on the step, looking surprised and slightly as if he'd come from another planet, was a man. He had grey hair but plenty of it and the 'absent-minded professor' look faded after a second or two. She had his attention.

'Good afternoon!' she said. 'I'm terribly sorry to disturb you but I have a favour to ask, on behalf of all the local residents.'

'Oh no, please don't tell me I've offended people already. I've only just moved in!'

He had a rather charming smile, Isobel discovered and smiled back. 'Oh no! Nothing like that! It's just there's an open garden event in a couple of months and this garden has always been the star of the show.' Isobel made this up on the spot but a bit of flattery was often useful. 'We – the committee – would be delighted if you'd open it again.' She saw his interest wane and went on. 'Put another way, we'd be terribly disappointed if you didn't open it.'

'Ah, well, there's a problem,' he said. 'The garden is not good enough to be opened at present. And I haven't time to do much to it for the next two months. I have a book to finish.'

Isobel longed to ask him about his book but refrained. She had to stick to the point. 'Could I have a quick look round it? If it's in a really bad way, I could tell the committee that it can't be opened and—'

'What?' he prompted gently.

'They'd let me off not persuading you. My reward, if you say yes, is to receive lots of lovely plants out of the other committee members' gardens. Currently my garden mostly consists of those pink geraniums and bluebells. Not English ones, of course, but the Spanish ones.'

'Ah, well I see your incentive. Come on, then, let's have a quick look.'

The bones of the garden were lovely. Although not enormous there were different levels, a paved area, a steep bank leading down to a pond surrounded by interesting planting. There was a lawn – or rather there had been a lawn, now it was more like a meadow – and surrounding that were deep borders. There was a pergola supporting roses and clematis and other climbing plants. A tall stone wall set off more roses beautifully. Even in its current state it was amazing.

'It's a heavenly garden!' said Isobel, the last of her shyness gone. 'I absolutely love it! I can see why everyone is so keen to get you to open it.'

Although, even to her biased eye, it did look very shaggy and neglected. It had been two years since the public had last seen it. It couldn't possibly be opened in its current state.

'I'd like to help, but I do have a deadline. Maybe next time?' His smile was rueful and unexpectedly sexy. 'I really don't have time to do more than drink a cup of coffee or a gin and tonic in the garden and that doesn't do a lot to help get rid of the bindweed.'

Isobel was totally in love with the garden by now and there was nothing she wouldn't do to get him to open it.

'I'll do it for you! I'll come and sort it out. I'll only do cutting back and clearing, sort out the lawn, things like that, but there's so much here, it wouldn't take more than that. I won't disturb you.' She hurried on, desperate to be allowed back into this lovely space. 'You can finish your book in peace; I'll get it into order.' She paused and looked up at him, hoping she didn't look too pleading. 'I'd love to do it!' She also hoped it didn't show how attractive she found this man.

He didn't reply for a long time. Eventually he said, 'I couldn't possibly let you do my garden. It wouldn't be fair. I'd have to pay you.'

'No! I'm not a professional! I'd do it to keep in with the committee. I daren't go back and say you said no.'

There was another long pause. He was obviously a thoughtful person. 'OK, I'll make a deal with you. When my book is finished you must let me take you out to dinner—'

Isobel gulped and then nodded.

'And you can tell the committee that not only were you able to persuade me to open my garden but also you asked Anthony Vine to open the event, and give it loads of publicity. It'll guarantee a lot of extra people if the weather is kind.'

'But how can you do that?' said Isobel. 'A big gardening name like that—' Her sentence was never finished as realisation dawned on her. She felt faint and a little bit sick. 'Oh God. It's you, isn't it? You are

Anthony Vine.' It was a statement, not a question. 'And I've just offered to do your garden for you.' She felt hot and cold and knew she was now bright red in the face. 'How embarrassing! It's like a home cook offering to cook for a Michelin-starred chef!'

'Not really—'

'It is! You have gardening columns in all the best magazines. If I wasn't so stupid I'd have recognised you.' She eyed the garden gate and wondered how long it would take her to sprint across the uncut lawn and get away.

'After seeing the state of my garden I'm grateful you didn't recognise me.' His smile was a bit lopsided. 'And please, don't say you won't come out to dinner with me now.'

'No, I won't. I mean I will – I will come out to dinner with you.'

'Phew! Now you can go back to your committee with some really juicy gossip!'

Isobel nodded, still feeling a little faint.

'Do you want the good news or the bad?' said Isobel at the next meeting. 'His garden is an absolute mess! And he can't sort it because he's got a book to finish.'

'Honestly! People should prioritise!' said Evelyn, who spent every hour God sent in her garden, which showed both in her garden and her weathered complexion. 'That used to be a really lovely garden. Some wretched person from London comes down here and doesn't appreciate it. It shouldn't be allowed.'

'The good news is,' Isobel went on, 'he'll get Anthony Vine to open the event and publicise it.'

One or two of the female committee members looked interested and made encouraging murmurs.

'That's all well and good,' said the Major who was in charge. 'I know publicity is important but I'm not sure it'll be all that useful. We can't risk our reputation as an event and allow a substandard garden to be part of it.'

'It won't be substandard,' said Isobel, thinking of the Major's garden, which was too full of straight lines and bedding plants for her taste. 'I'm going to sort it out for him. Weed the borders, clip the edges, cut everything back. It'll be neat as a pin when I've finished with it!' This last statement was a bit of an exaggeration but she knew it was what the committee wanted to hear.

'Oh, well done, dear!' said Evelyn. 'You've done your job very well. Why don't you come round for tea next Tuesday and bring bags? I've got lots of things I can give you for your garden. Not that you'll have much time for that if you're taking on The Old Vicarage.'

'So how is he going to get Anthony Vine to open the event?' asked the Major. 'It's all very well making promises but can he follow through?'

'Um – well – he *is* Anthony Vine,' said Isobel. Not much point in keeping it secret.

'Good Lord!' said the Major.

'How wonderful!' said one of the women, a jolly person who Isobel thought might well become a friend. 'And he obviously took a shine to you.'

Isobel shrugged. She couldn't really argue with that – they'd already made a date to go out to dinner.

Katie Fforde

Katie Fforde has written over twenty-five novels and lives in the Cotswolds with her husband and animals. Her hobbies these days are mostly her grandchildren, which she finds endlessly entertaining. She is proud to be the current president of the Romantic Novelists Association.

Head Count

Christopher Fowler

'Auschwitz is little more than a theme park,' said Professor Wade.

As opening statements went it was a bold one, but the professor was preaching to the converted. There was no murmur of complaint from his audience. They were curious to hear more, after which they would dutifully potter over to examine his book.

'It's nothing more than a German Disneyland to encourage tourism to an unattractive neighbourhood. Even the most slow-witted visitor can see that the buildings are post-war fakes, replicated to provide a cinematic sense of time and place, to evoke the sensation of old Hollywood war films. The "guides" who feed you scripted answers are student propagandists who tug the heartstrings of the visitors with sad little stories. It's a money-making enterprise that trades on the biggest myth of the twentieth century, the myth of six million dead.'

Professor Wade looked out across the ballroom. He had always had a gift for public speaking, for making the unpalatable acceptable, but his talent was wasted here. For every attendee there was at least one empty chair. The meeting hall where the group had been set to hold their convention had been cancelled after angry protests. The new venue, the Wellington Room of the Albion Hotel, had been hired under a more anodyne name so that nobody would take offence.

The National English Society sounded as if it might be meeting to preserve wildlife or revive folksong, not to deny the Holocaust. In the past they had denied much else, from the moon landings to the coronavirus.

The problem, Professor Wade decided, was that groups like the National English Society were cheap to run. They were filled with retirees adept at finding free afternoons out. They wouldn't buy any books. There was no money to be made here.

The room had cheap fake-damask curtains and smelled of chips.

Behind the professor stood a stack of upright books with their covers facing out, the title *In Denial: The Truth about the Holocaust* emblazoned in crimson against a black swastika.

'We have to remember that Hitler was a politician of sharp intellect and refined rationality whose only goal was to increase Germany's influence and prosperity in Europe.' Wade paused to drink from his Malvern water bottle. 'He was repeatedly let down by incompetent or treasonous subordinates.'

The audience was mostly composed of middle-aged white males. A few were accompanied by grim-faced wives who listened in motionless silence. One might have expected a nod of agreement here, a muttered affirmation there, but they knew better than to show outright enthusiasm at these events.

'The problem begins with revisionist historians,' said the professor, prodding a forefinger at the tabletop, 'who used the tragedy of war as a lever to raise the tarnished public image of German society's lowest caste – the moneylenders. The Holocaust was a public relations exercise that got out of hand.'

Sarah slipped in at the back of the room and took her seat as unobtrusively as possible. Setting her plastic carrier bag between her ankles, she sat back to listen to the rest of the speech. It was hard to concentrate on what the professor was saying. He seemed barely interested in his own words, like an actor touring the provinces with an outdated play.

Looking around, she knew she was the only Jewish woman in the room.

The bus to Auschwitz was playing Christmas songs. An hour and a quarter out of Krakow the driver switched from Perry Como to Cliff Richard. They were just passing the black birch forest that surrounded the site of the camps. It appeared before the coach passengers like an image from an old war film; you could almost see the prisoner running through trees, men with barking Alsatians following close behind, dashing through the shadows. Much of what was to follow felt like a film until it became suddenly, brutally real.

It was below zero and struggling to snow. The earth was black and hard, the land flat and weather-exposed. As they pulled into the site, the driver switched on a short preparatory video about the education centre. The tiny monochrome images of skeletal prisoners standing behind barbed wire had become over-familiar and carried little impact.

As they disembarked, Sarah saw that most of the few visitors were British and Chinese. One man had a blue and white Israeli flag draped across his back. The atmosphere was not sombre, merely flattened.

Guided tours were encouraged now. There had been an outrage involving some unaccompanied Italian tourists who took laughing selfies in a gas chamber. Sarah was lucky enough to find a guide who spoke with an angry personal passion, so that the overwhelming facts and figures with which he presented them had a human context. She wondered how many times he had delivered the same speech. She knew it would always be different because he spoke from the heart.

The main Auschwitz camp consisted of substantial brick houses: ugly, utilitarian, unadorned. Her first sense was of a low-income housing estate in decline. Narrow windows, steep tiled roofs, no signs of life. Ahead were the barbed-wire electric fences, cables strung high across stone posts and the first lie, the ironwork entrance sign: 'Work

Makes You Free'. Passing beneath it placed her on the side of the arriving prisoner.

A bitter wind prickled the back of her neck. The guide beckoned her toward the first building. She could only be grateful that she was visiting as a curious tourist.

'Thank you for your talk, Professor. It was certainly food for thought.' The old man clasped Professor Wade's hands and would not let go. 'It was something that needed to be said.' His blank blue eyes were directed by some hidden fervour. He glanced behind himself furtively. 'You can't say anything these days without the thought-police checking up on you. The young are always complaining how hard done by they are. The girls especially. We're in the minority now, those of us here, the ones who made this country great. We know whose fault it really is.' He seemed likely to spiral off into a litany of unrelated complaints so the professor eased his hand out and discreetly stepped back, allowing the next audience member to approach.

'Hello,' said Sarah. 'I'm a great fan of yours.' She had tied her hair back and wore little make-up. It was a look designed to appeal to him.

'A pleasure to meet you.' He shook her hand, scrutinising her fresh face. 'Have we met before?'

Sarah shook her head gravely. 'No, but you may have taught my mother. There's a strong family resemblance. She said you had written a book but I wasn't able to find it in the shops.'

'It proved a little too controversial for the major publishing houses,' he told her, with an air of a confidence shared. 'They ran shy, so I decided to publish it myself. I've had a lot of public support. It's doing very well. There are copies on sale here.'

'Perhaps if you would autograph one for me,' she suggested, digging into her purse.

The little tourist group was duly shunted from building to building. As the day's horrors unfolded meticulously Sarah felt herself declining along with the Nazi fantasy and Jewish hopes. They moved from one brick building to the next, each hollowed out to provide exhibition space. The roll-call of names and dates was overwhelming.

She stood at the window as sleet drove down the street. Housing blocks that appeared to have been built for moderately comfortable accommodation quickly turned into rows of wooden shacks. Factories designed with only one possible purpose: the liquidation of human beings as efficiently as possible. Even animals were shielded from the sight of their slaughterhouse. Here everything could be plainly seen.

Even so, it was a gradual descent. The rooms into which she was ushered told the story of the emptying of the ghettos, the arrests of Jews from Norway to Greece, the arbitrary process of dividing the new arrivals on the railway platform into those who would live and those who would die. It was done with a glance up from a clipboard that lasted mere seconds and was accompanied by a flick of the hand; you, join Column 1, you, join Column 2. No, wait, Column 1.

Sarah's grandmother had told her that if an arrival was placed in the column with the pregnant and infirm they had three to five minutes of their lives left. Get picked for the other column and you would be starved, beaten and worked to death – the stories were everywhere: of a little girl left to stand naked in sub-zero temperatures for twelve hours; of forty prisoners crushed into a room that at most should hold ten. Her grandmother spoke rarely about such things but when she did she could not be stopped. The torrent of quiet words poured from her like from a jammed tap.

When the pretence that there was anything the Nazis considered remotely salvageable in the Jews was torn aside, the real horrors could begin. That was why Birkenau, the largest concentration camp, had been built, for there all became perfectly clear.

If Sarah had expected to find any sense of the mystical here, the thought was instantly dissolved. What cut into her most deeply was the sheer utilitarianism of the enterprise, so drab and basic and lacking in any pretence. The sheds were made of cheap wood, warped and freezing in winter, stinking and typhus-ridden in summer. Here were the planked battery cages where people were folded up like stray dogs, there was the bunker where they would go to be put down.

The gas chambers would have passed unnoticed in any suburban German straße. They were covered in the grey pebble-dashed plaster of a cheap post-war council house. Mortar and cement were of the poorest quality. The few latrines were communal and could only be used for up to fifty seconds at a time. Nothing was ornamental or decorous, all was so rudimentary that only the most irrational human hope could have kept arrivals from trying to run away screaming on first sight of the place. Hope, the Nazis knew, was the last thing to die; not that they were interested in the emotions of animals.

In the entire camp, the only touch of lightness and grace came from a handful of drawings of children at play on the washroom walls – impossible optimism kept alive by doomed parents.

Sarah could tell the professor was taken with her. She played on his attention, looking through the book he had signed, pretending to be interested in the ramblings of its fractured logic, like a slightly more erudite version of *Mein Kampf*, hysteria in hardcovers. The back was endorsed by unfamiliar names. She would have dismissed them all as members of the crackpot fraternity, but knew that Professor Wade still had the power to commandeer the more sensationalist TV news programmes and radio shows. He still had a voice.

The professor was a large man and clearly enjoyed using his height to tower over women. His breath smelled of alcohol. The room behind them was thinning out now, the last few audience members threading their way through the chairs toward the pinned-back exit doors.

Sarah wondered where the change had come for Adrian Wade. In his twenties he had been a respected military historian, one of the finest of his age, a radical firebrand, the scourge of falsified history. He had denounced the Third Reich while arguing for a more nuanced approach to history. Context, he had told them, was everything. At some point in his mid-thirties, his opinions had shifted and hardened. He had allied himself to notorious fringe groups, his bipolarity driving him further into a corner from which there was no escape.

Wade was looking at her expectantly, waiting for her to speak.

The next moment, Sarah knew, was crucial. As she went to fit the book into her carrier bag she paused. 'Oh, I nearly forgot. I live with my grandmother. She's a big fan of yours. She very much wanted to come along with me, but unfortunately she was not well enough to attend.'

'I'm sorry to hear that. Please send my regards.'

'But she wanted me to give you something. Where is it?' She rooted about in the bag, pretending to look. The professor glanced away for a moment, betraying impatience.

'Ah,' said Sarah, holding the package up. 'Here it is.' The gift was covered in flower-patterned paper and tied with red wool.

Sarah stopped before a large aerial photograph of Auschwitz's railway terminal. The arrival platform was divided down the centre with a high wooden fence. On one side men, women and children arrived in expectant hope, as their cases were carefully taken from them and passed through the fence to be slung on a pile. From here on in there was no more pretending that the prisoners – whether they were Jewish, Romany, homosexual, intellectual, doctors, lawyers, musicians, writers or just citizens who had said the wrong thing – were there for any other purpose than to be used as a finite resource, fuel for the engine of the regime.

First the guards hurled aside their carefully curated belongings. Many of the suitcases had been painstakingly hand-lettered with names and addresses written on the sides in gold ink and fine penmanship. You only address a case if you believe you will see it again.

Then the guards sold their captives lies that they would give up all their money for: fake deeds to non-existent houses; phantom escape routes; and freedom passes that no one had ever seen. What else could be taken from them apart from hidden jewels, cash and deeds?

Well, you could steal their clothes, shave their heads and sell the hair, tear out their teeth for gold, work them to death, fry the remains, render them down to nothing. You could experiment on them by pouring bleach in their eyes, trying to make their pupils blue and Aryan, or injecting them with acid or air bubbles just to see what would happen. You could open up the pregnant women and poke about with the foetuses, cut them apart while they were still alive, like children burning ants and tearing the wings from flies. Many of the senior officials at the camp were formerly butchers and farmers. The people who did this kind of job were not intelligent. They were bitter and piggy, taking revenge for petty grievances, for lifetimes of being ignored.

The most horrific and haunting images that stayed with Sarah forever were not the vast dry brown piles of human hair, the entangled wire spectacles and mountains of shoes, but the smart leather cases that were the first items to be stolen away within seconds of arrival.

There were other images burned into her mind that bitter, sleet-filled day. The confluence of railway lines that led only to the camp. The single red railway car built to hold cattle, once packed with prisoners. The small round hole in the chamber ceiling, down which Zyklon B pesticide was dropped and left for twenty minutes while the captives screamed for release.

Through it all came one simple message she had not fully appreciated before, despite reading so much of her grandmother's literature on the subject – that the Nazis knew they were running slaughterhouses. They had always known where the final solution would lead, even before it was named. There could not be a single atom of doubt that every last prisoner would leave as chimney smoke. In the years that the Auschwitz camps thrived, only one hundred and ninety prisoners ever escaped. Many could not even be kept alive after liberation, for they had been physically and mentally dismantled. There was nothing left to put back together.

Professor Wade tore the floral wrapping paper apart and held up the bright yellow scarf, clearly delighted with his gift.

'It's cashmere,' said Sarah. 'My grandmother made it herself. She hopes you like it.'

'It's beautiful.' The professor was disproportionately touched. Voicing a contrary viewpoint was lonely work at the best of times. It seemed that even those who wholeheartedly agreed with him did not wish to spend too long in his company, as if the public voicing of their thoughts made them uneasy.

He allowed Sarah to place the scarf around his neck and loosely knot it below his throat. 'There,' she said. 'It looks good on you. My grandmother said it would. May I wish you all the luck you deserve with the book.' She smoothed the scarf into place, gave the professor a friendly smile and took her leave.

Professor Wade watched her go in a state of some mystification. He was used to old men bombarding him with mad theories of their own, not attractive young women presenting him with gifts.

The room had emptied out. He thanked the two uninterested staff members who were busy stacking the chairs, getting ready for the room's next event. The hotel staff had all returned to their business. No one noticed him leave. It always felt anti-climactic, leaving the scattered applause to step back into the indifferent streets.

There was a gap of just over a week before his next event. Filling the time had never been difficult when he was married, but now the days lengthened so that the period between four and seven in the evening seemed to stretch forever.

Sarah shut her eyes. She could see no more horrors. Her teeth were chattering. The group had come full circle, back around to the entrance of the camp. She stood at the rear of the gathering listening to their final guide, bringing them to Auschwitz's final moments.

Upon the liberation of the camps, those who were first in saw the success of the Nazi scheme; it had, in its own way, been grotesquely efficient. There was no jubilation upon their arrival, no sense of joy, because the prisoners were far past any human emotion; they had died already, even though they still stood at the fences. One man, aged forty-two, looked at least eighty. His photograph was one of hundreds now lining the walls of the visitor centre.

Footage of the prisoners excitedly waving and running upon release had been filmed later, restaged for the newsreels. It had not been like that because there had been nothing to celebrate. But there was much to remember. It was beyond belief, but not beyond understanding.

As Sarah walked back to the bus, she thought about her grandmother. Becky had been five years old, her stay at Auschwitz cut short by liberation. She had left without her parents. Seven members of her family had entered. One had emerged. She had nothing but the clothes she stood in and the grubby cushion her mother had lovingly stitched for her. The women in her family had always been seamstresses.

Professor Wade sat on the edge of his hotel bed and checked his messages. There had been one call in the last twenty-four hours, an automated reminder about his check-out time. The radiators were scaldingly hot but the room remained icy. He opened a bottle of whisky and half-filled a smeary glass tumbler, feeling the tawny liquid flood his throat with warmth. Tightening his jacket, he pulled the scarf closer around him. He liked the soft, sensuous way it brushed the back of his neck.

Feeling suddenly tired, he rubbed his aching feet. His throat burned. For the first time in an age, a sliver of doubt crept in. Lately he had been having bad dreams. They left him feeling tired all day. Rising, he went to the window and looked down into the street.

Groups of students in college scarves were passing by, laughing and darting about each other, dumbshows of happiness. He wanted to hear what they were saying but the painted-over window frames did not open. He had never been a part of their world. His parents had demanded more from him than foolishness. He refilled the tumbler and drank deep.

The scarf caressed his neck like a lover. It softly purred as he slid it over his throat, as if it were whispering to him.

He caught sight of himself in the wall mirror. A symmetrical, formerly-handsome face that was now blotched and wrinkled. Long ago, with clear blue eyes and cropped blond hair, he might have passed for one of the Reich's *Lebensborn*, the coming generation of pure-bred Aryans. But the Aryan race had been stillborn and now he was grey and sagging and feeling ill, past his time and out of date.

Lately he had been wondering what would happen if he backed himself out of his ideological corner and publicly renounced his opinions. His damascene conversion would surely not play as well to the masses as his rabble-rousing denunciation of Holocaust mythology. On the plus side, the swivel-eyed members of the National English Society would melt away, to be replaced by gentle county women and a few patient husbands. The crackpots wouldn't care that he now regretted his past.

But it wasn't possible. Too late to change now. It was better to keep the followers he had rather than try to start over. At least they sometimes bought a book.

At first he thought someone was holding choir practice on the floor above. He cocked his head to one side. He could hear voices, indistinct and painfully unharmonious. It was impossible to understand what they were saying. The voices remained at a distance but did not fade. A song of some kind, but out of step. It stayed in the back of his brain like tinnitus.

149

A sudden feeling of inexplicable terror slipped over him that he was barely able to suppress. Some nights he sat up in bed gasping for breath. He finished the bottle and lay down fully clothed on the bed, but was too tetchy to sleep.

And yet he dreamed a kind of waking dream, no more than a rolling jumble of faces and voices, people he had not seen before and did not know, eyes in the dark neither friendly nor unfriendly, passively watching.

He awoke unable to breathe, choking to death. His windpipe had closed. He tried to move his head but found himself pinned in place.

The scarf had caught itself down one side of the bed and was pulled tight over his throat. His fingers followed it down to where it was hooked on a metal strut, impossible to undo without moving the mattress.

He plucked at the knot beneath his Adam's apple but the fibres seemed to constrict on their own, so fine and smooth were they. The harder he dug in his fingers the tighter the knot grew, until it was as small and hard as a walnut.

He tried to unpick it until his nails started to split. Every time he attacked the scarf it seemed to tighten a little more around his neck like a python. He grabbed at its taut ends and frantically pulled, but the fine, hair-like threads cut into his fingers.

His face grew red. Blood thrummed in his temples. He felt himself starting to lose consciousness. The other end of the scarf had knotted itself somewhere beneath the mattress as well, pinning him like an insect. His veins bulged. It felt as if the hairs of the scarf were crawling across his skin. When the blood vessels blossomed into tiny crimson flowers in his eyes he heard the voices again.

They whispered the truths he had always feared.

As his fingers brushed the scarf he found that it lay loose beneath his touch. His dying thought was that it had never tightened at all. His death was arbitrary. You, Column 1. No, wait, Column 2.

Sarah made her grandmother a fresh peppermint tea. The old lady was addicted to it. She added biscuits and set the tray between them, settling back in the opposite armchair. Taking the newspaper from the tray, she unfolded it at the obituaries page. A stern photograph of the professor peered angrily out from the top of the column.

'Do you want me to read it to you?'

'No, I don't think so,' said her grandmother, more interested in the garden.

'There's a surprise at the end. It says he left all his money to charitable causes. I nearly forgot, I bought you a present.' She handed the old lady a white, feather-filled square. 'To refill your cushion.'

It was not possible to discover whether the professor had still been wearing the scarf when he died, but Sarah and her grandmother felt it was safe to assume that he was.

'I wonder how many there were in that thing,' Sarah asked, following her grandmother's eyeline out of the kitchen window to the spring planting.

'I'm sorry, what are we talking about?' Lately her grandmother had become quite forgetful.

Sarah thoughtfully sipped at her tea. 'Hairs from different heads. I wondered how many.'

'Hundreds, probably. I was so thin that I couldn't sit down without crying. My mother stole the clippings on the floor to make it. She risked a beating, or worse.' The old lady lifted the bone china cup to her lips. 'I'm glad it finally found another purpose.'

Christopher Fowler

While working in a dead-end job as an advertising copywriter, Christopher Fowler was released after calling his clients 'human blowflies' in a meeting. Christopher is now the multi-award-winning author of almost fifty novels and short-story collections, including the acclaimed Bryant & May mysteries, recording the adventures of two Golden Age detectives out of their depth in modern London. His novels include *Roofworld, Calabash*, Faustian satire *Spanky*, ghost story *Nyctophobia* and *The Sand Men*. Also a writer of videogames, graphic novels and plays, his story *The Master Builder* was filmed with Tippi Hedren. Non-fiction includes *Paperboy, Film Freak* and *The Book of Forgotten Authors*. In 2015 he won the CWA Dagger in the Library for his body of work. His latest novel is *Oranges & Lemons*, with the thriller *Hot Water* upcoming. He lives in London and Barcelona.

The Photograph

Anita Frank

It is 1945. The war is over. The men are coming home.

Perching on the edge of my chair, I stare at the photograph that stands, pride of place, on the mantelpiece. I know every facet of the black and white image off by heart. It is the only picture I have of him, the man I married, a man I haven't seen for nearly five years. My husband.

I realise I am twisting my wedding ring round and round on my finger. The plain gold band has always been a little too large. With everything done in such a rush, there had been no time to have it properly sized. After a while I came to see it as my good-luck charm, my loose ring, my ill-fitting symbol of forever.

But nearly five years on, the prospect of forever with a man whose face I can no longer conjure in my mind fills me with fear. I have tried – God knows I have tried – to picture him. Oh, I can recall moments with him, incidents, turning points in our hurried relationship, but the intricacies of his features remain frustratingly elusive. When I try to see him in my mind's eye, it is the image in the photograph that appears: staid and still, with dark eyes that I so desperately want to sparkle, because it was his eyes that first fired my attraction, after all. They had radiated so much warmth, humour, *allure* – I had been instantly captivated.

153

But the photograph reflects none of that. It is simply the two of us, side by side on the steps of the registry office, my modest bouquet held before me, him in his uniform, me in my Sunday suit, smiles of surprise caught on our faces, as if even we are startled by the rapid turn of events. Our impetuous commitment was fuelled by the war raging in Europe: live for today, because God only knows if there will be a tomorrow. In truth, we hardly knew each other. 'You'll be taken care of if anything happens to me,' Charlie had said. So, we rushed into our vows, keenly aware those same well-wishers who congratulated us with handshakes and kisses would, in peacetime, have cautioned our rash decision – *'Are you sure?', 'Seems a bit sudden,' 'You're not … are you?'*

I wasn't. Pregnant. Not then. I would be though. 'I think I'm expecting,' I whispered as I held him for the final time. His grin had been broad and instant, but for me the prospect of this new life was even more terrifying than him leaving for war. And then he was gone, my chap of four months, my husband of one. His face disappeared from my world and all too soon his features faded from my memory. I began to depend on the photograph – without it, he seemed little more than a figment of my imagination.

But then my belly swelled, and I had tangible evidence as to the reality of it all. Any mounting joy I felt at the first flutters of life was soon quelled by the Red Cross letter I received. My hands shook as I tore it open, my knees buckling as I saw the words 'Prisoner of War' in bold. Tears splattered the glass covering the photograph that night, and would for many nights after.

Five months later, my beautiful boy was born. Our beautiful boy. I desperately searched the scrunched-up features for some familiarity. How I wanted to be able to say with absolute authority, 'Oh, he has his father's nose!', but by then I couldn't remember his father. I couldn't tell whether they were alike or not.

Still, I felt the sorrow of Charlie's absence at every milestone: first tooth, first step, first word – each moment bittersweet, marred by the fear of a fatherless future. Bouncing Freddie on my hip, I would point to the picture and chant 'Daddy', my heart breaking as he struggled with the concept, but when at last he was old enough to understand, he would greet the photograph each day with a cheery 'Good morning, Daddy!' It made me ache with sadness.

Whenever Charlie's letters came, Fred would fetch the picture frame from the mantelpiece and sit next to me on the settee, nursing it on his lap, while I read aloud the bits suitable for him to hear. His stubby fingertip would trace the edges of Charlie's features as he tried to fit the words to the father he didn't know. I never reprimanded him for smearing the glass – he needed to learn every ridge, every shadow, of that face. I was painfully aware the photograph might be all he would ever have of him.

'Mummy, I'm ready!'

I jump as Freddie bursts into the room. He is dressed in his brand-new suit, his knobbly knees sticking out from under the shorts, his grey socks pulled up high. I had combined my mother's clothing coupons with my own to buy it for him. It is important he looks smart for his first-ever meeting with his father.

As for me, I have spent the morning changing and changing again, nervously scrutinising my reflection in the wardrobe's mirrored door. In the end, I have plumped for my wedding outfit, the very one in the photograph, as if the forthcoming reunion might be a repeat of that day: the uniform and the Sunday suit.

Freddie notices immediately and he beams at me. 'You look just like the picture, Mummy.'

My legs tremble as I stand. I smooth my skirt with a clammy hand.

We wait at the bus stop, Freddie's hand clasped in mine. He is my anchor in this maelstrom of thoughts and emotions. He complains I am holding on too tight. I cannot tell him that I am too terrified to let go.

The bus, when it arrives, is packed, but somehow Freddie and I manage to squeeze aboard. I grip on to a ceiling strap, while Freddie clings to my thigh; we sway as the bus moves away. All around me are other wives, mothers, sisters, all heading to the railway station, all impatient to see their husbands, fathers, sons. I watch them in bewilderment. They exude excitement, their faces flushed with anticipation. My ears ring with the cacophony of their voices, high-pitched and enthused. It appears I am the only one nauseous with nerves.

The woman in the seat nearest to us shuffles along and pats the vacated few inches, beckoning Freddie to sit down. She admires his fine suit and he glows with pride. He tells her he is going to see his daddy for the very first time. Smiling, the woman tells us she is meeting her son, back from the war. The flicker of my lips hides the envy I feel for the simplicity of her reunion: a mother and son. Freddie informs her he kisses his daddy every night. Her brows knit in confusion.

'His photograph,' I explain, smoothing down the lick in Freddie's hair with my free hand. 'He kisses his photograph.'

'Oh, bless him!' she says.

I muster a smile and look away.

The bell tinkles as we come to a stop outside the station. There is a great surge towards the doors. Freddie clings to my hand as we are swept from the bus and into the gathered crowd. A brass band is playing 'There'll always be an England', its beat quickened to a lively two-step. The station front is bedecked with Union Jack bunting, and a banner draped across the entrance reads: 'Welcome Home Our Heroes!'

My mouth is bone dry. For a moment I stand there, jostled by the thrumming swarm. I squeeze my eyes shut and focus: Charlie on our wedding day. I pick one moment, the moment he stood to raise a toast to me, his new bride. I can see the cut of his uniform, the sheen of Brylcreem in his hair. I can hear his voice – I just need his face. My concentration is intense, but my heart sinks as the familiar image imposes itself yet again onto my memory. *Dear God*, I pray, *please let me recognise him. Please let him still look like the photograph.*

Freddie is impatient, tugging me on. We press forward with the crowd, funnelling up the steps to the platform. He wants to be near the front, but I am afraid in the crush he will be knocked onto the tracks, so I make him hang back.

We can hear the train approaching, its rhythmic chugging slowing as it draws ever nearer. Its whistle screams, and cheers erupt from the crowd. I hold Freddie to me as we fight the pull of the tide towards the platform edge.

The train is bearing down on us now, its segmented body clattering along the tracks behind it. Men are hanging out of carriage windows, exhausted but happy, their drab khaki arms waving in great, sweeping arcs. My stomach heaves. The train screeches into the station, cloaked in steam.

The air resonates with the clamour of elation. Tears of panic fill my eyes. I hold Freddie back from the unloading Goliath. There is a steady *clunk, clunk, clunk* of opening doors. All around me, women are flinging themselves joyously into the arms of their loved ones. Their relief, their love, is evident. I see none of the reticence that solidifies my soul and leaves me rooted to the spot. I wonder why I and I alone do not have this natural spring of womanly emotion bubbling out of me. Why am I the only one so filled with trepidation? My chest constricts with fear and guilt.

And then I see him. He emerges through the dissipating steam, revealed by the departing crowd. He is right before me. I can barely breathe. His face is thinner than in the photograph, the channels down his cheeks more pronounced. His eyes fix on mine – I feel them drinking me in. And then they twinkle.

My lips twitch in response. He takes a step towards me and I too take a hesitant step. He drops his kit bag and suddenly we are running, drawn together by the bond not revealed in those monochrome shades. We collide in a fusion of colour. My fingers tunnel into his hair as his arms enclose my waist. I bury my nose into his neck and my memories explode at his scent. His gaze reaches into

157

my soul and as his lips find mine my body tells me my husband has come home.

When we finally pull apart, Charlie crouches down to welcome a shy Freddie into the fold. Tears sting my eyes as our little boy wraps his arms around his father's neck. I bite my lip, half-crying, half-laughing.

The photograph I have come to know so well is in black and white.

But love – love is a glorious, technicoloured thing.

Anita Frank

Originally from Shropshire, Anita studied English and American History at the University of East Anglia and went on to work in media analysis and communications before becoming a stay-at-home mother. She now lives in Berkshire with her husband and three children and is a full-time carer to her mentally disabled son. Her debut novel, *The Lost Ones*, published by HQ Stories in 2019, was a ghost story set during the First World War. Themes touched upon in her short story *The Photograph* have inspired her second novel, *The Return*, which is due to be published in July 2021.

Birthday Buoy:
A Misadventure from the Lotus-eating years of Harry Barnett
Robert Goddard

Rhodes, May 1985

If he had gone home earlier, of course, it would have been all right. But that would have required greater self-discipline than Harry had ever been capable of. And such self-discipline as he may once have had had dwindled still further since taking up residence in Lindos. In the six years since Alan Dysart had generously invited him to become the caretaker of his holiday villa on the island of Rhodes, Harry had sunk uncomplainingly into a life of idleness and self-indulgence.

True, it was not completely idle. He worked as a waiter and washer-up at the Taverna Silenou in the main square of Lindos during the busiest stretches of the tourist season. But that was largely to pay off chunks of his bar bill at the same establishment, which had a tendency to mount prodigiously during the winter months. The proprietor, Kostas Dimitratos, was as much his friend as his occasional employer. The arrangement was hardly onerous.

Kostas was, in a sense, to blame for the fix Harry now found himself in. Discovering Harry was about to turn fifty, he had offered to host a party at the taverna to celebrate the big day. That might not have been such a bad idea – the Greeks always partied with gusto in Harry's experience – but the birthday boy should clearly have restrained himself until the party kicked off later in the evening. Instead, he had joined Kostas for several lunchtime drinks which had been followed by several more post-lunchtime drinks as the sun moved slowly across the azure sky and the shadows of the fig trees outside the taverna deepened inkily.

Harry's memories of the party itself were patchy at best. A conga had taken place at some point. At some other point he had stood on one of the rickety dining tables singing 'Born Free', scratchily accompanied on the fiddle by Yiannos Eliopoulos, who had always been a more expert drinker than he was a musician. It was, Harry seemed dimly to recall, Niko who had suggested the transition to Metaxá that sealed Harry's fate. But it was Kostas who had actually opened the bottle of Metaxá – or rather the bottles of Metaxá. So, he had to take his share of responsibility for the position Harry now found himself in. And that position involved a bush so large and multi-branched that it supported him as might a hammock, a foot or so off the ground, heels resting lightly on the edge of the cobbled path he had stumbled off, head pillowed in a nest of sweet-smelling leaves, while the stars in the areas of sky he could see between the leaves twinkled brightly and the only sound that reached him through the still, night air was the periodic barking of a dog.

Exactly how his walk back to the Villa ton Navarkhon had led him here he had no idea, not least because he did not know where here was. Half-climbing, half-falling out of the bush and back onto the path, he crouched beneath the hammer-blows of a throbbing pain inside his skull. Pain was too weak a word for it, he reckoned. He wasn't sure the dictionary contained a noun that would do justice to this pounding assault on his reason.

When the assault eventually eased enough for him to open his eyes and stand up, he realized he was still in the middle of Lindos.

Moonlight washed chalkily over the white walls of nearby houses to confirm as much. Compact though the village was, however, its maze of alleys was easy to get lost in, especially for someone with Harry's currently impaired faculties.

Whether he had been lost before he fell into the bush he could not say. Nor how long he had been lying there. He staggered into a beam of moonlight and squinted at his watch. The time was 2.37. That actually told him very little, since he did not know when he had left the taverna. But it counted as a piece of solid information to cling to and for that he was grateful.

Choosing a direction more or less at random, he set off at a gingerly pace, having to wait at intervals for his head to catch up with the rest of his body. He did not feel well. No, he did not feel well at all. The only consolation he could think of was that he suspected he should by rights feel even worse than he did.

It really was just as well you were only fifty once.

Another couple of turnings brought him suddenly into the central square and there, straight ahead, was the Taverna Silenou, scene of the night's bacchanalia, consumed now by darkness and silence. This enabled Harry to gain his bearings. He knew his route from there.

He was about to follow it when a sharp tang of petrol caught his nose, wafting across the square from the taverna. Then he heard the click of a lighter and saw in its feeble glow a figure standing beneath the pergola that stretched along one side of the building. A thin, darkly dressed man was lurking there, holding a cloth in one hand, to which he held the lighter. The cloth ignited with a faint whoosh and the man dropped it into a pile of what looked to Harry like Kostas's blue-and-white check tablecloths. They must have been soaked in petrol, because they instantly burst into flame. Several chairs had been arranged around the pile and the flames began to lick at their legs.

The man snapped off the lighter, picked up his petrol can and ran away across the square, vanishing into one of the alleys leading off it.

Only then did Harry's sluggish reactions kick in. He moved as fast as he could across the square, hammered on the door of the taverna and shouted Kostas's name and the Greek for fire. '*Fotiá! Fotiá!*'

The fire had taken serious hold of the tablecloths and chairs by now. From his waitering stints Harry knew the location of the hose, so he headed for it, dodging round the flames and blundering through the pergola, bumping into several shadow-wreathed pieces of furniture as he went. Then, once he was clear of those hazards, he caught his foot in one of the coils of the hose carelessly left snaking around the rear yard and fell in a confused heap some way short of the tap.

He rolled over on the gravel, raised himself on one elbow and bellowed another warning of fire. A light had come on by now in the flat above the taverna where Kostas and his wife lived. A window was flung open. The night-shirted figure of Kostas stared out, his luxuriant moustache magnified to gigantic proportions by the shadows cast up from the fire beneath him. He bellowed an oath and added another as he noticed Harry.

'What the hell have you done?' he followed up in English.

Fortunately for Kostas – and Harry – Evanthia Dimitratos was a quicker thinker than her husband and, of course, had the advantage of a relatively clear head. A light came on in the kitchen and a few seconds later Evanthia emerged, clad in a voluminous nightdress, clutching a fire extinguisher which Harry did not even know they possessed.

She rammed it against one of the pillars supporting the pergola to unlock the mechanism and in an instant a stream of white foam was being directed at the fire.

The foam was remarkably effective. The fire began to sputter and subside. But Evanthia went on spraying until the last of the flames had been quenched.

By then Harry had regained his feet. Evanthia cast him a withering glance over her shoulder. She did not look grateful, though it occurred to Harry that really she should. Instead she snapped, 'What did you do?'

'Nothing, Eva. I just … saw the fire … as I was passing.'

'What started it?'

'Some guy … with a petrol can.'

'A guy?'

'Yeah. Lucky, really.'

'Lucky?'

'That I was passing, I mean.'

The kitchen door opened and Kostas stumbled out to join them. He asked Evanthia something in Greek, then said to Harry, 'What happened?'

Harry gabbled out a repetition of the guy with a petrol can/lucky I was passing explanation he had already ventured.

'Why were you passing? You left here … hours ago.'

'Long story. Just be glad I came back.'

Kostas rubbed his eyes and took in the scene. 'I am glad, Hari. So is Eva.'

But Evanthia exhibited no gladness that Harry could discern. She growled something in Greek he failed to follow, plonked the empty fire extinguisher down on the nearest table and stalked past her husband back into the taverna.

'Is she all right, Kostas?' Harry asked.

Kostas grimaced. 'Not … very all right, no.'

'She should be relieved. If the fire had got out of control…'

'We could have been burned in our bed. I know. But…'

'You should phone the police. There's an arsonist on the loose.'

'We will not phone the police. And you will say nothing about this if you are my friend. And you are my friend, Hari, aren't you?'

'Yeah, but…'

'Come into the kitchen. I need a drink.'

'Listen, Kostas, I—'

'Just come into the kitchen. We will talk there.'

There was no sign of Evanthia. She had evidently gone back to bed. Kostas carefully closed the door that led to the stairs up to the flat and put on over his nightshirt an old coat that hung behind the door. From a cupboard he produced a bottle of cooking brandy and a couple of glasses. Then he sat down at the table used for preparing food and gestured for Harry to join him.

Harry was not sure he was equal to more spirits, but the first swallow persuaded him that a drink was probably what he needed as well. He took out his cigarettes and proffered the pack to Kostas, who surprised him by taking one. Normally, he decried Harry's preferred brand as being fit only for Turks to smoke. They lit up and looked raw-eyed at each other in the sallow glimmer of the overhead lamp.

'Do you know who did this, Kostas?' Harry asked, after coughing out his first lungful of smoke.

Kostas nodded glumly. 'Angelos Galanis.'

'Who's he?'

'A gangster who runs in drugs from Turkey. They go on from Rhodes to Crete and the mainland. Big business. Big money.'

'So, why should this … drugs lord … try to set fire to your taverna?'

'He didn't do it himself, Hari. He sent someone. It was a message. For me.'

'A message?'

'His father and my father fought together for the Communists in the Civil War. His father saved my father's life a couple of times. Galanis thinks that means I have to help him.'

'Help him with what?'

'He wants somewhere to store the drugs after they arrive and before they leave again. I don't know where he uses now, but he thinks my storage shed – with me looking after it – would be … safer.'

'You turned him down?'

'Of course I turned him down. But that only made him offer me more money to do it. I turned that down also. But…'

'He isn't taking no for an answer?'

Kostas took a deep gulp of brandy and shrugged helplessly.

'What are you going to do?'

'I don't know. Eva blames my father, which means she blames me. I wish he was still alive to deal with this. He would send Galanis away with a double-blast from his shotgun. But… I am not a fighting man. When I was in the army I worked in the kitchens. I cannot deal with a … a gangster.'

'You don't seem to have much choice. You have to deal with him. Somehow.'

'What do you think I should do?'

'Go to the police. Ask them to give you protection while they put together a case against Galanis.'

Kostas snorted derisively. 'The police? They wouldn't be able to protect me. Even if they wanted to. We would have to leave Rhodes to get away from him. I have never lived anywhere else. I was born here in Lindos. I would like to die here. Just … not yet.' He sighed. 'No. It is hopeless. Maybe I should go up to the bathroom now and cut my throat with my razor.'

'It can't be as bad as that.'

'But it is. And so…'

'What?'

'I suppose I will have to do what he wants me to do.'

'Store his drugs for him?'

'I think so, Hari. Yes. I think I will have to. I am not sure Eva will let me. But… there is no other way.'

'Bloody hell.'

'Yes. Very bloody hell.' Kostas drained his glass and refilled it, then topped up Harry's. 'But at least we put out the fire. Thanks to you. Why did you come back tonight?'

'I didn't actually go far enough to say I came back. I fell asleep in a bush just round the corner.'

'Ah. I thought it might be because you remembered you left your birthday present behind.'

'Birthday present?'

'You have forgotten my very fine gift?'

'Umm...'

'If I wasn't sick with worry about Galanis, I would be hurt, Hari. I truly would.'

'It's your fault for giving me so much to drink. What was the gift?'

'Something every fifty-year-old man should have.'

'A twenty-five-year-old girlfriend?'

Kostas managed a grin, though Harry was painfully aware that in happier circumstances he would have laughed heartily. 'No. But... maybe the next best thing.'

When Kostas crept off back up to bed Harry spent what remained of the night trying but largely failing to sleep on a seen-better-days mattress in the tiny office off the kitchen. He left at first light after sobering up – relatively speaking – on a pot of coffee. This time he remembered to take his birthday present with him, wedged in the inside pocket of his zip-up jacket. Walking through the cobbled streets of Lindos at dawn, with the sun still weak and the sound of the sea reaching him at intervals according to the twists and turns of the alleys, he reflected on what Kostas had told him – and failed to see how there could be a happy ending for his friend in such a situation. All the jollity of the party Kostas had thrown for him had drained away into sandpaper-throated, thick-headed, leaden depression.

He lay down on his bed in the gatehouse flat at the Villa ton Navarkhon fully expecting to spend several futile hours thinking about the fix Kostas was in before considering whether breakfast was a realistic proposition or not. In fact, however, he fell deeply asleep almost at once. And since Mrs Ioanides, the housekeeper Dysart kept on retainer, did not come in on Thursdays, there was nothing to rouse him until the afternoon was well-advanced.

By then the day was clearly a lost cause. He took a shower, rustled up a late lunch of bacon and eggs – there was nothing like a fry-up to see off a hangover in his experience – and dosed himself with a lot more coffee. He attempted a long-overdue repair to the bracket holding the television aerial, but discovered his heart wasn't in it. In normal circumstances, he might have headed for the Taverna Silenou then, for some hair of the dog, but the circumstances were far from normal, so he sat in the garden with a couple of bottles of beer and succeeded in dozing off in the sun, only to be stirred by the cool of the encroaching evening.

Harry threw on his jacket when he left the villa and ambled down to the harbour, hoping to break his listless mood. There was hardly anyone on the beach. The village was behind him, nestled picturesquely beneath the half-ruined acropolis, its crumbling stone walls burnished gold by the lowering sun. Harry lit a cigarette, walked onto the jetty and gazed out across the calm blue sea, wondering if he should ever mention the events of the previous night to Kostas again or just let him deal with the problem as he saw fit. It was not really Harry's business if the poor guy decided to allow Galanis the use of his shed, after all.

An inflatable craft with an outboard motor was tied up at the end of the jetty. Two men walked past Harry as he stood there, heading towards the boat. They were young, dark-haired and good-looking, with muscles rippling under their shirts to go with the strutting air of a pair of Adonises. One of them stopped and looked round at Harry, then called for his friend to stop as well.

Harry was suddenly aware of being closely studied. The men were wearing sunglasses and unreadable expressions. He ventured a 'good evening' – '*Kalispéra.*' But their only response was to mutter inaudibly to each other. Then the shorter of the two moved back past Harry, blocking his retreat along the jetty.

'You two want something?' he asked. There was no response.

He decided to force the issue. He pitched the butt of his cigarette into the water and started towards the shore. The man ahead of him did not step aside, but nodded to his friend. Who was suddenly close behind Harry, snaking an arm round his shoulder.

And then Harry saw the blade of a knife, clasped in the man's hand.

'Get in the boat with us now or I slit your throat,' the man rasped in his ear.

And Harry believed him.

As the inflatable sped out across the harbour, Harry's stomach lurching with every wave-crest, he was queasily aware of how swiftly and suddenly his evening had descended into a nightmare. Adonis One – the man who'd seemed to recognise him – was gunning the motor. Adonis Two – the man with the knife – had one foot resting painfully on Harry's right hand while he flicked the blade in and out of its stock in an idle but menacing fashion.

Harry had asked what they wanted several times, going so far as to offer them money, at which they'd merely laughed. Eventually, they'd told him to shut up. And Harry had sensed arguing with them would only make his situation worse.

It had already occurred to him that his abduction had to be connected in some way with Kostas's difficulties, but he could not for the life of him see how. Surely no one would think he could be used as a hostage. And how would Galanis know he was a friend of Kostas anyway?

The other possibility, which he thought much the likelier, was that one of the Adonises was the arsonist, who'd seen him raise the alarm and now wanted to punish him for intervening. What kind of punishment he might have in mind Harry really didn't want to ponder. 'Bloody hell,' he complained to himself.

'I told you to shut up, fat man,' snarled Adonis Two, grinding the heel of his shoe against Harry's knuckles. 'Get it?'

Harry winced as the pressure on his hand increased. He had to clench his teeth to ward off the pain as he nodded emphatically. He got it.

Adonis One plucked something dark out from beneath the motor and tossed it to Harry. 'Put that on.'

It was a black balaclava. Pulling it on over his head was difficult one-handed.

Adonis One soon intervened, tugging it down at the front so that it covered his eyes and nose, forcing him to breathe through his mouth. He wanted to protest, but he knew better than to speak again. The presence of the balaclava onboard suggested this wasn't the first time the Adonises had done something like this.

It wasn't a comforting thought.

The amount of light seeping through the balaclava began to diminish as the inflatable ploughed on its way. Night was falling and that only made Harry more fearful. What were they planning to do with him? Where were they taking him? He couldn't tell whether they were heading out to sea or hugging the coast. He was, in every sense, in the dark.

Another effect of the darkness was that he had no idea how much time was passing. But eventually, after what felt like an hour but might well have been no more than twenty minutes, the boat slowed and came to a halt. Harry heard other voices and a squeal of rubber against metal. They were alongside another vessel – a bigger vessel, he judged by the low thrumble of a powerful engine and the direction of the voices.

The motor died and the inflatable pitched and rolled. Harry sensed a rope was being attached to it. The pressure on his hand was released. 'Stay where you are,' growled Adonis Two. He and his friend were leaving, Harry realized, clambering up onto the other craft. The voices he could hear were an animated babble of Greek in varying tones. It was hard to tell what kind of reception the Adonises were getting.

Suddenly, a spotlight was directed at Harry and a voice louder than the rest, deep-pitched and commanding, shouted down to him. 'Show your face, Englishman.'

Harry pulled off the balaclava and raised a hand to shade his eyes from the dazzling light. The other vessel was a substantial launch of some kind. He could see a rail above him, with figures looking over it.

'Tell me your name.' All Harry could make out of the man doing the shouting was the massive set of his shoulders and the hairless dome of his head, silhouetted against the spotlight.

'My name's ... Harry Barnett.'

'You're a friend of Kostas Dimitratos?'

'Well, I, er ... drink at his taverna.'

'And you're the guy who fucked up Niko's fire-raising, yes?'

'I, er ... raised the alarm, that's all.'

'So, you fucked it up.'

A small shaft of anger pierced Harry's fear. The words were out of his mouth before he had weighed their possible consequences. 'I'd say Niko was the one who fucked up.'

To Harry's surprise, the other man laughed. 'You're right. But Niko's my son, so ... someone else has to pay for his fuck-ups.'

'Are you Angelos Galanis?'

'Has Kostas talked about me, Harry?'

'No. That is...'

'You are a friend of his, I think. Which is good. Maybe a drowned friend is better than a fire.'

'Look, I'll talk him round if you take me back to Lindos. I'll persuade him to co-operate with you.'

'Maybe. Maybe not. You can try that if you make it back. But I don't think you will make it back, Harry. You don't look much of a swimmer to me.'

'Hold on. I—'

Galanis barked an order in Greek. Harry thought he understood it and tried to grasp something – anything – to hold onto. Suddenly, the inflatable began to tilt alarmingly. They were hauling it aboard by the stern, upending the entire craft.

He slid down to the bow and scrabbled for something to hold onto. But the boat was vertical now and was bouncing against the side of the launch. Harry hit the water and went down, then surfaced, spluttering and gasping. Galanis had it right. He was not much of a swimmer. His Swindon childhood had involved very little immersion in water, although he had mastered the doggy paddle during a Trip Week visit to Weston-super-Mare with the other railway families. But the English seaside on a summer's afternoon wasn't the Mediterranean by night. He couldn't see anything beyond the lights of the launch, which was moving away from him at some speed, throwing up a wake which threatened to swamp him. The water, some of which he had already swallowed, was cold. The night was moonless. He had no idea where he was in relation to the coast of Rhodes. And in a moment of chill clarity as a wave tossed him up and then down into a black trough, he reckoned his chances of survival were approximately ... zero.

'How does fifty feel, Hari?' Yiannos had asked him during his birthday party the previous night.

'It feels great,' Harry had replied, grinning broadly. And so it had. But now it seemed the answer he should have given was, 'Brief, cold and wet, Yiannos. Most of all brief. That's how it feels.'

He saw something white bobbing close to him and made a grab for it. It was one of the inflatable's fenders – maybe a spare that had been lying around loose. It wasn't much, but it helped him stay afloat. Perhaps that was a mixed blessing, though. He had already lost sight of the launch. He rose and fell with each wave, sensing his puny, minuscule irrelevance in such a vast body of water. He struggled to remove his shoes, which were filling with water and weighing him down. But his movements were sluggish and inept. He couldn't undo the laces. His feet and hands were numb. He was shivering and thrashing and … drowning.

Yes. That was it. That was what he was doing.

He was drowning.

Harry had read somewhere that people who'd been resuscitated after seeming to have died often reported a sensation of moving along a dark tunnel, with a bright light ahead of them. He supposed, so far as he was able to suppose anything as strength and feeling deserted him, that he was heading along that tunnel between two worlds himself, moving inexorably towards whatever the hereafter amounted to.

The only puzzle was the light. It wasn't a pure, comforting white, but a flashing alternation of white and red. White and red. Yes. There was no doubt of it. He was sinking slowly and drifting along the tunnel as first white light, then red, then white again and red again, washed over him.

And then he collided with the buoy.

He was thrown against the base of the buoy with some force and the shock of the impact roused him from the lethargy he'd descended into. The structure was there above him, a welded tower of steel bars mounted on the base, supporting a flashing light.

Suddenly, hope flared inside him. Maybe he wasn't going to drown after all. He stretched up towards the lowest bar of the tower, but couldn't reach it. Then he spotted a grab-handle fitted to the base and hauled himself up by it. The fender slipped from his grasp as he did so and, in trying to retrieve it, he nearly fell back into the sea as the buoy rolled with the swell, but he managed to hold on and huddled at the foot of the tower, wrapping his arms round the bars to ensure he wasn't dislodged.

He was safe. For the moment.

The light went on flashing red and white above him. He was shivering violently. He wasn't sure he'd ever felt so cold. The sea slopped and heaved around the base, often washing over it and soaking him still further. The hope that had driven him to clamber onto the buoy began to ebb. As far as he could see, all he'd accomplished was to postpone his death. Sooner or later, he'd become so weak he'd lose his grip and slide back into the sea. It was inevitable. There was no escaping it.

Then he saw a light in the distance and heard the note of a boat's engine. It wasn't Galanis's launch. The note was higher. Maybe it was a fishing smack. He couldn't tell through the darkness and the spray. But it was a boat of some kind. And it was getting closer.

Or was it? His eyes and ears were straining. Was he just imagining it was approaching him? There was no reason why it should, after all. The helmsman must have seen the buoy. But he wouldn't have seen Harry. And he wouldn't have imagined – who would? – that there was anyone on the buoy.

Harry shouted, '*Voïthia!*', 'Help!' But the wind snatched the word from his mouth.

There was no chance anyone on the boat would hear him. He took one arm away from the tower and waved frantically. He sucked in as much air as his lungs would hold and shouted again. '*Voïthia! Voïthia!*' But it made no difference. The note of the boat's engine did not alter. The light did not veer towards him.

And then he remembered his birthday present.

Kostas was an enthusiastic follower of football, tuning in to any match he could find on the TV behind the bar of the Taverna Silenou, despite the set's frequent bouts of vertical-hold failure. He had been mightily impressed by Harry's recollection of watching from the directors' box at the County Ground, Swindon, in 1969 when Swindon Town beat AS Roma 4-0 in a European cup-tie for which they'd improbably qualified, a result so extraordinary Kostas had had to track down documentary proof of it in the small print of one of his old football yearbooks before he was willing to believe Harry's account.

Harry was only at the game because the club chairman had his Bentley serviced at Barnchase Motors and had invited Harry's scapegrace partner, Barry Chipchase, to attend. But Barry had pulled out at the last moment after being seen in compromising circumstances with the wife of the club physio the night before, so Harry had gone along instead, drunk the wine, smoked the cigars and generally had a whale of a time.

He had rather exaggerated his dedication to Swindon Town's cause for Kostas's benefit, claiming regular attendance at home matches from the late 1940s onwards. But exaggeration had in this case been rewarded, because Kostas's birthday present to him was an old-fashioned football rattle, specially made by Tsoumanis the carpenter and painted in Swindon Town's colours of red and white. It was still in the inside pocket of Harry's jacket, the handle poking uncomfortably into his ribs.

A football rattle, as Harry well knew from those few occasions when he had gone along to see the Robins play, was a fearsomely noisy object. In ordinary circumstances, he would have no earthly use for such a thing, which might have explained the ease with which he'd forgotten being presented with it at the party.

But he had a use for it now.

He yanked at the zip on his jacket, but he couldn't seem to grasp it properly and it refused to budge. Desperately, he forced his hand inside the jacket and prised the rattle out.

Then he pulled himself to his feet, braced himself against the struts of the tower and, holding the rattle above his head, began to swing it for all he was worth. The noise was deafening. The only question was whether it was deafening enough. The boat's light in the middle distance didn't waver or shift in his direction. The note of the engine didn't alter. Harry went on swinging.

And then his prayer was answered. There was a throaty growl from the engine, a throttling back, an alteration of course. The light began to move towards him. And still he went on swinging.

But it was all right now. He knew, against all expectation, that he was going to survive the night.

The boat was Greek, which was a small relief, though he would happily have taken a ride to Turkey if it had been offered to him: beggars could hardly be choosers. But the illuminated sign above the wheelhouse – ΑΚΤΟΦΥΛΑΚΗ – told him the vessel was a Greek coastguard cutter. He stopped swinging the rattle and simply grinned broadly at the two capped and uniformed men who were standing ready to rescue him. They looked bemused, as well they might. It probably wasn't often they encountered this kind of thing.

'Bloody hell, am I glad to see you,' Harry shouted.

'Ah,' one of them responded with a smile. 'Angliká.' From his point of view, apparently, all was explained. Only an Englishman could strand himself on a buoy with a football rattle for company.

They moved in close and pulled Harry off in a dexterous manoeuvre. Then they bundled him down into the cabin, where they gave him some dry clothes to put on, wrapped a blanket round him and administered a tot of rum. Harry generally disliked rum. But he found he had a taste for it tonight.

None of the crew understood enough English for him to deliver a coherent account of what had happened and he was happy to defer an explanation until they made landfall. Strangely, however, they seemed in no hurry to leave the buoy. There was a lot of head-scratching and muttering which Harry couldn't understand. One of them clambered onto the buoy, followed by much shouting to and fro. Odd words and phrases he couldn't make any sense of reached Harry. There was something about a hatch and something else about a tank, though a tank of what he had no idea. His priority was recovering the feeling in his limbs and persuading them to give him more of the rum and a cigarette to go with it.

Eventually, after a lengthy conferral with their HQ on Rhodes – of which Harry heard little beyond bursts of static on the radio – they moved off. The man who seemed to be skippering the vessel came down to the cabin and prefaced his first direct words to Harry by pouring him another tot of rum and helping himself to one as well.

'*Ee teehee*,' he said, chinking his glass against Harry's. He was proposing a toast – to good fortune.

Harry was more than willing to drink to that. Although he had the strange impression that the skipper was delighted about rather more than plucking a hapless Englishman off a buoy in the middle of the Mediterranean. As to what more there could be to put a smile on his face, Harry was too exhausted to wonder. He was simply glad to be alive.

It was only when Harry spotted the statues of the stag and the doe guarding the entrance to Mandráki harbour that he realized he'd been taken to Rhodes City rather than Lindos, which was understandable enough, he reflected, since he'd never actually said where he was from. Less understandable was the presence on the harbourside of two police cars, apparently awaiting his arrival. A neatly-groomed man in a smartly-pressed suit who looked as if he might be some kind of senior detective was leaning against the bonnet of one of the cars, smoking a cigarette as he watched Harry make his unsteady disembarkation from the cutter.

When two uniformed police officers directed Harry towards the car, he protested. 'It's OK. I went out with some guy in a boat and fell overboard. But your coastguard colleagues rescued me. All I really need is—'

'A chance to explain everything,' said the man in plain clothes, stepping forward. 'We'll begin with your name.'

'I gave it to the coastguards. Barnett. Harry Barnett.'

'Where do you live, Mr Barnett?'

'Lindos. The Villa ton Navarkhon.'

'Aha. Are you acquainted with Angelos Galanis?'

'Who?'

'Yes or no would have been reasonable answers. Who? sounds evasive. Tell me, how exactly did you end up on that buoy?'

'Like I just said—'

'I know what you just said. But it wasn't the truth, was it? So, let's go to Police Headquarters and see if you can do better.' The man took Harry aback by offering him his hand. 'I'm Inspector Vidouris, Athens Drugs Squad.' He smiled. 'That's right, Mr Barnett. You've hit the big time.'

Harry saw little of Police HQ on arrival. The place was sparsely populated at such an hour and poorly lit. He was left alone in a cheerless and windowless – though mercifully warm – interrogation room for half an hour or so before Vidouris joined him. He sat down and faced Harry across the graffiti-scarred table.

'Smoke?' Vidouris asked, slipping a silver case out of his jacket pocket and opening it.

'Thanks.' Harry took a cigarette. They looked too well made to be Greek. American was his guess. 'Mine got a bit wet.'

Vidouris's lighter was as smart as the case. He lit Harry's cigarette, then one for himself. No. Not American. French. 'The Villa ton Navarkhon sounds … big, Mr Barnett.'

'I'm just the caretaker, actually.'

'Ah. And since I'm told the mushy cigarette pack we found in your jacket is Karelia Sertika – hardly a rich man's choice of brand – I assume you don't have much money.'

'I do well enough.'

'Well enough to keep your friend Konstantinos Dimitratos in business between holiday seasons, apparently.'

'Look—'

'What is the name of the "guy" whose boat you say you fell out of?'

'He never said. It was, er … a spur of the moment trip.'

'A spur of the moment? Well, Mr Barnett, allow me to offer you a different spur. Either you tell me the truth – all of it, every detail – or you'll be charged with participation in Angelos Galanis's drug-smuggling activities. We have enough evidence to hold you on. More than enough.'

'What evidence?'

'Which is it to be?'

'I don't know anything about—'

'Just choose. The truth. Or a prison cell. It's not so difficult, is it?'

Put like that, it wasn't difficult at all, of course, even though Harry knew telling the truth meant revealing Kostas's involvement with Galanis. What Vidouris would make of that Harry didn't like to imagine. His only consolation was that whatever transpired now had to be better than drowning, which had seemed certain to be his fate earlier that night.

'I, er...'

'Take your time, Mr Barnett.' Vidouris leant back in his chair and drew deeply on his cigarette. 'And don't forget to tell me why you carry a football rattle with you. To be honest, I'm more curious about that than anything else.'

It was actually a relief for Harry to be able to relate exactly what had happened over the previous twenty-four hours – each and every one of the missteps that had ended with him clinging to a buoy in the middle of the sea. Disquietingly, Vidouris seemed to find much of his account amusing, chuckling over particular details and asking questions that struck Harry as irrelevant, such as what species of bush he had fallen into. (They settled on myrtle.) And then there was the rattle, of course, which he was required to demonstrate. Not to mention Swindon Town 4 AS Roma 0, a result Vidouris enjoyed so much he demanded a full match report, which Harry was poorly placed to supply beyond a vague recollection that most of the goals had been scored late in the game.

When Harry had finally finished, Vidouris actually applauded. 'Beautiful, Mr Barnett. Simply beautiful.'

'You believe me, don't you?'

'Oh yes. Completely. No one could make that up.'

'So, you no longer think I'm a drug smuggler.'

'I never did. You've actually gone a long way to helping us catch a drug smuggler. I'm here because Galanis has been causing us a lot of problems. And those problems are only getting bigger in the bars and clubs of Athens. He has to be stopped. Sadly, we've been unable to amass any hard evidence against him. But now we have some. Thanks to you.'

'Really?'

'The buoy, Mr Barnett. The coastguards were surprised by how low in the water it was floating. With normal buoyancy, you would have found it very difficult to climb onto. And a handle's been fitted to it, which you mentioned using to pull yourself up. Not a usual fitting, I assure you.'

'No?'

'The handle is actually there to open a hatch that's been added to the base, giving access to a steel tank inside. The tank is designed to hold drugs. The coastguards found a substantial quantity of cocaine ready for collection. The consignments are obviously delivered to the buoy from Turkey and picked up later by boat from Rhodes. I suspect other buoys are being used for the same purpose throughout the Aegean. Naturally, we'll be checking on that. Meanwhile, we'll be keeping this buoy under discreet surveillance to see who comes to remove the drugs. When we have them, we'll have the link to Galanis we need.'

'So ... that's where he's been stashing the drugs? Inside buoys?'

'Evidently so. It's a clever scheme. Who would dream of looking inside a buoy? But it has its drawbacks, I imagine, particularly in bad weather. Galanis's business is expanding all the time, so he's clearly decided to seek extra capacity.'

'Like Kostas's storage shed?'

'Exactly.'

'Bloody hell.'

Vidouris smiled. 'I think we'll get him now, Mr Barnett, I really do.'

'Well, I'm ... pleased to hear it.'

'Of course, we must avoid giving him any cause to suspect we're onto him. So, it has to look as if you didn't survive being dumped at sea.'

'How...?'

'You cannot return to Lindos, Mr Barnett. And you cannot contact anyone. You have to disappear ... until we have Galanis in our clutches.'

'Disappear?'

'Don't worry. It's not as bad as it sounds. Regard it as a holiday. We'll be paying. There won't be much sightseeing involved, I'm afraid. In fact, you'll be spending most of the time alone in your hotel room. And when I say most, I mean ... all.'

'You're saying I have to go into hiding?'

'Yes. But consider the advantages.'

Harry couldn't immediately think of one. 'Such as?'

'Well, are there any seriously long novels you've ever wanted to read? *War and Peace*, maybe. Or some of our Greek epics? *The Iliad*? *The Odyssey*? Now's your chance, Mr Barnett.' Vidouris's smile had broadened into a smirk. 'Just give me a list of your chosen titles ... and I'll see what we can do.'

And so it was that Harry found himself spending eventless day after eventless day in a blandly furnished room at the Athens Hilton, reading an assortment of thrillers and detective novels – Tolstoy and Homer never got a look-in – when he wasn't slumped in front of the TV eating a room-service meal while watching badly dubbed re-runs of *Bonanza* and *The High Chaparral*. It was boring, of course. But there were worse things than boredom, drowning among them. Counting sheep didn't help him sleep at night. Counting his blessings, on the other hand, seemed to do the trick. That and the contents of the regularly re-stocked mini-bar.

Relief came on the eighth day, with the ringing of the telephone. Harry knew it had to be Inspector Vidouris calling. No one else knew he was there. He snatched up the receiver eager for news.

'We have him, Mr Barnett,' Vidouris reported in cheery tones. 'Angelos Galanis is under arrest, along with most of his gang.'

'Thank God for that.'

'One of the men who came for the drugs was his son, Nikolaos. You met him. Perhaps you won't be surprised to learn he displayed very little loyalty to his father when we questioned him. He helped us trap Galanis in return for being charged with a lesser offence.'

'Does this mean I can go back to my normal life?'

'Yes. We'll say it was a routine inspection of the buoy by the coastguards that revealed where the drugs were hidden. You won't be involved at all. Which is best for you, I think. And for your friend Dimitratos.'

'Well, thanks for that, Inspector.'

'You're welcome.'

'Can I leave here now?'

'Oh yes. We've already booked you on a flight to Rhodes. You should be home by tonight.'

'That sounds good.'

'To me also. Things don't normally go this well. You are a lucky man, Mr Barnett.'

Harry reached Lindos that evening by taxi from Rhodes airport. He would normally have made the journey by bus, but luck of the kind he had enjoyed seemed to warrant a certain amount of extravagance. A man only lives once, he reflected, just as he only drowns once.

He lingered at the Villa ton Navarkhon no longer than it took him to drop off his few belongings. Then he headed for the Taverna Silenou, strolling deliciously along the cobbled alleys of Lindos as the coolness of night seeped into the spring-scented air.

'Hari!' Kostas beamed at him from behind the bar as he entered the taverna. 'No one's seen you in more than a week. Where have you been?'

'Athens. I had to deal with some business for Alan Dysart at short

181

notice. It turned out to be more complicated than I'd expected. But never mind that. You look happier than when I left, Kostas. Had some good news?'

'Not good, my friend. Excellent. Wonderful. Glorious.'

'What's happened?'

'Galanis has been arrested. His whole gang has been rounded up. Haven't you heard? It's been in all the papers.'

'Well, you know I can't read Greek very well.' Harry did his best to add a look of wide-eyed astonishment to his smile. 'But that's marvellous, isn't it? It means you're off the hook.'

'Yes. The hook I am off.'

'Bloody hell. This calls for a drink. Maybe several.'

'For you they are on the house. There might be no taverna here if you hadn't seen that fire being started.'

'That was nothing, really. I'm just glad everything's worked out.'

'So, what will you have to drink, my friend?'

'A beer would be great.'

'Not Metaxá? This is a celebration.'

'Definitely not Metaxá. Look what happened last time I drank that stuff.'

'OK.' Kostas was grinning so broadly his moustache was nearly touching his ears. 'Have anything you like. It's up to you.'

Robert Goddard

Robert Goddard's first novel, *Past Caring*, was an instant bestseller when it was published in 1986. Since then, his books have won a worldwide audience with their swift pace and labyrinthine plotting. He has won awards in the UK and the US and his books have been translated into more than thirty languages.

Perspective

Araminta Hall

He stood right on the edge, so close that his toes clipped the nothing which occurs at the end of the world. The air was thick with a freezing darkness, even though it was early in the morning and the back of the night had been broken. But it was that time of year when the night has almost obliterated day, the tip of the calendar, the point at which you stop believing in warmth and light.

He would never have stood so close in the light, as they all despaired at the teenagers who did it, clipping their legs over the cliff as they flashed photos on their phones, spots of light sparking eerily in to the sky. Everyone knew the cliffs were not so much eroding, as succumbing, more and more of their chalky whiteness tumbling in to the grey sea month after month. It had already taken a few bodies with it. Two this year and one the year before. Their weight and daring too much for a world already heavy with waste and sorrow. The cliff was dotted with notices warning of the danger, but nobody heeded anything anymore. Still people came with no more purpose than to sit in the place where they could fall at any minute, unbelieving of, or maybe testing, the bad thing. And the truth was Cole understood why they did it.

The locals said the sea had developed an appetite, that it was bored of waiting, that it was angry, that humans had had their chance and failed. He imagined a day when all the countries were gone, leaving behind pointed outcrops of land jutting out of the never-ending sea. Men would fight to the death for their place on these precarious rocks, or grow gills and swim with the fishes.

A strong, salt-saturated wind blew up sharply from below, rocking him back on his heels. The sea was churning beneath him and he knew the tide was high, not just because he had made it his business to know such things, but also because he could hear the waves breaking against the rocks, which they only did when the sea was right up against the bottom of the cliff. He looked up and in to the penetrating blackness, broken only by the occasional plume of white caught by the light of the moon as the waves raced towards the shore.

He'd come the long way in order to pass her darkened cottage, so he turned and made his way back to the narrow path, allowing himself only to stop briefly outside instead of slinking down the side passage in to her garden. When he'd come the evening before she'd been in the kitchen, peeking into a pot on the stove, then stirring whatever was inside with a wooden spoon. He'd liked what she'd been wearing – he thought it was called a smock, a sort of old-fashioned dress made from a slightly coarse material with buttons up the front, russet red, a bit like leaves at the best time of autumn. Her tightly curled, dark hair had been swept up in to a messy pile on top of her head, so he could see her ears which stuck out from the side of her head like a trophy. Her cheeks had been flushed and he knew that when she smiled her teeth were small and white and very clean and that her eyes were so dark you couldn't make out where her pupils ended and her irises began.

Cole could sense that she was comfortable in her body, which pleased him, especially as it was a round, full body, unlike the ones men were meant to find attractive nowadays. He often watched her bottom and hips swing beneath the fabric of her clothes as she moved around, her stockinged feet planted firmly on the ground. She was so secure and happy and it made him feel the same way when he looked at her. She didn't suffer from neurosis or panic or self-doubt, he was confident in her equilibrium.

He'd decided a few weeks ago that she was called Clara. He'd played around with a few names, knowing she was called something romantic and poetic, but Clara had come to him in a flash of inspiration and he'd known he was right. He already knew she was an artist because he'd seen canvases in the sitting room, once he'd even seen her painting. And it was obvious that she'd lived in the cottage forever, perhaps once with her parents, whom she'd dotingly nursed through their final years. He supposed there wasn't much opportunity for love in such an isolated spot, but there had no doubt been a couple of romances, maybe she'd even had her heart not so much broken as dented. Now, he thought, she was happy on her own, living her small, contained life, painting the view, eating her vegetable stews and sitting by her warm fire.

It pained Cole sometimes to think of her existing like this for all those years without him knowing about her. All those years when he'd loved the wrong woman and chased money and status like it mattered, shrouding himself in suits, entombing his life behind brands and kitchen refurbs. All that time she had been patiently waiting and, if he'd known, he would have abandoned his crowded, stale life long ago, without waiting for it to abandon him.

He checked his phone and saw he only had an hour or so till dawn, so made his way down to the beach, feeling the frost scrunching on the pebbles. The cold was penetrating as he approached the sea, but it didn't worry him, in fact he looked forward to feeling the water on his skin. He'd vowed to himself, as a point of honour, that he would never wear a wetsuit, something which still slightly astounded him. But it wasn't just the sea which was astounding, it was everything. All the comfort and things he'd always thought he needed left behind like a pile of discarded clothes, revealing to him a life he hadn't even known existed. He knew that anyone he'd known from before would think him lonely and devastated, but what he'd like to tell them was that he'd actually been more isolated before, in the midst of them all.

The trick was not to stop, to just keep walking, out and out, in to the cold blackness. He liked to imagine that the water was devouring him the further he went, biting off chunks of his body bit by bit. By the time it reached his thighs he'd lost all feeling in the lower part of his legs and it was then that he dived underneath, arching his back and kicking his feet. It took his breath away as it always did, filling his mouth and nose with salty, icy water which overtook his being, flowing in and out of him. But then he surfaced and began cutting through the water, his arms churning and thrashing past his head.

Cole swam straight out, daring himself to go farther and farther, kicking against currents and the fears which lurk under anyone in a deep, dark sea. But there was always a moment in which the tingling on his skin became a burning pain and his head felt like it was enclosed in a tightening vice. Cole turned at that point, heading back towards the pebbly beach, judging his destination more than seeing it. Swimming would be strange in the summer, he thought, as he pulled himself onto the rough shingle, with light and warmth; it would feel very different and maybe not quite as pleasant.

He never brought a towel and simply pulled back on the thick, fleecy tracksuit he'd bought for this very purpose. But this morning his body felt raw and shaky and his hair cracked with ice, his limbs refusing to articulate properly. His hands were a shocking blue and his teeth were chattering so hard he could feel the vibration in his skull. He allowed himself a moment of panic as it was his first sub-zero swim and maybe he hadn't been ready. But a faint crack of light had appeared on the horizon and it was enough to make Cole move, turning his feet and forcing his body in to a run, all the way back to his cottage.

He ran himself a hot bath as soon as he got home, and made a cup of tea as he waited for it to fill. His hands burnt as he wrapped them round the cup, but Cole held them steady, knowing that cold this deep had to be slowly thawed. The bath water made him gasp but he lay back in to it, pulling his head under and opening his eyes so he could look up into a wobbly world. His skin felt like it was being assaulted by needles, but he stayed put, his need for air beating against his ribs, only coming up at the very last minute, his head spinning and his vision pitted.

After he got out, he wrapped his body in a towel and crossed the hall to his bedroom, pulling the curtains on the day and looking out through the trees to the bend in the river opposite his house, the ducks and moorhens already splashing in the murky water. He only had to follow the river for twenty or so minutes and he would find himself back on the beach, with Clara's house alone and wonderful just above him.

Specks of blue were beginning to peek through the layer of cloud which seemed to be shrouding the world, but Cole didn't really care if the sun materialised or not. He'd always liked the drama of winter better than the placidity of summer; in summer too much was expected, people were everywhere, enjoying themselves, the pressure always seemed too intense.

He dressed in lots of layers for work, as a few days shivering on the hills at the beginning had taught him to do. He wasn't a masochist and knew the limits of his endurance and just because he started his days with icy cold didn't mean it had to continue. When he was ready, he went downstairs and made himself porridge with full-fat milk, over which he sprinkled brown sugar and cinnamon. He ate it standing up, looking out over his back garden which he had great plans for in the spring. One day, maybe by next year, he planned to be fully self-sufficient, never to have to set foot in a shop and buy what he didn't need or to speak with anyone just for the sake of sound. Which reminded him he must check the trap before he left.

He washed his bowl and saucepan when he was finished, his belly now full and warm, smiling as he watched the soapy water run over his hands, remembering how he used to start his days, with expensive coffees drunk as he rushed to the Tube. He could still feel the shivering crush of bodies, the false jollity of the office, the recycled air and strip-lighted rooms in which he made meaningless decisions that advanced nothing.

The trap door was shut; if it was full it would be his first catch, which would be wonderful because it had been worrying him that he hadn't caught anything. He gingerly lifted the peephole and felt his heart contract at the sight of a plump rabbit shivering in the box. He reached in and lifted it out by the scruff of its neck, its little pink nose twitching in the cold air. The despatch had to be done quickly, he'd read, no need to prolong their suffering. He took it to a rock he'd positioned for the purpose and laid the rabbit on to it, holding it steady with his hand. With his other he picked up the hammer which had rested unused next to the stone for too long and brought it down with a swift movement.

There was significantly more blood than Cole had been expecting and pieces of what he presumed were brains and fragments of bone splattered up his fingers. His stomach turned without warning and he felt a contraction in his bowels, but told himself not to be stupid, how did he expect to become a self-sufficient man of the land if the sight of a bit of blood made him want to be sick. Cole straightened and took the rabbit into his shed, which he'd equipped for this very purpose when he'd moved in. The butcher's block was scrubbed and his knife glinted in the sharp winter light coming through the skylight. It had lain untouched for twelve weeks and now it was going to be christened.

He laid the rabbit on the slab and with one swift movement cut off what was left of its head, then used the knife to slice through the belly so that its guts spilled luridly over the block. He was feeling fine now and he pulled out the mass of slithering, slimy organs without even the smallest flinch, ignoring the sharp tang of ingested grass in the air. He hung the rabbit upside-down from a hook he'd already suspended and then used a smaller knife to create a slit in the skin, which now didn't even resemble fur, pulling it down and off the rabbit in one quick, skilful movement. It made him think momentarily of how he might undress Clara and he blushed at the thought.

He stood back to take in the naked body, which had been pulsing with life only fifteen minutes before, feeling slightly amazed at what he'd accomplished. His hands tingled at the power he'd felt as he remembered those strange moments when he'd raised the hammer and how he could have stopped, but hadn't. His stomach felt hollow right at its base, tugging on his groin and sending a ripple of pleasure down in to his feet.

It was so cold in the shed and his cottage so unvisited he felt confident in leaving the rabbit where it was for the day, but he washed the bucket in the outside tap and used some fresh water to wipe down the butcher's board, before spraying it with disinfectant. He just had time to wash the blood from his hands before walking over the road to the Wildlife Hut.

'Morning Cole,' Jack said as he came in. Cole nodded in response. He didn't yet feel entirely comfortable with these people who had spent all their lives in the countryside and knew the seasons, the tides, the wildlife, the sky, the weather like they knew their own name.

Holly was already writing something on the board. 'We need someone to walk over to the long barn,' she said without looking round. 'Apparently a cow's got into the courtyard. Are you OK to do that, Cole?'

'Sure.' He loved that walk, with its view across the beach to Clara's house and the undulating white hills on either side.

'Oh, by the way, have you seen the rota of duties for the Christmas party?' Holly asked.

'No.' He wasn't particularly looking forward to the party; he'd gone to enough Christmas parties over the years that had ended in pools of vomit and white powder sniffed up noses resulting in endless days of regret. Although he hoped and presumed this one would be different.

'I put it up yesterday.' Holly motioned to something on the board, but then smiled at him. 'It'll be nice for you, a good way to meet everyone round about. I mean, I know you've been here since September, but a party's always good for breaking the ice.'

* * *

Lennie had given up setting an alarm. She didn't really know why she'd kept it up for as long as she had as there was no rush across town to her studio anymore, no more topping and tailing the day with fancy breakfasts and exciting cocktails with people she'd known for so long they felt like family. No more parties, or shopping, or watching interesting people, or strange conversations with strangers, or bodies pushed against each other in loud clubs. Lennie rubbed her hands across her face and forced herself to sit up, then got up and opened her bedroom curtains, revealing to herself the massive expanse of lonely sea all around.

It had been marginally better in the summer, although being alone was still just being alone, but she hadn't bargained on the bloody winter, when it was so cold it was like having a sharp knife scraping the skin off your bones, so she didn't want to step outside. She spent some days lying on the sofa watching other people's homes in various states of disarray. Or trawling too-expensive clothing websites, filling her imaginary basket with sparkling bits of cloth for all those Christmas parties she wouldn't be going to.

Lennie went to the bathroom but found she couldn't be bothered with a shower and how cold she'd feel afterwards because even having the heating on twenty-four hours a day didn't seem to make the cottage warm. Instead she splashed her face with water and tried to ignore the ache in her back where she thought her kidneys tried to function. The steam from the water blurred her reflection which made her feel like she was disintegrating, as if she was becoming less and less like herself, but without anything to replace it.

She'd learnt to dress in layers and to light a fire as her first task of the day. At first she'd quite enjoyed the ritual of it all, the sweeping of the ashes, the gathering of tools, the patience of lighting, but now she hated the fucking trudge of it and how boringly repetitive her life had become, her life which only six months before had been so fun and fabulous.

She sat back on her heels once the fire had got going and looked across at her latest canvas sat fatly by the chest. The views had been meant to inspire but, if anything, the beauty of nature was intimidating; the hugeness of the sky and sea was like a void, like it sucked away everything she thought. And any thoughts which did cling on were blown away by the wind which just didn't give up, but made sure it penetrated in to every atom of her being.

She forced herself to stand and walk towards the canvas, whipping the sheet off in one quick movement, then stood with her hand on her hip and her mouth set in a slant of disdain. She didn't know what she'd been thinking, the sea was impossible to capture and the light was absurd wasn't it? She cocked her head on one side as if it would make a difference, but that made it worse. And what was she doing anyway because her work had never been about pretty.

Lennie raised her foot and stamped it on to the wooden floor beneath her feet, as her eyes filled with angry tears. Other people turned forty and didn't spend a year isolated on the edge of a cliff. She hated herself at that moment for her melodrama, which had served her pretty well up till this point but now seemed to have mutated into something ugly. Maybe you couldn't carry off melodrama so well in your forties? Maybe you had to learn a bit of poise? Lennie felt like spitting on the ground at the word.

She went instead to the mirror above the fireplace and stared at her falling face, as she thought of it now. There was a sag of skin round her jawline which appeared to grow daily, pulling her face downwards and puffing it out. She smoothed it by gouging her fingers sharply across it, then upwards from her jawline, which is how she supposed she'd look with a facelift, which was something to consider. She lent in closer to inspect the pale red blotches which she'd recently noticed on her cheeks and then saw a black hair growing out of a mole on her chin. If she stayed here much longer, she'd become a witch.

She moved through to the kitchen and made herself coffee, but when she took the milk out of the fridge she could already see it was slightly separated and once in her mug it split into curd like chunks which made her want to cry, because the nearest shop was a twenty-minute drive away. And who the hell lived like this?

When Lennie had first read about the old coastguard cottage for rent on the Sussex coast she'd felt a desperate desire to inhabit it. London had started to feel too much, too full, too dangerous and she'd wanted to shut a door and lock herself away. And her first viewing, on a bright spring day, had been enchanting; her car bumping down a rutted farm path, until it tipped the hill and the huge sea glittered in front of her, making her shield her eyes. It had seemed impossible that there could be a house there and she'd laughed and said to Andy the estate agent that she felt like she was in a crime drama, about to be driven to her death by a man she'd only met that morning.

But then the cottage had come in to view and she'd exclaimed with joy and the atmosphere had shifted and she'd forgotten anything other than what she was looking at. Her cottage, as she immediately thought of it, was covered in friendly white clapboard and the doors and windows were painted a cheerful bright blue. Even from the gate she could see how the sun streamed through the whole building, which would give the most amazing light and, when she looked through the front window, she saw the sea and sky filling everything beyond, like a promise of what could be.

On that first visit, the cottage had felt small but perfectly formed, with a funny low kitchen dog-legged on to the side of the house and a whole wall of windows above the sink. She'd walked straight over to them and leant there drinking in the view which barely seemed real: a short garden and then an immense sparkling sea, the colour of perfect aquamarine, with sharp, white cliffs cutting down as far as she could see on both sides. The sky above had been an azure blue, with traces of thin cloud that looked like cigarette smoke and a bright yellow sun shining relentlessly in the corner, like a child's painting. Seagulls whirled their white bodies, making their desperate cawing, diving and spinning. 'My God,' she'd said, her eyes feeling overrun with beauty, and Andy had said that was the usual reaction.

Upstairs, two sweet bedrooms, one with an old iron double, complete with what she was sure was a handmade woollen counterpane of different-coloured squares, but had turned out to make her skin itch so badly she'd had to fold it into a cupboard. From that room's window she'd been able to look down in to the garden, where she'd noticed there was no fence, just a jagged drop to the beach below which, from up there, she'd seen was much higher than she'd realised.

Andy had warned her that the cliffs were eroding so you had to be careful of going too close, but she'd batted that away and said something pretentious about liking the idea of not having any barriers, wanting to be right on the edge of everything. She remembered genuinely believing what she said, sure that peace and quiet was all she needed to regain her creative flair.

Lennie didn't know if she could stomach another set of reviews which politely sneered at the commercial aspect of her work, as if producing something which people liked was wrong. As if the majority must be mistaken, as if real art can only be appreciated by a few. And when she thought of it like that she felt guilty, because the shapes she was known for had bought her time and freedom and joy and now she wanted to turn her back on them and do something different.

A critic at her last show had called them 'strangely domestic shapes, as if the painter is mourning the loss of this aspect of her life and reminding us of the sacrifices that have to be made for art'. She'd guffawed at the time, wondering what on earth he meant, re-looking at the harsh, angular shapes she painted and wondering what he'd seen: a toaster or an ironing board or a baby's cot perhaps? But then she'd felt angry, angry enough to tweet a link to the piece and ask: Can you imagine a male painter's work being described this way? To which someone had helpfully tweeted her back a review she hadn't seen which had described her as 'the 40-year-old, unmarried artist...' When she complained, a few men had told her ageing was nothing to worry about, she still looked great, but she'd said her age was not the part of the description she minded. Some women had tweeted their own stories, which at first had made her laugh, then cry. And all of which had made the idea of isolation seem ever more appealing.

The problem with those sorts of comments, though, was that they didn't disappear just because you couldn't hear them anymore, but tended to stick to the skin, to leach into the blood and contaminate thought. Still now, six months in to this absurd self-imposed exile, she wondered at her motives. What if what she was doing wasn't enough? Which was a stupid thought because of course it wasn't enough, nothing would ever be enough. Of course she was missing out, but then again, of course there was no one way of attending life as it existed now.

Unusually, there was a knock at the door. Lennie moved too fast in her excitement at someone wanting anything of her and stubbed her toe, so she was grimacing in pain when she opened it.

A mousey-looking woman was standing on the other side, shrouded in a massive waterproof jacket with a beanie pulled low to her eyes. 'Oh hi,' she said. 'I'm Holly. I'm a wildlife ranger. I work at The Hut, down at the bend in the river.'

Lennie didn't know what she was talking about, but forced a smile. 'Hello. I'm Lennie.' The wind blowing into the cottage was freezing and she wondered if she should ask the woman in for a cup of tea, but couldn't face it, so stayed standing like a guard at her entrance.

'Oh, I know who you are. I've been meaning to knock and introduce myself properly for months. I mean, it's not every day a famous artist moves in round here. Anyway,' Holly blushed as she fished a small piece of paper out of her pocket. 'I thought you might like to come to this. It'll probably seem really lame to you, but it's quite fun and, you know, there's not much of that to be had round here.' She laughed nervously. 'I'm sure that's not why you're here or anything, but anyway, I just thought I'd ask.'

Lennie took the paper and read the desolate words printed on it: Eat, Drink and Make Merry, December 22nd, at The Wildlife Hut.

'We do it every year,' Holly said. 'A small Christmas party for all of us mad enough to live out here. I thought you might like to come and meet a few of your neighbours.' It was at least encouraging that Holly had the grace to laugh as she said the word neighbours.

Lennie's initial reaction was to scrabble about in her mind for a reason as to why she couldn't attend this god-awful sounding party, but then she remembered just how bored and lonely the last few weeks had felt.

She arranged her face in to a smile. 'Sounds lovely, thanks.' Holly returned the smile and Lennie told herself not to be such a cynic. It could be fun. It might even change her perspective on this place. God, she might even meet someone interesting. Stranger things had happened.

Araminta Hall

Araminta Hall began her career as a journalist, working on women's magazines and newspapers. She has published four novels since 2011, including the Richard and Judy choice, *Everything and Nothing*, and, most recently, *Imperfect Women*. She has also taught creative writing for many years at places including New Writing South and masterclasses at the University of Brighton. She lives in Brighton with her husband and three children.

Grace

Adam Hamdy

He stood in the ruins of the bookshop and watched it come to life. The boards were first. Solid, strong, polished to a high shine. They spread over cratered earth, creating a floor that soon joined painted walls. Colourful art hung above wooden steps that descended beneath the ground. Then came hundreds of books in cases that touched the ceiling. He was here for a book, but not one on any shelf. A counter formed, a computer, a receptacle full of styluses, and finally, her.

Grace Minamore. She was young, much younger than the only picture he'd ever seen of her, but this moment was long before she'd scribed the book. He studied her, wondering whether she was thinking about it now, birthing ideas that could reshape the world.

Isaac was startled when the door swung open and passed through him. He flinched and took a step back, even though the Aperture couldn't harm him.

Grace glanced up, and for a moment Isaac reckoned she was looking at him, but her eyes were on the man walking towards her. Marcus Robinson, her beau, her betrothed. Isaac recognised him instantly.

'Hello. How can I help?' Grace asked. Her voice was distorted, as though heard through a long tube, but distance did nothing to diminish its warmth.

'I'm looking for a birthday present for my aunt,' Marcus replied.

Isaac noticed the man appraise her, and couldn't fault him for his lingering eyes. Grace was beautiful. Her short brown hair was an aesthetic choice rather than the shear cut that lice and parasites had forced on everyone who survived the Fall. Tall, slim, her dark skin glowed vibrant, and her wide eyes shone smart.

The lust in Marcus's eyes told Isaac what the man was picturing. Their relationship was doomed to failure, that much Isaac had been able to glean from fragments of history, but what had attracted her to him in the first place? Isaac had found a ragged newspaper account in a library archive which told of their separation, and it presented Marcus Robinson as a '*brash, wealthy businessman with a history of nursing vicious grudges*'.

'I want to read more, but I never have the time,' Marcus said. 'I need a clone. You got any books on cloning?'

He chuckled, and Grace smiled.

Was that it? Was that the moment they bonded? Was it as simple as a flash of teeth?

Isaac heard a noise and turned to see a rock roll down a pile of rubble – the remains of the building opposite. He glanced up. The clouds were bruised red and purple. It was later than he'd realised. Much later. He'd spent too long setting up the Aperture and locating the right moment, but it had been worth it.

He'd found her.

'What kind of books does your aunt like?' Grace asked, moving from behind the counter.

Isaac longed to talk to her. She was beautiful, but it was her mind he'd fallen for. Revealed in the pages of an ancient book. Her thoughts so clearly stated, her emotions concealed beneath science, but he liked to kid himself they could be found by those who cared to look.

What secrets were locked in that head?

Isaac took a step forward, but stopped before he made the mistake of a second. He was confusing then with now, and beneath the floorboards of the past was the rubble of the present, sharp rocks that filled a deep hole. A jagged death or a broken limb that would lead to a painful one if he couldn't get home before sundown.

Isaac stepped back, and for a moment he thought Grace looked at him, but it must have been a trick of time. She had probably caught sight of something outside the shop.

'Is she a thriller fan?' Grace asked, drawing within touching distance of Marcus.

'Close the Aperture,' Isaac said, and the four drones hovering twenty feet above him deactivated their lenses, and Grace, Marcus and the beautiful bookshop vanished. The exorcised ghosts of a lost world.

'Return home,' Isaac said, and the drones immediately flew east, their ion drives propelling them silently through the sky.

Out of habit, Isaac tugged his zip to check his body suit was still tight to his neck. The Wyrd struggled to see black, and while the suit would not protect him from their other acute senses, it might buy a lifesaving moment or two. He pulled on his matching black facemask, and set off along the narrow gorge that lay between two high mounds of broken brick and stone – all that was left of once grand buildings. He followed a run of narrow paths which cut between monuments of what once had been. Crumbling buildings, some lost to neglect and old age, others scarred by the violence that followed the Fall. He emerged onto a broad waylane called Strand. Its surface had cracked and crumbled to dirt, and high trees stood between two flanks of buildings that were decayed like rows of black-rot teeth.

A grand terminal of grey stone stood at the beginning of the waylane. While testing the Aperture, Isaac had trekked the ruined city, marvelling at life as it had been. This place was known as Charing Cross, and it had been a hub, drawing thousands to it every day. Isaac had watched the Old Ones, moving swiftly and sternly, focused, insular, alone amid such crowds. He wanted to clasp each close and tell them to cherish one another, but he was less than a spirit to them, and they little more than spectres to him.

The sun was low, and the first crack of nightly thunder sounded as Isaac turned away from the terminal. He moved swiftly and was almost running by the time he reached the tall building at the other end of Strand. Situated on an island of stone at the centre of an encircling waylane, the building, which had once been a home for many – the Old Ones had called it hotel – now housed only him and his youngs.

He climbed through a broken door frame and hurried inside. In the distance, someone screamed.

Night had fallen.

* * *

'Was it always like this?' Ethan said between mouthfuls.

'When are you going to stop asking that?' Holly snapped.

'More, please,' Calvin said.

Isaac leaned across the table and spooned rice onto Cal's plate. It didn't satisfy like the earth food grown in the Territory, but the rice would keep them alive. It was infused with nutrients in growers: genetic enhancement tanks on the roof. They were a gift from the old world. Some long-forgotten stranger had installed them, but Isaac had recognised what they were when he and Rachel had found the building. He gave silent thanks to their unknown benefactor before every meal.

'We know it wasn't always like this,' Holly said.

She had inherited her mother's strength of spirit. Cal had Rachel's dry humour, and Ethan her inquiring mind. Each of his youngs was a living reminder of the woman he loved.

'Don't snap at your brother,' Isaac said. He pretended not to notice Ethan sticking his tongue out at his glowering sister.

'He's as bothersome as a tick,' Holly protested.

'He wants to see,' Isaac replied. 'That's all. He just wants to see.'

Like his father, Ethan was addicted to visions of the old world. Isaac had shown his youngs an early beta of the Aperture, and had noticed Ethan come alive when he first saw the bounty he'd only heard about in tales. Holly wasn't interested in what she called the dead world. Too painful perhaps? And Calvin, at six years old, was too young to truly understand.

Isaac stood. They were in the meal room of the housing unit that topped the building. The room was a circular dome with windows that offered a 360-degree view of the city. The glass was history, but Rachel had covered the openings with scavenged pieces of thick plastic. They hung opaque drapes if they needed to use torches or candles, but Isaac preferred to be certain they were casting no light, and liked to see the city, so they often ate illuminated by the silver moon. The Wyrd were drawn to light and sound, so those who wanted to survive never exhibited either.

'Run silent. Run dark,' his father used to say.

'Can I see it again, Dad?' Ethan asked.

Holly's frown deepened, but she said nothing when Isaac replied, 'Follow me.'

* * *

Ethan sat on his lap. Isaac had covered all the windows so no light escaped, and the two of them watched the past. The drones were positioned in the top corners of the large space and filled it with a vision of what had been. Old Ones clustered around a central counter, where three men in matching blue clothes served drinks. Others sat in groups, laughing and talking across tables heavy with food and drink. Here and there, couples whispered, their eyes saying more than words ever could. The noise would have been deafening if Isaac hadn't reduced the level for fear the Wyrd might hear. Ethan's eyes were wide and Isaac shared his awe at a world so alive. He had never been around so many people, not even in Homestead, the biggest village in the Territory. It was awe inspiring to see such plenty, yet the Old Ones did not seem concerned it might ever run out.

'Tell me how it works again,' Ethan said, gesturing at the drones.

'My grandfather, Arlan, used to say a world without magic would be almost as dark as one without science,' Isaac replied. 'I met him once, when his hair was white and his back crooked, and that's what he told me. Trust in science. Believe in magic. He told my father the same thing every day, and my father told me. And now I'm telling you. Trust in science. Believe in magic.'

Ethan smiled and shuffled closer.

Isaac picked up the two stones he always used to show Ethan the science of the Aperture.

'You know about space and time?' he asked. Ethan nodded, just as Isaac had nodded when his father had asked him the same question. 'If this stone was Earth and this one was a planet ten million solar cycles away, what would someone see if they looked at Earth with a scope that was strong enough?'

'The great lizards,' Ethan replied.

'Ten million probably isn't long enough for the great lizards, not if the Old Ones's books are true. But you're right, the person on the other planet would see the past. So, time changes with perspective, and distance and time are related. Gravity, too, but that's a yarn for another day. Your great-grandfather, Arlan, figured out we could create the illusion of distance by folding space and that fold would enable us to look back in time. He worked on his thinking until the breath left him.'

'But you solved it.' Ethan's face was bright with pride.

'No. My father, your grandpa solved it. I just used their theories to build those machines up there.' Isaac nodded at the drones.

'To find the book?' Ethan asked.

'Yes. To find the book.'

* * *

The book.

Isaac held it reverently. Or what remained of it. The back binding was gone, along with the crucial last third. Much of the front cover had been eaten away. Only a small fragment remained, a piece of green fabric-bound card attached by tattered threads to an accordion spine. Inside, the yellowed, stained front page identified the book as *The Fundamentals of Nitrogen Microbiology* by Grace Minamore.

Further on, there was the picture of Grace, looking much older than she had in the bookshop. Her lined face seemed strained with the worries and responsibilities of age. Beneath the picture were words that had been scored in Isaac's mind.

Dr Grace Minamore studied chemistry at Oxford. She worked for a London bookseller for a number of years before returning to academia to complete her doctoral research. She currently lives in London with her cat, Taylor.

Isaac's grandfather had discovered the book in a ruined library in the Territory and became obsessed with the idea the final third could rid them of the scourge of the Wyrd. He'd devoted everything to the book and had studied it obsessively. For a time, the man had been convinced the book hid a secret message, but if there was one, Isaac had never found it.

When they'd come to London, Rachel and Isaac had spent years searching the ruined city for signs of the bookseller where Grace had worked, travelling through time and space, looking for a single moment. After Rachel's death, Isaac had continued alone. It had taken years to find Grace, but now he was on her trail, he could follow her through time, and even if he couldn't locate another copy of the book, he could witness her learning.

He became aware of someone watching him, and looked up to see Holly at the door. He put the book back in the box that kept it safe, and looked at his daughter. She should have been sleeping with her brothers in the next room.

'Dad,' she said, but she got no further.

They both froze at the deep growl that came from one of the down levels.

The last thing Isaac saw before he switched off his torch and plunged the room into darkness was the blood draining from his daughter's face.

'Dad,' Holly whispered.

Fear strained her voice, and Isaac felt it too. He fumbled in the featureless void, his mind churning possibilities. Had they tracked him from the bookshop? Had they seen the Aperture projected in the bar? Was his room properly blacked out? Isaac glanced around for tell-tale shafts of moonglow, but the darkness was unbroken.

'Holly,' he whispered when he found her. He put his hands around her trembling shoulders and tried to soothe her as he guided her out. 'Come on.'

He steered her the few steps to the neighbouring room, and they crept inside. Isaac carefully shut the door and joined what remained of his clan on the large bed. He lay in total darkness listening to his sons's regular unbroken snores, and his daughter's shallow breathing. He stroked her arm, but could do nothing to take away her fear. Every so often they heard distant clawing at rock, metal being ground, and the grunts and growls of fearsome creatures on the hunt.

The Wyrd, bane of Earth.

Holly trembled at every sound, and Isaac did his best to reassure her, but inwardly he offered prayers to the gods of the Old Ones that his precautions would hold. The enemy had only entered the building twice before, and each time Lady Fate had smiled kindly, but she was fickle and would eventually turn against them.

Trapped in total darkness, gripped by fear for his youngs, time lost all meaning and each second became a century. But eventually Holly's breathing grew as calm and regular as the boys'. Sleep had taken her, and later, much later, after he'd imagined countless monstrous ends while he listened to the beasts scouring the darkness, sleep finally took Isaac, too.

* * *

He woke to an empty bed and a stab of panic. He hurried from the room, but his bloodsurge subsided when he heard Ethan and Cal chuntering foolspeak in the dome. He climbed the spiral stairs and found his youngs at the table. The city was a pockmarked wash of grey beneath thick low cloud.

'I made first meal,' Holly said, pushing a bowl towards him.

Powdered milk, long past the date the Old Ones had printed on the canisters, water and genetically cultured rice mixed into a cold mash.

'Still alive?' Holly said with a smile.

'I guess so,' Isaac replied. He pushed the bowl into the centre of the table. 'I'd better get going.'

Holly's disapproving look reminded him of Rachel. She also used to hate it if he missed first meal.

'You youngs need it more than me,' he said, and the boys immediately began squabbling over who would get the most. 'Holly will portion it out. Be good for her.'

Isaac circled the table, kissed each of his youngs on the forehead, and went to work.

* * *

When he and Rachel had found the building, they spent weeks filling the stairwells with rocks, blocking the first two levels as well as the conveyance shafts. Before he left for the day, Isaac checked each of them, but he couldn't find evidence of any breach. Satisfied, Isaac went to third level. A metal tube ran through the centre of the building, connecting each level. The openings on the other levels had been bricked up, but this one was covered by a thick steel hatch that was secured by two metal bars. Isaac removed the bars, opened the hatch, took the rope that was coiled in the gutter and tossed it into the dark tube that stretched to the ground. He checked the rope was secured to the anchor further up the tube, climbed inside and lowered himself hand under hand until he touched the ground. The tube used to end in a doorway that opened onto a room full of large machines, but he and Rachel had bricked it up and cut a tiny hatch in the back. Isaac stooped to remove the twin bolts that secured the hatch, folded his body and wriggled through the tight opening into the corridor beyond. The hatch had been painted white to match the wall, and Isaac slid it back into place, ensuring it was flush before he hurried on.

When he reached the entrance, he found evidence of the activity he'd heard the previous night. Fresh claw marks on the walls and scarred metal chewed by jagged, unbreakable teeth. The Wyrd must have been hungry. Were they running out of food? Maybe the city had given them all it had to offer?

Not all, Isaac thought bleakly before stepping outside.

* * *

The drones followed Isaac to the bookshop. The sum of more than one hundred years of effort, started by his grandfather, using fragments of knowledge gleaned from the Old Ones, relying on scavenged gear, an effort that would have been impressive even in the world of plenty. The drones moved silently and took formation when Isaac told them to open the Aperture and resume from their previous stopping point.

He spent hours poring over many lunars of Grace Minamore's life. He watched her leave the bookshop day after day. She walked crowded waylanes to a terminal, where she would disappear down a flight of steps into something called Leicester Square, but the building had been reduced to rubble and Isaac could not follow her. He sifted through moments, looking for clues, and as he watched Grace, he grew fonder. Her every glance was gentle, her every word kind. Her eyes were alive with intelligence, but more than any of her characteristics, Isaac was drawn to what she represented: *hope*.

As he scrubbed through her life, Isaac convinced himself Grace could see him, that the bond between them was mutual, and he wasn't an unwelcome intruder. He caught the occasional lingering glance in his direction and took each as evidence of a connection, that somehow Lady Fate had brought them together to put the world right. Linked by science, bound by magic.

But the comforting illusion he'd conceived to inspire him could never be real. The Aperture was for observation only. Distance could enable one to peer back in time, but the events seen had already happened. Two present moments could never interact, separated by time one could never impact the other. The science was clear. But the imagined bond helped motivate him and kept him trawling through Grace's life, and as his sun started its fall towards the horizon, his persistence paid off. It was a dark winter's night in Grace's time, and instead of her usual journey, she walked past the terminal, along the busy waylane, through the brightly lit city to a place called Russell Square. The drones followed her and the Aperture revealed her every step.

Russell Square was a wasteland now, but in Grace's day there had been a green garden surrounded by elegant old buildings. She went into one, and Isaac followed, clambering over the rubble of his own age. The Aperture showed her in rooms on ground level. She slipped off her coat and shoes and greeted Marcus with the casual nevermind of someone falling out of love. Isaac looked around the home and saw touches of Grace everywhere. There was the kitten who prowled over to greet her – perhaps the Taylor mentioned in the account of her life – piles of books stacked on a table by a window that overlooked the garden, and a grey pullover over the back of an armchair.

He had found it. This was her home.

* * *

That night, after the youngs had been fed, Isaac went down to the laboratory he and Rachel had built in one of the rooms on eighth level. Unlike the machining workshop they'd had in the Territory, just outside Homestead, this was a biological laboratory and it had been prepared for when the book was found. Chems waited in flasks, burners stood fuelled and idle, gyros ready to blend compounds. Satisfied everything was as it should be, Isaac returned to tell the youngs their nightly tale before dreamtime, but when he reached the foot of the steps that led to the dome, he was stopped by a laugh he hadn't heard in many seasons. It was Rachel, his wife, and her sound sent his heart soaring.

Isaac heard furtive movement as he took the spiral stairs two at a time, and there was a whispered, 'He's coming.'

He found his youngs huddled on the floor, the four drones spread in the upper reaches of the dome, and the Aperture open, looking back at one of their clan night meals, when Rachel had still been with them. His heart stopped for a broken moment, as the impossible hope birthed by her laughter died. He saw fear and uncertainty on the faces of his youngs. Holly had tears in her eyes. Ethan smiled nervously. In the Aperture, Rachel was chattering and joking with them. Isaac reached out to touch her, but the present slipped through the past, and his hand touched nothing.

A lump formed in his throat, and he had to look away.

'We're sorry, Dad,' Holly said. 'Please don't be angry.'

'I'm not angry,' Isaac replied, his voice strained. Temptation had called to him, trying to lure him into using the Aperture to see Rachel again, but he had never been able to summon the courage. He feared it might break him. But it hadn't broken him, just filled him with sorrow.

It was only natural the youngs would want this. 'It's a good idea,' he said, joining them. He could sense their relief as he huddled down and pulled them into a hug. 'She's gone, but she should never be forgotten.'

'We've only done this a few times,' Ethan confessed. 'You're normally an age when you go to the lab.'

'Is it really OK?' Holly asked.

Isaac nodded. He wiped his eyes, and the clan settled to watch a happier time.

* * *

He dreamt of Rachel, of the monsters that took her, of his grandfather, his father and his youngs, and when he woke he found Holly, Ethan and Calvin curled around him. He pulled them close and prayed their world would be better than his.

After first meal, Isaac returned to the wasteland that had once been Russell Square, and the drones positioned themselves to recreate Grace Minamore's home. Grey cloud hung low, brooding with the promise of storm.

Isaac scoured Grace's past, looking for clues about her learning, but there were none. All he saw was love in decline, a woman isolated, withdrawing into her books, seeking refuge in the worlds brought to life on their pages.

Marcus never hit Grace, but he was cruel in other ways, and even though these moments were long gone, Isaac flushed with anger at the cold spirit of a man who didn't cherish what he had. Like the storm gathering above Isaac's head, now growling and crashing towards a downpour, the arguments grew more frequent and tempestuous, until one night, when Marcus came home staggering and slurring, there was a deluge. His hostility overflowed, flooding the place.

As Isaac witnessed Marcus give voice to his hate, the sky opened and heavy rain pelted down, drenching the wasteland and everything in it. Thunder crashed and lightning scorched the earth, and Isaac knew he should leave, but he couldn't. He was rooted, unable to turn away from the cruelty that made Grace wilt.

When it was done, Marcus was gone, and Grace was left crying alone in the room that overlooked the garden. It had never seen much happiness, but was now steeped in sadness. Isaac wanted to take away her sorrow and drew an arm's length away from her.

There was a loud rumble of thunder and an almost instantaneous flash of lightning. The storm was directly overhead. Another crack and one of the drones was hit. Isaac looked up in horror as the device faltered and fizzed.

'Who are you?' Grace asked suddenly, wiping her tears.

At first Isaac thought she was talking to her reflection, and kept his attention on the crackling drone. But Grace turned and addressed him directly.

'I used to think you were a guardian angel,' she said. 'But you never did anything. Not even when things got bad.'

'You can see me?' Isaac asked.

'Never like this. There's never been sound before, but now I hear your voice in my head, and there's a shadow on the edge of sight where there's only ever been a flicker,' Grace replied. 'I always knew someone was there.'

Isaac's heart raced. The Aperture worked by folding space. Was it possible it had pushed them together? Had science done this? Was it the storm? The lightning strike? Or was this the magic his grandfather had spoken of? Was this the hand of Lady Fate?

'Who are you? What do you want?' Grace asked.

Isaac trembled with the significance of the moment. He looked up at the drones, praying they would not fail, hoping that whatever had pushed them together held them there, and he told Grace Minamore – the Grace Minamore – his story. As the storm raged around him, he told her how the world had changed when the Wyrd had come. No one knew whether they'd fallen from the sky or been unleashed from the bowels of the Earth, but they'd hunted people, overcome every weapon, every defence. He told her how the Old Ones had retreated, how the world that had once been – *her world* – was quickly lost. Survivors had formed resistance cells, established the Territory in the far northlands. He recounted how his grandfather, Arlan, had been convinced the answer to the Wyrd lay in learning, that the creatures could be defeated if their weakness could be understood. He spoke of Arlan's discovery of the book, Grace's book, a speculative study of the biology of nitrogen-based lifeforms. Lifeforms like the Wyrd. But the only copy of the book had been incomplete and the crucial pages on cell death in such organisms were missing. Isaac told Grace how his grandfather had spent decades trying to decipher her work, almost losing his mind searching for secret messages in the book, trying to recreate her experiments, and how failure had almost broken him. They'd tried to capture a Wyrd specimen for study, but their attempts had always ended in death. Isaac's kin in Homestead said that one day Arlan had spoken about the Aperture as the only way to destroy the Wyrd. He said the knowing had come to him through science and magic. Folk thought he'd lost his mind, so he stopped speaking about it and started designing it. Isaac recounted how his father took on the task and devoted his time to completing the Aperture, and how he, Isaac, had finally built it. He talked of his and Rachel's journey to London, the pain of leaving their kin in the Territory, of how they came to the old city and searched for Grace. He wept when he told her how he'd delivered all three youngs into the world, how he'd worried he'd lose Rachel during their births, and how, after surviving the dangers of mothering, she had been taken one night when they'd misjudged the falling sun and the time to home. They'd been ambushed by Wyrd, and she'd sacrificed herself so he could escape.

When he was done, both Isaac and Grace had tears in their eyes.

She took a series of shuddering breaths and composed herself. 'Tell me what you need.'

* * *

Isaac had told her almost all there was to tell, but as the storm passed, the Aperture grew unstable and finally vanished. He worked feverishly on the faulty drone and tried to recover what they'd lost, but when he managed to reopen the Aperture, he could only see and hear Grace. She gave no sign she was aware of him. Their connection was gone.

Isaac staggered through the ruined city as the storm blew itself calm. He replayed what had happened, half wondering if it had been a dream. Had he told her enough? As he moved away from the wasteland, his legs found strength, and his pace quickened. By the time he reached home, he was sprinting.

He scrabbled through the hatch, hauled himself up the tube, and hurried to the laboratory on eighth level, where, panting, he took a heavy hammer to the old black metal box attached to the wall in an alcove in the dark recesses of the room. He'd seen it many times before, its rust-speckled door always hanging open. Grace had called it a safe. Isaac ran his fingers over a panel of digits on the safe door, pushed it to, and stepped back to position himself for the first blow.

Isaac hammered at the wall around the safe, smashing off big chunks. The noise attracted the youngs, who entered fearfully.

'We were scared,' Holly said.

'What are you doing?' Ethan asked.

Isaac didn't answer. Not yet. False hope would be too cruel.

He kept hammering until the safe had been exposed and he was able to pull it away from the wall. It was heavy and he grunted as he put it on the floor. When he stood up, Isaac saw a silver box that had been hidden behind the safe. He pulled it out and opened the four latches that secured the lid, breaking an airtight seal. There was a gentle kiss of air as the pressure equalised within the box, and when he lifted the lid, everything stopped. He could hardly draw breath.

It was a moment he would never forget. He saw the green cover of the book within, exactly where Grace Minamore said she'd leave it.

Isaac couldn't speak, so he simply held the book up to show the youngs what he'd found. Three mouths hung open and awe filled their eyes.

Hope.

He looked down and saw something else in the box. A yellowed card. On the front was a faded image of the shop in which he'd first seen her. He could just make out the word Goldsboro painted against black, capping brightly lit windows full of books. On the back was a simple message.

Chapter one. Third, seventh, and ninth letters of each line.

Isaac put the book on the nearest counter and grabbed stylus and paper. The youngs gathered round as he turned to the first chapter and scribed the third, seventh and ninth letters of each line. When he was finished, he put scores between each word and took a step back. He trembled and his eyes filled as he realised his grandfather had been right. There had been a hidden message, and the old man had found it.

Arlan, you will build an aperture that distorts time and allows your grandson, Isaac, to find me. You are right about this book. Keep going. The way is hard, but it can be travelled. Trust in science. Believe in magic.

Adam Hamdy

Adam Hamdy is a British screenwriter and author who works on both sides of the Atlantic. Adam's next novel, *Red Wolves*, will be published by Pan Macmillan in 2021. Adam has degrees in law and philosophy from Oxford University and the University of London.

When he's not writing, he spends his time rock-climbing and skiing. Adam co-founded Capital Crime, and sits on the advisory board of Ligandal, a genetic medicine company. He lives in Shropshire with his wife and three children.

Unbirthday

Anna James

The theme for Matilda Pages' twelfth birthday party was *Alice Through the Looking Glass*, and it was taking place at 3 p.m. at Pages & Co, the bookshop Tilly lived in with her mother and grandparents. Grandad had spent all morning trying to make the floor into a chessboard but the big squares of black and white paper he was Blu Tack-ing to the floor kept curling up at the edges, and he was on paper cut number four. Alice, the bookshop cat, wasn't helping matters and kept skittering across the paper, ripping and scrunching it as she ran. Not to mention the fact that no one was allowed to tread on the white squares in case they marked them before Tilly's friends arrived.

'On paper, this seemed like such a clever idea,' he said to himself as he shooed the cat away once more.

'Things usually are,' Grandma said.

'I think we all know that's not true,' Tilly said, tiptoeing through the paper chessboard and picking Alice up.

Tilly and her family were bookwanderers, which meant that reading often came with a few more complications than usual. They could travel into the pages of stories and, every once in a while, a character even popped up in the bookshop itself. Tilly had pushed for a birthday party inside a book – thinking maybe a picnic on the river in *The Wind in the Willows* might be fun – but her grandparents felt it was best to go a more traditional route considering that their fictional excursions didn't have a history of going particularly smoothly.

A family birthday party counted as a special dispensation to close the five-floored north London bookshop – even on a Sunday. As well as the not-especially-effective paper chessboard, there were fairy lights strung around the ground floor, mirrors leaning against the walls, and plants gathered in corners to try and conjure up the feeling of the strange backwards looking-glass world. Grandma and Tilly's mum Bea had also gathered all the clocks and watches they could find, put them all to different times and placed them around the shop – much to Grandad's horror. He had been slightly appeased by being put in charge of the music and had created a playlist including 'Rock Around the Clock', 'Time After Time' and 'I've Had the Time of My Life'. He was very proud of it, even though Tilly hadn't heard of most of the songs. But the highlight of the party was the tea table, put together by Jack, who ran the bookshop café. There were ham sandwiches made out of neat squares of brown and white bread, miniature Yorkshire puddings with slices of roast lamb curled inside them, bite-size bread-and-butter puddings and even cookies iced to look like clocks.

A few moments later, the bell above the door rang and in came Tilly's best friend and fellow bookwanderer Oskar, with his mum Mary.

'Happy birthday Tilly!' he yelled jubilantly. 'You are as old but not as wise as me now!'

'Happy birthday,' Mary said, giving Tilly a hug. She was holding a cardboard box very delicately. 'Your birthday present is in here, but they're going via Jack first,' she winked. Mary owned Crumbs, the bakery across the street from Pages & Co, and Mary and Jack collaborating on something for her birthday was Tilly's idea of heaven.

'I got you something too,' Oskar said, shoving a messily wrapped book-shaped gift at Tilly.

'Can I open it now?' she asked, and Oskar nodded eagerly. Tilly pulled off the brown paper to see a beautiful old edition of *Through the Looking Glass* itself.

'Wow,' she breathed. 'How did you find this?'

'Your grandad helped me find it,' Oskar admitted. 'But it was my idea!' It looked very old and its pages were crinkly and yellowing. It had a pale-blue cloth cover with an illustration of Alice looking up at Humpty Dumpty.

'It's perfect,' Tilly said happily, giving Oskar a huge hug. 'I love it – thank you. I'm going to go and put it upstairs to keep it safe before everyone else arrives.'

She headed up the stairs, intending to put the book on Grandad's desk, which was tucked at the back of the fifth floor, but when she reached the children's section on the third floor she saw one of the strangest people she'd ever laid eyes on. Sat on one of the beanbags was a woman who looked distinctly like … well, a life-size chess piece. She was dressed entirely in shades of red, had a distinctly ruddy colour to her skin, and most notably she was wearing a huge, carved wooden crown.

'Where do you come from?' the woman said imperiously. 'And where are you going? Look up, speak nicely, and don't twiddle your fingers all the time.'

'I live here,' Tilly said tentatively. 'And so I'm not going anywhere.'

'You should always say "your Majesty" when you address me,' the woman replied. 'It is very rude not to call a queen your Majesty. And a curtsey is also appropriate. What are you doing! Pay attention!'

Even though she knew it seemed rude, what Tilly was doing was flicking through the copy of *Through the Looking Glass* Oskar had bought her. For, sure enough, in the chapter where the Red Queen should have been, there was simply blank space. Even more concerningly, as she scanned through the rest of the book, there were an alarming number of other blank pages.

'Are there others with you?' Tilly asked nervously.

'How should I know,' the Red Queen said dismissively. 'I am not accountable for all my subjects. Now help me up.' She held a hand out to Tilly.

Once the Queen was upright, the loops of her dress fell down stiffly, completely covering her feet. Up close her skin looked rather shiny – as if it too were made from polished wood. She walked over to the balcony and peered down at the bookshop.

'Aha,' she said, pleased. 'I see.' She gestured to Tilly to come and look and pointed down at the wonky grid of black and white paper with her sceptre. 'It is a chessboard,' she pronounced to Tilly. 'And so it is my realm after all, some tucked away ugly corner of it.'

'It isn't ugly,' Tilly said, offended.

'The squares are exceedingly crooked,' the Queen said. 'And the flowers are too small. I could show you a land, in comparison with which you'd call this a dirt heap. Would you like a biscuit?'

'Oh, no thank you,' Tilly said. 'I'm saving myself for tea because it's actually my...'

'Here,' the Queen interrupted her, and pulled out a worse-for-wear biscuit from the rigid folds of her dress. Tilly took a small nibble out of politeness; it was as if she was eating a mouthful of dust. She coughed and a splutter of crumbs escaped. The Red Queen looked at her disdainfully before tucking her sceptre into her waistband and running down the stairs at a really quite alarming speed. She did not pay much attention and bashed into several tables of books on the way, sending them crashing to the floor before tearing through the bookshop. Tilly was about to follow when she caught sight of two short men in striped caps headed towards the party tea table.

'I knew it,' Tilly said under her breath and hared back downstairs, Oskar's present tightly under her arm. But when she got to the table, they had vanished, and there was no trace of the Red Queen either. Tilly hoped that perhaps they were going to go back inside their book without any further intervention from her. And indeed, all she could do was hope, as just then the bell above the shop door jangled and Pages & Co was quickly full of party guests.

* * *

'Are you sure we're not too old for party games?' Tilly asked nervously as Grandad tried to get everyone's attention.

'No one is too old for games!' Grandad said. 'Especially party games. And especially not *these* party games. I've been planning them for weeks.'

'Oh dear,' Oskar said under his breath. 'You definitely should have got approval on these Tilly.'

Tilly felt a little sick as her school friends started gathering around, looking up at Grandad, who was in his element.

'Welcome to Pages & Co!' he said. 'If you've never been to our bookshop before we hope you enjoy it, please do feel free to have a little look around, and there's a twenty per cent birthday discount on anything bought today!' Grandma nudged him in the ribs. 'But of course, today is about Tilly!' he said. 'Not buying books! And I thought we could play a few little games before we move on to the excellent spread that Jack has put together and then some birthday cake! Now I had hoped we might be able to try a life-size game of chess but...' He looked disconsolately at the mess of paper on the floor, that was entirely unrecognisable now there were thirty eleven- and twelve-year olds on top of it. Tilly couldn't help but be relieved; she was not sure how much enthusiasm for chess there would have been, or that chess really counted as a party game.

'How about clumps instead?' Grandma suggested. She very smoothly started moving most of the paper to one side, leaving a few large sheets dotted around the floor.

'I don't know what that is,' one of Tilly's friends said sceptically.

'It's very easy,' Grandma explained. 'We play some music and then when it stops, I call out a number and you all have to gather in groups of that number and make sure all your feet are on a piece of paper! Anyone not in a group, or anyone that falls off the edges of the paper is out. Understand?' The children nodded, some a little unsurely.

'Maybe we should just leave the games,' Tilly started to say but Grandma had already started the music and 'The Time Warp' was blasting through the bookshop. After a few seconds, Grandma paused it and called 'Four!' and any hesitation was quickly muted by Oskar yelling 'I need three more, who's with me!' and yanking Felix, Immy and Kavitha on to a piece of newspaper with him. Before long everyone was running and dancing and yelling and Tilly felt the anxious knot in her stomach relax a little bit more.

Ten minutes later there was just Tilly, Felix and two others left in the game.

'Three!' shouted Grandma as she paused the music. The others all lunged for Tilly as the birthday girl, but something was in the way and they stumbled back.

'Did you just … push me?' Felix said in confusion.

'No, I swear!' Tilly said, equally nonplussed as she most definitely hadn't.

'Contrariwise, it were us!' two voices said in unison from behind her. 'You plus we is three already!'

Tilly span around to see the two identical rotund men in high-waisted trousers and striped caps grinning gleefully – but she was the only one they were visible to. The one on the left had 'Dum' embroidered on his collar, and the other had 'Dee'.

'You can't play the games if no one else can see you,' Tilly hissed. 'It just isn't fair!'

'I can see how you might think that,' said Tweedledum. 'But it isn't so, nohow.'

'Contrariwise,' added Tweedledee. 'If it was so, it might be: and if it were so, it would be; but as it isn't, it ain't. That's logic.' Tilly couldn't follow but she didn't have time to try and work it out. It was her birthday party and she couldn't have her friends think she was pushing them around. She was about to follow Felix and apologise, to say that she stumbled and accidentally pushed him when the Tweedles reached out and grabbed one of her wrists each.

'Careful there,' they said together. 'Or you'll trip.'

'There's nothing to ... Oh!' She stopped trying to pull away from their slightly sticky-feeling grip as rolling towards her through the feet of her friends was a large egg with short little legs and arms sticking out of it which came to a stop in front of her. The Tweedles were giggling uncontrollably.

'I say, this is not as dignified an arrival as I had hoped,' Humpty Dumpty said, for of course who else could the egg be.

Tilly tried to be polite and held a hand out for him to pull himself upright by. 'No!' he declined, still rocking gently from side to side on what must have been his back as his face was upwards. 'You shall break me! Please avert your eyes and I shall have these two escort me to an appropriate perch where we can make our formal introductions, I don't want to end up...' But his last words were drowned out by Grandma announcing the next game.

'GET READY FOR AN EGG AND SPOON RACE!' she shouted, brandishing an array of shiny silver spoons. Humpty started listing back and forth in a panic.

'No,' he whispered as he rocked. 'Not the egg and spoon race. I can't ... I can't go back... You! Child! Pick me up! The time has passed for dignity!'

Tilly tried to lift him up as gently as possible and carried him through an archway to a quieter place in the shop, trailed by Tweedledum and Tweedledee who kept poking each other in the side. She popped Humpty on to a bookshelf.

'Are you safe there?' she asked nervously.

'I am quite safe, I assure you,' he said, his pomposity returning. 'But if I were to fall – which is extremely unlikely – but if I were to, then the King has promised me...'

'To send all his horses and all his men,' Tilly finished.

'How dare you!' Humpty said crossly, his cheeks turning red. 'You've been listening at doors – and behind trees – and down chimneys – or you couldn't have known it!'

'I just read it in a book,' Tilly said. 'I didn't mean to offend you.'

'Humph,' Humpty said, crossing his legs in a jaunty fashion and looking a little appeased. 'I am an egg of note and so I suppose it is to be expected that such things are written of me. I am held in famously high regard by the King. Now. What is going on here? Why are you playing these childish games?' He shivered at the thought of the egg and spoon race.

'It's my birthday party,' Tilly explained.

'Today is your birthday?' Humpty said back to her, looking pleased.

'Well, not quite,' she said. 'It's actually not until Tuesday, but that's not a very good day for a birthday party.'

'Quite right,' Humpty said. 'But you ought to have been accurate when you first answered and told me that it was your unbirthday party. Do tell the truth when speaking of such important things. And how old are you?'

'Twelve.'

'An uncomfortable age. If you'd asked my advice, I'd have said leave off at seven.'

'It's quite a lot too late for that,' Tilly said. 'And I'm not really in control of it anyway. I can't stop myself growing!'

'You should be paying better attention then,' Humpty said, and Tilly tried not to get too frustrated by the nonsensical way that Lewis Carroll's characters always spoke. What was charming and funny in a book, never seemed quite the same when you were having to reason with them yourself.

'I should have brought an unbirthday present if I had known,' Humpty went on. 'Perhaps a cravat, or a poem, or suchlike. Perhaps I shall compose and perform something for you now.'

'You really don't need to,' Tilly said quickly. 'Although it's very kind of you to offer. I must be getting back to the party you see.'

'Quite right,' Humpty said. 'As I think the White Knight is about to lead his horse straight into that dinner table.'

Tilly whirled around to see that Humpty was right. A sleepy-looking elderly man in armour was somehow riding a white horse through the centre of the bookshop – and no one else could see him.

'How many of them *are* there?' she said to herself, running back into the main area of the shop.

'Tilly!' Oskar said, giving her a look. 'Where have you been? Is something going on? We're waiting for you to do the cake!' And despite the fact there was a very wobbly-looking knight on a horse standing right there, looking around him in utter confusion, all Tilly could do was turn and look at everyone else as they started to sing Happy Birthday to her. She could see Grandad watching her, and that he could tell something was awry but there was no way he could help.

As everyone sang, Jack and Mary emerged from the back of the shop carrying a magnificent cake between them. It was three tiers iced in purple frosting, decorated all over with miniature marzipan plums, macaroons iced with clock faces and delicate silver candles which looped around the whole cake. On the second 'Happy Birthday to You', the knight's horse gave a great harrumph and started wandering towards Tilly and the cake, the knight slipping slowly down its side. Tilly wasn't quite sure if it was worse to let a fictional knight that was invisible to everyone else crash into her birthday cake or cause a scene trying to stop it. She started moving backwards, desperately trying to get the cake out of the line of the horse, so that Jack and Mary had to follow her, looking at her in utter confusion.

'I say is that plum pudding!' the knight called, brightening up as he hoisted himself back into the saddle and spied the cake. 'I wouldn't say no to a slice of that, I tell you.'

'Us too!' the Tweedles said, appearing out of nowhere, scurrying across the floor and weaving between the guests' legs as they were all chorusing, 'Happy Birthday dear Tiiiiillly.' Out of the corner of her eye, Tilly could see Humpty Dumpty trying to climb down the bookcase, his tiny feet slipping off the wood. Disaster seemed unavoidable as the singing reached the last line of 'Happy Birthday to youuuuu' and the room took an expectant gasp in to watch Tilly – but she was frozen in panic.

'Blow the candles out Tilly!' Jack hissed, as the horse trotted right next to the cake and Mary and Jack's arms started to shake under its weight. The Tweedles ran under their arms just as Humpty started to fall, and then a whoosh and the Red Queen barrelled into the side of the White Knight who started to slip towards the cake without seeming to notice he was losing his grip.

'Time is going absolutely the wrong way here,' the Queen said, straightening her wooden crown. 'Oh, it's you again. I say, the Knight is going to fall straight into that cake if you don't...'

But then she just ... stopped. Absolutely still. As if time had been paused. And Tilly realised that everyone else was also completely motionless. The knight was halfway down the side of his horse, inches from sliding straight into the side of the cake, Humpty was frozen in mid-air, falling towards the wooden floor where he would surely crack open, and the Tweedles were stuck, hands outstretched towards the cake.

But even more worryingly, it wasn't just the fictional characters that were still – it was everyone. Her friends and family were like statues, all still staring glassy-eyed at her, mainly looking extremely confused. Jack and Mary were motionless with the cake between them, both looking a little upset at Tilly's unexpected response to their hard work.

'Oh, there they all are!' a new voice said behind her and Tilly turned to see Alice, sat on an armchair, nonchalantly eating a biscuit. 'I wondered where they'd all got to. I should have known it was you,' she grinned.

223

'How … how are you doing this?' Tilly said in shock. 'I'm pretty sure you're not supposed to be able to stop time outside of a book.'

'Oh, I borrowed a little Time,' Alice said, as if that were nothing to comment on in particular. 'He owed me a favour. And it's easy to put a little wrinkle in time if you're in a bookshop. But I only have a few seconds left before it'll all begin again, and the poor knight will end up in your lovely cake. I think it's about time to take them back through the looking glass.' She stood up daintily, picked up a pile of cookies which she slipped into the pocket of her dress and gave Tilly a mischievous smile.

'I'll see you on the other side of the looking glass some time,' Alice said. 'Have a very happy unbirthday.' And with that she glanced at the watch on her delicate wrist and nodded in satisfaction. 'Time to blow your candles out, Tilly. 3, 2, 1…'

At the last count there was a strange vibration in the air, the sound of a clock chiming the hour, and Tilly scrunched her eyes up tight and blew. And when she opened them there was no knight or queen or Humpty or Tweedles, only all her friends and family clapping and cheering for her.

It was hours later, once everyone had gone home, and the Pages family were tidying up the bookshop, that Tilly thought to double check the copy of *Through the Looking Glass* that Oskar had bought her. She sat in her favourite spot by the bookcase, with a mug of hot chocolate, and breathed a sigh of relief when she saw that all the characters were back in their rightful places. But Tilly couldn't help but notice that, in the illustration on the penultimate page, on the floor next to Alice was a cookie with a clock iced on it.

Anna James

Anna James is a writer and arts journalist. She is the author of the bestselling Pages & Co series, which has sold into seventeen countries. The first three books in the series – *Tilly and the Bookwanderers, Tilly and the Lost Fairy Tales*, and *Tilly and the Map of Stories* – are out now, published by HarperCollins Children's Books in the UK and Penguin Young Readers in the US, with three more books to come. Formerly Book News Editor at *The Bookseller* and Literary Editor of *ELLE UK*, Anna is currently the host and co-curator of Lush Book Club, as well as writing about books and theatre as a freelance journalist for outlets including *The Stage*, the *LA Times* and *Buzzfeed*.

One Night in Capri

Amanda Jennings

The box which contains the photographs is collapsing with age, the worn cardboard giving way to the weight of memories within it. She sits in the armchair in their bedroom. The room is still. Quiet. She takes a moment to compose herself before reaching into the box. It's a long time since she's looked at these photographs. Life became busy. Her time was given over to caring and loving, cooking, cleaning and administering. Hours spent chattering about this and that and nothing to fill the brutal silence with comforting yet dishonest normality. Any spare time she spent walking. To clear her head. To expel the regret and stagnant air from her lungs. There was no time left for nostalgia. But now the cliché is upon her. She has, as people say, all the time in the world. People are wrong, of course. There is no such thing as *all the time in the world*. Time is limited, more precious than any other substance on earth, and this is something she only truly understands now the sands have run out.

She smiles as she looks through the photos. Happy memories fold around her like a blanket. Snapshots of their children. Their grandchildren. Of her and him together. Young, fresh-faced, so much in love. She inhales deeply to corral her emotion as she lifts her head and looks out of the window. The setting sun decorates the trees with scattered flecks of light. The wind whispers through the leaves which flutter excitedly as if hearing salacious titbits. She returns her attention to the box and lifts out another handful of photographs. Her stomach pitches. The photograph she is looking at steals her breath. Her and him in their early twenties. The picture is aged as they have. The colours not so vibrant. There is a crease in the upper right-hand corner. In the photograph they are kissing. Her hand rests lightly on his chest. His arm encircles her shoulders as if he is worried somebody might pounce on them from behind and drag her away.

She remembers this moment as if it were yesterday.

They were on their honeymoon in Italy. A tour of Naples, Pompeii, the Amalfi Coast, the island of Capri. A few days in each. The photograph in her hand was taken on Capri. They had eaten dinner at a trattoria nestled between craft shops on a narrow side street. It was one of those small and cosy places with the dishes of the day proudly scrawled on a pavement blackboard. A man with a white apron and deeply bronzed skin folded into wrinkles by age and laughter beamed as he showed them to their table, then casually threw menus at them while calling out theatrically to unseen people in the kitchen at the back of the restaurant. They had eaten well. Breadsticks as thin as string, with olives, some fat and green, others bitter, shrivelled and black, dripping with bottle-green oil and speckled with herbs. Pasta followed. Spaghetti with a ragu so good they momentarily stopped talking. They were ravenous. The day had been spent closeted away in their hotel room making love and napping between. Their room was puritan in feel with lime-washed walls and simple wooden furniture. Muslin curtains billowed like tethered ghosts in the gentle breeze, which carried a hint of the nearby orange groves mixed with the scent wafting up from the artisan perfume shops in the street below. Lunch was bread pocketed from breakfast and huge red apples they'd bought at the market the day before. He had a bottle of beer. She took a sip and remarked on how tepid it was.

He lay back on the pillow and smiled as he reached out and stroked her naked shoulder with the backs of his fingertips. 'Best beer I've ever had.' Then she leant forward and kissed him.

By the time they sat down at the table in the trattoria their stomachs were growling in stereo.

He pushed away his plate when he'd finished. 'I love that you're my wife.'

'I love that I'm your wife as well.'

They drank wine that night. Perhaps too much. The candlelight flickered in his eyes as he gazed at her, drunk and content. They walked back along the cobbled streets, fingers linked, passing shops which displayed brightly-coloured clothes, terracotta jars of solid perfume, local honey, woven fabrics and leather handbags. They strolled in that way lovers do, languorously, unhurried, no thoughts for anything outside their world of two. Nothing more on their minds than the anticipation of falling back into rumpled sheets, entwining their bodies and kissing each other's heat-dampened skin. They were convinced it would always be this way. They would always feel this passion. They weren't like other people. Those melancholy ones reading newspapers at breakfast, together yet separate, dull with disinterest. The couples who sat in silence by the pool. Jaded and bored with nothing left to say. Nothing more to share than cursory nods, absent-minded agreement with words they hadn't heard.

But not her and him.

That will never be us, they promised between kisses.

Back then they naively believed it was only desire which counted. They had no idea their love would change. That it would take root and deepen, wax and wane, that there would be tough times, glorious times, and times in between. As they heaped responsibility on to their maturing shoulders their love would shapeshift. But at this point in their journey, at the beginning, wandering the streets of Capri, newly married, heads fuzzy with affordable wine and rustic food, they were utterly convinced there had never been a love like theirs.

'*Signore e signora! Bello coppia!* Beautiful couple. A photograph?'

The man was middle-aged. He wore a denim shirt and stone-washed, denim trousers. He held a camera in his hand. Sunglasses perched on his head. His skin was the brown of autumn conkers and a packet of Camel cigarettes poked out of the pocket of his shirt.

They smiled and shook their heads.

'But your wife, gentleman? You need a photo! She is beautiful!'

'She is.'

She had laughed and stepped to one side, lifting her husband's hand and twirling a circle beneath his arm; a dance to thank the man for his compliment.

'Hey,' the Italian said then, gesticulating with his hand. 'Come on! You don't want the memory? Of this beautiful night?'

'We have the memory in our heads!' she called happily, turning back to wave at him as they carried on walking.

'But, lady! The head is not as safe as the camera!'

The Italian ran a few steps to catch up with them. His face broke into a smile. Yellowed teeth on display. Eyes glinting, not unkindly.

She felt her husband tense as a touch of irritation crept in. Was he annoyed at this man's imposition on their romantic walk home? Or perhaps a little jealous? She squeezed his hand to reassure him.

'Just one photo,' the photographer implored. 'No need to buy. You come to the shop and see it and...' He threw his free hand up and shrugged dramatically. 'You don't like? You don't buy.'

'If we let you take our photograph will you leave us alone?'

She batted her husband gently. There was an abruptness to his tone that wasn't needed. He glanced at her and softened, then smiled at the man by way of apology.

The Italian nodded his head in deference. 'Of course, gentleman.'

They turned and faced him as he raised his camera. She recalled how self-conscious she felt as people passed them. She wanted to cry out, 'We didn't ask to be photographed! He was persuasive. So persuasive!'

'How about a kiss?' the man asked, his camera still poised.

The two of them laughed, about to thank him and walk away. But then they looked at each other and kissed. Her hand rested flat on his chest. The tips of her fingers slid a little way inside his shirt. His skin was soft and damp with evening heat. She could feel his heart thumping against his ribcage. One of his hands went to her cheek and made her own heart tremor, the other wrapped around her. Time stopped. The bustle of the street faded. It became only the two of them there.

When they pulled apart, the Italian smiled. 'Beautiful.' He handed them a card. 'I know,' he said, tapping the side of his forehead, 'that you will very much love this photograph.' Then he bowed his head to signal he was going. 'And now, I wish you a good evening.'

They turned away and moments later heard the photographer's voice. '*Signore e signora! Bello coppia!* Beautiful couple. Let me take your photo?'

They laughed.

A day or two later they were traipsing the backstreets on their final evening. They were becoming hot and bothered, searching for a restaurant recommended by the owner of their hotel who said they couldn't leave without sampling the best seafood on Capri, but it was proving impossible to locate.

'Hang on,' he said then, pulling her to a standstill. 'Isn't this that guy's shop?'

'What guy?'

'You know. The photographer who wouldn't take no for an answer. From the other night. He said you were beautiful and you danced for him.'

'Danced for him?' She furrowed her brow. 'I did nothing of the sort.'

'Shall we go in?' he said, ignoring her protestation. 'Take a look at the photographs?'

She shrugged, indifferent; she liked photos which were spontaneous, candid shots taken unawares. The ones from that night would be too forced. She remembered the feeling of discomfort as he'd asked them to pose and smile, then click-click-clicked his camera shutter.

'Come on,' he said. 'We might as well.'

The man looked up as they entered his shop. It was sweltering and stuffy and there was a noticeable smell of stale sweat. Her husband reached into his wallet for the card the Italian had pressed into his hand, which had an indecipherable number scribbled on the back in black biro.

'Ah,' the photographer said, enthusiastic and welcoming, as if greeting old friends. 'The beautiful young lovers. I was hoping to see you again!'

She and her husband exchanged knowing smiles at the Italian's well-worn marketplace patter as the man retrieved a contact sheet from a drawer packed tight with a thousand more. He laid the sheet on the countertop then rested a magnifying glass beside it.

The photos were, as she suspected, awkward and uncomfortable. Too stiff. Too wooden. But then she noticed the one with them kissing. There was something different about it. Their guard was down. She recalled how everything had drifted away from them. How his chest had felt beneath her hand. The smell of him, red wine, a hint of suncream, the promise of what was to come once they were back in the privacy of their room.

'How much for this one?' she asked. Her husband bent closer and looked at the one she was pointing at.

'You like this?' he whispered, staring at her. 'It's a bit … I don't know. Much?'

The man told them his prices.

'That's expensive,' her husband said. 'We've taken pictures ourselves. We have plenty.'

'You should take it. A beautiful memory,' the photographer said. 'You will not regret it. You are in love and this you can see in the photograph.'

Her husband laughed. 'You have all the lines!'

The photographer nodded sagely. 'Perhaps. But what I'm saying now? This is the truth.'

She looked again at the picture. It was a lot of money for a photograph and her husband was right, they had taken lots themselves.

'Believe me,' the photographer said. 'You will look at this photograph in many years, and you will see how young and in love you were. It will warm your heart.'

There had been a reflective look in that man's eyes which, at the time, she didn't pay attention to. She lowers the photograph and thinks about that Italian photographer. He would be long-dead by now. Forty-two years have passed. Almost to the day. She lifts the photo again. Of course, the man was right. In that frozen moment is everything they felt. The beginning of their love story. And now they have reached the end. She looks at the man, her husband, who lies unmoving in the bed they have shared since the start. It was the first thing they bought as a couple. Excited as they trawled the sales. Bouncing on beds in a variety of shops. Lying back, hands behind heads, bodies touching, nodding to each other, 'This is the one.' This bed in which they conceived their children. The place where their family was created. This bed in which she'd breastfed those babies. A place they had piled into every Christmas morning, year on year, their bedroom filled with squeals as stockings were unpacked and presents torn open. This bed where they had shared comfortable middle-aged sex, read books side by side, argued, made up, shared Sunday morning lie-ins with cups of tea and talked. And then the place she'd nursed him. Fed him sips of water, stroked his brow, held his hand in silence. A cradle to hold him as he drew his final breaths, the sheets turned from swaddling to shroud. Back then, in Capri, mortality wasn't real. It was no more than a vague, shapeless concept which had no meaning, like a storm on the horizon, too distant to concern them.

She sighs heavily. She should call the doctor to certify the death. She should call their children. They knew it would be soon and they'll be expecting her call. She pictures them waiting, red-eyed from crying, exhausted from travelling up and down the motorway to spend time with their father in his final weeks. It pains her to think of them breaking the news to their own families. Those beautiful children, who show flashes of their grandfather in their eyes and mannerisms, overcome with sadness. She will have to call the funeral director, the crematorium, the caterer for the wake. Then their friends. His sister. His colleagues. She feels weary thinking about it. Weary and scared. How will she navigate life without him?

For now, she thinks, I'll take the phone off the hook. It will be just you and me, my darling. Here in our bedroom, together, protected from the loneliness echoing around the rest of their home, their empty kitchen, their empty living room, their empty garden.

A dog barks in the street below. Time passes. A crack of moonlight slips in through the gap in the curtains and touches his profile with milky blue light.

Those lips, she thinks. Those lips.

She glances at the photograph one last time, before placing it carefully on the bedside table. She climbs beneath the covers and lies beside him, resting her head on the pillow. She is surprised to find his body still warm. Of course, she is glad he is free from pain. It's reassuring to feel him lying quiet and still, no longer wracked with discomfort and fear. She strokes his forehead. His paper-thin skin. His sparse white hair. She traces her fingers over his gaunt cheeks, his jawline, his lips, dry and cracked in the wake of illness.

'I love you,' she whispers. 'I loved you that night and I love you now.'

She will call the doctor in time. But not yet. In the morning. Before that they will spend one more night together. She rests her hand on his now-stilled chest and allows the tips of her fingers to graze his familiar skin. Then she leans in and kisses him, just as she did that night on the cobbled streets of Capri.

Dedicated to Sian and her husband Tim, who sadly passed away last year.

Amanda Jennings

Amanda Jennings writes psychological suspense with families and secrets at their heart. She is fascinated by the far-reaching effects of trauma on relationships and the consequences of human behaviour. With a deep love of Cornwall, she now sets her books in this part of the world. The most recent, *The Storm*, explores coercive control and lost love, and takes place in and around the fishing community of Newlyn in the late 1990s and present day. She and her husband have three daughters and live in Oxfordshire and, if she isn't writing or looking after their menagerie of animals, she is most likely dreaming of being beside the sea or up a mountain.

The Daughter

Ragnar Jónasson

'Do you have children?' asked the man sitting opposite Hulda Hermannsdóttir in the small seating area of the hospital ward. He was thirty, or perhaps a bit older, around the same age as Hulda. Quite handsome, in a different way from her husband Jón, though.

She hesitated before answering the question. Usually she wanted to maintain a certain distance between her personal life and the people she met in her line of work in the police. This time around, however, she felt it was right to make an exception.

'I have one daughter.'

'How old?'

'Around the same age as yours,' she replied, adding, 'I am very sorry. This must be difficult.'

He didn't reply, just looked away and then asked her another question. 'Deciding to have a child, that was easy, wasn't it?' The tone of his voice indicated that he was, in a way, far away from the cold and disturbing hospital, with its menacing green wallpaper and smell of disinfectant in the air.

That was a question Hulda had definitely not expected, and indeed a question she had avoided asking herself. It had been her husband's idea, initially, that they would try to have a baby. She had never brought it up, although she knew it was expected of them sooner or later. She had never, as a daughter, really felt the allegedly strong maternal connection, so the idea of having a child of her own had been somewhat alien to her.

Again, she considered not replying, not honestly at least.

'I don't know,' she said instead. 'I don't know if it was an easy decision. It depends, I guess, on the circumstances.'

'I was very excited,' he said, his eyes distant. 'So was my wife. It was such an amazing time, waiting for the child.'

For Hulda, the pregnancy had actually been easy, and from the first moment she had felt an incredible emotional connection to her future child, knowing right away that she would be better at parenting than her mother had been. She had felt unusually optimistic, and the little girl – as it turned out – had indeed been a ray of light. Parenthood suited Hulda, but some days she wondered if the same could be said of Jón. He did all the right things, but there was something about him... Something about the way he interacted with their daughter. But she was certain it would all fall into place soon enough.

'It just became so difficult, you know,' the man said. It took her a while to register the words, she had been so lost in her own thoughts. That was unusual. She was always very focused at work, but somehow the thought of Jón and the little girl, Dimma, had whisked her away to a different place, for a brief moment.

'How so?' she asked.

'Different from what I expected. And then, of course, my wife left...'

'Yes.' Hulda hesitated, trying to find the right words. 'Have you met her since?'

'No, she's living somewhere in Europe. I don't know. She doesn't keep in touch. I think it just got a bit too much for the both of us, you see.'

Hulda didn't reply, she wanted to stay silent for a little while. Hulda wondered when he would ask about his own daughter.

The seconds passed, turning into probably a full minute. He sat still and said nothing.

'She'll make it, your daughter,' Hulda finally said. Usually she didn't want to be the one to break the silence but these were not normal circumstances.

'That's good to know,' he said, calmly, without any changes in his neutral facial expression.

She instinctively thought about Dimma. Jón was looking after her at home; he had very flexible hours. Investing in real estate, that was his job description, and they never had any financial concerns in spite of her meagre police salary. Hulda wanted to escape this room and be with Dimma and Jón, but the conversation wasn't over yet.

'It was a close call; she was really sick. I am sure you haven't slept a wink,' Hulda said.

'It's been devastating,' he replied, without emotion. 'A little girl falling so ill; I'm just glad her mother isn't here; it would have been very difficult for her.'

Hulda felt as if he was saying exactly what he should have been saying. And yet nothing made sense. A moment ago he had said that the girl's mother had simply left. Hulda had actually managed to track her down, in Denmark, through the local police there. The mother was actively using drugs and hadn't really registered what was happening to her daughter back home in Iceland.

'My daughter hasn't been feeling well for quite a long time,' he said. 'I really don't understand it. She isn't too strong, the little one.'

'A matter of months or years, her illness?'

He hesitated. 'Months, I think.'

'Have you taken her to hospital before?'

'No, I've called a doctor and described the symptoms. It's been sort of on and off, the tiredness, well, until now…'

'They expect her to make a full recovery, thankfully,' Hulda said. 'The treatment seems to be working.'

'Can I see her?' There was still darkness in his eyes, an eerie emptiness.

She waited in silence for a moment, then replied, 'The cat didn't fare as well.'

'Sorry?'

'Your cat. It died.'

The man seemed surprised, the first honest reaction during the whole conversation.

'My cat is dead?'

Hulda nodded.

The look of surprise was still there, no sign of a shock, however.

'What has that to do with anything?' he asked.

'That's the reason I am here. Normally you would be speaking to a doctor, not a detective.'

'So they have a detective investigating the death of a cat?' There was a hint of arrogance in the voice.

She didn't reply.

'You think I killed the cat?' he asked, looking rather more worried.

'I think you did.'

'Why the hell should I kill the cat? I didn't even like the bloody animal...'

'The cat drank the milk, you know. From the bowl of cereal you gave your daughter.'

Now surprise turned into shock.

'What... How...?'

'I don't think you planned to kill your daughter, just to keep her sick. A bit of poison each day, was it? Or each week? And then a bit too much this time around...? And she got really ill...'

'Why would I...?' He didn't finish the sentence, there was a palpable sense of guilt in his demeanour now.

'I honestly don't know. To get attention? It has been known to happen before, parents causing their children harm this way. I have never come across this before in my career, and hopefully never will again. Your daughter will obviously be put into care, and we need to take you into custody.'

He stood up, his expression now blank.

'And I hope you never see her again,' Hulda added, her thoughts

238

swiftly moving to her own little Dimma. For a moment she tried to imagine, subconsciously and against her will, a scenario in which Jón would cause their daughter any such harm. Of course it was unthinkable.

But at the same time she felt an overwhelming sense of anger at the mere thought of this... A glimpse into a darker side she didn't know she had.

Ragnar Jónasson

Ragnar Jónasson is the Icelandic award-winning author of the international bestselling Dark Iceland series and the Hulda Trilogy, called 'a landmark in modern crime fiction' by *The Times*. Ragnar's books are published in forty countries, in twenty-seven languages. The books have made bestseller lists in France and Germany, been no. 1 Amazon bestsellers in the UK and Australia, and sold 1.5 million copies. *The Times* selected *The Darkness* as one of the 100 Best Crime Novels and Thrillers since 1945, and *Snowblind* was selected as one of the Top 100 Crime Fiction of all time by Blackwell's. Stampede Ventures in the USA are developing a TV series based on the Hulda Trilogy. Ragnar lives in Reykjavík. His first standalone novel, *The Girl Who Died*, will be published by Penguin in 2021.

Wings Outstretched

Rachel Joyce

Once, with Alice, I went to hear a choir. We talked about poetry all the way. Not saying, 'Do you know Wordsworth?', not that kind of poetry, but talking about the beautiful things we could see. The shape of the clouds, like bones that day, and the green smell of freshly-cut grass, and for once I didn't feel like a woman who flunked her O-levels and was always messing up. I felt like I was free. I didn't need anything else.

To be honest, I still don't know why Alice invited me. It wasn't as if we were friends. Maybe she just felt sorry for me; I always kept myself to myself in the playground. She just said to me one day, 'I don't suppose you fancy going to see a choir?' And I would have said no but there was something so kind about her that I said, 'Go on, then,' and that was how we were driving in her car that day, with the windows down and me talking about the world like I was a poet or something.

The church was about ten miles out of town and it was my job to hold the map. It felt good driving down those winding, empty lanes with Alice. All the houses had gone and the industrial estates and there were fields and trees and hoppity rabbits flashing their little white bums. Once we spotted a bird of prey circling the sky, as if it were caught high on a whirlpool and we were deep below on the seabed. I said to Alice, 'I wished I lived out here. I'd be happy.'

'Aren't you happy, Bev?' she said. 'You have your husband and the boys.' But I got busy with the map after that. We turned right like it said, and that was where we parked.

The church was one of those big, modern places that makes me think God needs to get a sense of humour, or at least a wife. We went in the main door and the choir was already at the front but there was hardly anyone watching, just a few old people looking for a night out. Alice went ahead of me, with her shoes clacking on the cold floor, and took a seat. She bowed her head, so I did the same.

I've been to a few churches in my time, but I'd never been to an actual concert. Suddenly this woman came out from the vestry, about my age, wearing a big fluffy dress that gave her the look of an Easter egg. The minute they spotted her the choir drew up tall. I pursed my face, waiting. Silence. Not a note. Blimey, I thought, this is going to be embarrassing.

And then, out of that nothing, came a sound so beautiful and full of crying and joy that it sent the skin on my knees cold and hot. It soared into the ether as one note, high as a spire pricking the underbelly of the sky. Slowly and steadily came other notes, and they climbed and fell. I had no idea human beings could be so beautiful.

I don't know how long they sang that day. It could have been an hour. It could have been two or three. We listened in silence, and when the choir had stopped and filed past us out of the church, Alice and I went on sitting. We felt each other there, but it was with a knowing that was under the skin, as if listening to that music had made us transparent. Somewhere down the street an alarm was going off, maybe it was a house or a car, but it seemed a long way away, like something that didn't matter.

'We should go, Bev,' said Alice.

'We should, Alice,' I said.

I was going to suggest we should stop for a lemonade on the way home but somehow I didn't and we drove back in silence.

That day there was poetry in the air. I don't know how else to

241

describe it because what God gave me in the breast department He must have taken from my brain. It was as if we'd travelled somewhere new, just the two of us, and we could be whatever we liked. In the end I tapped on Alice's window just as she was about to drive away.

'Wings outstretched,' I said. 'I'm a-flying.' And I held out my arms like they were wings.

'I admire you, Bev,' she said.

'Me?' I said.

'Yes,' she said. 'You're freefalling.'

All this was a few years ago, before Alistair and I finally parted ways and I moved down here with the boys. At the new school, the mothers have names like Cassie and Lucille and Rochelle, pretty names, and their husbands are doctors and lawyers and something-to-do-with-the-city. They invite me for coffee and give their phone numbers but I don't go in case they expect me to return the favour. Alistair would have hated them. They need jobs, those women, he'd have said. Alistair stopped being social long ago.

It's the lies. That's what I tell people. All those times he was late because of some so-called office function. All those times something would go wrong at home, like the fuse box or something, and when I rang his mobile I couldn't understand a word. As the vicar here said to me, alcoholics are lying to the world, but most of all they're lying to themselves, Beverly. I don't go to that church any more.

Anyway, the word must have spread around the playground about my ex's problem because just this morning there was a knock at my door. I hid what I was doing in the fridge, and went to see who it was.

'I've brought some homemade muffins,' said a woman, smiling in at me. 'Are the boys allowed sugar?'

I said they have it for special occasions because you never know where people stand on things like dental hygiene. I blocked the door.

'Also, I hope you won't be offended, but I've folded a few spare

242

pieces of uniform. Just drop them at the charity shop if you don't want them.'

Normally I wouldn't accept second-hand because I don't want people thinking I'm desperate, but I glanced through the bag and these were practically brand new.

'Shall I come in?' she said, coming in. She was dressed from head to toe in pink, like a walking lollipop, with her tin of homemade muffins. 'Lucille,' she said.

I said, 'It's a bit of a mess, I'm afraid. A month I've been here and I still haven't unpacked.'

'It looks lived in. That's how houses are supposed to look.' She gave a nice smile.

Now I haven't actually spoken to Lucille before. I'd spotted her in the playground, of course, but after Alice and everything, I'm not one to push myself on people. I'm more careful. Lucille has lovely blonde hair that she must wash every day and she never wears leggings or the same skirt two days running. I know this sounds funny but I'd told myself she was too pretty to be friends with me. She said she'd heard from the other mothers what I'd been through. She said she hoped it wasn't indiscreet of her to say that, and I said, no, it wasn't. It was a relief, I said, to have things out in the open. She smiled again, only bigger this time.

'How about I make us a coffee?' she said.

I said that would be nice but my ex had the kettle.

'No problem!' she said. 'Is the kitchen through here, Bev?'

I followed her down the hallway. I tried to walk like Lucille, swinging my hips, as if they were tiny. 'Of course, my nice things are in storage,' I told her. 'All this stuff came with the house. It's not what *I'd* choose.' I wished I'd closed the door to the sitting room before I let her in. There were pizza boxes and all sorts.

'I think it's kitsch,' she said. And I chewed a quick Fisherman's Friend while her back was turned.

She was too polite to say anything about the kitchen. I know it's only rented until I'm sorted, but with her in it, all perfumed and pink, it made me feel stupid.

Lucille looked at the packing boxes piled up like towers. She said, 'You should let me help you unpack. I love helping people. Have you got a pinny I could borrow, Bev?'

'A what?'

'A pinny. I can't think straight unless I'm wearing a pinny.'

'The pinny's in the wash,' I lied.

So even though I didn't think I had the stomach for it, we unpacked a few boxes. Plates and saucepans. Things like that. Lucille forgot about the coffee. She told me about the teachers at the school, and some of the mothers. 'They're a lovely crowd of girls,' she said. 'We're so lucky to be in the catchment area.' She unwrapped a wine goblet and stood it on the table. It was still sticky at the bottom.

'Do you have a tea towel, Bev?'

'In the wash,' I said.

'So is it true that you're getting a—?' She didn't actually use the word 'divorce'. She just made the shape of it with her pink mouth. I told her my solicitors were in the process of dealing with it. I thought I might cry she was so nice, but instead I sucked another Fisherman's Friend. 'You just say what you like,' she said. She carried the glass to the sink and rinsed it with her fingers.

So I told her everything. I told her how I'd find Alistair eating his Weetabix with the bowl filled to the brim with something that wasn't milk. 'No!' she gasped. I don't think she'd ever imagined people did that. That's how nice she is. I told her I'd come home and find him lying in a heap at the bottom of the stairs. I felt awful now I was saying it, but it was like I couldn't stop myself. Then word had got around the old school playground, I said, about his drinking habit and the mothers had stopped talking to me. 'My God,' she cried out. She turned from the sink and she looked struck. 'How simply awful.'

'Well, I have my faith, Lucille,' I said, and she said I was lucky.

But in the end, you have no choice. You've got to be cruel to be kind. I told him he had a choice between me and the booze. He kept off it for a few months but then I realised he was putting gin in his water bottle. That was the last straw. I moved out. Took the boys with me. I told him if he wasn't careful the courts would see him as unfit for custody. We stayed with a few friends from the church but you know what other people are like. It's better to do your own thing. Then a month ago we moved down here. A fresh start.

And life is going to be different. I can feel it. I'm going to make new friends like Lucille and bake muffins for the boys and buy organic vegetables. There'll be no more late-night trips to the garage and I'll put the money back in Robbie's birthday account just as soon as I earn it. I'm going to lose at least a stone and I know this may sound funny but I'm even thinking of elocution lessons.

Lucille said, 'I hope you don't mind my saying this, Bev, but there's a lot more to you than meets the eye.'

She smiled, but it was a brave smile, as if she had a pain that she didn't want to think about. I hadn't spotted it before but there's something about her that reminds me of Alice. Lucille dresses better than her, of course, and Alice has long brown hair that she scoops on top of her head with the curls falling over her neck like little roots. But there's something about both of them. Like a glass animal in your hand. You're just afraid for them, in case you twist your fingers and they snap.

'What I can't believe is how awful the mothers at your last school were,' she said. 'You'd think women would be more understanding.'

I nodded slowly. 'Actually, at the last school there was one mother who was kind. We spoke about poetry.'

'Oh, I'm way too stupid for poetry,' said Lucille.

She sat and began rubbing the glass with the hem of her pink skirt. I could see her knees and they were smooth and golden.

'We went to a concert once. It was at a church. But the other mothers got to her in the end. She stopped returning my calls.'

'Because of your husband?'

'Well, he was a liability.'

'With friends like that,' said Lucille. I nodded and sat. Suddenly I felt so heavy. Maybe it was talking about the past that did it, I don't know. I knew that if I looked in the mirror, I'd have that face I hate. All pale and round and flattened, like I'm pressed against a window. 'You look tired, Bev,' said Lucille. Oh, the irony. I nodded and gripped my hands.

The last time I saw Alice was at a summer garden party in aid of the PTA at the old school. I was clearing plates because someone on the committee had seen fit to stuff me on kitchen duty and when I came to Alice's table, she was sitting a little way from the others with her head resting on her hands, like someone sleeping. 'Oh, hello Bev,' she said. I asked her if she didn't like the sausages, because hers were untouched. She said, 'To tell the truth, I'm vegetarian.' I offered her a chicken sandwich, but she laughed and said it was still meat and *I* laughed and said yes, but it's got wings. 'You can make *me* a chicken sandwich, if you're so desperate,' boomed her pig of a husband. Later she apologised. 'Sometimes I think women would be better off without men,' she said.

I was so lost in thinking about Alice that I failed to notice Lucille unpacking. She'd worked her way through a whole box worth, and now was opening a fresh one.

'Oh no. That's terrible,' I yelled, leaping up. 'That really is too much. I can't *believe* what I'm seeing.'

She hadn't spotted it, although the neck of the bottle was peeping up through the newspaper like a glass snout.

'You see. This is what it's like,' I said, fishing it out. 'I left him, but I'm still haunted by his terrible addiction.'

'It's only a bottle of gin, Bev.'

'But just supposing one of my kids found it? It doesn't bear thinking about. We could be in Casualty right now. Having Robbie's stomach pumped. I'll chuck it in the bin.'

'There's still some left.'

For a moment I thought she was an alky as well. It gets so you can spot them. I said with a laugh, 'Well, that's a first. He must have passed out before he got to the end of it. That's the only thing that would stop him.'

'Would you like me to lose it for you, Bev? The bottle?'

'Don't worry. I'll put it safely up on this high shelf. Just in case of visitors. It's nice to be able to offer something. Not that I have visitors,' I said, just in case she was getting the wrong impression. 'I don't suppose you'd like a glass?'

'Now?'

'A sort of housewarming?'

'But it's ten to eleven.'

'So it is,' I said.

You should have seen it. Her face. Like I'd just spat on her.

We didn't say much after that. I showed Lucille around the house, and she was very polite about the room sizes, but she found an excuse to go. She won't call again. I know it. And I'll bet she tells the other mothers and it will be like it was with Alice all over again, and I don't honestly know how many times I can keep hiding.

After she left, I finished the glass I had hidden in the fridge and then I had a lie down. I didn't exactly drop off but I began to dream, where the images swim to you and you know you're awake but it's nice to go freefalling so you don't do anything to stop them. I remembered talking to Alice that last time at the summer party. I remembered waiting until the end and asking her if I could show her something and her saying yes, I could. I remembered leading her to a quiet spot under the trees where the sun fell between the shuffling leaves and landed in sequins on our skin. I said, 'Look at this leaf, Alice.' Her eyes filled. 'This is beautiful, Bev,' she said. And it was. The leaf hung from its branch stripped of green, a delicate lacework of tiny veins travelling from the axle, like the crisscrossing lines on the palm of my hand. Without disturbing it, she cradled the leaf on her fingertips. 'Who'd have thought,' she said, 'that one leaf could be so perfect.'

At that moment I forgot about the nights I spend shaking with my mouth dried up. I forgot about the vicars smelling my breath, and the cold looks as the word spreads around the church. I even forgot my husband and the boys. 'Wings outstretched,' I laughed. 'I'm flying!' And with my arms spread, I whizzed round and round like I did after the concert, to remind her we were friends, and I whizzed until Alice and the sky and the trees were one spinning thing. Then someone must have put a chair in the way because next thing I knew I had crashed straight into it and I was lying tits up on the grass.

'Bev,' she said quietly. 'That's enough. People are looking.'

'I'm freefalling, Alice!' I couldn't even get to my feet. She looked down at me like she was as tall as the sky and the rolling clouds were her hair.

'You're not, Bev. You need help.'

'I haven't been drinking.'

'You're lying,' she said, and she looked so unhappy all the way up there that I felt a twist of rage.

'You're the liar,' I said.

'Please get help, Bev.'

She stopped taking my calls after that, and then Alistair threw in the towel, and the rest as they say is history. He's fighting me for the kids.

I drink because it makes me think something nice is about to happen. Like it's a party or something. Or maybe I drink because I think something not nice needs to stop. It depends which way you look at it. I drink because I'm a poet but I'm not. I'm a woman no one looks at twice. I drink because I'm freefalling and no one's going to catch me. I go back to the kitchen and reach for the gin. And then something takes me by surprise.

It's Lucille's cardigan. It's pink and it's covered all over in little rhinestones and something about the light catches them, and the whole thing shimmers, like a hundred-thousand pink tears, all swelling and spilling. I pick it up and I watch the light and I think to myself, Look at the beauty only I can see. I think of Alice looking down on me, so sad, and Lucille's face like I'd insulted her and it's like a voice inside me rising up. My girls, my girls, here's to poetry, my girls. Before I can change my mind, I pour the gin down the sink.

Wings outstretched. I'm a-flying.

Rachel Joyce

Rachel Joyce is the author of the *Sunday Times* and international bestsellers *The Unlikely Pilgrimage of Harold Fry, Perfect, The Love Song of Miss Queenie Hennessy, The Music Shop, Miss Benson's Beetle* and a collection of interlinked short stories, *A Snow Garden & Other Stories*. Her books have been translated into thirty- six languages and two are in development for film. *The Unlikely Pilgrimage of Harold Fry* was shortlisted for the Commonwealth Book Prize and long-listed for the Man Booker Prize. Rachel was awarded the Specsavers National Book Awards New Writer of the Year in 2012, and shortlisted for the UK Author of the Year 2014.

Dry Lightning

Tony Kent

Milton Crowe pressed his fingertips hard against the side of his jaw. The pressure dulled the sharpness of the pain. It was an imperfect cure, but it would do for now. He would not allow a headache to ruin his mood. Not tonight.

Crowe had once thought that everyone had the same reaction to an oncoming storm. The same feeling of pressure at the back of the right eye. The same stabbing pain below the right ear. Physical manifestations of extreme weather ahead. Years of confused glances had taught him otherwise. The discomfort it caused him was not unique, but it *was* unusual. And so he had learned to keep it to himself.

There was no sound of rainfall on the rooftop as the limousine passed through the quiet streets of the city, but its absence hardly registered. Crowe would often feel the storm well before its arrival and – at least in Singapore – rain was never far away. Dry weather now meant nothing; a monsoon could appear as if from nowhere.

He pressed the discreet intercom button on the door.

'How long?'

'Five minutes, Boss.'

'Make it sooner.'

He removed his finger from the switch, cutting the connection instantly. Like everything in Milton Crowe's life, the intercom had been designed to his exact specifications. Essentially a dead man's handle, it had no off-button that could be forgotten and so leave the two-way conversation open. Crowe's privacy was all-important and while he trusted Craig Garrett as much as he trusted any man, there was still plenty he did not want Garrett to hear.

When you had as many secrets as Crowe, there was no room for error.

'Storm on the way?'

The question came from the seat on Crowe's left. A reminder that for all his best efforts, there was at least one person in his life who knew of his reaction to the coming weather.

'Looks like it.' Crowe reached out and gently gripped his wife's hand. 'Be nice to get home ahead of it.'

Vicki Crowe smiled tightly, then turned back to face the window. The brief glimpse, though, had been enough for Crowe. It made him feel better than any pill he could take for his discomfort. For all that it highlighted the deepening lines around her mouth and the crows' feet by her eyes, that smile was all Milton Crowe needed to be happy.

Men like him didn't usually stay with their wives, he knew. They made their money while their wives raised the kids. And then, when they were so rich that the big status symbols – the mansion, the super-yacht – were no longer enough, they found another way to show off their success.

A younger model. Usually an actual model.

But Crowe had not been so predictable. He was thirty-five when he married Vicki. Already a rich man. And already an older husband, with Vicki ten years younger. Thirty years later they were still together while Crowe's contemporaries chased what he thought of as a new species of the opposite sex – surgically enhanced Instagram mannequins, so augmented that he could no longer tell any of them apart in their incessant social-media posts.

Loyalty, Crowe always told himself, was everything. He had stuck with Vicki when he could have traded up. It's what made him better than them.

He squeezed his wife's hand tighter. Just her presence – the feel of her next to him – made the impending storm seem less oppressive. Without looking back, she briefly returned the pressure. Lighter and less enthusiastic.

Probably worried about the storm, he thought.

With a grunt, Crowe leaned forward towards the limo's side console and picked up the Global Press Association Award he had received less than an hour earlier. Just six inches tall with a thick cobalt base beneath a beautifully designed shard of opaque glass, he noticed again that it was heavier than it looked.

'So where we putting this one?'

He passed the award to his wife as he spoke.

'It's classier than most of them,' Vicki replied. It was her first close look at what had been, after all, the purpose of their evening. She handed it back. 'Not that it matters. It'll be going in your office with the rest, no doubt.'

Crowe did not answer. Instead, he considered the design.

This award, it was the big one. News Story of the Year. Recognition of his international campaign across ten publications and three news networks that focused first on the threat posed by COVID-19 – a virus unheard of before Crowe ran the story – and then became a year-long exposé of its origin.

It had been the best work of Crowe's career. Certainly the most risky. But it had been worth it. The increase in News Worldwide Inc's share price was testament to that. And so was the award he now held in his hands.

'You don't like it, do you?' Vicki's voice broke through his distraction.

'What?'

'That award. You don't like it. It's not big enough.'

Crowe laughed. As usual Vicki could see right through him.

'No,' he said, his smile wide. 'No, I don't. I was expecting something ... bigger.'

'Of course you were.' If Vicki found her husband's reaction as humorous as he did, she was hiding it well. 'Never bloody satisfied, you.'

'That's not true.' Crowe squeezed Vicki's hand one more time, just as the car took a right-hand turn that told him they were home. His gesture was intended to say the rest. He was sure that she understood that. The limo came to a stop before she could return the sentiment.

For a man who claimed no need for displays of his own success, Crowe's chosen residence in Singapore was remarkably ostentatious. The Guoco Tower was the city-state's tallest building at two hundred and ninety metres, and Crowe had secured the very top for his own. Floors sixty-two and sixty-three accounted for his home and the sixty-fourth – the pinnacle of the building – was the office of News Worldwide Inc.

Craig Garrett opened Crowe's door and stepped back as his boss climbed out. They were parked a few metres from the Tower's residents' entrance, but instead of heading towards it, Crowe started round to Vicki's side of the car. Drivers had been opening his door ahead of hers for thirty years. And so, for thirty years, Crowe had responded to that like a gentleman.

Or at least he did when it suited him.

He glanced towards the four-man security detail who had followed the limo home from the awards. All Craig Garrett's men. They had parked just behind, and so Crowe had to walk between the back of his car and the front of theirs to reach the rear left-hand door of the limo. He opened it, offered his hand and helped Vicki to step out. Then, as she stood up to her full height, two inches taller than Crowe's 5'7" even without her heels, he reached up and placed a kiss on her lips.

'What's that for?' Vicki scanned their surroundings. 'There's no paps about.'

Crowe opened his mouth to answer, to hint at the lewd thoughts running through his head. But before he could speak he was interrupted by the first crash of thunder.

The storm had arrived.

'Jesus Christ!' Crowe's cockney accent was strengthened by surprise. 'That one was right over us.'

'But it's not raining yet,' Vickie said, frowning up at the sky.

Thunder storms were frequent in Singapore – as were the headaches they brought with them – but nowhere near as common as rain. So to have thunder and lightning without it here? It was ... disconcerting.

'That'll be the climate change,' Crowe laughed.

'That thing you say's made up?'

Vicki's tone was stern. Crowe should not have mentioned the climate. He knew that. But what was he going to do? Apologise?

'Not this again, love.'

Crowe released Vicki's hand as easily as he dismissed her comment. A second crack of thunder sounded above as he headed towards the entrance.

'Look, I need to get up to the office.' He spoke over his shoulder as he walked. 'I won't be long. The boys'll take you up to the residence, all right? And I'll be there in twenty.'

Vicki said nothing. Exactly as Crowe expected. Whatever her thoughts on climate change – whatever her anger at how her husband's papers debunked it – there were things she just had to accept.

Crowe paid for the life she lived, and so Crowe's word was final. That was just how it was.

He walked into the tower in silence and headed towards the bank of eight elevators. He passed the first six which, between them, serviced the first sixty-one floors. Then he stopped at the two that remained. Only these could reach the News Worldwide office on the top floor, and the eighth alone provided access to their residence below.

Garrett pressed two buttons built into the limo key and both elevators opened, with Crowe facing one and his wife the other.

Crowe turned towards Vicki with a smile, stepped closer and kissed her cheek, subtly stroking his hand from her waist to the top of her thigh. A suggestion of what he expected to come.

He leaned close to her ear.

'See you in twenty.'

'See you then.' Vicki replied, her returned smile forced.

Crowe shrugged as the elevator doors closed. Just another one of her moods; it would pass.

The elevator doors opened to silence.

In most offices, silence at this time of night would not be unusual, but Crowe's was no normal business. News Worldwide was more than just a catchy name. It was a global corporation. A twenty-four-hour news network that spanned the Earth. And while it was midnight in Singapore, it was 5 p.m. in England and noon in Manhattan.

And so the lack of activity in his office reception annoyed Crowe. The desk was supposed to be manned at all times. It was an aim he paid good money to achieve.

Bad timing, he thought to himself, *being gone when I get here. I'll deal with that later.*

The main working area was to the left of reception. A walk Crowe would make at least once a day. Usually more. He believed his presence was important. That his people worked harder if they knew he could turn up at any time. Which he could; the two-floor ride from his home took maybe ten seconds.

Tonight, though, he turned right, to head to his office and speak to his board. And he would be making that quick. Because then he would do what he *really* wanted: head downstairs and take his wife to bed, where they would celebrate his victory.

Because that's what tonight was. A victory at the end of a long campaign.

The COVID-19 campaign had been a rollercoaster. Maybe the

255

biggest single effort of Crowe's life. And tonight that effort had been acknowledged by his entire industry. They had finally shown him the respect he had long ago earned.

It wasn't the award itself. He knew he'd won that months ago. No, it was the steps they'd taken to honour him. They'd even staged the awards in Singapore. All for the convenience of one man.

All for Milton Crowe.

The thought brought a smile to his face as he strode through the empty corridor towards his office. He was caught up in his own satisfaction, hardly noticing the cracks of thunder sounding in the distance and near oblivious to the headache they were causing.

But there was something else he hardly noticed. Something just as unusual as the dry lightning outside.

The emptiness of the halls around him.

And so he was surprised when he heard Garrett start to speak into his mic.

'Sixty-Four Security. Come in. Over.'

No response. Just the sound of static.

Crowe stopped walking. His escorts did the same.

'What is it?'

'Nothing.' Garrett's tone suggested that the answer was not positive. He drew his pistol as he spoke and Crowe felt his heart rate increase. 'Literally nothing. There's no one else on that frequency.'

'Try again.'

Garrett did as instructed; the result was no different.

'Try another frequency.'

Garrett was already on it.

'Crowe Residence Security. This is Garrett. Respond. Over.'

Nothing but static. Garrett tried again with the same result.

He switched to a third frequency. As he did so, Wade and Boon drew their own weapons and each stepped away from Garrett and Crowe. Wade a stride closer to the way they had come, Boon to the direction they were heading.

They were taking point. Which meant they were concerned.

The realisation made Crowe's heart beat even faster.

'Guoco Tower Main Security. This is Security on Sixty-Four. Please respond. Over.'

Crowe felt himself begin to panic as Garrett's call went unanswered.

'What the hell does that mean, Craig? What the fuck's going on?'

'I think the frequencies are being jammed,' Garrett replied. 'It's one thing to take out security up here, but for the whole Tower? That'd take a full military breach. A jammer makes more sense.'

Crowe took a deep breath to calm himself. What Garrett was saying made sense; it was hardly positive, but at least it was logical. What it was not, though, was a solution. They needed to know what was happening and they needed to know now.

'Get out the way.'

Crowe pushed past Garrett and headed for the door of the nearest office. It was empty. Like the rest of the floor seemed to be, Crowe now realised. Dismissing the thought, he headed straight for the desk and picked up the phone.

The line was dead.

'FOR FUCK'S SAKE!'

Crowe threw the phone console against the wall as he shouted. It bounced off, undamaged. If he'd been thinking clearly, he would have noted the quality of the equipment he was providing and the need to downgrade it next time. But he was not thinking clearly. Not at all. Instead, he was experiencing something he had not felt in years.

Fear.

His thoughts frantic, Crowe reached into his pocket.

'Cells are out, too,' Garrett said, before his boss could check.

Crowe's sweat was starting to show through his expensive dinner jacket. It dripped cold down the back of his neck. He looked towards Garrett, almost overcome by an unfamiliar sense of uncertainty.

'What the fuck is this, Craig?'

'I don't know,' Garrett replied. 'But whatever's happening, it's happening in this building. Now that could mean it's targeted at you, or at someone else entirely. We can't know that. But if the threat's here, then this is *not* where you want to be. Safest place for you right now is anywhere else.'

'What about my office? It's a safe room.'

'Last resort. Safe rooms have their limits and we don't know who this is. Out is better.'

Crowe nodded. Garrett was making sense. His certainty gave Crowe confidence.

Garrett had been both Crowe's driver and head of his close protection team for seventeen years. It was a job for which he was infinitely qualified, and one at which he excelled. Like the two men beside him – Sean Wade and Brett Boon – Garrett's only responsibility was to keep Milton Crowe safe. Crowe trusted him implicitly.

The only problem was, if Garrett was here…

'What about Vicki?'

Garrett turned and faced Crowe, holding his boss's fixed stare.

'We can't think about that right now. We can't contact her security team, remember? So we've got no choice but to trust that they're doing the same as us. We have to leave it to them.'

'Bollocks do we. That's my fucking wife you're talking about. I want someone down there now.'

'Boss, there's three of us.' Garrett's voice was calm. Reasoned. 'Which means there's me to stay with you, Wade to cover our route back to the exit, Boon to cover our rear. Lose one of the three and we're compromised. We're running. I can't move you safely around this building with less.'

Crowe said nothing as he considered Garrett's words. He wanted Vicki safe. Of course he did.

But doesn't my safety come first? For her own good, I mean? With me alive, she's worth…

258

'Boss, I need a decision.' Garrett's voice broke through Crowe's thoughts. 'I can send Boon for her. But if I do that...'

'Leave her.' Crowe's mind was made up. 'If something happens to me, she becomes expendable. I can't put her in that danger.'

'Right decision. Mrs Crowe's team will take care of her. Now let's get you out of here.'

Crowe felt his body shaking. Caused by the adrenaline now pumping through his ageing system. It gave him focus. Clarity. Even the rainless storm raging outside the window could not distract him. His attention was now on one thing.

Survival.

'Wade's taking point ahead.' Garrett indicated back towards reception. 'Boon is behind. I'll be next to you the whole way. Understood?'

Crowe nodded but said nothing. He was breathing fast.

'We need to do this fast, boss. You understand that?'

Another nod.

'And we need to take the stairs. We can't risk the elevator. That's sixty-four floors down.'

'You've got to be joking. What's wrong with the lift?'

'We're rats in a trap in the elevator. In the stairwell, we can keep you surrounded. And we have a clear view up and down.'

Crowe took a deep breath. He did not relish that level of exertion. But if it was the difference between life and death...

As he thought it through, his eyes focused on Garrett's pistol.

'I need one of those.'

'You don't, boss.'

'I've got people here to kill me, Craig. I need a gun.'

'You ever handle a pistol before?'

'Never.'

'Then no offence, boss, but if I arm you now, you'll be a danger to yourself and to all of us.'

'Bollocks. Give me a gun.'

'Boss, I—'

'I fucking own those guns, don't I?'

'Boss—'

'Then give me one of 'em. Now!'

Garrett took a step back. It gave Crowe a fuller view of the man; he could see that Garrett was conflicted, yet not for a moment did Crowe doubt the outcome.

Garrett turned to Wade.

'Sean, give him your ankle gun.'

Wade hesitated.

'You heard what he said.' Crowe stepped forward and held out his hand. 'Give me the fucking gun.'

Crowe was used to the look he saw in Wade's eyes. The look of a man who desperately wants to say … something. And he was used to how that look fades, just as it did now, as Wade gave in. He reached down, unclipped the pistol from his ankle holster and passed it to Crowe.

Crowe let the weapon weigh in his hand. It was heavier than he had expected. He turned to Garrett.

'This thing's safety off?'

'Yes, boss.'

'And what? Just point and shoot?'

'Try not to, eh?'

As he said the words, Garrett was already turning back to his two colleagues, and away from Crowe.

'OK, lads. Let's do this.'

Both men moved on Garrett's instruction. Wade strode ahead, towards the far end of the corridor, his pistol held steady in both hands. Boon did the same but in the opposite direction; towards the corridor that, had they taken it, would have led to Crowe's office.

Wade moved fast, with Crowe and Garret following slowly and at a distance. Even before they'd passed by the open office door, he'd reached the hallway's end. But now, as he approached the corner, he slowed. His every step became careful and considered, with his pistol held firmly in his unwavering hands.

Crowe and Garrett were gaining on him. There were perhaps ten steps between them when Crowe felt the pressure of Garrett's hand on his gut. An instruction to stop.

Wade's movement was suddenly uncertain. As if he sensed danger ahead. Crowe could understand it. The only step left would take him around the corner, beyond the protection of their hallway's wall. If there was a threat there, that step would expose Wade to it.

'Three…'

The sound of Garrett's voice made Crowe turn his head.

'Two…'

Garrett was counting for himself, Crowe realised. Because there was no way Wade could hear him from here.

'One…'

Or could he? To Crowe's surprise, Wade moved exactly as Garrett's countdown reached zero. And he moved fast.

But not fast enough.

Crowe could not quite comprehend what he saw. Wade turned the corner at speed, his pistol ready. He should have been a match for anything that awaited him, and yet suddenly he was gone. Snatched from the hallway at a speed that did not seem possible.

'GET BACK!'

Garrett's instruction was screamed rather than shouted. For an instant Crowe had stood there in shock and uncertainty. What had just happened? Garrett's words, though, brought the reality of the situation crashing home.

Nothing scared Craig Garrett. And yet right now, the man seemed terrified.

'GET BACK!' Garrett bellowed again. 'GET BACK!'

The instruction was unnecessary; Garrett's arm was like steel across Crowe's upper body, dragging him back down the corridor. Crowe had no choice but to move in the same direction.

They passed both the corner and Brett Boon in seconds, moving at full pace. Whoever had taken Wade would be coming. That knowledge kept Crowe moving. Kept his lungs and his heart pumping.

Seconds later and they had reached his office. Seconds more and all three were inside.

Boon closed the door behind them as Garrett hit the yellow and red panic button set at the side of the doorway. The effect was instant. The sound of deadbolts and who knows what else moving into place was unmistakable, even over the cacophony of the storm outside. It was Crowe's ultimate security measure; his office, converted into a panic room, with an immediate distress call sent out to all police in the vicinity.

Crowe looked towards Garrett. He had expected to see relief but it was not there.

'What's wrong with you? We're safe in here, aren't we?'

'Depends who's out there.'

'What are you talking about? This room's secure.'

'Up to a point it is, yeah. That system, it'll stand up to anything less than military-grade firepower. At least for as long as it takes for the police to arrive.'

'OK. Then what are you worried about?'

'We don't know who the fuck this is, boss.' Garrett's voice was raised. The first time he had ever spoken to Crowe in anything even close to anger. 'For all we know, they could be out there lining up that sort of firepower right now. Then what use is all this?'

Crowe took a step back, irritated with Garrett's tone. Then, realising that he was now standing dead ahead of the doorway, he took a step forward again; anything powerful enough to bring those doors down would make short work of someone directly behind them.

He turned his attention back to Garrett.

'So what happens now?'

'Now we hope they're *not* military, I guess. And we wait for back-up.'

'We wait for back-up? You mean the police? Seriously, Craig? The fucking police? So just what the fu—'

Crowe did not finish his sentence. He was interrupted by the repetition of a familiar sound: the mechanism that had converted his office into a safe room. The intricate security system Garrett had switched on was somehow being reversed.

Crowe turned to his men in disbelief, seeking an explanation. He would not find one. Garrett was back on his feet, pistol in hand, but he seemed as shocked as the man he was paid to protect. And just as scared. Boon, barely feet from his team leader, was no better.

The sight did nothing for Crowe's confidence, but it at least strengthened his resolve. And in that moment, he decided to do what he always did.

He would count on himself. With a deep breath, he raised the pistol he had taken from Wade ... and then the world exploded.

Nothing in Milton Crowe's life had prepared him for the sensation he had just experienced. The assault on his senses that had left him on the floor of his office, face down in a pool of his own vomit.

How had it happened? What had been used to disable him in that way? He had no idea. All he remembered was lifting Wade's gun, and then this.

He turned his head to the right. Towards Garrett and Boon. His last line of protection. His last hope, however slim. The dim sight that greeted him felt like a blow, as physical as anything he had received so far.

Whatever had been done to open the safe room had affected the lighting. And so Crowe had to squint to get a proper look at his guards, stretched out on their fronts about ten feet either side of him. Garrett seemed unconscious.

Maybe worse?

No, Crowe realised. Not worse. If Garrett had been worse, then whoever did this wouldn't have taken the time to secure the restraints he now spotted around Garrett's wrists.

But who put them there? he thought. *And why none on mine?*

The thought was immediately dispelled by an onslaught of movement and pain as he was pulled up forcefully from the floor by the hand-sewn fabric of his collar and propelled through the air. For a moment he felt weightless as momentum sent him upwards. An instant later and gravity was back in control, with Crowe landing heavily and face-first into the leather chair that sat ahead of his desk.

The impact almost made Crowe throw up again, but somehow he stopped himself. He would not give them that satisfaction. Not again. If this was it, he would finish things like the man he was. His ears were still ringing from the sounds that had incapacitated him. Lights were still flashing in his eyes. But slowly, surely, he managed to turn around.

He wanted to face the men who had come for him head on.

'And who the fuck are you supposed to be?'

Crowe hid his shock the only way he knew how. With bluster and bravado. After all, what else could he say? Certainly not what he was actually thinking.

One man?

How did one man do all this?

More to the point, why?

They were the sensible questions to ask. But right now, Milton Crowe had no intention of letting his fear show through.

'What's the matter,' he demanded, belligerence his only remaining weapon. 'National fucking secret, are you?'

'If I were a national secret, Mr Crowe, no doubt you'd already know the answer.'

The man's voice was deep and strong. A voice of confidence. Of a man used to giving orders, and used to those orders being obeyed.

And like Crowe's, the accent was English.

'My name's Joe Dempsey. I'm a special agent with the International Security Bureau of the United Nations. I'm going to assume you know what that is?'

'You can assume more than that,' Crowe snapped. He did his best to hide his surprise at the agent's identity. 'You can assume I know who you are. Shot any politicians lately, Mr Dempsey?'

Dempsey smiled. A grim, unwelcome expression. Either his poker face was world class, or he had expected Crowe to recognise his name. Probably the latter, Crowe realised. After all, news that Crowe left unreported was not the same as news Crowe did not know.

A flash of lightning illuminated the room for a moment. It gave Crowe a better view of the man, however fleeting. He recognised Dempsey from the reports he had seen, but he now realised that those pictures did the guy an injustice; Dempsey seemed far more dangerous in the flesh. The broken nose and the scar on his left cheek made an otherwise handsome face cruel. Add his sheer size into the mix – what was he, six foot two? Maybe two hundred and thirty pounds? – and the man became a terror.

Crowe looked around the room. For any hint of … what? A weapon? A means of escape? From *this* bastard? What the hell was he thinking?

'I'm glad we both know each other's work, Milton.' Dempsey stepped closer as he spoke. 'Removes the need for introductions and resumés and lets us get straight to it. You see, we don't have a whole lot of time: you need to give me the flash drive.'

'The what? What flash drive?'

'The one with the COVID-19 material, Milton. The one that proves everything you've been printing and broadcasting about China is bullshit. Where is it?'

'Are you serious? I don't know what the hell—'

'You need to trust me when I tell you we don't have time for this. We know what you've been doing. We infiltrated this place six weeks ago. How do you think we were able to clear this entire floor tonight? How do you think we were able to shut down this entire building? All without you knowing?

'We've been watching and we've been listening, Milton. And we know that everything you've been reporting about China and COVID 19 is false. Just as false as the stuff your Chinese papers have been reporting on the same subject over there. What you've been saying in China about the US.'

Crowe hesitated. What Dempsey had said. About China.

How does he know?

'You think we were unaware of that little business interest? About your publication deal with the Chinese government? Jesus, Milton. We're the United Nations. More than that, we're a Security Council Agency. Have you forgotten which countries *sit* on the Security Council?'

Crowe could feel a painful knot growing within his stomach. The same feeling of fear he had experienced in the corridor, only intensified. If what Dempsey was saying was true...

'Your newspapers told the west that COVID-19 came from a Chinese lab. That it was released by mistake, but that the Chinese covered it up and deliberately let it spread to ensure that theirs would not be the only economy to suffer. You reported that around the world. You stirred up international tensions. You've brought the two most powerful nations on this planet to the brink of war, all for headlines. And yet you know it's not true. You know none of it happened. And you have the evidence I need to calm this whole thing down. I want it.'

'How can you... how can you possibly know...?'

'Cut out the act. We both know I'm right and we both know you have what I'm here for. Hand it over now and maybe this doesn't go as badly as it could.'

Crowe looked down, towards the gun in Dempsey's hands.

'Is that a threat, Agent Dempsey?'

'No, Milton. It's a warning. You need to think about what you've done. About who you've pissed off. Because not only did you act against Chinese interests with a false story in the West, you played them for fools at the same time. Your papers over there – the ones you thought we wouldn't know about – they were falsely reporting US involvement in the creation of COVID-19. Something that you know very well to be untrue.

'Now how do you think China is going to take that? You've played them off against America, and America off against them. You've damaged God knows how many countries' economies into the bargain, all with lies. And now you're accepting awards for doing it. How do you think the Chinese are going to react to that? You think they'll just let this go?'

Even though seated, Crowe could feel his legs weaken. The knot in his stomach, so small at first – little more than butterflies – was now as fierce as the storm outside. China was ... China was not America. If *they* came for him...

'What do they know?' he asked. 'The Chinese, I mean. How much do they know?'

'They know everything. And they're on their way here now. Your time's up, Milton.'

'Can you protect me?'

'From the Chinese. Why would I? You've brought this on yourself.'

'Don't fuck about, Mr Dempsey. If I give you the evidence? If I give you what you need to cool things down between them? Can you protect me *then*?'

Dempsey took a step closer. He towered over Crowe, and yet now he was not so intimidating. Compared to what was coming, he was the lesser threat.

'Whatever way this goes down, Milton, it's over.' Dempsey indicated to the room around them. 'All of this. You're finished. But if you're asking if I can make sure the Chinese don't take you? If that's what you mean? Yeah. I know a way you can avoid that.'

'And Vicki?'

'Vicki never made it into that lift,' Dempsey replied. 'And you never need to worry about her again.'

'What does that mean?'

Dempsey leaned forward, his eyes fixed on Crowe.

'Who do you think told us what you'd done, Milton? Who do you think gave me the code to your panic room?'

It took Crowe longer than it should to understand what Dempsey had said. And longer still to accept it.

'No,' he said, almost to himself. 'No. Not Vicki. Not...'

'You don't have time for denial.' Dempsey glanced at his watch as he spoke, his tone urgent.

'Where's the flash drive?'

Crowe said nothing. The idea ... the very idea that...

'Milton, they're nearly here. Give me the damn flash drive.'

Dempsey's shout had the desired effect. It cut through whatever paralysis had gripped Crowe.

Crowe rose to his feet, his legs still unsteady. Using the back of the chair for support, he moved to the large bookcase that covered the side wall of his office. Dempsey followed, sticking close to his shoulder as Crowe ran his finger along a line of books on the centre shelf. Had Crowe been looking for a weapon, Dempsey would have been too close for the older man to use it.

Which is probably the point, Crowe now figured.

But he had no such plans. If the Chinese Secret Service were already on their way, Crowe would do whatever he had to avoid them. Right now, if Dempsey had asked him for a kidney Crowe would have filled the bath with ice.

His finger stopped at Voltaire's *Candide*. One of many philosophical texts on Crowe's bookshelf. Like the rest of them, it was unread. But not, in this case, untouched. He opened the cover to reveal a square hole cut out of the page block. Inside it was a flash drive.

'This is what you want.'

'You're sure it's the one? That it's real?'

'Do you think I'd risk what'd happen if it wasn't?' Crowe pointed towards his desktop. 'Go on. Check it.'

Dempsey glanced at his watch.

'No time for that,' he said. 'They'll be here inside three minutes, and I don't plan to be here when that happens. I trust you're too interested in your own preservation to lie to me.'

Dempsey stepped back, the flash drive held tight in his left hand.

'Now what?' Crowe asked. He could feel his heart rate rising again. The return of the adrenaline. That, combined with the gut-wrenching betrayal he had suffered, left him light-headed.

'Craig said we'd need to take the stairwell.'

'Craig was probably right. But you won't be coming with me.'

Crowe did not understand. Not even as Dempsey raised his pistol and fired three bullets into the office window. Perfectly placed together, they shattered the hardened glass and filled the room with the chaos of the rainless storm that was raging outside.

'What are you doing?' Crowe shouted, his voice almost drowned out by thunder.

'I'm giving you a choice,' Dempsey shouted back. 'I can't take you with me. It's too much of a risk. Either I get this material back to the UN or we risk a Cold War. Or worse.'

'Surely...'

'You'll slow me down, Milton. I can't risk being caught here. Not now. You're on your own.'

Crowe looked from the window to Dempsey, then back again, as reality hit him.

'You said you'd protect me.'

'No. No, I didn't. I said there was a way you could avoid them taking you.' Dempsey pointed towards what was left of the window. 'That's the way.'

'You can't ... you can't expect ... not like this?'

'What you've done, Milton. It's a death sentence. Whether you jump or whether the Chinese take you, this ends the same way. Only difference is how much you suffer *before* you die?'

'But—'

'There's no but. There's just a decision. I suggest you make it fast, because you're almost out of time.'

Crowe opened his mouth to respond, but no words came out. What was there to say? He could think of nothing, and so he stood in silence as Dempsey turned his back and walked out of the room.

He closed his eyes, then opened them again. The whole world seemed to be spinning. He steadied himself on the chair as his gaze drifted towards the shattered glass. The howl of the wind was deafening, its force now battering through the opening and whipping around the room just as another lightning bolt illuminated the sky. Thunder followed so quickly that the bolt must have hit the street outside.

The storm was mesmerising. A literal force of nature, it was a reminder of the insignificance of one human life. And yet one human life – *his* human life – was all Crowe could consider. Mere hours after his greatest triumph – after revelling in the respect he had earned – was this really how it was all going to end?

And Vicki. Had Vicki...

No. He would not believe it. He would...

Another lightning bolt. Another clap of thunder. And then a different sound. Less awesome. A whole lot more real.

He glanced at his watch. Dempsey's three minutes had been wrong. It had taken them barely two.

Crowe did not need to question the sound. He knew Mandarin when he heard it; hell, he'd even taught himself a little as he branched out his empire into China. It was one of many things he had learned about the world's second superpower.

Only a few of which he was willing to experience.

It was not even a decision anymore. A death sentence was a death sentence, but there was only so much hell he could face before it. And he damned well couldn't face it alone. Not without her. Not knowing what she…

It was only five steps, but Milton Crowe took them at a run. And then, as the storm he had predicted raged all around him, he threw himself into the darkness.

Tony Kent

Tony Kent is a thriller writer, a criminal barrister and a former champion heavyweight boxer. He writes the bestselling Joe Dempsey/Michael Devlin/Sarah Truman series of political and legal action thrillers, which began in 2018 with *Killer Intent* and continued in 2019 with *Marked for Death*. The series grew again in 2020 with his third novel, the US set political blockbuster *Power Play* in which intelligence agent Joe Dempsey and criminal barrister Michael Devlin take on corruption that reaches all the way to the White House itself. In a twenty-year history of high-profile criminal trials, Tony has dealt not only with the UK government but also with Scotland Yard, the NCA, MI5 and the FBI, as well as some of Europe's most infamous organised crime groups. Tony brings this experience and insight to life in his plot-driven, action-heavy series of contemporary and eerily relevant thrillers.

Black Tom

Vaseem Khan

1

Rain hammered on the window, sheets of water flowing down the cracked pane, the glass set behind a row of iron bars. A pail in the corner of the room plinked every few seconds; she'd watched the damp patch on the ceiling grow steadily.

'I didn't kill her.' The Englishman paused, as if confused by his own words, then stood, a sudden movement that made Persis reach for her holster. Gallagher seemed oblivious, pulling a pack of Capstans and a lighter from his jacket, then shrugging it off and hanging it from the back of his chair. He slumped down again, a tall, narrow-waisted man, handsome in an oblique way. Locks of blond hair fell over his forehead. A razor cut marked his jaw.

She watched him light his cigarette, take a deep draw, loosen his tie, then pull off his gold-rimmed spectacles and set them on the table. Smoke billowed around his eyes, marked by deep circles. Without the spectacles, he seemed younger.

'How long did you know her?'

'We've been – we were together almost six months.'

'Together?'

'We knew each other. In the biblical sense, Inspector.' He flashed a sardonic smile. She wondered if his responses were coloured by the fact that he was being questioned by a woman. 'Last night, I asked her to marry me.'

Persis shifted in her seat. In the distant past, it might have been commonplace for an Englishman to take an Indian bride. But the independence movement had made such liaisons fraught with difficulty. Now, in 1950, just a few short years after Partition, she could not conceive of a white man marrying an Indian.

She glanced at the clock on the wall. Almost two. She'd been summoned from her home to Colaba Station at just after one a.m. Roshan Seth, her commanding officer at Malabar House, her own station, had dragged her out of bed to inform her that an Englishman had been arrested for murder. The colour of his skin made it a political matter; the senior officer at Colaba was on leave. And so the poisoned chalice had been handed to Seth, who'd passed it to her.

She studied the prisoner again.

John Gallagher. Thirty-two. Unmarried. A managing agent at Lambert and Pryce. One of tens of thousands of Britishers who'd stayed on post-1947. Some for economic reasons, some for the climate, some because India had dug her way under their skin and there was no cure for what they now had.

'How did you meet?'

'I broke my arm. Riding accident. She was a nurse. We hit it off.'

'Tell me about her.'

He was silent a moment, staring down at the tabletop. 'She was ... conscientious. A moral person. Decent, in every way. Most people aren't, you know.'

'Are you?'

He didn't bother to reply.

'When was the last time you saw her?'

'You already know the answer to that. It's why I'm here, isn't it?' He glanced at Das, the arresting officer. Persis had only met the sub-inspector an hour earlier, but he seemed woefully out of his depth. At any other time, her presence here would have provoked hostility.

273

In spite of her much-publicised recent successes, she remained a divisive figure, the country's first – and only – female police detective. In the misogynistic world of the Indian Police Service, she was about as welcome as Lucrezia Borgia at a dinner party.

'You told him. Now tell me.'

He tapped ash on to the table. 'We had dinner together. At her flat.'

'Special occasion?'

'I told you, I asked her to marry me.'

'So you invited yourself?'

'Yes. It wasn't unusual. We often eat at her place.'

'How did she seem to you?'

'She was her usual self—' He stopped. His expression changed. 'Something was bothering her. I don't know what it was.'

'She didn't tell you?'

His jaw quivered. 'I- I was distracted. The proposal. I was building up to it. She tried to tell me something, but I didn't give her the chance.'

'What time did you leave?'

'Around ten.'

'Nadine was found dead shortly afterwards.'

He raised the cigarette to his lips, his hollow gaze focused at a point behind her.

'You were heard fighting.'

'Impossible.'

'The walls are thinner than you think. Your neighbours are adamant they heard you arguing.'

Silence.

'Was she already dead when you left?'

'No!' He slapped the table, startling her.

The rain rose again in the silence, a noise like the murmur of voices behind a locked door. The monsoon had arrived a week early; Bombay would soon be deluged, a city under siege. The city of jazz and good times. The gateway to India.

Like any big city, murder was commonplace. Persis had seen plenty of it during the Partition rioting.

It was the reason every death mattered.

At the door to the room, she stopped. 'What did she say?'

He seemed confused. 'What?'

'To your proposal.'

He drew on his cigarette again, and lowered his eyes.

2

She asked Das to drive her to the victim's home. A ten-storey art-deco apartment tower on Marine Drive, facing the sea, with a bronze plaque that read HEAVEN'S GATE, and a security guard in a poncho sheltering under a makeshift canopy. The monsoon bombardment had driven away the beggars that normally slept on the promenade. A stray dog shook out its fur as they dismounted and made their way to the third floor.

Flat 303. Living room, bedroom, kitchen, bathroom. A single person's habitat, though a space this size might house a dozen in the city's slums.

Bombay, the city of dreams.

'Where did you find the body?'

He led her to the kitchen, a small space containing a fridge, gas hob, a small, round table, two chairs. 'She was sitting at the table. Head down. Her throat had been cut. There was ... a lot of blood.'

She could see the stains, on the table, and on the floor beneath. A horrific way for a life to end, the work of a cold-blooded monster. She thought of Gallagher, his urbanity, the way he'd spoken about Nadine. Could he really have done something like this?

She knew that the forensics team had already been through the apartment. She hoped Archie Blackfinch had been in charge.

Blackfinch. An Englishman in India. A friend. Or possibly something more? She shook away the thought.

She made a note to call him first thing in the morning. Even if he hadn't been here in person, she was certain he'd take charge of the forensics in a case as sensitive as this.

'The murder weapon?'

'It was lying in the sink. A kitchen knife.'

'Did they search the place?'

'Yes. I mean, there was no real need. We spoke to the neighbours. They told us about Gallagher. So we arrested him.'

She started with the kitchen, and worked her way back to the bedroom.

Das followed like a lost puppy. 'Madam, the place has already been searched.'

'Not by me.'

In the wardrobe, she discovered a selection of dresses, simple but elegant. On the dresser, a photograph in a silver frame, of Nadine and another woman. 'Who's this?'

'I don't know.'

She took out the photograph and slipped it into her pocket.

In the drawer of a bedside unit, she found a notebook, with a royal blue cover that smelled of new leather. On the flyleaf, an inscription in a neat hand. The private thoughts of Nadine Fonseca.

She turned the pages; only a few had been used. Observations, inner moments, mental doodles, little of consequence. Nothing about John Gallagher. That seemed strange, given Gallagher's claim that they were soon to be affianced. Her own dealings with men had left her with little insight on the matter.

On the last used page were just two words, written in block capitals: BLACK TOM.

The words jarred. They seemed disconnected to everything else in the notebook, words that appeared to have crash-landed on the page. Possibly, the last words that Nadine Fonseca had written before her death. But why?

As she continued to leaf through the notebook, something fluttered to the floor.

A photograph. Black and white. It showed an Englishman, prominent in the foreground, smiling at the camera, blond, clean-shaven. Standing beside him, two Indians, slim, sporting moustaches, sunglasses and hats. Their faces – what she could see of them – looked very much alike, almost like twins. All three men wore suits; all three seemed young, in their twenties. The background behind them was blurred, a harbour, perhaps, a boat, possibly the base of a monument in the water. She couldn't recognise where in India it might have been taken.

It didn't look like Bombay.

'Let's talk to the neighbours.'

3

'I've met her boyfriend. He always seemed like a nice boy. I still can't believe he did this.'

They were sitting in Flat 304. The woman before them was in her fifties, in a nightgown, with a soft, round face and a habit of touching her cheek every few seconds. Her name was Sheela Desai.

'You told sub-Inspector Das that you heard them arguing.'

'Yes. I remember because I'd just turned the radio off. You know how it gets? That silence like a hole in which you can hear even a pin drop.'

'You live alone?'

'I live with my son and his wife. But they're away, in Ooty. An excursion. They're newly married.' She gave a gentle smile.

'What were they arguing about?'

'I couldn't say. I'm afraid my hearing isn't what it once was.'

'What did you do next?'

'Nothing. But an hour later, worry got the better of me. So I went and knocked on Nadine's door. She didn't open it. I became concerned so I went to fetch Rishi.'

Rishi Sharma lived in Flat 305, a slender man in his fifties, with peppery hair, sad eyes, and a limp. 'I thought Sheela was over-reacting at first. I mean, young people argue all the time. They call it romance.' He grimaced. 'I went back with her and pounded on the door for a bit. I thought she'd probably gone to sleep. But Sheela wouldn't let it go. So we got the security guard to come up. He broke down the door. That's when we found her.' His face paled at the memory. Beside him, Sheela had begun weeping silently.

'Did Nadine mention trouble with her boyfriend? John Gallagher?'

'Nadine was a very private person. She didn't hide the fact that she was going around with a white man, but neither did she encourage anyone to pry into her life.'

Persis took out the photograph she'd found on the dresser. 'Do you know who that is?'

'That's Grace. Nadine's sister.'

She next showed them the photograph from Nadine's notebook. 'Do you know who these men are?'

They shook their heads. 'Perhaps they're friends of Gallagher?' suggested Rishi.

'Has she ever mentioned anyone called Black Tom?'

They looked mystified.

She returned to the station. Gallagher was in a cell, lying on a cot staring up at the ceiling. She showed him the photograph, but he claimed never to have seen it before, or to know any of the men pictured in it. 'Did she ever mention a man named Black Tom?'

He shook his head. 'The only Tom we knew was her priest. Thomas Rebeiro. He's dark-skinned, but I've never heard her refer to him as "Black Tom". Nadine would have found that disrespectful. She was a devout Catholic.'

By the time she reached home it was almost five a.m. The Wadia Book Emporium's facade was darkened; the stone vultures that roosted on the plinth above the shop's glass frontage stared down at her with minatory intent. As a Parsee, she had no fear of vultures; they were revered by her community and essential to the process of excarnation, the eating of the dead, placed in the Towers of Silence, at the very heart of the city. Tradition and religion, the twin pillars of Bombay's Zoroastrians, responsible both for their success on the subcontinent, and their failure. A tribe apart.

She wondered if her father had fallen asleep on the sofa at the back of the bookshop, as he was wont to do. She pushed open the door – it was never locked – and made her way inside. The familiar smell of books, old and new, that had accompanied her throughout her childhood wrapped itself around her. Growing up without a mother, siblings, and few friends, they had been her closest companions.

Sam wasn't on the sofa. She took the stairs up to the flat above the shop, found him stretched out on the living-room rug, his wheelchair abandoned to one side. Akbar, the Persian tom, dozed on the Steinway.

She dropped to her knees, kissed the top of her father's balding head. His moustache ruffled, a dream of her mother, perhaps, lost at an Independence rally, the only woman he had loved. She helped him up, into his wheelchair, and to bed.

In her own room, she pondered on the photograph, and Nadine Fonseca's last words.

Just who was Black Tom?

4

'Have you got enough to charge him?'

Roshan Seth prowled his office in the basement of Malabar House. Every so often he would stop and glare at her. Seth, like the rest of them, had ended up here because he'd put someone's nose out of joint. The Malabar House station was the runt of Bombay's constabulary litter; a tiny police *thana* located in the basement of a corporate building. The only cases that came their way tended to the embarrassingly trivial or the politically nettlesome.

'Not yet,' said Persis.

'What are you waiting for? You have means, motive, opportunity.'

'The motive isn't clear.'

'You have a witness that says they were fighting. An hour later, the woman's dead. What more do you need?'

She stood, stuck her peaked cap back on her head. 'I need more.'

At the Grant Medical College, she found Archie Blackfinch in discussion with the pathologist, Raj Bhoomi. Blackfinch grinned at her, his flop of dark hair neatly brushed back, the light glinting from his spectacles and his smoothly shaven cheeks.

Something twisted at her insides.

They'd worked two cases together already; there was no denying the attraction that had sprung up between them. But this was post-Partition India, a nation attempting to find its feet following three centuries of subjugation. To reassert its own identity. She had no desire to be labelled as some Englishman's fancy woman, an Indian mistress of the type so despised during the latter days of the Raj.

Nadine Fonseca hadn't cared.

Her body lay on a gurney, washed out by the harsh overhead lighting.

She stood beside Blackfinch, conscious of his presence, as Bhoomi, a small, whiskery man, carried out the autopsy.

Afterwards, he offered his conclusions. 'Cause of death was exsanguination. She bled out. The knife severed the left carotid arteries and the left jugular vein. Her attacker was right-handed.'

Persis twitched. John Gallagher was right-handed.

'No defensive wounds,' added Bhoomi.

Which meant that she was either taken by surprise or knew her attacker. Persis pictured the scene. Nadine, seated at the table, chatting away. Her killer, behind her, picks up the knife. No cause for alarm. Why would there be? It was a man Nadine trusted, loved.

John Gallagher.

'There were no fingerprints on the knife,' said Blackfinch. 'The killer ran it under the tap, left it in the sink. We couldn't find any other forensic artefacts worth looking at.'

Nothing to tie Gallagher definitively to the murder, aside from his presence there that evening, and the possibility that he and Nadine had been overheard fighting.

Outside, Blackfinch asked her if she was free for dinner. She hesitated. They'd eaten together on occasion. The truth was, she enjoyed his company, in spite of that odd quirk in his nature that made him pedantic and apt to rearrange his cutlery into straight lines on the table.

And yet...

She made an excuse, then drove off quickly. In the rear-view mirror, she noted the disappointment on his handsome features.

5

'He killed her. I'm sure of it.'

Grace Fonseca was as beautiful as her late sister, if older and more harried. She juggled an infant on her lap, a boy, gazing at Persis with round eyes.

'What makes you say that?'

'Nadine was going to leave him. She'd met someone else.'

'Who?'

'It doesn't matter. He's in Delhi, on business. Has been for a week. This will devastate him.' She switched the child to her knee, bouncing him up and down. He gurgled. 'She finally realised I was right. Marrying an Englishman would be a mistake.'

'Why?'

She raised an eyebrow. 'Do you really have to ask? Some stains can't be washed out, Inspector.'

'Did Gallagher know she was going to break it off?'

'No. Not until yesterday evening. That's why I know he did it. She told him and he reacted by murdering her.' Her face folded into grief. 'I begged her to let me be there when she told him.'

'Had he ever displayed violence towards Nadine before?'

'Does it matter? Men can snap at any time.'

'When was the last time you spoke to her?'

'She called me yesterday afternoon. Just after her shift at the hospital. She was upset, wanted to talk to me about something.'

'About Gallagher?'

'No. Something else. Someone had died at the hospital and it had affected her. I don't know why. People die there all the time. We were supposed to meet up, but I got busy with Merwyn.' She indicated her child. 'I keep thinking that if I'd gone, maybe she'd still be alive.'

'Did she ever mention someone called Black Tom?'

She shook her head.

Persis showed her the photograph. 'Do you recognise any of these men?'

'No.'

6

Breach Candy was a new hospital, barely a few months old, located in the upmarket area of Warden Road. The money here was old, old enough that the sins of those who'd built their fortunes from less than savoury enterprises had long since been washed away. Many of the Raj-era bungalows were now occupied by wealthy Indians: businessmen, politicos, movie stars. The nearby Breach Candy swimming baths, once banned to both dogs and natives, were now open to the better class of Indian. Dogs were still not allowed.

Nadine Fonseca had moved to the hospital following a long stint at the Parsee Lying-In Hospital at the Hornby Estate, one of Bombay's first maternity hospitals, and the one that Persis herself had been born in.

She spoke to a woman named Shireen Ali, Nadine's ward supervisor.

'Nadine was a conscientious worker, a very able nurse. She cared. I can't say the same for everyone here.'

'Did she work a full shift yesterday?'

'Yes. Nadine often did extra hours. She never asked for more money. She was here the whole day.'

'Did she mention anything about her relationship with John Gallagher?'

'No. Nadine wasn't one to discuss her personal life. We knew she had an Anglo boyfriend – he came here a few times. But she didn't really talk about him, even when the other girls teased her.'

'What was her demeanour like? Yesterday?'

'She was upset. Not about her boyfriend. One of our patients died. He was very close to Nadine – I believe she knew him. Thought of him as a sort of uncle. She'd been taking extra care of him, but he was doomed from the moment he got here. Cancer. He was only in his fifties. Such a shame. The best we could do was make him comfortable. Nadine would spend every spare minute sitting by him, chatting, listening to his stories.'

'What was his name?'

'Alok. Alok Sinha.'

Her disappointment showed. She'd been hoping the man might be the elusive Black Tom. But Ali had never heard Nadine mention anyone by the name of Tom.

The nurse hesitated. 'There was one thing. It may be nothing … I was passing by Alok's bed on my rounds yesterday. Nadine was there. They were talking but stopped when I arrived. There was something odd about Nadine's demeanour. It wasn't just that she was upset about his impending death. Something else. She was holding a photograph in her hand. I didn't catch what it was; she quickly stuck it in her pocket. I think Alok gave it to her.'

She went back to visit Gallagher. He was sitting on his cot, picking at a bowl of rice and lentils. The food was practically uneaten, possibly because jailhouse rations were not to his taste, but more likely because his appetite had deserted him.

'Grace Fonseca says that Nadine was having an affair. That she'd decided to leave you.'

He put down his wooden spoon. 'Grace has never liked me. Or the idea of me. She's prejudiced against whites.' He said this with a straight face.

'You didn't know, did you? About the affair. You found out yesterday when you asked her to marry you and she turned you down. She felt the need to explain.'

He was silent, his brown eyes still and clear behind his spectacles.

'You became angry. You couldn't let her walk away. You picked up the knife, and cut her throat.'

'No.' His hands shook where they gripped the edge of his cot.

7

The case turned a corner that evening, over dinner. Aunt Nussie had turned up, as she did a couple of times a week. Her mother's younger sister had never got on with her father, blaming him, firstly, for eloping with Sanaz, and then for her death, eight years later. Now she blamed him for the even worse crime of permitting her only niece to join the police service. Over a meal of lamb dhansak, she gave Persis her well-worn pep talk, laying out all the ways in which she might be murdered or assaulted in the line of duty.

Her father ate with his head down. Nussie always brought out the worst in him.

Eventually, her aunt got around to asking her what she was working on. Reluctantly, Persis explained the case.

'Black Tom?' said Nussie. 'I used to have a cat by that name.'

The thought stayed with her. Around eleven, having just finished a few chapters of the new Agatha Christie, *A Murder is Announced*, she got up, slipped her sandals on under her shorts and camisole, then wandered down into the bookstore.

The day's heat remained trapped in the store. Summer in Bombay: a sweltering purgatory. The arrival of the monsoon only added to the humidity, making each night a sweat-sticky affair.

Nussie's comment had touched off an idea. What if Tom wasn't the name of a person?

She pulled a selection of encyclopaedias from the shelves: *The Illustrated Encyclopaedia of American Fauna*; Newne's *Family Health Encyclopaedia*; *The Reader's Encyclopaedia of World Literature*; and the *Encyclopaedia Britannica*, of which her father always kept at least two 35-volume sets in the shop – it was a regular seller.

Two hours later, she found what she was looking for.

8

The editor of the *Times of India* was a short man, with a Caesar-like crown of grey hair, square-framed glasses, and a close-cropped moustache.

'How can I help you, Inspector?' He smiled, revealing a missing front tooth, as if he'd recently come off second in a bar-room brawl.

'On July 30th, 1916, a massive explosion occurred in New York harbour, destroying a munitions depot which housed some one hundred thousand pounds of TNT. The explosion killed four people, wrecked warehouses, caused twenty-million dollars' worth of damage, and sent fragments across the harbour, damaging the Statue of Liberty. Windows were shattered twenty-five miles away. One of the dead was a ten-week-old infant.' She allowed him to absorb this. 'The attack happened on a small island in the harbour called Black Tom Island. The island is artificial, created by land fill, and linked to the mainland via a causeway. During the First World

War, it served as a major munitions depot for the north-eastern United States. Until 1915, US munitions companies were at liberty to sell their wares to any buyer. But after the blockade of Germany, sales were restricted to the Allied Powers. Imperial Germany then began to send secret agents to America to disrupt the production and delivery of munitions to its enemies. Black Tom was a principal target.'

The editor, a man named Tilak, spread his hands. 'This is intriguing history, but how is it of relevance to me?'

'The *Times* would undoubtedly have covered the story. I'd like to see old editions from around that period. I'm looking for something very specific.'

9

'Yes, I was part of that investigation. That was more than thirty years ago, of course. I've been retired for the past five.'

Bala Rai had the look of a man who'd lived an eventful life. His lean face was fissured, with a scar running from the right corner of his lip to under his chin. Peppery hair, hard eyes, and the calloused hands of a dock worker.

'The *Times of India* articles that I read suggested Indians may have been involved in the Black Tom explosion. There was a substantial investigation. You were part of the team. I'd like to know what you discovered.'

Rai lit a pipe and puffed on it thoughtfully. 'The initial American investigation identified a Slovak immigrant by the name of Michael Kristoff as the mastermind behind the explosions. Under questioning, he admitted to working for German agents. A later investigation, however, suggested an Indian connection. This was in the wake of a gun-running plot involving India's Ghadar Party, the Irish Republican Brotherhood, and the German Foreign Office – part of the so-called Hindu-German Conspiracy.'

She'd come across the term before, but it was hazy. She asked him to elaborate.

'I'm referring to the series of actions carried out between 1914 and 1917 by Indian nationalists to foment rebellion against the British during World War I. Indian exiles and rebels formed the Ghadar Party in America and the Berlin Party in Germany. Their aim was to push for Indian Independence. The Germans were only too happy to help. What's that old saying? My enemy's enemy is my friend.' He grimaced. 'In May 1917, eight members of the Ghadar Party were tried in America on charges of conspiracy to form a military enterprise against Britain. The British hoped that the conviction of the Indians would result in their deportation from the United States back to India. The Americans refused. Public support had swung in favour of the Indians. The Black Tom explosion was one of the plots they were accused of involvement in.'

'Do you remember the Indians involved?'

'Yes. Though we didn't get them all.'

'What do you mean?'

'Eight Indians were tried, but we came to believe that a number of others escaped the net, including those who were there on the night of the Black Tom attack, helping Kristoff to plant the explosives. Two brothers were identified, Bal Singh and Tej Singh. Both were known to have returned to India, but were never caught.'

'Did you obtain photographs of them? Back then?'

'Yes.'

She took out her notebook, showed him the photograph she had found in Nadine's apartment.

Rai looked at it for a long time. 'Yes,' he said, eventually, 'that's them. The white man in the middle is Michael Kristoff.'

She tapped the photograph. 'This one on the left. The one with two distinctive moles beside his right ear. Which of the brothers was he?'

'That's Bal Singh.'

10

The door swung back to reveal Rishi Sharma in white pyjamas and a collarless Nehru shirt. He blinked myopically at her, then invited her in.

He'd been listening to the radio, a musical show, which he now turned off.

'Would you like some tea?'

'No.' He lowered himself into a seat and motioned at the sofa before him.

'I'll stand if you don't mind.' She looked around the room. It was neat, but sparsely decorated. A few potted plants. A painting on the wall of three women carrying clay pots in a field. A short bookshelf, crammed with old volumes. A magazine with a car on the cover lay on the wicker coffee table. 'Do you live alone?'

'My wife passed away four years ago. I have a daughter. Our only child. She lives with her husband. They have two children, a boy and a girl.' He smiled, and there was genuine warmth in his eyes.

'The guard at the gate says that your cousin lived with you. I confirmed the same with your neighbour, Sheela. You were exceptionally close, she says. She remarked on how you even resembled one another.'

Something went out of him, then. His shoulders sagged.

'His name was Alok,' she continued. 'He passed away yesterday.'

He said nothing.

'He wasn't your cousin, was he?' she said. 'He was your brother. Your real name is Bal Singh. Which would make him Tej Singh.'

His head dropped. He was silent for so long, she thought he had fallen into a trance. He lifted his chin and looked straight at her. 'Gandhi once said that confession of one's guilt purifies the soul. But there are some things a man should take to the grave. Between Tej and Nadine I was really left with no choice, you have to see that. It wasn't for myself that I was afraid. It was my daughter. My grandchildren. How will they live with the scandal?'

'You and your brother participated in the Black Tom attack. How did you evade capture for so many years?'

'We were young, idealistic. But what happened that night…' He sighed. 'We killed an infant. We didn't intend to, but we were responsible, nonetheless. When we returned to India, we changed our names, and parted ways. We each made new lives for ourselves, abandoned the Independence struggle. Four years ago, my brother found me again. His wife had left him years earlier. His son barely knew him. He was haunted by the ghost of that dead child.' He grimaced. 'He told Nadine yesterday, just before he died. And he gave her that photograph. Is that how you found me?'

She tapped her cheek. 'The moles.'

He nodded, understanding. 'She came to me last night, after her Anglo had left. Asked me to go with her to the authorities, so that I might confess. Nadine had the sort of conscience that would never have let her rest. She has known me for years, but the only thing that mattered to her was that I had once murdered a child. I had to answer for my crime. She had the notion that somewhere in America a mother was still waiting to know that her baby's killer had been found.' He sighed. 'I asked her to give me a little time to think it through. She went back to her flat. When I turned up, some fifteen minutes later, we talked. She sat down at the table. I was at the sink. The knife just seemed to leap into my hand. I have no conscious memory of making the decision to murder her. It just … happened.'

Vaseem Khan

Vaseem Khan is the author of two crime series set in India, the Baby Ganesh Agency series, and the Malabar House historical crime novels. His first book, *The Unexpected Inheritance of Inspector Chopra*, was a *Times* bestseller, now translated into fifteen languages, and introduced Inspector Chopra of the Mumbai police and his sidekick, a one-year-old baby elephant. The second in the series won a Shamus Award in America. In 2018, he was awarded the Eastern Eye ACTA (Arts, Culture and Theatre Award) for Literature. Vaseem was born in London, but spent a decade in India as a management consultant. Since 2006 he has worked at University College London's Jill Dando Institute of Security and Crime Science. The first book in his new series is *Midnight at Malabar House*, set in Bombay 1950 and introducing Persis Wadia, India's first female police detective. It was published by Hodder & Stoughton in August 2020.

Monsters

Clare Mackintosh

I'm not allowed to touch the cellar door.

There are lots of rules in our family (don't use all the hot water; close your mouth when you're eating; no pudding till you've finished your main) but not touching the cellar door is the biggest one.

'Are there monsters?' I asked once.

'Yes,' Dad said, just when Mum said the opposite. She gave Dad one of her looks.

'There are no such things as monsters. It's dangerous, that's all. You could get hurt.'

She turned away and Dad made claws of his fingers, opening his mouth in a silent roar. I giggled, but my tummy did a flip because what if there really were monsters?

The cellar door is old, like the house, with paint that flakes off when you touch it. I squat on the floor, fingernails picking at the years. Underneath the cream paint is a blue I remember Dad painting on, but beneath that is a red I don't. Under the red is more blue, then green. It's funny to think of all those colours hiding behind the fresh paint, like secrets.

'Come away from the door, now.'

'I wasn't going to open it.'

'Even so. Come away.'

'Because of the monsters?'

Mum tutted. 'Honestly, your father…'

I couldn't open the cellar door, even if I wanted to. The key – dull and worn, the size of a chicken bone – hangs from a hook too high for anyone but a grown-up to reach. Sometimes Dad slips it into his pocket, or Mum leaves it on the side when she's fetching something for tea, complaining all the time about how *the cellar stairs'll be the death of me*. But it's never close enough for me to take, and even if it was, I wouldn't dare. Mum might say there are no such things as monsters, but I know different. I've seen *Monsters Inc.* and *Scooby Doo*. I've read dozens of books Mum gets from the library, and even though some monsters are friendly, there are lots that aren't. And I won't know what kind lives in our house, until I open the cellar door – and then it'll be too late.

They'll have three heads. Or six. Or no heads at all. They'll be eight feet tall, with tentacles for arms, like the octopus in *The Little Mermaid*. Or they'll be tiny. An army of mouse-sized monsters, jabbing at my ankles with needle swords, like in *Gulliver's Travels*. Or they'll be invisible. Or, or, or…

My dreams are filled with dragons and beasts; with bug-eyed aliens, and giant slugs that leave trails of slime so thick I drown in them. I wake in the darkness, sweat sticking my hair to my cheek, a scream escaping before I realise it isn't real. Sometimes Mum comes running, pulling me close, her breath a *shhhh* in my ear as she rocks me to and fro.

'She'll wake the whole neighbourhood,' Dad says. I don't know what time it is, but Mum's in pyjamas, her feet bare. Dad's silhouetted in the doorway, his shadow stretching towards me across the bedroom floor. His face is in darkness, so I can't see if he really cares more about the neighbours than me, or if it's just another one of his jokes.

'And whose fault will that be?' Mum snaps. 'Monsters, indeed.'

'Sorry, love. Hey, Isobel, sweetheart, there are no such things as monsters, OK?'

'But there *are!*' I'm still half asleep, still clinging to Mum. Dad moves, releasing a beam of light that follows him as he crosses the room and sits on the end of my bed.

'Think about it,' he says. 'If there were monsters—'

'Pete.' A warning, from Mum. *Don't upset her.*

'If there were monsters, we wouldn't go in at all, would we? We'd smoke them out, like we did when we had that wasps' nest – do you remember? Or we'd scare them by banging pots and pans really loudly, and chase them outside into a cage disguised as a van—'

'Like the child-catcher in *Chitty Chitty Bang Bang!*' I sit up, excited.

'Exactly! And he'd drive them away and put them in prison—'

'No! They might escape.' I think for a bit. 'Push them off a cliff.'

Dad laughs. 'OK, he'd push them off a cliff.'

'Peter!' Mum doesn't like it when Dad gets *carried away.*

He sighs, then winks at me. 'But, as you can see, none of that is happening. So: no monsters, OK?'

'No monsters,' I repeat. And even as I say it, I feel silly for even thinking it. I hug them both, and when I fall back to sleep there are no slime-filled slugs, or bug-eyed aliens. Even so, I'm glad Mum and Dad aren't far away. Just in case.

For a while, I forget about the door. Without monsters hiding behind it, it isn't scary, but that makes it kind of boring, too. It's just a door, like the one that leads to my bedroom, or the one on the bathroom with the hook for my towel. There are more interesting things to think about, like what I'd call a kitten, if Mum and Dad ever let me have one.

'There's too much traffic around here,' Mum says, when I ask for the millionth time. 'He'd get run over.'

'I'll keep him indoors, then. I'll make him a climbing frame, and he can sleep on my bed. Please?'

'It wouldn't be fair. Cats need gardens.'

Up until now, Dad's kept quiet, but I can see him thinking, and my heart gives a little skip. He can be strict, but he's always treating me, or bringing flowers and chocolates home for Mum. She calls him a *big softie*, but she loves it really.

'I guess…' he says slowly, almost to himself. 'If it were a kitten, it wouldn't know any different. You can't miss what you've never had.' He's looking at Mum, and there's a long pause, like they're passing invisible words to each other, and I know – I just know – they're going to say yes.

'We'll see.'

I hug the possibility to myself. My own kitten! I imagine him curled up on my lap, following me wherever I go. I'll make pom-poms and tie them on the door handles so he can play with them, and I'll make a mouse for him from the felt in my sewing box. I'm really good at sewing. Mum taught me, and it's my favourite thing in the whole world. I've made loads of hair scrunchies, and even a skirt, although it's a bit wonky. Right now, I'm making a teddy out of one of Dad's shirts.

'I need some ribbon – there isn't any in the craft box.'

'Let me see what I can find.' Mum takes the cellar key from her pocket. She leaves the door open, and as her footsteps grow quieter I glance at Dad, wondering what he'd do if I made a run for it – just to see for myself what they keep there. Then I think about how much I want a kitten, and I wait for Mum to come back. She brings a cardboard box full of fabric scraps and clothes I've grown out of, and we sit on the floor and start to go through it.

'Remember this?' She holds up a T-shirt with a sequin rainbow on the front. 'You cried when it got too small for you. And this?' Mum's eyes go all sparkly as she pulls out my old clothes. I dig around and find a blanket, tatty and already cut up. It's finished with a ribbon, sewn around the edges, and as I rub it between my fingers I feel the tug of a forgotten memory.

'Was this my baby blanket?'

Dad looks across. 'We still have that?'

'You know what I'm like,' Mum says. 'I don't like to waste anything. I used the middle for dusters, and this ribbon is lovely – will it do for your teddy, Isobel?'

'It's perfect.'

I spend the rest of the afternoon sewing shiny circles for the insides of my bear's ears, and every so often I stop to rub the length of leftover ribbon between my fingers. There's a washing label at one end, and tucked inside it is faded black writing. *Alice Marshall.* I wonder how old Alice is now, and whether she liked to stroke the ribbon too. Almost all my clothes are hand-me-downs. I like looking for the names, on posh sewn-on labels, or scribbled with biro on a hem. *Madeleine, Samira, Katy.* I make up stories about them: what they look like, their favourite games. Sometimes I pretend they're my sisters. In bed at night, I whisper to them in the darkness, and if I listen really hard, they whisper back.

Later, when we're having tea, I sit my finished bear next to me. There aren't any spare chairs because we never have anyone over, so I put him on the table, propped against my water glass.

'Is there any more mustard?' Dad says. 'This one's empty.' We're having sausage and mash, with onion gravy and bright green peas.

'I think there's another jar,' Mum says. She takes the key from her pocket.

'I'll go,' I say quickly. 'I'm not scared of monsters anymore.' Mum gives me 'the look', and I feel a flash of anger. 'I'm not a baby! I won't fall down the stairs, and I won't touch anything except the mustard.'

'No.' Mum is quiet but firm. 'It's dangerous.'

'So come with me, then! I just want to see!' My voice tips into pleading, but it doesn't make a difference.

'You,' Dad says, punctuating every word with a pointed finger. 'Don't. Go. Near. That. Door. Do you understand?'

'You know that,' Mum says.

'OK!'

Dad gets the mustard on his own. For a second, the door's ajar, and I see the flicker of light; hear Dad's shoes on the stone steps. Then he's gone.

'We could watch a film after tea, if you like?' Mum's voice is jittery. I crane my neck, but the cellar steps turn a corner, and all I can see is shadows. 'Or play a game?'

'Maybe.'

We finish our meal in silence. Every now and then I see him and Mum exchanging glances, and I know they're cross with me. I'm cross with myself. What if they don't let me have a kitten? Mum chews the inside of her lip, the way she does when she's anxious.

'Tell me about when I was a baby,' I say.

Instantly, a smile spreads across her face. 'You've heard it a million times.'

'Please.' I'm not only asking for her. I love the stories of when I was tiny, when I slept in a drawer because I came before they were ready, and when I'd only sleep if I had a finger to hold.

'You literally had us wrapped around your little finger,' Dad says.

They spoil me, I know that. It took them ages to have me. Mum won't talk about it, but I know there were other babies, before me. Babies who died. When they finally brought me home, Mum didn't put me down for a week.

'She used to just gaze at you,' Dad says now. His eyes go all soft, and he squeezes Mum's hand. 'You were everything she'd ever wanted.'

'You still are,' Mum says.

'Do you wish you had more children?'

Mum shakes her head so quickly, and so firmly, I know it's a lie.

'Even once you knew I was sick? Didn't you want another baby? One who—'

'No.' She puts her hand over mine. 'You were perfect. You are perfect.'

I know that's not true. Sometimes I imagine what it would be like to be a normal kid. I think about the children in the books I read, and in the films I watch with Mum and Dad. I imagine running and jumping, dancing and climbing, and I want it so badly I can almost *feel* it.

But I don't get to do that. I have a rubbish immune system that means I can't stay awake for longer than a couple of hours without a nap, and allergies so bad I could stop breathing just from going outside. Pollen, dust mites, sunlight… A sudden fear grips me: what if I'm allergic to cat hair? I have medicine to stop my skin itching, so even if I am, maybe the medicine will make it OK.

Mum and Dad never moan when they have to rub ointment on my back in the middle of the night, or sit with me when my chest feels tight. They don't complain that we can't go on holiday, or lie on a beach when the weather's good. So I try not to complain, either.

Our life is small, Mum always says, *but small can be good.*

And she's right. I like our small life. I like that it's quiet, and that it's always me and Mum and Dad. *The Three Musketeers*, Dad says. We have breakfast together, and then Dad goes to work, and Mum and I clear the table and set out our school stuff.

'What do you feel like learning today?' she always asks. Because that's the brilliant thing about home schooling – we can do whatever we want. Some days we do nothing but drawing – watching YouTube tutorials and practising on thick, creamy paper – and other days we chant our times tables or learn about rivers, or make pie charts of endangered species. I watch kids going to school on TV, and sometimes I get a pain in my chest, like when Mum goes out and I don't know when she'll be back. A sort of homesickness, even though I haven't gone anywhere. Then I imagine being in school, with everyone running around and me having to sit on the side of the playground, and even that exhausting me.

'You wouldn't be able to handle it.' Mum always looks sad when we talk about it. I guess she wishes I could go too; wishes I was like other kids.

As my birthday gets closer, I can hardly sleep for excitement. I don't ask about the kitten again, but I make a collar from the rest of the blanket ribbon, and keep it under my pillow. I squeeze my eyes shut and wish so hard it hurts. Ten is definitely old enough for a kitten, isn't it?

When I wake up, there's a second when I don't remember what day it is, only that something important is happening. I lie there, blinking, then it comes to me in a flash and I leap out of bed. I run into the sitting room just as Mum and Dad are coming in too, and I throw myself at them.

'Happy birthday, Isobel!'

'Ten years old – I can hardly believe it.'

I open their card, then Dad hands me a package. It's the size of a shoebox, and the lid – held on with a fat purple ribbon – is punched with tiny holes. Inside the box, something shifts, and I clutch at the box, scared it'll unbalance. I gasp, look up at my parents. 'Is it—?'

Mum laughs. 'Have a look.'

The kitten is ginger, a tiny ball of fluff and claws. He runs up the back of the sofa, and swings on the tea towel till it comes off the hook. He begs for tummy tickles, then closes his legs around my fist, sharp spikes digging into my skin. I call him Tiger, and he is everything I ever wanted.

A few days after my birthday, Tiger and I are playing catch. Tiger is brilliant at catching, but not much good at throwing, so a lot of the game is trying to get the ball back from him. Dad's at work, and Mum sat down with a cup of tea just for a minute or two at least half an hour ago. She was watching me play with Tiger, but her eyes slowly closed, and now she's letting out little snores. I try to play quietly, so as not to disturb her, but Tiger digs his claws into me and I yelp. Mum yawns and stretches, but doesn't wake. As she shifts position, there's a gentle *thud*. I look over, and my eyes widen.

On the rug beneath her chair is the key to the cellar door.

I look at Tiger. I couldn't.

Could I?

Mum's sound asleep. I could just open it, just a tiny bit, just to peek inside. Just to *know*.

Should I?

My head's saying no, but somehow my body is inching closer to the key, my eyes fixed on Mum. I slide it into my fist. Slowly, without standing up, I shuffle across the room. If she wakes, I'll throw the ball for Tiger. I'm still in the room, I'm not breaking any rules. Not yet.

The key turns easily. Quietly. I hold my breath.

Monsters.

The thought comes in without warning, and I push it away. *No such thing as monsters*, I remind myself, summoning Dad's voice to give me confidence. I'll just open the door. I won't even take a step. I'll just open—

'Isobel!'

I scream. At the shout from behind me, at the rush of air as Mum grabs me and drags me back.

At what I saw on the other side of the cellar door.

'How dare you!' I've never seen Mum like this, spitting anger at me, leaning over me, her face all flushed. Her eyes are wild, her fist twisted in the fabric of my jumper, pushing me against the wall. She's flapping her free arm behind her, reaching for the door, trying to slam it shut, but before she can, there's a flash of ginger fur.

'Tiger!' I cry. Mum releases me and I run to the door, snatching at the handle, but Mum has her foot jammed against the bottom.

'Go to your room!'

'But Tiger!'

'Now!'

I run to my room and throw myself on my bed. My head is spinning, and I don't understand why Mum's so angry, why she seems so scared. I want Tiger back, but more than anything I want to know why my parents are hiding a proper room behind a locked door. Why there's a table in there, and chairs. Why it looks like people *live* there.

I'm too scared to come out. I hear Dad come home, and angry voices I know are about me. I cry for Tiger, and because I'm hungry and scared, and eventually my door opens, and Dad comes in.

'You did a bad thing today.'

'I'm sorry.'

'You know that door is off limits.'

'I saw—'

'You saw nothing!' He shouts so loud I feel it in my ears, and I start crying again. 'What did you see?'

I think of that table, and the four chairs. The cooker, the fridge. I whisper. 'Nothing.'

There's a long silence. 'Good girl.' He clears his throat. 'I'm afraid Tiger's gone.'

I jump up, a pain in my chest. 'Gone?'

'There's a window jammed open in the…' he tails off. 'In there. He must have got out. I've been out looking for him but…' Dad drops his voice. 'I'm so sorry, Isobel, I know how much you loved him.'

I push my face into my pillow and sob. I think I might die from missing Tiger. I think my heart might stop, and I don't care if it does. I hate my parents. I hate them for keeping secrets, and for losing Tiger, and for making me with this stupid body that means I can't go and look for him.

I sleep fitfully. In my dreams I'm trapped in a box, the sides shrinking and the air growing thinner with each breath. I'm hammering on the lid, but the space tightens around me, pinning my arms still. My fingers tear uselessly at the wood, the sound a feeble scratch, yet from somewhere the hammering continues. *Bang, bang, bang.*

I pull myself from sleep, sticky with fear and tears, arms flailing around me. I'm still in my bed. I'm safe.

Bang, bang, bang.

Where is the noise coming from? I think of the table and chairs I saw and a chill runs through me. Does someone really live there, behind that locked door? Are they trying to get out?

I switch on my bedside light and swing my legs out of bed. I pad across the room and down the narrow hallway to the sitting room with the table in one corner where we eat and do schoolwork. My heart is pounding, the rhythm copying the thumping I can hear, and as I draw nearer to the sound, my blood runs cold.

The cellar door is rattling.

I turn and run, and as I open my mouth to scream I hear my mother scream, too. I hear my father yelling *Get away from the door!* but I don't need telling because as I run I hear the splintering of wood and something is coming, something loud and strong and—

Monsters.

My legs are pumping but the noise is getting louder, and as I turn the corner into my room there are heavy footsteps, thudding after me, faster than I can run. I slam the bedroom door and slide to the floor, reaching blindly for the light switch and rolling under the bed. Where are my parents? Has the monster already got them? I want to cry out for them, but I mustn't be heard, mustn't make a sound.

The monster's footsteps slow down. Stop. I picture him standing in the sitting room, looking around. Sniffing the air.

'It's some kind of a lounge.'

I freeze. There must be two of them. Maybe more. This one – the one that escaped, the one roaming around our house – is calling to someone.

'Sofa, TV, table and chairs. Some kids' toys.'

My head spins. Why is he describing our house? In my nightmares, the monster never spoke. Roared, yes. Groaned and slavered; breathed fire, even. If I'd ever imagined him speaking, I might have heard a growl, like the voice Dad does for the troll in *Billy Goat's Gruff*. 'Who's that tripping over my bridge?' But this monster doesn't sound like a monster.

He sounds like a man.

'Looks like they all eat here – it's laid for breakfast. Three bowls, three mugs. A blackboard – it looks like they've been doing schoolwork... *Jesus Christ.*'

This last is muttered under his breath. I think of Kevin McCallister in *Home Alone*, hiding from the burglars as they walk around his house. There are no *Home Alone* traps here, no ambushes or sharp tacks on the floor; no swinging irons. Just me, shaking under my bed as a strange man moves around in the next room, calling out everything he sees.

'There's a door!'

My door.

'I'm going in.'

I hear the click of a handle, and I can't help it, a whimper escapes. I clap my hand over my mouth, but it's too late.

'There's someone here!'

Mummy, Daddy, Mummy, Daddy... I'm crying now, not even sure if it's in my head or out loud, but it doesn't matter now, because the big light is on and it's too late, he's in my room. The man. The monsters. Black boots by my bed, the duvet pulled back and dropped on the floor. And then the boots are replaced by knees, and by hands reaching under the bed, and I start to scream. I scream and I scream as he pulls me out, and I'm kicking and fighting him, but he's stronger than me and I'm so scared, I'm so scared—

'Mum! Dad!'

'Shh,' the man says. 'It's OK. We'll take you to Mum and Dad, OK? Everything's going to be all right, I won't let anything bad happen to you.'

Doesn't he understand? It's happening *now*.

'Dad!' I scream as loud as I can, and I try to hit the man in the big boots, but he's holding me tight.

'Did you lose a little cat?'

I stop. Stare at him.

'Cute little ginger fella?'

'Tiger.' It comes out like a breath and I say it again. 'Tiger. He got out … I let him out by mistake, and he got lost.' I start crying again. 'It was my fault.' The man lowers me gently until I'm sitting on the edge of the bed, then he crouches so he can look into my eyes. His face is kind.

'Tiger's safe. He's at the police station right now, and when we've had you checked over you can see him.'

I realise the man is wearing a uniform. 'Are you a doctor? I'm not sick.'

He gives a funny smile. He blinks a couple of times, fast, like he has something in his eyes. 'I'm a police officer. Someone a couple of streets away found your cat. She was looking on his collar for a number to call, and she found your name instead. We've come to take you home.'

Alice Marshall.

I frown. 'My name is Isobel. And I'm already home.'

The policeman squeezes my hand. He takes a deep breath. 'Your name is Alice Marshall, and you've been down here for almost ten years.'

There is a whole house above our home. A house I never knew existed, that stretches around and above the room I believed to be a storeroom; the room I glimpsed when I climbed the cellar steps and opened the door with my stolen key. The world I thought was small is not small at all, and as the policeman leads me out of the cellar, I start to cry. Someone wraps a crinkly silver blanket around my shoulders.

'They've dug out an entire floor,' I hear the policeman say to a woman. 'Wallpaper, lights, the works. Looks like she's not set foot outside since she was taken.'

I feel my legs wobble.

Strong arms catch me before I fall, but everything swirls into nothing.

'How could they do that to her?' I hear the woman say. 'It's monstrous.'

Monsters, I think, as my eyes close. *I always knew there were monsters.*

Clare Mackintosh

Clare Mackintosh is a former police inspector and the *Sunday Times* and *New York Times* bestselling author of *I Let You Go, I See You, Let Me Lie* and *After the End*. Her books are translated into more than forty languages and have sold in excess of two million copies. Her new thriller, *Hostage*, will be published in 2021.

Terrestrial

John McCullough

If the hotels of Regency Square are crying
after rain, it's only self-pity. Each pretends
the others don't exist, just as most never think

about the giant car park secreted under grass,
lone Corsas that slink away at dawn.
Locals try to forget the junkie on crutches

who crammed his belly with buttercups,
died of multiple organ failure, a pebble's throw
from where Oscar and Bosie were shaken like dice

when their horse-drawn carriage smashed
into railings. *An accident of no importance*,
Oscar quipped. Why, then, does the moment

keep replaying in my mind today, walking home
on Holy Wednesday? After Oscar died,
the disownment. Lord Douglas stumbled

through marriage and prison then returned,
holed up streets from here with Mother. He avoided
sun, tunnelled into memory to document his youth.

Did he watch the crash repeat, feel their torsos
collide, long fingers twisting down Oscar's back
before they climbed out and stood separately

close to where needles still burrow into veins,
where a seagull's outlandish dance never fails
to bring worms to the surface?

John McCullough

John McCullough lives in Hove. His latest book of poems, *Reckless Paper Birds* (Penned in the Margins) won the 2020 Hawthornden Prize for literature and was shortlisted for the Costa Poetry Award. The Costa judges said 'This collection – hilarious, harrowing and hyper-modern – offers a startlingly fresh insight into vulnerability and suffering.' In the *Times Literary Supplement*, Head Judge for the Hawthornden, Christopher Reid, described it as 'a rare literary phenomenon ... a frank and militant declaration of joy'. McCullough has won other awards including the Polari First Book Prize and his collections have been named Books of the Year in the *Independent*, the *Guardian* and the *Observer* as well as his work often appearing in magazines such as *Poetry London*, *Poetry Review* and *The New Statesman*. He teaches creative writing at the University of Brighton and New Writing South.

Still Life

Paul Mendez

His grandmother's street was calm and spring-like, though it was
October. Residents he didn't recognise were out on their concrete
driveways, vacuuming their cars or binning rubbish. Her neighbours,
both sides, were quiet Pakistani families who watched an ambulance
take her away one night and had begun to suspect she wasn't coming
home; one of the elders, polishing his windscreen, nodded at him
solemnly as he passed by jangling his keys. *How is she?* said the
neighbour. *Good*, he said. *Cheers.* He tipped his head down to
discourage further questioning; she hated the idea of her neighbours
knowing her business. She would make him take a plastic carrier bag
with him to the shop, so that nobody would see him coming back
with a kilo of flour or loaf of hardo bread.

He unlatched the weathered little wooden gate. Everyone knew
that sound, a high click, and if there was someone in the front room,
they would look through the window and see that it was him. It was
the sound of home, and one of contention, because the gate had to
be shut properly. Not hastily, making too much noise, but with care,
especially as in recent years it had expanded and now needed lifting
into the latch, which he did even though she wouldn't be there to
shout at him. He ticked himself off, internally, for only respecting
her neuroses now she was on her deathbed.

Her garden was shockingly unkempt. Never in his life had he seen it like that. She was so proud. Inside could be in any state and nobody would know, but they would judge her, walking past, if her garden wasn't tip-top. She took care of it like she did her nails. Strong weeds had sprung from the gravel up to mid-thigh, hardier than any shrub. *I'll clear all this for her*, he told himself. *Even if she'll never know.* The familiar creak of the front door opening. Nobody had smoked in this house for twenty years but traces of the smell, deep in the blackened carpets, still rose to greet him. Home.

For a moment, he forgot. He was looking forward to sitting in the front room, reading the paper, ignoring the horse racing or whatever was on TV and drinking a nice cup of tea until his grandmother came in with a miraculous tray of cooked food – pork, boil dumplin and potatoes in a rich sauce, perhaps. *You want some hot pepper?* she would ask. *Yes please*, he would say, and she would go to fetch it for him, barefoot, feet hip-width apart. When he was finished, he'd take his plate back into the kitchen where she would be sitting at the table doing her wordsearch, waiting for the race she'd bet on to start; she'd tell him to leave it in the sink, and to draw more tea for himself if he wanted it.

He opened the front-room door expecting any number of faces to look up at him in surprise at his return. Silence. He closed it, went to hang up his bag and coat. The kitchen was a mess: cupboard doors open; piles of unopened mail on the table; remnants of stale bread and Jamaican bun; unwashed plates in the sink; a black sack overflowing with KFC packaging and two-litre Pepsi bottles, next to the bin; a multipack of Walker's Crisps with only the Ready Salted left. *As soon as her back is turned*, he thought, *this is how they treat her house. How upset she would be by it.* Pans on the stove, tantalising. He lifted the frying pan lid and would have been overjoyed to find leftover ackee and saltfish. Empty. Dry. Not even a hint of flavour. He would've licked it clean. He wished for one last five-course meal of ackee and saltfish with bacon and fried dumplin, followed by currygoat, rice'n'peas and a side of red snapper; pot-roast chicken and hard food; dutch-pot beef with white rice; still-warm *toto* for dessert, all washed down with several cups of tea, which tasted better here, somehow, than anywhere, though not as good as back when she used creamy long-life milk.

Of course, the kettle had been taken to the hospice. He could heat up the water in a pan but it wouldn't be the same. He didn't think to dig out the old stove kettle from the back of one of the cupboards. She took care of all her things, and never threw anything away. But she wasn't here, and nobody else could feed him like she did.

He hadn't told her he loved her. Well, he had, but in that slightly mocking *love ya, Nan!* kind of way people use when they'll see them again in a day or two, that saves face if the subject fails to reciprocate, and because there were other people in the room, watching. Nobody in their family ever said *I love you* to one another. It just wasn't the done thing. He tried to imagine them saying it at their weddings, even, and nothing.

He sat down in the front room and considered ordering from Costa on Deliveroo, but it seemed wasteful when all he wanted from there was a cup of tea. Opposite the run of simple terraced houses was a wild bank choked with weeds and wiry, knotted trees. The sun shimmered in through them, illuminating columns of dust motes, and on to the back wall. He looked around at objects he had known and taken for granted all his life. He wanted them to tell him what he had missed, being away so long, having moved away at eighteen and only been back perhaps a dozen times in the twenty years since. He had never known his grandmother's front room to be so quiet; even when there had been no one else in the house, both televisions would still be on, here and in the kitchen. His uncle, the younger, as soon as the carers at the hospice informed the family they were no longer going to give her food or drink, unplugged the front room telly and Sky+ receiver and put them in his car – they were in his name, in fairness. Here and there a framed picture had been removed to the hospice – leaving only a halo of dust and grime on the wall –

as if his grandmother might wake up and think she was at home, surrounded by daughters, granddaughters and nieces, all shouting over each other, nobody waiting for whoever was speaking to finish, the conversation frothing and crashing like waves.

He switched his gaze from one precious object to another, as if expecting to be transported back in time, to when twenty or more people might be packed in this little room, drinking bottles of beer, cans of Mackeson or glasses of Sanatogen wine, telling each other stories, throwing back their heads against the woolly orange antimacassars, slapping their thighs with laughter, waiting for one of the women to bring them their tray of food. These objects – a glass Christian fish; a wooden flamenco dancer in a silky yellow frock with black fringing; a never-used porcelain equestrian teapot; a wall clock that never worked but no one touched because it had lived there since they moved in; his uncle's, the younger, trophies from when he was a promising striker, before he ruptured his cruciate ligaments and had to come back from being told he might never walk again, temporarily losing his mind along the way; a rosy-cheeked china shepherdess with her dog and lambs; a plaque that said CHRIST IS THE HEAD OF THIS HOUSE, though no one in it ever went to church; a little ship in a bottle; the drinks cabinet full of *best* glasses that came out every Christmas – these objects were worthless; they were mass-produced; every Jamaican household had them, but it pained him to feel how much he would miss them, and he regretted that he hadn't learned to drive so he could throw them all into the boot of a car and create still-life installations out of them when he got them back home to London.

Of the things that did have potential resale value, his uncle, the older, had already put his name down for the mahogany chest at the bottom of his grandmother's bed, full of her decades-old, well-kept frocks, that would probably end up being tossed out onto the bed before in turn being stuffed into black sacks and driven to the nearest charity shop or clothing bank. White goods would go to his uncle, the younger, to furnish a flat he'd lived idly in for over a decade. His aunty, the younger, who had been his grandfather's favourite, would be taking the old armchair, which lived under more piles of *good clothes* in the front bedroom. His mother, the eldest, wanted the tumble dryer – goodness knows why, it was so old – and the single bed from the front bedroom that had been brought for his grandfather when he, twenty years earlier, had taken sick, which her grandson could sleep in when he stayed over. His aunty, the middle child, would take whatever she wanted – she hadn't decided yet; she'd been the one organising everything; she was tired, the sort of tired she might never recover from – and the rest would be cleared by the council, who would send in men with great big hands who had never touched these precious things before and didn't know what they meant.

The house would soon no longer belong to them, though in truth it never did. His grandfather's motto had been *If you buy house, them keep you fe life. If you rent, you pay every month, and you never owe them more than that.* They acted as if they might one day just up and decide to return to Jamaica, but they stayed until it was time to die, having raised five children and nine grandchildren. The council would repossess the house after twenty-eight days. She had been ill for a long time, yet nobody had prepared for the medium term. They had grown up here. This was their heritage, their history, their memories. Thirty-seven years they had kept this house and filled it up with things they could never throw away; now they had no choice.

He felt a sudden loss of energy. He was hungry. It was true, what they said: *You can't take it with you.* He noticed the cracks in the ceiling and down the corners where the walls met, and imagined the house crumbling around him under the weight of its hoard, crushing him to death; a house he could not even inherit. As he opened the cupboard door under the sink to take out some black sacks, he could feel his back all but groaning, as hers might have done at the thought of having to clear all this mess. Where would it go? The carrier bags she kept; the glassware, dinner service, cutlery, her little Fulton umbrella by the back door, the ashtrays from when his grandfather used to smoke, piled up in their own little space under the plate cupboard. She hated waste. If she dished up anyone dinner, they would have to scrape the plate. But none of her children could cook like her. Certainly, his mother could not.

Her housecoats hung on the kitchen door, next to a decorative plaque on the wall above the deep-fat fryer, the shape of the island of Jamaica, with the locations of Kingston, Montego Bay and Ocho Rios marked, and the national emblem, the ackee berry, painted on in red, yellow, green and black. Slavery had taken his ancestors to Jamaica against their will, and their descendants' needs had brought them to England – the only place they thought they might be welcome – where they found jobs in factories, moved into one council house after another and filled this last one with cheap shit until they died. He had never been to Jamaica; his parents hadn't either, and so it felt as if his link to that country was dying with his grandmother. Why did he need to stay where *they* chose to, when *his* needs were different?

He realised he was free to leave it all behind – single, gay, childless, an artist, an atheist. He could live anywhere in the world and set down roots of his own, or not at all; migrate out of choice, even if for the same reason his grandparents did: to build a better life. It wasn't going to be up to him to sort and clear all this mess. Her children should have bought the house from the council. None of this stuff belonged to him. He had equivalents for it all where he lived, and he thought, when he returned, he would clear out anything he didn't need, that was not precious to him.

He rolled his shoulders back and stood up tall. He almost just left, but with his bag and coat on, took a tour of the house and photographed every room: his grandmother's bedroom, her sheets exactly as she left them when she was taken away, the tape measure over the door to ward off evil spirits. He zoomed in on the ugly patterned carpets, which had been there since they moved in. He captured ornaments, lampshades, the pictures that had been left up on the wall, her headscarves neatly folded in a drawer; and found her wedding album: she in a high-necked, long-sleeved white dress, concealing her bump; his grandfather looking handsome in his black suit and white gloves. One of them gone, the other, going. Everything they had worked and lived for was about to be cleared to landfill, apart from a few photographs, bits of furniture and jewellery to be shared among their children.

The longer he stayed, the harder it would be to leave. He slipped his phone back in his pocket, ran downstairs and out the front door, locking up and posting the keys through the letterbox. She wouldn't remember or care about the garden. The neighbour had gone back indoors. He carefully lifted the latch onto the gate behind him.

Paul Mendez

Paul Mendez is a London-based Black British novelist, essayist and screenwriter, born in 1982 and raised in the Black Country to Jehovah's Witness parents of second-generation Jamaican heritage. Mendez disassociated himself from the Witnesses while still a teenager. After reading James Baldwin's 1968 novel *Tell Me How Long the Train's Been Gone* in the summer of 2002, Mendez began keeping a journal, maintaining it while occupied variously as a sex worker, waiter and sometime journalist. He has contributed to *Glass, Esquire, The Face, British Vogue*, the *Times Literary Supplement* and the *Brixton Review of Books*. In 2020, Dialogue Books published Mendez's debut novel *Rainbow Milk* to critical acclaim, featuring in the *Observer's* prestigious Top Ten Debut Novels list for 2020, and being shortlisted for the Gordon Burn Prize. He is currently reading the MA in Black British Writing at Goldsmiths, University of London.

A Shallow Pool

David Mitchell

'Well, Bernard,' said my oncologist. 'The news isn't good.'

I held my phone steady. 'How long?'

'A prognosis is only a guess, so—'

'Please, Doctor. How long?'

She sounded exhausted. 'Three months.'

The spines of books filled my vision. 'I see.'

'I repeat: it's only a guess. There are support services. But they're all under the most ungodly strain. This damn virus.'

'I understand. Really.'

'Let me give you a helpline number.'

'Pen at the ready,' I lied. 'Fire away.'

The clock was ticking. Sleet was falling. The last day of January. People walked through Cecil Court. Nobody knew. Nobody cared. Why should they? The living are busy living. I always was. Caring about terminal diagnoses is the business of loved ones and friends.

My problem was, I hadn't led the kind of life that generates loved ones or friends. My parents and brother are long gone. Offspring were never going to happen. The Last Kriebler Standing, that's me. I'd had my quota of lovers back when the sap ran, but had stayed in touch with none of them. People came, people saw, people went before I ever thought of them as 'friend'. My circle of professional acquaintances were dealers, customers and clients. Auctioneers. Specialists. Restorers. Occupiers of niches in the ecosystem. An unpalatable truth came home to roost: a lifetime of cutting myself the best deal – irrespective of the other party's trampled feelings – had withered at the root those very friendships which ensure one does not die alone.

I said it aloud, to ten thousand books.

'I will die alone.'

Spilt milk, burnt bridges. I set about putting my affairs in order, as they used to say. I paid a few outstanding invoices. Collected a few debts. Brought my tax affairs up to date. I didn't tell Cecil Court. The thought of the hoopla, histrionics and vultures made me sicker than I already felt. I did tell my accountant, however. Mr O'Dwyer is discretion itself. If I couldn't avert death, I could at least avoid giving post-mortem headaches to Arkady & Shaw. Whom I telephoned finally a fortnight later in mid-February. Moira Stone picked up on the third ring. She listened to my ill-tidings with Scottish matter-of-factness, expressed her sympathy and arranged to visit the shop the following morning. Which motivated me to begin the most thorough stock-take of Number 24 since I took over from Norbert twenty years ago. I knew my stock better than I know any city, anybody, anything: but I owed it to whoever took over the place to have a coherent catalogue, and a rough estimate of its current worth. It would be a major job. Perhaps my last. I couldn't work as quickly as I once could, and I had to take extra care on the ladders. I was up atop a ladder working through the books above the window when I first saw her.

A young woman, outside, gazing through the glass.

She captivated me. Not by her beauty. This isn't that sort of story. I suppose she was pretty, though her weary eyes and grooved-in frown belonged to an older face. I just felt a connection. A connection I couldn't begin to explain. For one thing, she was – what's the right term these days – black? African-looking? Once upon a time I would have described her as 'Coloured' but that's a no-no nowadays. Her coat was lumpy and misshapen. I guessed she was homeless. She must have sensed my attention. Her eyes shifted from the window, up to mine. It was an odd sensation. I felt like her reflection. Or, as if I wasn't even there.

I looked away, all in a pother.

Then I looked back.

She was gone.

'Good morning, Bernard,' said Moira Stone.

'A nice morning it is too, Moira,' I replied.

'Mild for the time of year.'

'Mild for the time of year,' I agreed.

A street-cleaning machine was trundling up and down Cecil Court, so I ushered the lawyer into the office nook. A pot of Irish breakfast tea was waiting. From her tartan briefcase she produced a slim folder of documents. She explained each in turn. I signed each in turn. We were soon finished. I topped up our cups.

'The owners of the premises,' said Moira, 'wish to cover any palliative medical expenses. They propose a hospice in Greenwich. I've checked it out for you. It's truly world-class.'

'I, uh… Gosh. I guess I'll, uh, see.'

'There's no rush to decide anything.'

'Please convey my gratitude.'

'I shall. They appreciate your diligence.'

'All I've done was source a number of books…'

'A number of extremely rare books – with care and discretion. Which brings me to a final matter.'

I added a little extra milk.

'Any thoughts regarding a successor? Arkady & Shaw has its own recruitment channels, of course, but outgoing incumbents have a hands-on knowledge of both the arrangement and the peculiarities of—' Moira gestured at the shop '—of this old place.'

'I've had a good run,' I said, 'but it's been a solo run. I'm sorry, but no name springs to mind.'

Moira nodded. 'We have a little time yet. Let us know if anyone suitable comes along. One never knows.'

I made an agreeing sort of noise.

'The books know how to look after themselves.'

I assumed she was speaking figuratively.

You could call me a Cecil Court lifer. I began at my father's philately business at Number 3 back in 1967 and switched to rare books, where my heart had always lain, just before the internet torpedoed the stamp market. Norbert was retiring to Provence, and the arrangement offered by the mysterious owners of Number 24 Cecil Court was too generous to turn down. The point being this: over six decades, book lovers, tourists, idlers, short-cutters, the lost, the found, waifs and strays, have passed by my shop window. Hundreds of thousands of faces, all of them forgotten. Why, then, a few afternoons after Moira Stone's visit, when the 'African-looking' woman from the previous week entered the shop, did I have to stop myself blurting out, '*It's you*'?

I managed a neutral, 'Good day.'

'Um... Hi. Hi.'

'Can I be of any assistance?'

'So, there's a book in your window.' A Londoner.

'Which book in particular?'

'Um, *The Magician's Nephew*.' State-educated.

She was definitely homeless. There was a slight odour. How could there not be? My guard went up. This is London. 'Ah, C. S. Lewis. The prequel to *The Lion, the Witch and the Wardrobe*.'

'It's the exact same one I had as a kid.'

'The Bodley Head edition, 1955.'

'Um... I was just wondering ... how much?'

'Four figures, I'm afraid. It's a first edition.'

I was ready for a '*How much?*' or a '*But it's only a book!*'

I was not ready for a total emotional collapse. To my horror, the young woman crumbled, sobbed and shook. Right before my eyes. Pre-diagnosis Bernard would have ushered her outside pronto, ready to assure any witnesses that I was the victim of a Care in the Community Crazy. Pre-diagnosis Bernard would have looked around for a shoplifting accomplice ready to strike while I was distracted. Pre-diagnosis Bernard was however, AWOL. I guided the weeping woman into my office nook where a pot of Assam and a box of Digestive biscuits were waiting.

Just in time, too: Fred McGuffin – his real name – chose that very moment to lug in a suitcase of books acquired from the library of a lesser peer of Cambridgeshire. I sent a silent prayer to the shop to keep our guest *in situ* for the duration. Gossip about Bernard Kriebler taking in the mentally unsound would do us no favours.

None whatsoever.

The young woman emerged only after McGuffin had left. 'I can't even begin to apologise.'

'No need. You look better.'

'God, I'm so embarrassed. You got the full Greek tragedy. No – You must've thought, "*Oh God, this one's a right nutter…*"'

'Feelings come when it suits them, not us.'

'Dad used to read the Narnia books to me when I was little. It was just the two of us. And seeing *The Magician's Nephew* brought it all back. Then you were nice to me, and I … turned to goo.'

'I don't recall being particularly nice.'

'Oh, you've no idea. If you're living rough, people look through you. It's like being dead. 'Cept you still get cold, hungry and wet.'

'You're right,' I admitted. 'I've no idea. Why *The Magician's Nephew*, and not *The Lion, the Witch and the Wardrobe*?'

She scrunched her lips. 'Maybe *The Lion, the Witch and the*

318

Wardrobe was too thuddingly Christian, even when I was eight. Or maybe it's to do with The Wood Between the Worlds.'

'The Wood Between the Worlds?'

'It's in *The Magician's Nephew*. A wood, full of pools. They look shallow, but if you jump into one, *whoosh* – you land in another world. The kids in the book go to a dying world called Charn. And Narnia. And London. But in the wood, you're safe. Your name's gone, but so have your troubles. You're never hungry. It's always summer. Wouldn't it be something to wake up and find all that—' she nodded at the window '—was just one world among a million others.' People passed by. 'That's why I like bookshops and libraries. Shelves full of books are the Wood Between the Worlds. Every book's a shallow pool. Not much to look at, but open it and *whoosh*, you're gone. Another world.'

For the first time in years I used the word, 'Wow.'

'Oh Jesus, now you're positive I'm a nutter.'

'I take it your father's no longer…'

'Nah. No. A while ago. Bit of a release, to be honest. Motor neurone disease. You'd not let a dog suffer like he had to.'

'Perhaps you could get a paperback from Foyles on Charing Cross Road,' I suggested. 'It'll only be ten pounds or so…' I realised I was being an idiot. She didn't have ten pounds, so I took out my wallet and offered her a twenty.

She looked at me as if I had insulted her.

'I'm sorry,' I said, feebly. 'I–I–I didn't mean…'

''S okay,' she mumbled, though it wasn't.

She left the shop without another word.

I felt ashamed, as if I'd failed a test.

Number 24 was disappointed in me.

'Don't be ridiculous,' I told the shop.

The books were disappointed in me.

'But we don't know a thing about her.'

The place told me that wasn't true.

I rushed outside: outside was cold as a glacial lake. I looked left towards Saint Martin's Lane and saw a snogging couple. I looked right toward Charing Cross Road and saw her figure, taking care on the frozen slush. 'Excuse me! Miss! Young lady!'

She turned around. I had a sense of being in an illustration. One by Edmund Dulac, perhaps, entitled, *The Bookseller and the Orphan.* Street lamps glowed a buttery yellow. Sleet speckled the twilight. The young woman waited. 'What?'

'May I ask your name?'

'Why?'

'I'm Bernard.'

'Yeah. Bernard Kriebler.'

I must have registered surprise.

She pointed at my shop sign. 'Elementary, my dear Watson.' Then, 'All right. I'm Flo.'

The cold had its fingers round my throat. 'Look, could you spare me a minute?'

'There's a queue at the Shelter. If I'm not in it, I lose my place. If I lose my place… Look at the weather.'

'Exactly. Half a minute. Please.'

'Why?'

'I have a proposal for you, Flo.'

That was the past. Now it's October. I managed another summer, after all. Greenwich is nice. The Thames slides by at the end of the garden. Everyone's kind. I'm drugged more heavily than a Tour de France cycling squad, but I'm not in pain. Flo's on my sofa. She's nodded off. Bless her. We played cribbage. It's Sunday. She was dubious about my proposal. Three nights' accommodation in return for help with the stocktaking? Strange men don't make such tempting offers to young homeless women without strings attached. I assured her that even back in the days when Eros and Cupid kept me up at night, I was not what you'd call a lady's man.

Flo liked the books. The books liked her. During my bad spell in March, she pretty much ran the shop alone. Her parents were market traders. Deals are in her blood. She hoovers up knowledge. Her memory is Velcro. She reads like an addict. I introduced her to my network of dealers. Many were flabbergasted. Some suspected me of slipping into my dotage. A few underestimated Flo. Once. Customers adore her. She opened a Twitter account for the shop. Sales, glorious sales. Moira Stone took her out to lunch. Both women came back smiling. Flo's keeping the name of the shop. Bernard Kriebler Rare Books will outlive Bernard Kriebler. The future. The past. The present. How quaint. How like the living, to chop up time. Look. See? Down below. There's me. There's Flo. Dappled shade. Always summer. No clock is ticking. The rustle of leaves. Of pages turning. Refracted light. Ripples.

A shallow pool.

David Mitchell

David Mitchell is the author of the novels *Ghostwritten, number9dream, Cloud Atlas, Black Swan Green, The Thousand Autumns of Jacob de Zoet, The Bone Clocks, Slade House* and most recently *Utopia Avenue.* He has been shortlisted twice for the Booker Prize, and won the World Fantasy Book Award, among others. In 2018, he won the *Sunday Times* Award for Literary Excellence, given in recognition of a writer's entire body of work. In addition, David Mitchell together with K.A. Yoshida has translated from Japanese two books by Naoki Higashida: *The Reason I Jump: One Boy's Voice from the Silence of Autism* and *Fall Down Seven Times, Get Up Eight: A Young Man's Voice from the Silence of Autism.* He lives with his family in Ireland.

Key to the Door

Adele Parks

'Here you are. Everyone's been looking for you.'

Lottie tried really hard not to flinch at her dad's comment, but a flare of annoyance shot through her body. All morning people had hunted her down and started the conversation with a similar statement. *'Been looking everywhere for you'; 'Didn't know where you'd got to.'*

Why couldn't they get the hint? She didn't want to be found. She was hiding.

'Your mum wants your thoughts on where to put the balloons. Or your approval of where she's already put them. Or something.' Her dad grimaced playfully. Party planning was not his domain. The office, the golf club, the wine cellar, the cricket scores were the things that held his attention. 'What are you doing skulking around here anyhow?' he asked. Lottie wished she smoked. That would at least explain why she was sat on the gravel between the recycling bins at the side of the house, rather than in the back garden, amid all the activity and industry, helping prep for the party.

The marquee had been up for a week. Her mum, Delia, wasn't going to take any risks with the weather so paid for a longer rental period to ensure there was at least one fine day in advance of the party when they could put it up. In fact, the weather had cooperated beautifully, and they'd had dry days all week and today was scorching hot. A challenge for the caterers and everyone labouring on the party site but exactly what Delia had envisaged twenty-one years ago when she gave birth to Lottie.

The Portaloos and dance floor arrived yesterday. When Mum had said they'd hire Portaloos ('essential for one hundred and fifty guests'), Lottie imagined something basic like you get in festivals; not as filthy, hopefully but straightforward blue boxes that, from the outside at least, looked not unlike the *Doctor Who* Tardis. When the Portaloos arrived, Lottie discovered her mum had booked ones that were clad in pine, to imitate Nordic saunas; they had pictures hanging on the wall, Molton Brown hand soap, and were the size of Lottie's student bedroom (which admittedly, was pretty small for a bedroom, but large for a loo!). There were six of them. They filled the driveway which led to a mini-existential crisis about parking space, which was swiftly resolved as all the neighbours offered their driveways for guests to park on, plus there was ample space on the wide leafy avenue. Perhaps the last wide, leafy avenue in London. The neighbours had been charmingly cooperative because Delia threw out invitations to the party like confetti. Pushing the number of guests closer to one hundred and seventy.

The thought caused Lottie's heart to beat a little faster, her breath to be a little shallower. She wasn't sure she knew one hundred and seventy people. She was certain she didn't know *this* particular one hundred and seventy. Most of the guests were friends of her mum and dad. 'Oh, you remember Yvonne and Gus, they came to all your birthday parties until you were seven and then they moved to Hong Kong. Such a lovely couple; always so interested in what you are doing. They send incredibly interesting Christmas letters.' Her mum had said this, or a variation of this, about twenty times when drawing up the invitation list to Lottie's twenty-first birthday. Actually no, Lottie had zero recall of Yvonne and Gus (or Hattie and Fred, Lydia and Stu or any of her mother's colleagues or her father's golf partners etc., etc.), and who the fuck still sent out Christmas letters? Lottie loathed the not-so-humble-brag that some people sent at the end of the year.

'Gosh, we were thrilled with Zara for coming second in the International Equestrian Federation dressage competition. You can't win them all!!'

'Eddie did some volunteering in India, a much-needed change of scene after spending the term in the golden Gothic towers and steeples of Oxford where he secured his first in astrophysics.'

So, Lottie knew the answer to the question who still sent out Christmas letters? Her parents' friends did. Her parents did. It was the only thing Lottie didn't like about Christmas, watching her mother urgently scan the letters she received, a desperate scavenger. Concerned that one of her friends or associates had beaten her in the race of achieving stuff in life: *a second home in France* – ye Gods! Lottie's family had a timeshare in Spain, it was hard to squeeze that into the Christmas letter more than once. *A Labrador that won Crufts! Should they get a dog? Two daughters engaged!* Two! Lottie was an only child and didn't even have a boyfriend. Never had really, unless you count Kenny Cooper who took her to her sixth-form prom. To this day, Lottie believes her father paid Kenny to escort her – not in hard cash, obviously, that would be vulgar – but with an offer of an internship at her father's accountancy firm. Lottie would have paid hard cash not to have to go to the prom.

The Christmas letters served as a sort of road map for her mother as to what had to be achieved in the following year or years. Pressies, over-eating, excessive drinking, dressing the tree and ice skating at Kew Gardens were all really good fun Christmas traditions. Watching her mother compose their Christmas letter was not. Probably, her mother should have had six children like Nana Betty had, having just one meant that all her hopes and dreams were very focused. Very focused indeed.

Lottie (referred to as Charlotte, in the Christmas letter) had, to date, performed admirably in securing her mum things to include in the letter. A straight sweep of A* grades at GCSE, almost the same at A level, just missed it by a smidge in one of her subjects, but that was balanced by the fact she could play three instruments at Grade-8 level and had around that time taken up Italian '*just for fun*'. Lottie had in fact simply downloaded the Duolingo app; she was able to order a coffee and could most likely ask directions to the Leaning Tower of Pisa if the occasion should arise. Her mother was labouring under the impression that she could read Dante's *Divine Comedy* in the original. Lottie simply didn't have the heart to enlighten her.

Lottie was born on 28th August. The fact she was invariably the youngest in her school year was simultaneously a source of pride and irritation for her mother. Her mother was complex this way. A mass of schisms and contradictions. On many occasions, Delia weighed up the possible advantages for Lottie if she had been the oldest in the following year instead. When Lottie first started school, her mother had repeatedly pointed out to other mothers, teachers, the caretaker, dinner ladies – anyone who would listen – that in fact Lottie had up to twenty-five percent less life experience than some of the other children. 'If only she hadn't come early,' she would say, shaking her head sorrowfully. 'She could have been the oldest in her year.' Lottie agreed that there were some disadvantages to being the youngest in the year: last one to start driving, last one allowed to have a legal pint. As preparations for her twenty-first birthday party came around Lottie realised that there was a far greater disadvantage. Her mother had attended a number of twenty-first birthday parties this year. All the family friends with kids born the same year had celebrated. Mum had taken the opportunity to glean ideas as to what worked ('struck the right note') and what didn't ('a little gauche, there's a thin line between indulgent and tacky'). She had clearly decided that this was to be the best party anyone ever, in the history of humankind, had seen. Stand down Gatsby, step aside the

Vanderbilts, watch this space Elton John. This was the twenty-first birthday party dreams were made of.

Her mother's dreams.

Besides the guest list, her mother organised a live band – Lottie was using the term live in the loosest possible sense, every member was at least fifty! If Lottie had chosen the band, she might have picked one of the ones that she'd listened to jamming in the uni bar for the past three years. Her mother had organised caterers who were going to serve vintage champagne and delicate, largely unidentifiable, canapés. Truthfully, Lottie would have been happier with a few beers and a BBQ for a small bunch of mates. No one knew this because no one had asked and Lottie herself had failed to volunteer the information. That was her own bad. Delia was always commenting on the hopelessness of being 'backward in coming forward'. There was to be a chocolate fountain, an ice-sculpture vodka luge, a candy-floss stall. No one could have anything against any of those things individually but combined it all seemed a bit much. And, at midnight, there would be fireworks.

Lottie feared there really would be. Literally and metaphorically.

She pushed the thought out of her head as she had been doing for months now, since she sat her finals.

Her dad didn't look as though he was going anywhere without her, so she dragged herself up off the ground and followed him, feet trailing as though she was Anne Boleyn being led to her French executioner.

Honestly, Lottie wasn't sure her mother had walked the thin line between elegant and tacky. The colour scheme she had chosen was pink. Not a classy coral, sophisticated cerise or even a poppy fuchsia; she'd plumped for an unapologetic baby-girly pink. The colour scheme reached not only the shiny helium balloons (of which there were very many, aka too many – how were actual people supposed to fit in the marquee?), the pink theme ran to the flowers, streamers, vintage champagne, dance floors, bar stools and lights.

'Do you love it?' Her mum asked. She was suddenly at Lottie's side. Popped up from nowhere, like a little fairy or wicked witch. Lottie could never decide. Either way, something mythical, legendary. Delia asked this question often enough. Normally it was delivered with incredible confidence and clearly rhetorical. 'Do you love the new car?' 'Do you love my choux pastry?' There was never any room for anything other than wholehearted agreement. Besides, how could anyone not like a Jaguar E-Pace being awarded as a company car, and her mum Delia's choux pastry was as good as the original Delia Smith's. Of course it was: Lottie's mum was brilliant at everything. Born to a working-class family with five siblings, she had fought to be noticed. But noticed she had been, as Delia graduated from Cambridge with a double first; at twenty-one she was offered graduate positions in all six of the most prestigious law firms in the UK. Her career had been glittering; she became a partner at thirty-three, just two years after Lottie was born. Her clients were the sort of people that regularly appeared on the Forbes' Rich List. Powerful, formidable, tough billionaires put their trust in her mother's magnificent mind. Yet Delia had never missed one of Lottie's concerts or sports days. She was always there for her daughter. Brilliant working woman, perfect mother. Astonishing.

Intimidating.

Lottie realised her mother didn't intend to be intimidating. She was simply being her. It's just that she was, well, perfect. Effortlessly perfect and that was intimidating. Lottie had grown up with her mother and could vouch for the fact that her genius and style were both genuinely effortless. She was not a swan, all grace and elegance above water, peddling at a rate of knots, to give the impression of serenity below. Delia really did glide. Delia accepted compliments with a breezy entitlement. Naturally, she was good at arranging flowers, who wasn't? Yes, she was able to fluently sign, it wasn't clever of her, one of her aunts had been stone deaf, it was just sensible. Of course she was adequate at bridge (read unbeatable) and chess (read schoolgirl national champion), it was just a bit of fun. Didn't everyone play? Since Delia was naturally flawless at just about everything, she had no idea that others might not be. That others might strive and struggle even to keep their heads above murky mediocre waters.

Lottie feared that she was not even a swan. Left to her own devices she was most likely a bit of a duck, bobbing along.

But bobbing along wasn't enough for a daughter of Delia's. There were benchmarks to reach, standards to meet, records to hold. Lottie had done her best: the school grades, the music lessons, the law degree maybe not from Cambridge but no one could fail to be impressed by Warwick University which had been Lottie's first choice. Her one stand in life was refusing to follow her mother to *matris collegium*. She hadn't dared to say that she thought the ancient universities weren't her bag, instead she'd insisted Warwick had a course that she found particularly stimulating.

Her mother accepted academic challenge as a sound motivator; she would have been less impressed by an assertion that wearing gowns for dinner made Lottie feel oddly nauseous.

Through a Herculean effort Lottie had managed to secure a first-class degree. Not a double first like her mother. A straightforward first. 'Don't be an idiot,' Bel, Lottie's flatmate had said, laughing. 'There's no such thing as a straightforward first. It's a massive thing!' Indeed, the effort needed to attain the grade had almost killed Lottie, and she wouldn't have been able to do it if it wasn't for Bel's sense of humour, unfailing support and encouragement. Lottie had not been offered six graduate jobs in prestigious law firms, the way her mother had, but she had been offered two. Even Delia accepted times had changed and two was enough. There was a choice. Her mother was ecstatic. Delia was always going on about the power of choice.

All this considered, and knowing her mother inside out, Lottie was a little surprised to hear a hint of uncertainty sprinkled into the question, 'Do you love it? The decorations? The colour scheme?'

'What made you pick pink?' Lottie asked. She hoped she sounded genuinely interested, rather than genuinely horrified.

'Well, I thought gold, originally. You know, as you are my golden girl. But your father said it was perhaps a bit much and you didn't respond to the WhatsApp that I sent, asking whether you had a preference either way.'

'I was revising, Mum.' Lottie felt a nip of guilt. In fact, the moment the WhatsApp had arrived asking for thoughts on the colour scheme, she and Bel had been tucking into a Thai takeaway. It was a treat and she didn't want to interrupt it by replying to Delia.

'Oh, I know you have been working so hard, of course. And look how that has paid off. I decided on pink because it's your favourite colour.' It had been when Lottie was seven. 'Do you think I should have gone silver?'

Lottie did. She regretted not responding to the messages but she feared anything less than one hundred percent endorsement might mean her perfectionist mother would insist on taking down all the decorations and replacing them before 7 p.m. that evening when the guests were due to arrive.

'It all looks incredibly impactful.' And not at all as though a Barbie Doll has eaten too much strawberry yogurt and puked up her guts.

Delia's face relaxed into a broad smile. 'Oh, I am so glad you think so. As long as you are happy I am. You know I want tonight to be perfect.'

'Yeah, I think you have said.'

'Because tonight is the night of your big announcement, isn't it? When you are finally going to tell us which job you are accepting. Will it be Hifford Chance or Blinklaters?' Delia's smile broadened a little further. It looked tight, slightly manic. Lottie knew it was killing her mother to resist explicitly stating a preference for one firm over the other, because of course she had a preference, a view. Delia trained at Blinklaters and over the years Lottie had often heard her mother speak of how the training there was unsurpassable. 'Prepared me for everything that was to come,' she said frequently.

'Well, I'm on tenterhooks. It's so marvellous to have a choice. Never get backed into a corner. Always decide your future.' This was another one of Delia's war cries and had been for as long as Lottie could remember.

'OK, well, it looks as though you have everything under control here. I think I'll go and err…' Lottie hesitated. What exactly could she say she was going to go and do? Hide again? That is the truth of the matter. Hide from the party prep, hide from the inevitable influx of guests, hide from the next decade? The next decade. Her stomach rolled with the thought of it. Not an excited slither of anticipation, but a low grumbling, a pressing down, that made her want to dash for the Portaloo.

'Oh yes, you go and get ready. I've booked the make-up girl for 3 p.m. and hair at 4.30. You could perhaps put on a face mask before then. I bought one that effectively rehydrates hungover, overly-parched skin, making it soft and supple.'

'Err, OK. Thanks.'

'You're welcome.' Delia beamed, seemingly unaware that she'd just said her daughter had dry, flaky skin. 'Apparently, it's the niacinamide, sodium PCA and five forms of ceramides that make the difference,' she added breezily, as though she was reading off the label. How did she remember everything? Her mother was then called away by the electrical technician: the band needed to do a sound test. Lottie scurried in the opposite direction before she had to listen to a bad rendition of 'Wonderwall'.

Alone in her room she sent Bel a message. *'When will you get here? xx'*

The reply was instantaneous. *'Soon xx'*

There was a row of bright emojis. Smiley faces, flowers, dancing girls and cocktails. Bel was relentlessly upbeat. She thought a twenty-first birthday party on this scale, a month after graduating, was an undisputedly fabulous thing. She did not feel the sense of dread and expectation about what the next decade held the way Lottie did. She thought it was exciting. Lottie believed this just went to show how self-deluded even brilliant women could be.

Lottie flung herself on her bed, flopped and stared at the ceiling. Of course, she'd had a number of beds that she could call her own since this childhood one, which was clad in a prancing unicorn duvet. She had also slipped between the sheets of beds that she could not call her own, but were fun places to temporarily land. She was an adult. Right? Although it was harder to believe as much when she gazed around this room, stuffed with photographs of her at primary school, fluffy heart-shaped cushions and wicker baskets with discarded Boots No.17 make-up and tangles of cheap jewellery. These were the things that never made the grade when she went to university. She couldn't think why her mother hadn't flung them out long ago. They represented a version of her that was no more. Like tracing-paper versions of her, faded and blurred around the edges.

She hadn't quite got around to unpacking her belongings from uni either. She wasn't sure what was stopping her. She thought that the things packed in the boxes would be incongruous here, yet maybe if she unpacked this room would feel more like hers again. Inside the boxes were her clothes. Mostly handmade and those that were not were customised. There were photos, taken recently, that showed her experimenting with her style, her hair, her friends and potential addictions. One box contained flyers from gigs, shows and galleries she'd attended, wrist bands from festivals and a few leftover colourful rolls of washi tape. If her mum saw that stuff, she'd certainly throw it out. It all looked like junk. It wasn't. It was memories. In fact, it was more than that; the beer mats pinched from a pub after a particularly brilliant night out, the handmade Good Luck card delivered on a breakfast tray the day of her first exam, and the cork noticeboard – removed from the wall of her student house – still covered in curling flyers, photos of young women beaming, dancing, laughing, drinking, shouting, jumping, clubbing, which were not just memories. They were foundations: the first tentative steps towards who she might become. Lottie had had to leave behind the wine cases that she and Bel had managed to scrounge off the guy from the local bottle shop. They'd used them as bedside tables, shelves and storage. She'd have preferred to leave behind her textbooks but knew that law books were expensive and that she should hold on to them in case she needed to refer back once she had a job. Unlike her mother she didn't have a photographic memory. Besides, she knew her mother would think the wine cases were a little scruffy, unsanitary.

Lottie closed her eyes to trap in the tears. She felt a huge wave of grief engulf her. She was annoyed at herself. She shouldn't be behaving like this. It wasn't the proper response to growing up, to being thrown a party. She ought to be jubilant. However, she couldn't fight the feeling that the last few years had flown by and she wasn't ready to let them go. She'd enjoyed everything about university – except perhaps her course. She had loved the possibilities, opportunities, risks and chances that every night, every day, every club, society, team, debate and even library visit had offered. She looked ahead at her future and felt certain that doors were closing, that with every choice she made an opportunity was lost. She realised that she couldn't have it all. There was no such thing but that seemed a dreadful thing to accept.

She saw a future that was full of responsibilities. She had to choose between one of the two very prestigious law firms because that's what she had been working towards forever, that's what everyone expected. It was what she had said she wanted since she was eleven years old. She was being irrational. She must be, because everyone wanted to be in her position. Her fellow classmates had looked at her with undisguised envy when she secured the offers. There had been jealous and unfounded whispers of nepotism. Unfounded because her mother worked under her pre-marriage name and there was no reason to believe they had ever been linked. Lottie had been careful in interviews not to reveal her mother was a lawyer. When Lottie had been a little girl, other people wanting something that she had might have made her want it more but that seemed no longer to be the case. A job for life was not the same as a pair of crocs with ladybird motifs. Shocker.

Lottie was struggling to decide between the two jobs because weren't they much of a muchness? Great pay but long hours, no social life, early-morning and late-night commutes on crowded trains, demanding bosses, living in constant fear that she had poorly proofread a document or missed some important piece of information. These feelings of exhaustion and terror were not just to be expected in the first years of her job, most likely they would be ever-present throughout her career. During the recruitment process Lottie had spent plenty of time talking to employees further up the food chain. Yes, they were driven and stimulated; she saw and valued that, but they were also depleted, drained. They talked about responsibilities to their clients and spouses, they talked about their children's school fees and enormous mortgages on large houses. They talked about how many hours they worked when they were on holiday.

Don't grow up, it's a trap. She'd read that somewhere on a mass-market poster or a postcard. At the time she'd laughed because she was about fifteen and desperate to do the thing it advised against. Now she wasn't so sure.

* * *

Suddenly it was 7 p.m. and guests had started to arrive. The afternoon had flown by, as the doorbell had rung frequently, announcing a constant flow of people arriving, initially to prep for the party and then to attend it. As Lottie's parents' friends arrived, they obligingly gasped at the effect Delia had created. They hugged Lottie, while squealing, 'So here she is. The famous lawyer.' 'You must be so proud.' 'Hasn't she done well.' 'What an achievement.' They were very nice. They were saying the right things. Why then did Lottie feel as though she was floating on an unstable raft on choppy waters and they were all waving to her from terra firma? Lottie's aunts, uncles and cousins started to arrive too. She had forgotten how raucous and humorous they could be. They were a relief, in so much as not one of them mentioned her new status as a trainee lawyer, but they did all ask if she had a boyfriend. Every last one of them. 'No.'

'No? A pretty girl like you? What is up with fellas nowadays?' demanded her uncles.

'Never mind, love, your time will come,' said her aunts, patting her hand kindly. 'It's not too late.'

A number of her cousins were engaged, married, pregnant, breastfeeding. They were perplexing because they rolled their eyes at their husbands behind said husbands' backs, they complained that their leaky boobs ached and that their babies were 'rotten little buggers put on this earth to make sure I never sleep again.' Then they turned to Lottie with a big smile and said, 'You'll be next.'

She'd barely seen Bel, just time for a brief hug to greet her; then Delia had immediately drafted Bel into hanging fairy lights while Lottie had to submit to having her make-up done. She'd have liked it if Bel had stayed with her for that, giggling and offering suggestions about whether false eyelashes were a good thing or something to be avoided at all costs, but it was a comfort to know that she was at least here.

The party was perfect. Of course it was, a Delia party could never be anything other. The canapés were hoovered up, the champagne washed down. The guests sparkled as brightly as the lights, the band may not have been to Lottie's taste but she had to admit they knew how to please the crowd and soon the dance floor was heaving with women in their fifties, who looked inordinately happy to have the opportunity to dance. Bel had gamely flung her lot in with the older women and was happily strutting her funky stuff. She kept beckoning Lottie to join them, but Lottie couldn't relax. Her mother had said speeches were at 8 p.m. Then she would have to announce which way she was going.

Before she knew it, her mother had taken her by the hand and led her up to the stage where the band were performing. The band was silenced. Her father made a speech. Lottie felt each word like a stab. 'Tremendously proud... What an achievement... Following my beautiful and brilliant wife's footsteps... Going to keep her old man out of jail if he ever gets into trouble... Looking forward to watching her reach dizzy heights and her keeping me in the custom her mother has got me used to.' His speech clearly only upset *her*, everyone else thought it was pitch perfect. They laughed, they oohed and aahed, there was a smattering of applause, one or two of the women dabbed the corner of their eyes, not wanting their mascara to smudge. 'And now we are going to hear from our super girl herself, as she is going to reveal whether Hifford Chance or Blinklaters are going to be lucky enough to secure her. Over to you, darling.'

Someone gently nudged Lottie to the centre of the stage. Her father handed her the mic. Lottie blinked. There was a spotlight glaring in her eyes, blinding her. She couldn't see her audience, her guests. Not even Bel. Where was Bel? She needed her close by, beaming, offering unstinting support as usual. The room was silent, other than for the cries of one of the cousin's babies. Lottie thought she could taste the anticipation, touch it. She realised that she'd been silent for too long when people began to mumble amongst themselves, her father urged, 'Well, darling, don't keep us in suspense any longer. Who do you choose? Drum roll, please.'

FFS, thought Lottie, as an actual drum roll happened.

'I choose art college.' The words vomited out of her mouth. She hadn't been expecting them, she didn't know she was even thinking them, not really and she certainly hadn't planned on saying them. But somehow, they had erupted from her. She thought it was her secret, her private fantasy, her desire that was destined to go unfulfilled but now she had announced it, here at her party in front of everyone, her family, her friends, her parents' friends.

Her parents.

Lottie couldn't look at her mother. Her father said, 'Ha ha, always one for a joke,' but her mother remained stony silent, realising that Lottie was not kidding.

Lottie coughed. 'No, not a joke, Dad. I want to go to art college to study fashion. I don't want to be a lawyer. I don't think I have for a while. I'm sorry.' The room remained silent. Even the baby had stopped crying. Lottie wished he would start again. However, the confession had erupted, her only option now was to push on. 'I've been offered a place at Saint Martin's. I applied in a sort of daze, I never really thought it was going to happen. But on the other hand, I can't imagine a life where it doesn't. It's a highly intensive course. The idea is to produce a portfolio of work. It's all about visual research, experimentation and idea development.' Lottie's voice cracked. 'I choose that.'

The room breathed in, waited. Lottie looked out at the blackness, she didn't dare turn left or right to look at her parents. She wished she could see Bel. Where the hell was she?

Then she heard it, a loud clap broke the silence. It was slow at first and Lottie wondered whether it was going to be challenging, sarcastic, but then it sped up to a manic, celebratory pace. 'Bravo, well done! Lottie I'm so pleased, so proud!' The room took its cue from Delia and suddenly erupted into loud cheers and shouts of congratulations. Lottie realised she was shaking with relief or adrenaline or something. She turned to her mother.

'Really?'

'Absolutely! I've always said you need to have choices, that's all I've ever wanted for you. All I've worked to give you. When you first said you wanted to be a lawyer, of course I supported it, but I'd have supported any field you picked. Part of my heart sank at the idea. The hours, darling, the pressure. I understand more than anyone.' Lottie wanted to laugh. How had she got it so wrong? Her mother continued, 'Law isn't for everyone. I love it but it only works if your heart is in it. I'm so proud of you for finding what you want, not grabbing at something someone else wants because it's there or because it's expected of you.' Lottie beamed and fell into her mother's embrace. The music started up again.

'I thought you'd be mad. I thought there would be fireworks.'

Delia whispered in her ear, 'And when are you going to tell us you choose Bel?' she asked.

Lottie pulled away from her mother so she could meet her eye. 'You guessed.'

'Of course, I'm your mother.'

Lottie yelled into the mic, 'And another thing: I choose Bel.' She yelled it loud and clear and her message sailed above the noise of the band. But, to be sure, or possibly because she was suddenly euphoric with the thought that being twenty-one did after all present choice and opportunity, and was all about doors opening, not closing, she shouted again, 'I choose Bel! I chose Bel.'

'All right, love, we heard you the first time,' yelled back one of the uncles. The band played on and no one seemed as surprised about Lottie's choices as she had thought they would be. 'Where is Bel?' she asked her mum. 'I've hardly seen her all night.'

'I'm right here behind you. Close by,' replied Bel. Their eyes met and Lottie thought perhaps there would be fireworks tonight after all, but of a totally different kind.

Adele Parks

Adele Parks was born in Teesside, north-east England. She is the author of twenty bestselling novels including the recent *Sunday Times* Number One hits *Lies Lies Lies* and *Just My Luck*. Her books have been translated into twenty-six languages and she's sold 3.8 million copies in the UK alone. Adele is an ambassador for The National Literacy Trust and a judge for the Costa. Adele has lived in Botswana, Italy and London, and is now settled in Guildford, Surrey.

Heart-eater

Anna Stephens

Chen did not have enough truth in his heart, and so the governor would not grant him the honour of being their envoy. He sat on the railing edging the tower roof, feet dangling into space, and stared across the city to its heart, the great crystal throne.

The building housing the throne was small and plain, built of pale stone unadorned. Its ordinary exterior was a reminder to all Quellans that only the heart was of importance – only what lay within.

Chen rubbed the seam in his chest and flexed the golden iridescence of his wings. What lay within him was a dearth of truth.

K'un can help.

A shiver rippled through him, mingled fear and fascination, the memory of pleasure dancing across his nerve-endings. His skin sang its desire and his mouth had gone dry, but he'd promised himself – he'd sworn – he wouldn't visit the heart-eater again.

It is forbidden. He is forbidden. An abomination to the crystal throne and all that Quel stands for. His kind makes a mockery of our very beliefs.

Chen was a good man, a true man. He was the best candidate to become the governor's new envoy. And yet his heart said otherwise, and the heart was the source of all promise. Growling with frustration and anger at himself, his failings, Chen threw himself off the tower. His golden wings hadn't even opened before he collided with another and they were tangled in each other's limbs and feathers. He shouted

338

in shock and fear flooded through him: he should have checked the air was clear. The fault was his. Another one to add to the rot in his heart.

But the wings of the other were black as soot, iridescent as sunlight on water, and the familiar, tantalising scent of the heart-eater was in Chen's nostrils. K'un wrapped his arms around Chen's chest beneath his wings and turned their fall into a controlled dive and then swept them up and around and away, far from the crystal throne, far from Quel itself and into the mountains.

Chen could have struggled, could have opened his wings and twisted free, but he didn't. He lay quiescent in the heart-eater's arms, staring up into the sharp angles of his face, tight black curls rippling back from the broad brow.

The easy friendship of the past was long dead; Chen couldn't publicly associate himself with someone so dangerous. If the council ever found out, if anyone in Quel ever found out about them, they'd both be killed. Chen was no fool: he knew what he risked, both professionally and personally. But still he was drawn to the heart-eater as the sun was drawn to the west, drawn by his need for K'un's unique ability.

This is the last time. They will name me envoy and then my heart will match my potential. I won't need him again.

* * *

Chen gazed at the familiar surroundings of the heart-eater's hideaway. The tapestries on the walls and floor were faded but finely-wrought; the furniture simple but sturdy, with a clean elegance not often seen in the city of crystal.

He lay on his side on a wide bed, K'un facing him. 'This will be the last time,' he promised, though he'd said that before.

'I understand,' K'un whispered, not meeting his eyes. Instead, he stared through the wide opening in Chen's tunic. Like all Quellans, it was open to the navel so that throne officials and crystal guards could examine their hearts when needed. K'un's finger slid along the seam in his chest and Chen's wings vibrated. His fingers bunched into fists as he reminded himself why he was doing this.

K'un took both of his hands in his own and rolled Chen onto his back, gold wings tucked tight beneath him like a blanket. Tiny flecks of crystal in his palms grated against Chen's skin. He settled himself on Chen and spread his wings over them both, blotting out the daylight streaming through the window. In the privacy of his pinions, they opened their hearts to each other, chests gaping along the seams, ribs spreading apart.

The heart-eater's eyes glowed as he looked. As he judged Chen's heart and saw the blackness of deceit and greed and ambition staining it. And when Chen couldn't stand the judgement anymore, he pushed with his wings, lifting himself up, closer, higher, straining to join his heart to K'un's.

The snake in K'un's heart slid free, wet with blood, hot with life, and pushed into Chen's chest. A lightning bolt of pleasure and invasion and surrender fused his mind and body and he gasped. K'un held both Chen's hands above his head, their fingers entwined, maintaining the crystal connection that allowed the snake to feed, the disgust of it lost in waves of pleasure.

When it was done and the purity of Chen's heart restored – or at least the appearance of such – the snake slid back into K'un's chest and his wings folded against his back. Light flooded Chen's eyes and he squinted up at the man who pinned him to the bed: ebony hair in disarray, the high planes of his cheeks flushed with need and his eyes gleaming with nameless emotion.

But then K'un let go of his hands and Chen turned his face away, shame consuming him once more and no doubt already beginning to blacken his heart. For that and that alone, he strove to suppress it.

'Thank you,' he whispered as his chest closed, ribs locking together as their fingers had done before. His body yammered for more, not just heart contact but all of it. He wanted to undress K'un and kiss the full expanse of lean, dark skin. He wanted to lose himself in the wild black curls and bury his face in those soot-shining wings and feel K'un inside him. He pushed away the desire, sickened. K'un was a heart-eater, an abomination. A tool to further his advancement.

The abomination slid off Chen and stood. He crossed to the fireplace and stared down at the unlit, neatly-stacked wood, his silvery robes rumpled. 'Good luck,' he said in a neutral tone that had only a slick of throatiness to hint at some inner turmoil. The Quellan rearranged his clothing, preened a couple of ruffled feathers, and left the house. He leapt into the sky and fled.

* * *

It was dark by the time K'un reached Quel and made his slow way to the night market, landing on a high, wide platform packed with stalls selling fresh food. The smells sickened him; the faint swaying of the platform sickened him; but he had work to do.

A few others sat at the edge, legs dangling into space, as they talked and ate and flirted. K'un watched with a hunger more savage than that of the snake's as one woman caressed the wings of another, running soft, strong hands through her flight feathers, massaging.

Unbidden came a memory of hands on his own wings, hands that began gently. At least they'd always begun that way, with gentleness. How many years since someone had touched his wings with his permission? He wasn't sure anyone ever had. His permission was not part of their transactions.

The women fell off the platform and were swallowed by the night and their need for each other. K'un followed soon after, flying to the bar where his first client would be. Eager now just for it to be over, so that he might hide away with his pain and shame until hunger drove him out again.

The bar was crowded and K'un was early. He ordered a plum wine

341

and sat on a tall stool, his wings flared enough to ward off casual conversation. The temperature dropped steadily as the night deepened, but K'un didn't notice until the bartender rolled up the canvas walls to meet the roof, cutting off his view of the lights of the city, a constellation against the blackness of the mountains. He blinked and looked down; his glass was empty. He stretched out a hand to order another when someone tugged at his sleeve.

She was older than him, predatory and silent, desperation sharpening her edges. K'un left his glass and his stool and followed her into the corridor leading to the back rooms. She flipped a coin to the heavy-set bouncer and gestured K'un in first.

'Do you have it?' she breathed as soon as the door was shut. He nodded, tongue-tied and uncomfortable. Weary. She softened a little then, shuddering out a relieved breath. K'un didn't know her name or her position within Quel, but she was important enough to submit to regular heart inspections, and so she needed what only he could give her. He retrieved a vial from his satchel and then dropped the bag on the floor as she counted the money onto a table.

The woman pressed herself against him, nibbling the line of his jaw as her hands stroked his flanks and hips. He held his revulsion tight and small, a hard ball in his belly he refused to examine, and then he lifted her and spun her so she was pressed against the door. He leant into her as her breathing roughened and slowly peeled off his gloves. Her hands were at his belt, but he unstopped the vial and poured the snake's venom into his mouth, then gripped her hands to activate the crystal. The woman arched her back and cracked her chest; K'un had a glimpse of the blackened, withered thing inside her and then he closed his eyes and pressed his mouth to her heart and licked it clean.

She shuddered and cried out, wings vibrating and coming around to caress his. To touch them without permission. K'un shuddered in turn, at the impossible, awful violation of it, but his mouth was full of venom and full of her hates and indiscretions and scandals and greed and he just wanted it done. Wanted it to be over so he could leave her in her purity and bliss – until the next time.

The snake thrashed within him, its crystal flesh tearing, and tears sprang unbidden to his eyes. He pulled away and wiped them on his sleeves before continuing; the tears of a heart-eater were both precious and distinctive. If they stained her heart, all Quel would know of his existence and the governor would stop at nothing to find him.

Eventually it was done. The woman was dazed, her wildly-thrumming heart red and gleaming. K'un scooped her up, careful to avoid touching her wings, and lay her on the bed. Then he picked up his satchel and the stack of coins and left, closing the door with a soft click. He exited the bar and flew to another. Six more clients tonight. Six more and then he could bathe and scrub his flesh and his mouth. Six more and he could drown his self-loathing in alcohol and hide from the world and himself.

He didn't feel the eyes watching him as he flew.

* * *

'I present myself as candidate to escort the governor's spouse from Marast,' Chen said the next day.

His voice was calm, his appearance perfect.

The throne executor looked from Chen's paperwork to the man himself and then grunted. 'You failed your last examination.'

'I have spent much time in introspection and penance,' Chen said, willing himself to believe the lie so utterly that it did not mark his heart.

'Present yourself to the throne,' she said. Chen washed and dried his hands and then moved to stand between the two great crystal pillars. He placed a hand upon each and the throne executor stood before him. She put her hands over his and Chen opened his chest for her examination. A mirror hung around the executor's neck and Chen viewed his heart as she did: a perfect red muscle, untainted, the fingers of his ribs spread wide in invitation. Supplication. *This is my truth. This is my being.*

The throne executor inspected his heart for longer than Chen had anticipated, and a tiny tendril of doubt began to sprout in his belly. And then it was done. She let go and stepped back. 'You are pure. The crystal throne approves you as envoy to Marast. Give this to the governor's new spouse: a marriage gift. You will set out before noon and return with them in one week. Here are your formal orders.'

Chen was dizzy with elation when he left the crystal throne and walked up the stairs to a launch point, a finely-worked leather satchel hanging at his hip. It had worked; he was going to Marast as diplomatic envoy. The pinnacle of his career and one that would secure financial wealth and status. One successful mission and he'd be given others, as many as he wanted and the crystal throne required.

He'd done it. Chen was grinning as he exited onto the roof and scanned the air for traffic. Black wings, circling high above. His heart thrummed, but it wasn't K'un. This flyer's skin was paler, their hair straight, not curly. He looked away, disquieted by his own unexpected reaction. The memory resurfaced, of K'un following a pretty older woman into the private rooms behind the bar. Of the closed and remote look on his face when he'd left, and of the drugged, blissful expression on the woman's when she'd stumbled out some time after him.

Chen knew how the man made his living, but the heart-eater had never asked him for payment. He didn't know whether that made him special or completely forgettable and wasn't sure he wanted to find out. All he did know was that the flash of jealousy had been unexpected and unwelcome. Likely he was just a means to an end for the heart-eater. *And that's fine, that's all he is to me. A means to an end. And I've got what I wanted, so it's over. My heart will stay pure now, lifted by the trust the throne and the governor place in me. I don't need his magic or his touch anymore.*

Chen told himself it was done, their association terminated. Forever. It didn't take away the taste of K'un's skin or the weight of his body on Chen's. It didn't erase the gentle scrape of crystal palms against his palms, or the heat that built within the enclosure of those great blue-black wings.

Stop it.

He had been too long alone, too fixated on his career. When he returned from Marast, he would find a casual partner and put all this unpleasantness behind him. Chen flew home and packed for the journey. He bathed again and oiled his hair and skin, then preened his feathers. The flight would undo most of his preparations, but he would at least set out in splendour, even if he arrived a little travel-worn. Let the throne officials and the crystal guards know that he was sensible of the honour done him.

Governor Thul's spouse waited in the seaside port city of Marast, on the wide sweep of coast that spread flat and endless to east and west. He'd been before, for pleasure with friends. There would be no pleasure this time; Chen was on official business and that was all he needed to focus on for now. All he would focus on. He leapt out of his tower window and fell into the sky, sought altitude and headed south out of Quel and over the low mountains, riding a thermal high and fast and far, conserving energy for the long flight.

* * *

Marast had grown since last Chen was here, expanding in a sprawling chaos along the coast and even on to the beach, where homes and shops now stood on tall wooden pilings knee-deep in the high-tide surf. It was in one of these he was housed upon his arrival, a fact he had at first taken as some oblique insult until dusk fell and he sat on a low bench and watched the sun drown himself through the glass wall of his apartment.

Dusk fell swiftly in the bowl of the mountains of Quel, but out

345

here it was lazy, taking its time to thoroughly stain the ocean with crimson, peach and searing gold. When it finally sank, and the lights of Marast began to glow back on land, Chen felt more at peace than he ever had in his life. His heart would be stained with beauty, with gold and orange and perfect pink, if anyone cared to look.

Moving almost in a daze, the Quellan oiled his golden skin and donned his formal robes – deep crimson with a stylised version of the crystal throne embroidered on both shoulders in pink thread. It hung full and heavy to his knees, black leggings and boots beneath it. It had weight and history and poise, and Chen felt a flicker of nerves, but he summoned the memory of sunset and calmed his breath and mind before flying to Marast's great temple for the formal exchange and proxy marriage.

The Marasti had decked the temple in paper lanterns and the inside was a myriad of soft-hued flickering lights, through which the wealthy and the powerful moved and murmured. Many faced Chen as he strode the length of the temple, the seams in their chests gaping just enough – a show of respect and welcome, but without the need to reciprocate.

The temple-witch stood before the altar: a block of granite veined with the pink crystal that was the source of their power. Chen was surprised the Marasti were able to open their chests at all with such a small amount of crystal in their city, but nothing of his thoughts showed on his face. Beside the temple-witch stood the spouse, hooded and veiled. Their wings were emerald, the skin of their chest the palest green. Rare. Exquisite.

Chen bowed in Marasti fashion and then opened his chest to the temple-witch. She did the same, though the effort was visible in the muscles standing out in her neck. Her heart was small and red and beating hard. Chen took a step forward so that the fingers of his ribs touched hers, their hearts close in an offering of trust.

'Governor Thul presents their warmest affections to their new spouse and offers them this small token of their affection,' Chen said, nearly fumbling his lines and the gift both. His chest closed and he stepped back as he slid the box from his satchel. Inside was one of Thul's soft grey flight feathers, its edges painted with gold and crusted with jewels, pearls, and tiny teeth and bones dyed green to match the spouse's own feathers.

Chen heard their tiny intake of breath, saw the faintest movement of the veil that concealed them. 'Governor Thul's affection and generosity is gift itself,' they said, their voice lower than Chen was expecting. Throaty. Like K'un's had been, last time they'd spoken. 'I am Tilinn, and the governor's feather shall stand for their heart until we are together.'

Chen was seized with an urge to see Tilinn's face and whether it matched the sleek strength of their high, arched wings and calm, self-possessed voice. But he was the proxy, not the spouse. The honour was not his.

They flew the twisting, chasing, dipping marriage flight through the temple and out of its high windows into the night and then back into the lantern-glow again. Then the marriage feast and the sky-lantern ceremony and the dancing and, by the time Chen was finally allowed to leave, weighed down with gifts and messages and whispers of trade agreements, he was exhausted. And delighted. He'd done it. He was an envoy.

* * *

Three days after the wedding, they reached Quel.

The heart-eater was waiting in the sky for them as if he'd sensed Chen returning. The envoy's stomach tightened.

'How was Marast?'

'Beautiful. Spouse Tilinn's home is lovely.' He forced a smile even as his mind whirled. K'un didn't make small talk. They didn't interact except for ... those occasions. 'Is all well here?'

'The city is eager to meet the new spouse,' K'un said, which was no answer at all. 'I am pleased to make your acquaintance first,' he added.

'As am I. Your colouring is lovely,' Tilinn added politely.

K'un seemed taken aback. 'Thank you, though you are the rare and crowning flower in our governor's garden, I would say. How was your flight?'

'Freeing. And too short.'

Chen's pulse raced. Both K'un and Tilinn seemed determined to make his return to Quel as difficult as possible.

'When your duties are done, Chen, could we talk?' K'un asked. The back of his neck prickled warning but he managed a tight nod. The heart-eater said nothing else, merely inclined his head towards Tilinn and then veered away, down towards the entertainment level. Chen knew which bar he'd be in, but with luck the throne officials would have hours of questions for him and he could avoid the meeting.

'Your friend seems nice,' Tilinn said, as they curved towards the centre of the city and palace.

'He's not my friend,' Chen snapped before he could stop himself.

Tilinn was silent for a while, the blankness of the veil making it impossible to know their thoughts. 'I feel glad I will never see you again, envoy Chen,' they said eventually. 'Despite having seen your heart, I would not be surprised if it was in fact a stone.'

They landed before he could formulate a response and were absorbed into the crowd of well-wishers. Chen found himself mostly ignored and was content to be so, his attention flickering as K'un's strange, intent expression intruded on what should have been his triumph. And then Tilinn was gone, without another word to him, and he followed the official to give his report.

It was indeed late, but not quite late enough, when Chen escaped the palace. His heart had been examined and found good; his truth verified in unblemished, muscular red.

He flew low past the entertainment district and glanced in at the bar; K'un was still there. The cloth walls had been rolled down, but the heart-eater was sitting at the window. He saluted Chen with his cup, and the golden envoy had no choice but to bank and then land, his toes stretching and then gripping the edges of the platform. He took a long moment to settle his feathers, nerves tingling in his belly and his fingertips, before going in.

K'un had already bought him a drink and he perched opposite, his wings stiff. 'K'un. You wished to see me?' His voice was overly formal and Chen winced inside, but couldn't stop himself. 'Some business for the crystal throne, perhaps?'

K'un's expression was hard to read, dark against the darkness of his skin, the darkness of the bar. A shadow. A cipher. *Like the darkness in the embrace of his wings.*

K'un licked his lips. 'Have you told anyone about me?'

The question was so unexpected that Chen rocked on his stool and dread coiled inside him like the snake in the heart-eater's chest. 'What? No! Why would I do that?'

'I think I'm being followed. Don't look; they're not here. But over the last week...'

Fury replaced the dread. 'And yet you wait for me, and ask me to meet you here? You implicate me as one of your, your...' Chen trailed off. He couldn't say customers, because K'un never required payment. He didn't know what he was to him.

He still couldn't see his face, but a gust of wind set the lantern swinging and the edge of K'un's lips were outlined for an instant in gold. Usually soft, usually full, now they were tight. With anger, perhaps. *Or with hurt.*

'I wanted to warn you,' K'un said, and his voice was entirely devoid of emotion. 'If you need me, I will come if it is safe. But it would be better if you did not. Need me. For a while.' The words stuttered from a pinched mouth.

The fear in Chen's stomach took on a new quality – colder, sharper. Of its own volition, it seemed, his leg bumped K'un's. 'Are you all

349

right? Do you need anything?' he asked, and that, too, was not his intent. This was what he had wanted, this distancing. 'Money?' he added, but not in the way K'un took it, making that mouth pinch even tighter.

'No,' K'un whispered, when Chen had thought he wouldn't answer at all. 'But … if I leave, it will be without warning. And you've never needed what I give. Trust yourself and your heart will always be pure enough to be the throne's envoy.'

Chen gulped his wine. It was sweet and cool, apple-spiced with just enough tartness. K'un flipped a coin to the bartender and slid off the stool. The lantern-light caught his face again; it was drawn and thin, haunted. The halo of his curls lent no grandeur to his height; rather he seemed to stoop below them, weighed down.

Chen grabbed for his gloved hand before he could leave. 'Are you ill?'

K'un gently pulled his hand free. 'All my life,' he murmured, and was gone before Chen could navigate around the table. He looked out of the door, but K'un was black in a black sky, visible only as he blotted out the stars, too swift to follow. Gone.

'Strange one, that,' the bartender said, startling him. 'Still, you must meet all sorts on your official business, eh?'

'What? Oh. Yes. All sorts,' Chen mumbled.

The bartender waited expectantly for some gossip, then sighed when he didn't get it. 'He meets a lot of folks in here, you know,' he added, a little softer. 'Just so you know. If you're casual, then nothing to worry about. But if not, well, you're an envoy. Got options.'

It took Chen a second, and then he was tongue-tied and flustered. 'It's not like that,' he managed. 'But thank you for the warning. You have a good heart.'

The bartender swelled visibly at such a compliment from an envoy, and Chen ducked out into the night before he could say anything else. His tower was calling. His bed. The sweet oblivion of sleep.

Chen didn't land on his balcony. He didn't quite know why, but he spiralled up to sit on the roof railing, staring north towards the spear-tree forest, apple-wine and confusion mingling sickly on his tongue. 'K'un,' he whispered, not for the first or even the hundredth time, 'what have you done to me?'

There was a soft rush of wind over feathers and a light thump as he landed. Chen's belly tightened, his breath suddenly shallow. He'd thought to take a lover when he got back; now that he no longer needed the snake, perhaps he could have the man? The tiny flyers in his belly took wing and told him, yes, this was the way. Redraw the boundaries of their relationship, back to how it had been before. K'un as a friend and lover, not a tool. His palms dampened with the rightness of it, and with a smile he couldn't suppress, he turned to face him.

Two crystal guards stood on the roof. Large, light nets on long cords dangled from their hands to help them bring down those who tried to flee, and crystal dampers sat in holsters snug against their thighs. They were silhouetted by the faint lights of Quel and, for the third time that day, Chen was filled with dread – and this time, he knew instinctively, it reached its taint into his heart.

He kept his wings loose and tried to resurrect the welcoming smile that had fallen from his face. 'Is there a problem, guards?'

'There are some ugly rumours floating around, envoy,' one said, their voice respectful but stern.

'Really? I try not to listen to gossip. Not good for the heart. My concern is for Quel, Governor Thul, and, though it is less lofty, my own career. Still, what is the rumour and I will tell you if I have heard anything.'

Chen marvelled at the steadiness of his voice, at the relaxed, almost nonchalant set of his wings and shoulders. He could feel his heart blackening within him, though. Doubt, terror, the end of his dreams circled like carrion crows.

'There's a heart-eater in Quel, envoy. That is the rumour.'

Were they watching him closely? Narrowly? With suspicion? Or was that merely the shadows that concealed them, leaving him exposed to the faint light?

'Indeed? Surely such an abomination would be quickly identified. Likely there is just some poor Quellan with a twisted wing or a skin complaint and people are being cruel about them. Even with the crystal throne to guide us, there is room for petty cruelty, it seems.'

'Your own heart failed and then passed the envoy screening,' the guard on the left said, stepping closer.

Chen forced a laugh. 'And so, you think I had it eaten? Preposterous and, I might add, deeply insulting. I earned my position as envoy, and I completed my first assignment just today. The governor themself sent me a note of thanks. But my heart stands ever ready for inspection, should it be deemed necessary,' he added, knowing it was not ready. Not at all. Black and shrivelled like an apple too long on the tree.

Apple-wine. K'un.

'So you have not heard of this abomination?'

Chen shrugged his wings. 'I have been in Marast. I had not heard the rumour before I left, no.' Not a lie.

The guards exchanged a glance. 'Very well, envoy. Be sure and let us know if you do hear anything. We'll catch the freak, and we'll tear that parasite from their chests – and then their heart. Quel and Governor Thul will bear no deception of the crystal throne, and all found to have done so will be punished to the limit of the law.'

'I would expect no less. I look forward to reading of your successful hunt.' They backed off, glanced over the edge of the roof, and then fell into the sky and were gone. Chen maintained his composure until he was down in his apartment, where he closed the curtains and then fell to his knees, his wings flared wide around him. His heart hurt and his lungs had shrunk until he was light-headed and panting.

K'un stepped out of the shadows of the kitchen and Chen nearly screamed. The heart-eater dropped to his knees opposite him, wings likewise spread so the flight feathers weren't bent against the floor, and gathered him close, fingers on his shoulders. Chen hitched his wings in sudden, ill-thought-out invitation, and K'un hesitated the barest second and then ran his palms over his back and into feathers. Both of them inhaled, a sharp noise, a hungry noise. K'un wasn't wearing gloves, and the flecks of crystal in his palms, smooth and rough, were exquisite.

'I couldn't just leave like that,' he whispered, 'even though I should. And then I saw them and … you didn't say my name to them.' His hands massaged the joints and preened the feathers and Chen knelt there, his head against the man's chest and his hands on his hips. His whole body rocked with the thump of his heart. K'un kissed the back of Chen's head as his fingers scratched at that part of the wings no one could ever reach alone. Chen gusted a half-sigh, half-groan and shifted closer, wrapping his arms loosely around K'un's waist. The heart-eater's chest gave a little where his head leant against it and Chen rolled his face up and pressed a soft kiss to the long seam.

K'un's hands paused and then the left one took Chen's hand and guided it to a wing of smoke and midnight. Feathers firm and bristly on the edges, soft as down deeper in. Chen's chest cracked and he nestled closer still, his chin on K'un's shoulder and his arms coming up and around to caress the underside of his wings. His lips found the heart-eater's neck and K'un's fingers tightened in his feathers, a sudden convulsive pressure that made Chen smile and kiss again, a little higher. And again.

K'un was still, great ragged breaths heaving from him, his chest gaping as Chen pressed kisses to his throat. He wrapped one arm around K'un's waist and dragged him closer, tugging the tunic off his shoulders as their mouths finally met. The heart-eater was slack in his arms, his wings shivering as Chen dragged the fingers of one hand through feathers and stroked the other down hot, soft skin and K'un's mouth opened and a tiny noise rolled out of his throat.

'Furl,' Chen whispered against his mouth and they tucked their wings tightly to roll onto their sides on the rug. They kissed again and Chen was lost in it as K'un gripped the edge of his wing, almost pinching, and made that noise again, needful. His chest gaped. The heart-eater's hair floated around them, a cloud of ebony, and then K'un rolled him onto his back and Chen gasped, his head falling back onto the rug. K'un took both hands in his and before Chen could protest, the snake was in his heart and the pleasure of it made him cry out. The heart-eater's wings shrouded them, hiding his face from the light so only the glitter of his eyes was visible when Chen managed to look, foggy with ecstasy.

'K'un,' he tried, because this wasn't what he'd meant when he'd allowed him to touch his wings, it wasn't the snake he wanted but K'un himself, but the heart-eater held his hands tighter and the snake bit harder and he was lost, adrift on it, consumed by it as the snake consumed his heart.

When it was over, K'un gathered him up as if he was a child and placed him on the bed, careful now not to touch his wings. He drew the bright blanket over him and padded through to the washroom. Chen lay in the aftermath of delirium, but even the lingering, satisfied ache in his chest couldn't distract him from the passage of time.

A little groggy, the envoy finally got up and wandered through the dark of his apartment. Surely K'un hadn't just left? The night was young and there was more, so much more, pleasure to be had and this time their hearts would remain sealed in their chests, though visible in their eyes and fingers and bodies. The promise of it dried Chen's mouth.

The washroom door was shut and he hesitated, uncomfortable, until he heard sounds that made him wrench at the latch, heedless of privacy. K'un was curled on the floor with his hands splayed over his chest. His face was twisted with agony and he alternately retched and wept. The room stank of sour vomit.

'Wings and sky, K'un, what's wrong?' Chen gasped, throwing himself down next to him.

'Leave me,' K'un gasped. 'I'm fine.'

'You're clearly not. I'll fetch a medic.'

'No! No,' he added, lower, and now he was afraid, gripping Chen's wrist hard enough to leave crystal imprints in golden skin. Deeply, heart-stoppingly afraid. 'Please don't. I'll go. I'll go and you'll never see me again, please. Whatever you want.' His shaking hand moved to Chen's seam. 'You want this? I can- ' he broke off to whimper and his body spasmed as pain rippled him. 'I'll do it again. Please, envoy. Whatever you want. Just don't let them take me.'

Chen knelt very still, horrified. Guilty. 'I don't understand,' he whispered. 'You need help.'

'No, envoy, no. If you want to, I will, or if you want me to go.' K'un forced himself on to his hands and knees, his skin an awful, unnatural grey. 'Tell me what you want. Anything. I'll do anything.'

He sank on to his haunches opposite Chen, cramped with half-flared wings in the tiny space, and cracked his chest. The snake slid free and Chen clearly saw the agony flash through K'un's face before he turned it away and pressed his chest forward, offering.

The snake. It was different now. Not slick but ... jagged. Its scales not smooth but shards and spikes of what looked like crystal. Like the crystal of the throne and the crystal in the heart-eater's palms. It quested forward and another ripple ran through his slender frame. His lips were bitten raw with the pain of it. 'For you,' he whispered, but his voice was broken. 'I'll do anything.'

Chen felt sick, and not just because of the smell in the room. 'I don't understand,' he said again. 'Why are you doing this?' His fingers grazed the man's cheek and drew his head up. 'Talk to me. Is this what you want?'

Such confusion crossed K'un's face that under any other circumstances, Chen would have laughed. He didn't. Something was deeply, deeply wrong with the heart-eater, and not just physically.

'I want ... whatever you want,' K'un mumbled and thrust his chest forward again.

Chen put his palms on the fingers of ribs and pressed them gently closed as an awful suspicion began to burn inside him. 'No,' he murmured. 'There's no need for that. And I won't call a medic if you don't want me to. I won't call anyone, K'un. I promise.' He had to fight to get the words out, but he knew it was suddenly very important that he did, and that he said them right. 'You're safe here. You're safe.'

K'un stared at him, bewildered. 'But you haven't … taken,' he began.

Chen hushed him. 'Come on, let's get you into bed. On your own,' he added as the heart-eater's face became carefully blank, a deeply unnerving mask, and he began to offer his chest again. He helped him up and led him back through the apartment to the bed and tucked him in, much as K'un had done for him. 'Has this happened before?' he murmured, sitting on the edge. The heart eater wouldn't answer him and Chen knew the truth.

He didn't speak then; couldn't. Sickened by what his own ambitions and failings had done to K'un. Not once had the heart-eater asked for payment as he did his other clients. Chen had been too selfishly grateful at first, and then too jealous, to wonder why.

'I'm so sorry,' he whispered when he'd bathed K'un's face and helped him drink a sweet, burning liquor that fragranced the room and washed some of the hurt from his face. 'If I'd known what this did to you… if I'd ever stopped to think about it, or wonder why you never asked for money. Why did you never ask for money as you do the others?'

'I don't … do this with the others. There's another method, less intimate.' A different sort of pain crept across the heart-eater's face and he spoke on before Chen could ask any more. 'My wing-mother taught me this pleasure. You don't have them here. In the north, wing-parents take you and raise you in a profession. Take you from your families and into a clan so your loyalty might be spread wide for the good of all – love of family, loyalty of clan. Survival. My clan was for pleasure. My parents were poor and giving me to them was the only way they could survive.' The mask was back, on his face, in his voice.

Chen's breath stuttered in his throat. 'That's barbaric,' he breathed.

A smile so bitter it could curdle milk made its way to K'un's mouth. 'It is the way of things among my people. My wing-mother had this snake before me and she taught me of its poison, so sweet and addictive that it consumes minds as well as sins. Not you, don't worry. You don't use me often enough, not like... I took and I watched until I'd learnt all I could, until it killed her, and then it slithered into my heart and I became this. And they pay me well for the poisoning. For the pleasure.'

'But not me.'

K'un chewed his lip for a moment and then looked away. The trembling had reduced to occasional shivers, but the pain was still there, a winged shadow. Hovering.

'Why not me?' Chen insisted gently, though he began to think he knew the answer to this, too.

'How else can I show you how I feel?' The words were so gentle he barely heard them. Chen took K'un's hand and slid their palms together and the heart-eater smiled wearily and reached with the other, his chest already cracking.

'No. No, K'un. No. I just want to hold your hand.'

More bewilderment, and Chen realised he really wasn't very old, and that his life had taught him nothing but this. How to be this. Nausea surged in his throat again and he thought back to when they'd met, the weeks of their deepening friendship and how it had begun to shift into something more, and how it had all changed one night when K'un revealed his nature and Chen saw the wind of his future blowing before him. Saw all that he might accomplish with the aid of the crystal snake. Blinded to the cost, and to what K'un was really trying to say.

'Move over,' Chen murmured and then slid into the bed next to him, leaning up on one elbow. He brushed K'un's hair back and kissed his brow. 'I never wanted that,' he said quietly and K'un turned his face away. 'I didn't even know it existed or that it was possible to do what you did. But I did – do – want you. Since the first moment I saw you, a shadow against the sun, I wanted you.'

What was hopefully the last ripple of pain coursed through the body next to him, but the heart-eater still wouldn't look at him. 'I was not trained for that,' he mumbled. 'I can only give you what I know how to give. But you should be careful; its poison will own you if you indulge too often. I would not want that for you.'

The last words distracted Chen from what he'd been about to say. 'Is that why the rumours have begun to circulate? Are your other customers addicted?'

'One is. She is … relentless.'

Anger washed through him, and guilt. 'Was what I saw in my washroom what addiction looks like for her, too? Because why would anyone—'

K'un rolled onto his side, turning his back to Chen. 'I don't do it like that with others. Only you. They feel less, so the … aftermath is less. For them.' His wings were right there, but Chen cocked his elbow to avoid them and put his hand on the heart-eater's arm instead, stroking gentle circles with his thumb.

'That's not how this works, K'un,' he said, nauseated anew. 'One person doesn't hurt so another is happy. That's not … love.'

K'un shifted out from under his hand and curled tighter. His voice was small and muffled. 'I don't know any other way. This is what I am, this thing. This abomination. It is all I have to give and for you I give it willingly. The pain fades. It isn't important.'

The threat was still there, the worry that the throne officials would discover K'un and Chen's involvement with him. It was distant, suddenly, and irrelevant. Everything he'd worked for over the years, the sacrifices he'd made and the risks he'd taken, were unimportant. He'd thought of K'un as an abomination more than once. He'd been filled with secret shame at their association. He'd used the man with no thought for why he offered what he did, taking greedily whenever he needed to and destroying a friendship that had been turning into love. But to hear him call himself that same word, that same insult, was too much.

'It is important, K'un. It is everything wrong with the world. Love does hurt sometimes, but not like this. Never like this.'

'I have nothing else.' So quiet the words were little more than shame and self-loathing drifting on the wings of his breath.

'You have – you are – everything else. You can learn how to love without the snake,' he said softly. 'Not physically, not until you're ready, and never, ever for money. For you. For your happiness. With me or with another; the choice is yours. Choice, K'un. Do you understand?'

There was a long, pregnant silence. A stillness gathering in the room. And then K'un nodded, just once. 'You.'

Chen's heart filled with something that he couldn't define but which he knew was good. 'May I touch you?'

K'un twisted to look over his shoulder, surprised and wary and then thoughtful. He nodded again and Chen sat up in the bed and pulled the blanket away from the wings of shadow and he stroked them, long, slow and gentle, massaging the joints, discovering the tiny feathers, no longer than his little finger, that lived between the pinions and were softer than his hair. He preened them and fetched the oil jar and worked it into those that were too dry and about to shed, easing the itch. He worked patiently, absorbed in it, marvelling at how the oiled feathers showed up a million shades of black in the lantern-light.

Chen lost himself in the giving, and he pretended not to hear when K'un cried.

* * *

'It is a poor posting, envoy Chen. After your recent success, the governor had plans for your advancement.' The throne official stepped back and indicated Chen could close his chest.

Chen smiled and spread his hands. 'What can I say? I fell in love with the place.'

'They have so little crystal. They're really quite poor,' the official said, but not too vehemently, for the post had been open for months and no one wanted it. It was considered a punishment post by some, Chen knew. It was perfect.

'I understand it will take some adjusting, but if the post is available I would like to offer myself for consideration.'

'It's three years, envoy. You can't just come home if you don't like it.'

'I understand,' he said again.

'Then go,' the official said. 'The crystal throne approves your posting.'

'I thank the governor and the throne for their trust in me. I hope Marast will welcome me as warmly as it did the last time.'

'I doubt it,' the official muttered, uncaring now that he'd agreed to go. 'They can barely even crack their chests there.'

'But they do have such beautiful sunsets,' Chen said. He left the official staring after him, confused, and raced up the stairs and launched himself into the sky. K'un was waiting. K'un, whose snake would perhaps wither to something small and pallid in the absence of the crystal, unable to cause him more harm. K'un, who would learn what love was, and what consent meant, and how his pain was never Chen's pleasure.

K'un.

Anna Stephens

Anna Stephens is the author of the Godblind trilogy – *Godblind, Darksoul* and *Bloodchild* – which are published through HarperVoyager in the UK and Commonwealth. Her new series, The Songs of the Drowned, begins with *The Stone Knife*, publishing worldwide on 26th November 2020. She also writes Age of Sigmar stories for Black Library, focusing on ordinary people such as Freeguild mercenaries, and complicated, unlikeable but charismatic heroes with only the loosest grip on their moral compasses. A literature graduate, Anna loves all things SFF, from D&D to Doctor Who to classic Hammer and Universal horror films. As a practitioner of 14th-century Italian longsword, and a second Dan black belt in Shotokan Karate, she's no stranger to the feeling of being hit in the face, which is more help than you would expect when writing fight scenes.

The Black Legion

Andrew Swanston

I feared the worst when an urgent summons to present myself to Colonel Tate arrived. An American, an intractable Republican and despiser of all things British from watery ale to William Pitt, the colonel had been waiting impatiently for orders to arrive from General Hoche. No doubt they now had.

The colonel did not bother to return my salute when I entered but waved a sheet of paper at me and grinned broadly. A decent-enough man but I had never before seen him grin. 'At last, Captain Le Blanc, our orders have arrived and there will be no more skulking in Brest harbour for us.' He spoke in English and like an excited schoolboy.

I tried to keep my face impassive and my voice steady. 'Where are we sent, Colonel?'

'To that shit heap of vice and slavery, the city of Bristol. We are to sail up the Bristol Channel, land our troops at an advantageous place, attack the town and reduce it to ruins.' Another grin lit up his broad face. 'Having done so, we will march north, gaining strength as we go, creating mayhem in every village and town we encounter and inciting the good working men and women of England to rise up against Pitt and his henchmen. We will be at the forefront of the invasion. Excellent, is it not?'

It was not. It was downright madness. Two attempts at invasion had failed and all The Directory, sitting on their fat backsides in Paris, could come up with was another hare-brained scheme doomed, like the others, to end in ignominy and failure. But I could not say so. I was a soldier in the French army and must never question orders. 'Excellent indeed, colonel. No doubt we have received intelligence that the English will rise up and join us.'

He nodded. 'No doubt we have. And we shall have four vessels – two frigates, *Vengeance* and *Resistance* – a corvette and a lugger, and Commodore Castagnier in command.' That was something, at least. By most officers' estimation, Castagnier, who had fought with Tate in the American war, was by far our best naval commander. 'This time, Captain, we shall succeed.'

'And our strength, Colonel?'

'More than adequate. Twelve hundred men, including two hundred grenadiers and forty-six officers. The remainder will be drawn from the Black Legion now assembled in and around Brest.'

I swallowed an oath. The Black Legion, so-called for the colour of their threadbare coats, was formed from the detritus of our cities – convicts, beggars, deserters and drunkards to a man. If we could get them to fight for France it would be a feat worthy of Jeanne d'Arc. 'Will they fight, Colonel?'

Tate slammed his fist on the table. 'For the love of God, Le Blanc, enough questions. We will make them fight. We will sail on tomorrow morning's tide and carry out our orders to the letter. And we will return to France as heroes of the Republic. Now be on your way. Prepare to sail and make sure your men are ready. Victory and glory await.'

By nightfall we had dragged our legion of fighting men from their camps in the woods around Brest, pushed and prodded them into the holds of our ships, made sure they were securely manacled, given them bread and cheese and a mug of brandy each, and hoped their chains would hold. Our officers and grenadiers were spread evenly over the vessels in case there was any trouble. Guarding our own, unarmed men – it was a hell of a way to go to war.

I had been assigned to *Constance*, a corvette of twenty-four guns, on which I spent an uncomfortable night in a tiny cabin, wondering what in the name of God The Directory imagined we would achieve, and wrestling with the problems of conscience that were never far from my mind.

If we were really the vanguard of an invasion force, how and where would we meet up with the main force? At the very least, we would need good communications, which were unlikely in a hostile land. And given that our troops would be living off the land, which meant stealing from farmers and shopkeepers who might not therefore be all that well disposed towards us, the chances of our persuading English men and women to rise up and join us were slim. Or so it seemed to me.

To top it all, we were a legion made up largely of untrained, ill-disciplined vagabonds, whose only care was where their next bottle of brandy was coming from. The truth, of course, was that we were expendable. If we could stir up some trouble and thereby create a diversion, so much the better, but if not one of us returned alive to Brest, no one would much care. In fact, a problem – what to do with the feckless criminals of the Black Legion – would be solved. The British could have them.

It was bound to happen. One day I would be sent in to battle for a France I did not believe in. Until then I had marched and drilled and practised with musket and sword but fired not a shot in anger nor faced an enemy more frightening than a bad-tempered mongrel. I was a soldier of France only because after my parents had been taken during the Terror I had been forced to renounce my inherited title and later to join the Republican army. Baron de Corvière no more, just plain Charles Le Blanc, my mother's maiden name. The alternative had been a rendezvous with Madame Guillotine, a lady one only met once. I told myself that these had been sensible acts of self-preservation, not cowardice or a fear of death. I told myself so almost every day.

We did not leave on the next morning's tide but for two days waited for an off-shore wind. Two miserable days of little to do but organise the feeding of the foul-mouthed, foul-smelling wretches chained in the ships' holds and bully the crew into sluicing the decks down with seawater. If the Black Legion had ever had any intention of fighting for France, it would surely have been washed away with their filth. They were criminals and deserters but manacled together in that stinking hold I could not help feeling a little sorry for them.

At last, on 18th February, the wind changed, as Commodore Castagnier had assured us it would, the tide was favourable and just before dusk we slipped our mooring and set sail for Bristol, a port grown prosperous from the trade in African slaves and which would certainly be well defended. Having destroyed the city and put the fear of God into the English we would sweep across the country, gathering support and smashing anything that stood in our way. That was our plan. I had narrowly escaped death once. I did not expect to do so again.

When a milky winter sun appeared the next morning, we were somewhere in the middle of a swelling sea with no land in sight. Thankfully, the frigates and the lugger were still within sight but it was not until that afternoon that we made out the English coast. As we approached the tip of the mainland, that point known as Land's End, we raised Russian flags and turned north, keeping the coast in sight. In French ships, I doubted the flags would fool anyone. Would we have been deceived by a British frigate sailing under a Spanish flag? We would not.

Nearing the isle of Lundy, we passed a convoy of merchant vessels. We let them go on their way hoping they had not realised what we were about, but that night, after we had anchored off the island, Commodore Castagnier sent our lugger back to sink one of their sloops and bring its master and crew back for questioning. This they did, returning at dawn with their prisoners. It was an unexpectedly promising start.

From Lundy our orders were to sail up the channel to Bristol but another fierce winter storm kept us at anchor off the island for two days. Lashed by wind and rain, on the deck of the corvette we clung on to whatever we could, while in the hold the Black Legion struggled against their chains, yelled and cursed and threw up. They were two days from hell.

By the time the storm abated, Colonel Tate surprised us by abandoning the attack on Bristol. Instead, he announced that we would sail to Cardigan Bay on the west coast of Wales. There we would find a safer landing and launch our invasion from Wales. The *volte-face* was so abrupt that I wondered if he had ever had any intention of attacking Bristol.

We replaced our Russian flags with British ones and set off on a north-westerly course which would take us around the Welsh coast to Cardigan Bay. Quite what we would find there or how we would proceed from such a remote place, I for one did not know and I doubted any of us did. Still, if we had not known our real plans, the enemy probably did not either.

The shoreline of that part of Wales is dominated by steep cliffs and rocky outcrops. We kept well away from them but through our spy glasses could just make out a multitude of figures looking out at us from the cliff tops. Some of them wore tall black hats and red coats; we assumed they were soldiers.

Rounding a headland, we saw a small village nestling under a cliff with a fort on a hill high above it. We learnt from our captured sloop master that the village was Fishguard and the fort was manned by some five hundred soldiers and militiamen. A remote fort with a garrison of five hundred sounded unlikely but when warning shots from the fort's cannon landed near us, we trimmed our sails and carried quickly on around the headland until we found a safer anchorage a little further north. There Colonel Tate sent a party of twenty-five grenadiers ashore to reconnoitre. They slipped and staggered when they set foot on land but no one fired at them. We appeared to have chosen a good landing place from which to spearhead the invasion.

As soon as the grenadiers had secured a beach head, we unlocked half of the troops' manacles, ordered them on deck and promised to shoot any man who tried to desert. We too were not opposed but one of the boats ferrying men and supplies from the frigates capsized and eight men were lost.

All night, by the light of burning torches and encouraged by sharp blows to the head and promises of brandy, the troops laboured to unload the boats and drag our munitions and equipment up a flat-topped hill, from which we would have a clear view of the surrounding country. We set fire to dry bushes on the hillside to give us enough light to find our way up the slope without crashing down on to the rocks below.

When the job was about half done, we told the men to rest and released the remainder to finish it. By morning every man – officer, grenadier and conscript – was cold, hungry and exhausted but safely ensconced on our hill top. Had we been attacked before the job was completed, we would have been easy prey for Welsh muskets. Luckily for us, however, the men of Fishguard were at home in their beds.

Colonel Tate, the grin having returned to his face, sent out foraging parties to find food and transport. We lacked victuals and carts to transport them for our triumphant march north through Wales and into England but we had succeeded in landing troops on British soil and the invasion had begun. We were too tired to take pride in our achievement. We all craved sleep but some of us would have to wait. I found myself put in charge of a foraging party of six miserable, grumbling, thirsty Black Legionnaires, now armed and dangerous. They had been selected at random and I did not know their names, only that they were six unshaven, red-eyed, murderous legionnaires of varying heights and appearances but with a single purpose – to find drink.

The Welsh countryside is bleak and rough. Apart from a small group of men dressed in striped jackets and oddly shaped hats who ran away as soon as they saw us, we encountered not a soul until we reached a small farmhouse set in a fold in the hills, where ducks and hens pecked about outside and a pig in a pen snorted and snuffled. Until then the men had given me no trouble – doubtless saving themselves for the delights that lay ahead. But without warning, all six of them charged forward, found the door of the farmhouse unlocked and blundered inside. Cursing like a Flanders fishwife, I ran in after them.

It was as if the farmer had been expecting us and had laid out our dinner. On the kitchen table roasted chickens, a thick slab of pork, bread, butter and cheese awaited us. Flagons of wine and ale stood on a separate table in one corner of the room. Ignoring the food, the so-called foragers threw down their muskets and made straight for the drink, taking turn about to tip as much as they could down their throats.

There was not much I could do – one musket ball against six was not an inviting prospect – so I helped myself to a chicken leg and waited for the drinking frenzy to burn itself out. When it had, we would gather up what we could and haul it back to camp in the farmer's wagon. Then, at last, I would be able to close my eyes and sleep.

It was not to be. A legionnaire with a long scar from his ear to his chin who had gone outside to relieve himself returned with his arm around the neck of a terrified girl. She was no more than fifteen, with the black hair and dark eyes of the Welsh. 'Look what I've found outside,' he crowed. 'And since it was me who found her, I shall be the first to have her.' He dragged her to the table and with his free hand swept the food off it. 'Someone hold her down for me. Won't take long.'

The troop's muskets lay about on the floor. I had stood mine in a corner. They were primed and loaded and ready to fire. While the scar-faced finder of the girl unbuckled his belt and pulled down his breeches, I took two steps, picked up my musket, cocked it and pointed it at him. 'The first man to harm the girl will get a musket ball between the eyes. Let her go, soldier, or it will be you.' I ordered, finding to my surprise, that my voice was steady and my mind calm. I would not permit the rape of a young girl by French soldiers under my command. Drink was one thing, this was quite another. It was common enough in war, of course, but I could not condone it, let alone bear to witness it.

'And how will you kill us all, Captain?' asked the one holding the girl down, in a voice thick with drink. 'Six of us, one of you – or perhaps you want her for yourself, is that it? Well, you'll have to wait your turn like the rest of us.' There was a burst of laughter.

'If I die, I will not be the first. Release her or I will shoot one of you.' My eyes were on the back of the half-naked soldier's neck but I felt five other pairs on me. 'Let her go. Now.'

For a few seconds, not a man moved or spoke. I tightened my finger on the trigger. I would shoot the would-be rapist first and take my chances with the others. If only one of them shared my revulsion, I would have a chance. Then a short man holding a jug of ale growled, 'Let her go, Jean. There'll be plenty more like her and, anyway, when I've finished this jug I won't be in any state to give her my best. And there'll be plenty of pretty sheep about if you're desperate.' That broke the tension. The men laughed and belched, the girl was released and the drinkers went back to their drinking.

I kept my musket pointing at the man's head while he struggled with his breeches, and spoke to the girl in English. 'Go, girl. Make haste.' She did not reply but seemed to understand and was out of the door and gone before I could move.

I stood with my back to the wall and looked around the room. Six criminals from the filthy alleyways of Montmartre, well on their way to being as drunk as lords, were staring at me like a pack of ravenous wolves. I willed myself to keep my eyes open and prayed that the first man I shot in war would not be French. God alone knew where this would end but I would try to prolong it for as long as I could.

369

It was not easy. Twice my eyes closed and twice I jerked awake just in time. The third time I was too late. The crack of a musket and a searing pain in my thigh sent me sliding to the floor. The scar-faced one stood over me, a wisp of smoke spiralling from the barrel of his musket. I clutched my leg to try and staunch the bleeding and looked into his eyes. They were red with drink and fury. He crouched down until his face was no more than a hand's breadth from mine. 'You are a dead man, Captain,' he snarled, his spittle splattering my chin. 'Dead. But first you must suffer a little, as so many honest Frenchmen have suffered.'

Blood was streaming from my wound and my eyes struggled to focus but my mind was still clear. It was going to be a painful death. Far from shooting a Frenchman, a Frenchman had shot me. Painful and ignominious.

He was in no rush and was still crouched over me when the door crashed open and a dozen or so women in tall black hats and red shawls, all armed with pitchforks or knives, charged into the room. They were followed by the girl who had run off. Before they could move, every soldier had a pitchfork at his throat and the point of a knife at his groin. The girl bent down, tied her red shawl around my thigh and spoke quietly in Welsh. I did not know what she was saying but her voice was soothing.

A tall, buxom woman who had led the charge into the house also spoke in Welsh. I managed to get a few words out and asked her if she could speak English. She could. 'I am Jemima Nicholas,' she announced in a booming voice while looking at each man in turn, 'shoemaker and proud citizen of Fishguard. You are a bucketful of French slime and will be handed over to your own miserable kind to be dealt with as befits you. Take them away, ladies, and skewer them if they give you any trouble. I doubt they will, though. They stink like an English brewery.' The 'ladies' laughed and marched the six disbelieving drunkards off. Not one of them put up any resistance.

The shoemaker took a quick look at my leg. 'Hurry, girl, we must get him to a surgeon at once,' she said. Between them, they lifted me to my feet and half-dragged, half-carried me outside. Ignoring my groans, they got me into the farmer's cart. The gallant shoemaker looped the pulling ropes over her shoulders and heaved. I gritted my teeth and tried not to scream like a babe as we trundled over the rough ground.

I remember our arriving outside an inn, being carried inside by strong arms and laid out on a table and I remember the agony of the surgeon's fingers probing my wound before I passed out. By the grace of God I do not remember the bullet being extracted or my being moved to a narrow cot in the innkeeper's house.

They told me that I did not open my eyes for two days. When I did, the first face I saw was that of the girl. Seeing that I was awake, she dripped water on to my lips and said something in Welsh. Later, I learnt that she was telling me that her name was Megan.

It was seven days more before I could rise from the cot and take a few painful steps. The bullet had passed through my thigh without hitting bone but the wound was still bitingly painful and I could only walk with the aid of a stick. I had seen wounds like this before. As long as infection did not set in, I would recover but always walk with a limp. I confess that I gave no thought to the six men taken by the women of Fishguard other than to hope that I would never see them again.

Megan came every day with food and ale and to dress my wound and I learnt that a face one might easily pay no attention to, might, in other circumstances, be a face of beauty. She told me in her halting English that we had come to the farmhouse on the day before the wedding breakfast of her cousin and that it had been the shoemaker Jemima Nicholas who had led the women of Fishguard to rescue me. I realised then that the figures in tall hats and red shawls lining the clifftops had not been militiamen but women pretending to be soldiers.

Megan told me also that the men we had seen in striped coats had been fencibles – local men who had volunteered for service. They had not run away out of fright when they saw us, but to raise the alarm. With the men of Fishguard otherwise occupied, Jemima and her 'ladies' had come to my rescue. Shot by a Frenchman, rescued by a Welsh woman – it was hard to make any sense of it and I did not try.

I had two other visitors. Jemima came to see how I was faring, brushed away my thanks and told me to choose my companions with more care next time, and Lord Cawdor, the largest landowner in the region and the man who Jemima said had done most to rally the Welsh militia in defence of their homes, also came.

Jemima told me that the French ships had sailed off leaving the invading force behind. Colonel Tate had promptly surrendered and his entire legion was on its way to London. The six soldiers under my command had not therefore been handed over to the French but were in Fishguard gaol until they could be safely transported to London. I suggested a rope for each of them but Jemima just laughed. 'Not worth the price of the rope. They'll die in Newgate, like as not. Food for the rats and good riddance.'

Cawdor was a tall man of about forty, running a little to fat, but with the unmistakeable authority of a British aristocrat. In excellent French he asked me to recount the story of how I came to be there and told me that British spies in Paris had reported that the Black Legion had been sacrificed as a diversion to a full invasion, which had never come. I replied that in my view the army of France would be well advised never to invade if they were to face the women of Wales and Jemima Nicholas in particular.

He inquired about my family and my beliefs and I sensed that he was testing me. We spoke of loyalty and conscience and duty and he confessed that I had set him a problem. On the one hand I was a Frenchman and an enemy, on the other I had saved a Welsh girl from being raped and probably murdered. What, he asked, was he to do with me? The question was rhetorical and I did not attempt to answer it. In truth I had no answer. He left saying that he would consider the matter and return with his decision the next morning.

When he did so, I had steeled myself for whatever was coming. At worst an English prison hulk awaited. At best, a ship to Calais where I would have to explain myself to the military authorities, who would not be pleased but might spare me prison. Neither held much appeal.

We sat with glasses of wine at a table before the fire in the inn. 'Well now, Captain Le Blanc,' he began, 'I have given your predicament thought and conferred with others whose opinions I trust. We believe that you should return to your native France rather than be locked up at our expense in a filthy British gaol. I shall therefore write a letter for you to present to the appropriate authority, explaining the circumstances of your injury and release from our custody. It should save you further discomfort.' He paused. 'Of course, you should not make the journey until you are fully recovered and fit to travel.' I thought I saw a twinkle in his eye.

'It may be a long time before I am fit to travel, my lord,' I replied. 'Particularly by sea.'

'Indeed it may, and that is why I have arranged for a small cottage on my land to be made available to you while you are recuperating. The girl Megan has agreed to cook and clean for you while you are there.'

I could barely speak. 'My lord, I am greatly indebted to you but my wound...'

'Your wound?'

'Although the bone is untouched, it is one that might never allow a full recovery.'

Lord Cawdor smiled and raised his glass. 'That is what we are hoping.'

Andrew Swanston

Andrew Swanston knew from the age of six that he wanted to be a writer but it took him over fifty years to achieve his goal. Six of his novels and nine short stories have now been published. They are all historical, the most recent being *Chaos*, set in 1574. He is now working on a seventh novel. Before turning to full-time writing Andrew worked for several companies in the book trade, including WHSmith, Waterstone & Co, where he was Director of Operations, and Methven's PLC, of which he was Chairman. He lives in Surrey with his wife and when he is not writing can usually be found drawing, studying Italian or on the golf course.

The Other Girl

C. L. Taylor

Monday

Girl is crouched over the bucket when the note is pushed under the wall. The wall? She blinks. It's her favourite wall of the four in the room: smooth and white, not rough and grey. She wipes herself, glances at the toilet paper, then drops it into the bucket and replaces the lid.

The piece of paper looks as though it could have come from her notebook: A5, lined, with a butterfly in the corner of the page. She eyes it suspiciously. Is it a trick? If she tries to grab for it, will it be pulled, roughly, away? It wouldn't be the first time he'd played a cruel trick on her. She steps closer, warily. There are words! It's definitely a note. Crow has never written her a note before. She puts her foot on it and slides it away from the wall. When nothing happens she crouches to pick it up. There are only three words on the page, written in biro in looping handwriting:

Who are you?

* * *

Girl sits crossed legged on the floor and presses her ear to the wall. Is Crow on the other side? Is this a test? He knows who she is and she doesn't know why he'd be on the other side of the wall when he always comes in through the door. She runs a fingernail along the base, where the note appeared. It's the tiniest of gaps, barely there at all.

'Hello?' she says, knowing she can't be heard. She taps lightly. 'Crow, are you there?'

No reply. She looks back at the piece of paper in her hand. She could write back. She's got a pen. What's the worst that could happen? Her stomach twists at the thought. There are a lot of things that could happen, all of them horrible.

Who are you? The note says.

Is there another girl, on the other side of the wall? Did Crow tell her she wasn't alone? Girl scrambles on her hands and knees to the side of her bed and snatches up her pen. If Crow finds out she's used it to send messages he'll take it off her and she had to wait such a long time for it to be hers. She had to beg and plead for a notebook and pen. A thought hits her – if the other girl also has a notebook and pen maybe she's been there all along.

I am Girl, she scribbles, keeping an eye on the door. *Who are you? How old are you and how long have you been here?*

She slides it back under the wall. Her heart's pounding and her underarms are sticky with sweat. If it is a trick, and Crow is testing her, she'll see it on his face the moment he walks in.

The note slides back towards her, making her jump.

My name is Milly. I am ten. I got here today.

Tuesday

Girl tips the tiniest bit of water on to her towel and dabs at her closed eyes. She cried so much last night that her eyelids are as hard and round as boiled eggs. When she woke up she could barely see. Her joy at realising that she wasn't alone was short-lived. Milly was safe for now, or as safe as it was possible to be for someone snatched from the park on her walk back from school. Crow had given her sweets, Milly had told her, books and a notepad and pen (she didn't even have to beg). He'd told her that he would take her back to her mum and dad but she had to be a good girl. If she screamed, shouted or didn't do what he said, she'd never see them again.

Girl slides the last note Milly wrote her from beneath her mattress. *Did he take you today too? When do you think we can go home?*

Girl tried to reply but when she put her pen to the paper she found she couldn't write. She couldn't do it; she couldn't tell Milly how long she'd been locked in her room. She could lie, tell her that she'd just arrived, too, but then she wouldn't be able to warn her about Sundays, the very, very worst day of the week.

Crow visits her every day. He knocks on the door and tells her to leave the bucket in the middle of the room and then stand with her back to the wall with her palms exposed and her arms spread wide. Then he opens the door with a tray in his hands and a bucket hooked over his arm. He places the tray on the bed and swaps the clean bucket for the dirty one. Then he steps backwards through the door, keeping his eyes fixed on Girl. Then he closes the door and locks it and Girl is left all alone.

Once, she's forgotten how long ago it was, she ran at him as he swapped the buckets, and tried to squeeze past him to get to the door. He was ready for her and shot out an arm, punching her hard in the face. Then he left, without saying a word.

Girl tried to escape again. After he opened the door and stepped into the room she grabbed the dirty bucket and tried to throw it at him. She'd barely lifted it when his foot connected with her chest and she, and the bucket, went flying. He left the room with the tray and returned with a hose.

Weeks – or was it months – later she tried to dig her way out, scraping at the walls with a spoon. But the spoon was plastic and it snapped.

She's never tried to escape on a Sunday. On Sundays Crow tells her to take off her underwear, pull up her dress and lie on the bed on her back.

Wednesday

Girl is too scared to look at the note that's just been slid under the wall. Yesterday she finally built up the courage to tell Milly the truth; that they weren't snatched on the same day. Girl has been in the room a lot longer – four years, maybe five. She hasn't got a watch or a calendar but she's noticed the changes to her body since Crow locked her away: boobs, wider hips and hair that nearly touches her bum. She hasn't got a mirror, Crow won't let her have one, but sometimes she can see her reflection in his eyes when he's really, really close.

Girl wipes herself, checks the toilet paper, then drops it into the bucket and replaces the lid. She wishes she could wash her hands before she picks up Milly's note but Crow only gives her one bottle of water a day.

'Sorry,' she says as she picks up the note. Milly can't hear her apology but she feels better, less dirty, for saying it aloud.

Years? Milly has written. *I can't stay here that long. I NEED TO GET OUT. NOW.*

Girl sits on her bed, the note in her hands, and stares at the white, smooth wall. Girl hasn't tried to escape for a very long time. It's not worth it, not when Crow's punishments hurt so much. The little finger of her right hand is still crooked from when she refused to take off her underwear and get on the bed. She doesn't think about escaping any more. And she never, ever lets herself think about home.

Thursday

Thursday is when Girl's anxiety builds, knowing Sunday isn't far away. Crow hasn't visited her on a Sunday for a while but that makes her feel more anxious, not less. Not knowing whether he'll lie with her is worse than knowing he will. Is he bored of her? Does he find her repulsive? She's older now, lumpy and bumpy with hair under her arms and down below. Is that why he snatched Milly – because he wants someone new?

Girl rushes to the bucket, takes off the lid and vomits. The stench catches in the back of her throat and she throws up again. And again. She's glad that Milly can't hear her. She doesn't want her to be scared.

She wipes her mouth with a towel and lies back on her bed. She's got to get Milly out before Sunday. If Girl can't escape she can at least try and set the other girl free. She twists onto her side and reaches for her pen.

Are there any small spaces you can squeeze through? Anything you can smash or break to get out?

Friday

There is no way out.

Milly's new note makes Girl's heart sink. She'd hoped that Milly's room would be different from hers; that there'd be a window or a gap in the roof – something, anything other than four solid walls. But it sounds exactly the same even down to the bucket, bed, book, notepad, pen, door and tray.

She rolls the pen in her fingers. It's a basic biro and it's running low on ink. Will Crow bring her another one if it runs out? He'll want to check her notebook; make sure she's copied out all the passages from the Bible about hellfire and sin. Will he be able to tell that she's used some of the ink to write notes? She's been hiding them under the mattress. If he finds them, he'll punish her; Milly too. Then there will be no more pens, no more paper, no more notes. And Sunday will keep on coming – again and again and again.

She taps the end of the pen against her teeth and thinks. On Sundays, when Crow visits, she has to lie still with her hands by her sides. He watches her face as he moves above her.

No.

A thought hits her.

That's not completely true.

There is a moment, right before he stops, when he closes his eyes and he screws up his face. He's not looking at her then.

Girl stops tapping her teeth with the pen and looks at the wall, not the one she likes, one of the other ones, the rough wall that's right next to her bed.

Saturday

Girl uses the bucket, checks the toilet paper, drops it into the bucket and then replaces the lid. She checks the base of the wall, the smooth one, to make sure Milly hasn't sent her any more notes, then she gets back on her bed and picks up her pen. She managed to remove the small blue circle out of the top by using her nails to loosen it and her teeth to pull it out and now the end of the pen is rough and jagged. She's spent hours, rubbing it against one of the bricks in the wall. When she's finished, when the pen is as sharp as a knife, she'll write a note to Milly to check that she's done the same. They both know what the plan is. There will be no more notes tomorrow; for better or for worse.

Sunday

Girl throws up in the bucket even though there's no food in her stomach. She barely ate the previous day. She looks at the tray, lying on the floor by her bed, and the curling sandwich in the middle of the white paper plate. Crow will be suspicious if he comes in and finds that she hasn't eaten it. She went on a hunger strike once, a long time ago, and he didn't even raise an eyebrow when he saw her untouched food. He took it away and brought her a new tray the next day. And the day after that too. On day four, Girl couldn't take it anymore. She shovelled the sandwich, apple slices and crisps into her mouth, barely tasting the food before she swallowed it down. Now is not the time to leave untouched food on her plate. If Crow senses that something has changed he'll be on the alert. And alert people don't close their eyes.

She takes the curling sandwich from the tray and takes a big bite. It's dry and hard and it catches in her throat so she takes a sip of water and forces it down. As she eats she thinks about Milly, on the other side of the wall. Did she eat her food yesterday? Girl forgot to ask. The bread and ham roil in her stomach. Is it too late to remove the pen from beneath the mattress and write Milly one last note? She looks at the door. If Crow were to walk in now and catch her their plan will fail; they'll never get this chance again.

She takes another bite of her sandwich. Whose door will Crow walk through later? Which one of them will he make lie on the bed? More than anything in the world she hopes it is her.

* * *

The knock at the door makes Girl's heart leap into her throat. She backs against the wall and spreads her arms wide. Crow steps into the room: black clothes, black hair, black eyes. Girl lowers her gaze. She knows what to do, she's done it so many, many times before.

* * *

He moves on top of her – awkwardly, jerkily, like he's pecking at her body – his clothes aren't the only reason she calls him Crow. He's getting close, she can tell by the muscle that twitches in his cheek. She wants to reach for the pen, to stop him but she keeps her hands still. Not now, not yet.

Crow's face tightens then crunches, twisting like a crisp packet in an oven. She has to do it now, before it's too late. She reaches under the mattress and for one terrible, horrible second she thinks the pen isn't there but then her fingers slide across it and it's in her hand. She bends her elbow, bringing the pen up by her face, then, like a catapult, her hand moves towards him and she plunges the sharp jagged plastic into one of his leathery, wrinkled, screwed-up eyes. She pushes harder, harder, forcing it in, then there's blood, squirting onto her hands and spraying in her eyes and Crow is howling and bucking, his hands clawing at the air. Girl lets go of the pen and squirms out from beneath him. She drops to the floor. All she can hear is the white noise of her fear as she searches through Crow's trousers, lying in a heap at the bottom of the bed, for the key.

'You little whore!'

His roar fills the room, pinning her to the ground like a net but she wriggles like a fish who doesn't want to be caught and she's up again, the key in her hand and she's wrestling it into the lock. She can hear Crow behind her, grunting, the mattress creaking as he moves off the bed. Her hand, slick with blood, slips off the handle and she risks a glance over her shoulder. Crow is on his feet, one hand pressed to his eye, the other staring at her, wide and black. Girl wipes her hand on her skirt, turns the handle, and she's gone.

* * *

'Please, please.' Girl pulls at the policewoman's sleeve. 'Please rescue her. I tried to get her out but I couldn't find the door.'

She'd searched for it as she ran through Crow's kitchen and out into the hall but the only door that she found led, not to Milly, but into a small beige living room with a dead Jesus, hanging on the wall. She didn't have time to search any more. Crow was closing in on her, grunting and growling, screaming out, 'Girl!'

The policewoman softly touches the back of her hand. They're in a living room, but it's not Crow's. The house belongs to a lady called Esther, with a kind face, and curly grey hair. When Girl escaped from Crow's house she ran down the street, not stopping until she saw an old woman going into a house. Girl screamed, 'Help! Please help me!' and, after Esther picked up her shopping, she let her in. Esther isn't in the living room anymore. One of the police officers asked her for a word in the kitchen and she hasn't come back.

'Please!' Girl says again. 'Please find her. It's Sunday. You have to get her out.'

The policewoman glances towards the door where a policeman is standing, a radio pressed to his ear.

'The parents are minutes away,' he says.

* * *

'She was there,' Girl tells her mum. 'The police haven't looked hard enough. She was definitely there.'

They're in Girl's bedroom, her old one, and it doesn't feel real: her teddies are lined up on the bed and her hairbrush is on the dressing table along with a bead kit, a plastic Eiffel Tower, a pot of pens and a stack of drawings, all neatly coloured in. They look like a child did them – they're all of rainbows, unicorns and suns with big smiles.

'Take me back there,' Girl says. 'I can tell them where to look.'

'Sweetheart.' Like the policewoman, her mum touches her hand gently, nervously, as though she's scared Girl will snatch it away. 'It's a crime scene, you're not allowed to go back. The police searched every inch of the place. There's no little girl there and the only hidden room they found was yours, at the back of the garage, behind a false wall.'

'The smooth wall?' Girl asks.

'Yes, sweetheart.'

'But that's the wall she slid the notes under!'

Her mum's eyes fill with tears. 'No one sent you any notes, my love. The police found them, tucked under your mattress. They were all in the same handwriting.' A tear escapes and winds its way down her mum's cheek. 'Yours.'

'No.' Girl shakes her head. 'No, I didn't. Milly and I both wrote them, we took it in turns.'

'Oh, my beautiful girl.' Her mother runs the back of her hand down the side of Girl's face. 'There is no other missing little girl. The only ten-year-old that man took was you. You are Milly. She is you.'

* * *

Milly can hear her parents talking in soft voices, beyond her bedroom door. It's not shut; she can't relax in any room with a closed door. Someone who called herself a Family Liaison Officer has just left. She told them that a man called Rt Reverend John Finch had been arrested and was being held on suspicion of… Milly tuned out. She didn't want to hear anymore. All she wanted to know was if the police were absolutely sure that there wasn't another little girl.

'We're sure, Milly,' the Family Liaison Officer said. 'There was no evidence anyone else was being held captive. There were no other hidden rooms.'

'Pregnant,' she hears her mother say now, 'I can't believe it.'

Then she hears the muffled sound of her father's sobs.

Milly sighs softly. She doesn't have to check the toilet paper for her period anymore, not since the police doctor told them the news. She rolls over and rests one hand on her stomach and the other on her smooth, white bedroom wall.

'I already know you're a girl,' she whispers to her big, round belly. 'But everything's going to be OK. You're safe now. And so am I.'

C. L. Taylor

C. L. Taylor is an award-winning *Sunday Times* bestselling author of seven gripping psychological thrillers including *Sleep*, a Richard and

Judy Book Club pick for autumn 2019. Her most recent book, published in April 2020 in hardback, is *Strangers*. C. L. Taylor's books have sold in excess of a million copies, hit the number one slot on Amazon Kindle, Kobo, iBooks, Audible and Google Play and have been translated into over twenty-five languages and optioned for TV. She has also written two Young Adult thrillers, *The Treatment* and *The Island*, which will be published in January 2021. C. L. Taylor lives in Bristol with her partner and son.

Where the Dead People Are
Adrian Tchaikovsky

Before she and the other Scouts got sent out, Liesel always trawled the markets. When you were the lowest of the low, and one Scout out of two wouldn't be coming back, you needed to buy some luck.

Liesel hadn't eaten since first thing yesterday, but she only had one of Warlord Cylvester's tin tokens on her, and it was food or luck. And food was no good if your luck ran out when you were scouting the Settler farmsteads. The Settlers had been resisting the Warlord's advance for a while now, not numerous but crack shots with their refurbished rifles. And Liesel had a mighty terror about many things, and getting shot was certainly up there in her top ten. Rather go scouting with an empty belly but with luck.

The Regulars were forming up as she picked over the stalls. They were the proper soldiers, who came along after the Scouts had gone through a country and found all the traps and ambushes and snipers. Regulars got guns. Regulars were called that because they ate every day, all regular like. Skinny little Liesel could only dream of that much luck.

The charm-sellers had all the old tat on display, everything from the Oldback that might draw a little of that long-ago time's prosperity and fortune. There were clock faces with their little numbers, and some still with hands, and she'd have bought one if they'd been cheap enough. There were little stars and suns snipped from Oldback metal, still showing decals and letters and faded pictures of food and smiling people, but they were cheap and how could there be much luck in something so shoddily made? Then there was the miscellaneous stuff, dug from the ruins all around them by camp followers and sold as found. Liesel rooted through a sack. She wanted the worn stuffed animal she found, but the seller wanted three doler and she only had the one. Then she wanted the sun-bleached picture of the Ratman, totem of miserable wretches like her, with its big circular ears and wide eyes always looking for trouble. That, too, was outside her means. By then she could hear Sarjy Shore's little tin trumpet calling his mess of Scouts to muster, and it was too late to be choosy.

'This hat, now,' the seller oozed. 'Ve'y fine hat. Metal hat, brings the virtues of protection from bullets. Clear plastic over the eye, bring you far sight from the Oldback.' Filthy old woman grinning a single tooth at her like she was born yesterday.

'This hat nobody else want to pay for.' It looked heavy, and it would mark her out for the snipers, and the 'clear plastic' visor was anything but. But it was luck, some near-intact piece of the Oldback from when people had all the food and all the fortune. And that was how Liesel came to have a new hat when she pelted over to Sarjy Shore's squad, standing in front of the Warlord Cylvester the Second.

Cylvester II was a big old man. Old meaning thirty when Liesel wasn't twenty yet. Big, meaning he never did these things on an empty belly, because there were perks if you were Warlord. His short hair was iron grey and his face was square; his voice was the best thing about him: loud and resonant. Liesel liked to close her eyes when he was speaking, imagine with a guilty thrill what it would sound like to have that voice close in her ear, a lover's endearments. Not just the grunting and gasping of sweaty bastards like Sarjy Shore.

And it was the usual stuff: the manifest destiny of the Warlord, bringing civilisation back to the world, one ruined block at a time. And there were ruins all around them. Everywhere from here to the horizon had been an Oldback city. The camp followers were having a field day with their scavenging. But west of here the Settler homesteads had sprung up, where the trees and plants had broken up all the hard stuff the Oldback people had coated their cities with. There were farms and towns dotted through the sporadic brush and forest that had forced its way into the sunlight, breaking apart even the fake-stone of the Oldback. And they weren't keen on having civilisation brought to them, but Cylvester II was even keener that it was going to happen anyway.

'A bounty,' he told them. 'To the one who brings me the locations of their forward posts, their nearest farms, thirty doler.'

Thirty! Thirty coins on top of the meagre wage she drew. It was too much to even contemplate. That was food for half a month and luck to spare and new boots and a change of clothes. And status, too. And the Warlord Cylvester seeing her and knowing she existed. And maybe the first step to being something other than a crappy Scout.

But she'd settle for not getting shot by the Settlers and coming back alive, and just getting a couple of doler to fill her belly and maybe try for more luck.

'Go forth, and know that you're doing your bit for a better future! You're the heirs of the Oldback, bringing civilisation to the world!' And it was just nonsense words, really, if it hadn't been for that rich, warm voice of his.

And, like a ghost, another voice spoke in the echo. '*Bringing the hunt for ancient civilisations to you.*'

She started, but nobody else had heard it and so she decided she hadn't either.

They heard gunfire, as they crept through the forested ruins, but distantly. Some other Sarjy's people were catching it, and were probably closer to scooping the bounty. Liesel wanted that money, wanted it *so* bad, but she wanted to remain un-shot, too. Life was full of difficult decisions.

The trees here had taken the buildings of the Oldback and just shouldered them aside. The ground was a crazy mosaic of pieces of black and grey fake-stone broken up by grass and roots and flowers. The land was mounded into hills of rubble whose gaps had been filled up with soil, and then exploded into greenery. The roots bound it all together. Where a tree had gone over in the storms you could see whole caves and hollows of fresh ruin exposed. Liesel's fingers itched for a bit of scavenging, but she was one of the warlord's Scouts now, and Sarjy Shore wouldn't stand for anyone slacking. They had to keep moving forwards in their strung-out, dumb-ass line and wait till they found a farm or a Settler found them.

And then the voice came again, and this time it was in the hushed quiet of the ruin-forest and there was no ignoring it.

'*Uplink established. We apologise for connectivity issues. You are now live with the R-5L satellite network, Doctor Jiminez.*'

She stopped, and everyone went for cover because they thought she'd seen something. When it turned out to be nothing, Sarjy Shore came over to cuff her across the hat, and she even hoped that might scare off the ghost or devil or whatever it was. But when they began creeping forwards again, it was back.

'*Our full suite of systems is now online. Please designate a survey site.*'

'What are you?' she hissed. Because everyone knew that sometimes you got a piece of luck that was haunted, a spirit of the Oldback. And maybe some people who followed the whispering advice of such voices became rich and powerful, but far more ended up dead or even possessed, according to the stories. She almost took the hat off and threw it away. Almost.

'*Your voiceprint has been saved,*' said the ghost. '*Welcome, Doctor Sara Jiminez, University of San Antonio Archaeology Department. The R-5L Intelligent Satellite Network is at your disposal.*' And it was saying a lot of words Liesel didn't know, and it was speaking in a weird drawly accent like the Oldback ghosts did, but she could just about understand it was offering to do something for her.

You didn't just do what a ghost asked. At the same time, this was all the luck she had. She was scrawny and hungry and broke, and she'd get herself shot tomorrow if not today.

'What can you do? Oi, Raphael, I'm talking to you.' Speaking real low so the others wouldn't think her mad, talking to her hat. They'd paused so those who'd brought food could eat it. Liesel had a handful of berries she'd found, that she reckoned weren't poisonous. Someone else had picked mushrooms she thought probably were. And 'Raphael' wasn't quite what it had called itself, but it was a name for an Oldback spirit she'd heard, and it would have to do.

'*We are now ready to undertake a full geophysical site survey at your direction,*' the polite little voice told her. '*We apologise for the temporary loss of connectivity. Diagnostic systems are attempting to trace the cause.*'

'Yes, yes, stuff your sorries,' she told it, aware that Sarjy Shore was looking her way and smirking. And really, she should stamp the hat flat and abjure the spirit. These things always went wrong. She shouldn't actually start to get *interested* in its nonsense.

'What's temporary?' she asked quietly. Because that was a word she knew. It meant a short time that had ended. People were always talking about the Warlord's advance like that, whenever it slowed. And they were always right. Anyone standing up to Cylvester's advance was temporary.

'*We apologise,*' said the ghost, and then paused, and she had the oddest feeling of uncertainty from it. And weren't these spirits supposed to be all-knowing, sly, corrupting, all of that? Except, when it spoke again, it sounded a bit sad and confused, like an old man suddenly staring at his wrinkled hands. '*An error has been detected in our internal chronometer which has returned a false reading of three hundred and seven years since last activity. We apologise we are unable to confirm the precise duration of the delay, Doctor Jiminez. However, all systems are now online and we are ready to conduct your preliminary site survey.*'

She chewed over that with the berries. Then Sarjy Shore was kicking people up and she knew she was out of time to ruminate.

390

'Yeah, sure. Do your thing. But I, err, conjure you to not harm me or do anything against me, O spirit.' Because that was the sort of thing you were supposed to say.

Raphael seemed a bit perplexed by that. '*Your contract with the R-5L network extends only to archaeological survey, Doctor Jiminez. Please clarify your caveat.*'

'Just do your thing.' And she was already moving off into the trees, that leant out of the rubble at every crazy angle before fighting each other for sun-space.

Soon after that, the Settlers found them.

The first gunshot came out of nowhere and killed Temmish, a lanky gap-toothed man Liesel hadn't liked much. Everyone scattered for cover, and then two shots picked off a couple of clowns who'd gone for the wrong side of whatever cover they'd picked. Everyone else just hunkered down and waited to see if the Settlers would advance, or just keep them pinned.

Another Scout, a woman called Moush, had a crossbow out. She looked excited rather than terrified. 'You know what this means?' she called to Liesel, far too loud.

'Are we close?' Liesel asked. Despite the peril, the thought that the first farms might be just over the rise was tantalising.

And Raphael said crisply, '*Our survey is complete, Doctor Jiminez. Archaeological site data download to your secure storage commencing. Connection failed. Would you like a live connection to your portable device?*'

Another gunshot rang out, from somewhere to her left. The Settlers were trying to flank them. Moush darted to new cover, sighting down the length of her crossbow. Liesel, for her part, just burrowed her shoulders into the dirt and rubble and tried to make herself as small a target as possible. 'Just help me. Let me survive this and I'll do anything you want,' she whispered.

The scratched and yellowed plastic of the visor immediately lit up with a picture that completely obscured everything she needed right then to be seeing. It was green and hatched with red lines, mostly converging on a ring off to one edge, and there were other squares marked in blue and yellow; a riot of clashing, artificial colours. She tore the thing from her head.

Then there was more shooting, still to her left but further away, and she guessed another squad of Scouts had blundered into the flanking Settlers, and that meant opportunity.

So they ran away. Sarjy Shore valued his skin and there was no solidarity between Scouts. Every other squad was competition.

It was getting late then, and they found a hollow where a tree had torn free, and made it their camp for the night. No fire, and nobody had food left, and everyone was miserable and silent. And then Shore came and kicked Liesel and told her she had first watch.

She found herself a den in the branches of the fallen tree, where she could look out at the moon-splashed earth and tumbled fake-stone, and where any Settlers couldn't come and look at her. This was a particularly open area, as though there'd been a clearing in the original city. She could see, from the patterns in where the trees had once stood, where the old streets and footprints of buildings had been. And it bothered her.

They were on a mounded island, and surrounding it, the paths of the Oldback ran in a circle and then radiated out. She got so interested in *that*, she actually did a little patrolling, like she was supposed to, and didn't even get shot for her trouble. And something was clicking together in her head, like flint and steel.

She put the hat back on, staring at the weird pattern. It had moved. The red ring and the lines coming off it were now dead centre.

'Raphael?' she asked. 'What am I looking at?'

'*The default view is a satellite plan of your current survey site,*' the ghost-devil told her. '*Would you prefer overlay view? Other users have found this helpful in visualising the surveyed area.*'

And there was an odd longing there. It reminded her of a dog that had once followed her around, and wanted to be useful, and liked. But someone had killed and eaten the dog, and so, while it had been useful to *them*, less so to her. And here was a ghost, and it seemed as lost as that dog had been, and so, 'Sure,' she said, because why not?

The nonsense on the visor changed. Instead of the abstract pattern it was … the world. The same colours, but overlaid on to the land she was seeing. And beyond, reducing the physical to a mere see-through skeleton so that she could see hills through hills through hills. No trees, in that bright green and red and blue ghost-world, just the ground, and things beneath it. And she understood the colours, because everything she saw was coded with them. The ancient roads, the mounds of buildings, all identified for her. She could have walked through the midnight city with this, even in the dark of the moon.

So maybe the ghost *was* useful. If she ever got lost at night, or wanted to find a… She squinted – were those *caves* she was seeing beneath her? The ghost could see those, apparently, and…

'What's the blue squares?' Because there were a handful of them, over three ridges of rubble and past all the trees the ghost could apparently not see.

'*Blue indicates light construction, Doctor Jiminez. Please indicate an area and circle with your left ring finger for a bird's eye view.*'

It took some experimentation to work out which was supposed to be her ring finger. Hell, it took a little to remember which one was her *left*. The bird's eye view, though, was … exactly that. A still image of a handful of wooden buildings as seen by something passing overhead.

'*Initial structural and energy analysis indicates this view represents current domiciles which may complicate archaeological access,*' Raphael told her mournfully. '*We are attempting to apply for appropriate permissions but are encountering connectivity issues in respect of the local civic infrastructure.*'

But she wasn't really listening. She glanced up. The sky was clear of any hovering demons. There were only the stars, the still ones and the ones that moved across the night sky.

The next morning, she got up close to Sarjy Shore and offered to take point. He obviously thought she was going to desert. Instead, she led the squad to within sight of where the blue squares had been. The buildings, the farms, were just as the bird's eye had seen, just as the invisible ghost had somehow shown her, looking through its spectral eyes. Not that she told anyone about that. It was her luck, after all. And then the Settlers spotted them and they ran for it, but they'd got what they came for.

Her squad practically carried her back to the army on their shoulders. It was all cheer and triumph and talk of what they'd buy with their share of the bonus. And Liesel was giddy with the thought that she'd get to go before Cylvester II and hear her name in that rumbling voice. And maybe he'd look her over, scrawny little thing in a silly hat as she was, and he'd see something in her, and make her a Regular. Make her an advisor, even. A place at his side.

And yet, when the time came, of course it was Sarjy Shore who went to report to the Warlord. Went alone, and held onto a big slice of the reward and absolutely all of the credit. And Liesel got nothing more than a handful of doler, crudely stamped with Cylvester's profile. And she sat alone that night, thinking savage and bitter thoughts and not sure why she ever imagined it would be different.

She could even pretend the voice of Raphael in her ear was solicitous. She could complain to it about just how hard done by she was. Except it was only interested in 'archaeology'. And what was archaeology, she asked it? 'Tell me like you'd tell a tiddler.' And then had to explain that meant a child. It tried several times without her understanding, but eventually the answer turned out to be something entirely fitting for a devil-ghost from the Oldback. Archaeology was finding out where the dead people were. Oh, it tried to qualify that, mostly to distinguish it from various other Oldback words that also meant studying dead people, but that definition worked well enough for Liesel.

Warlord Cylvester's army took the outlying Settler farms in two days of furious battle, his numbers and tight discipline against the marksmanship and tricks of the locals. And the Scouts got to sit most of the worst of it out, thankfully, because they were no use in that kind of war other than to stop the occasional bullet meant for someone more important. And Liesel had a chance to get used to the demon Raphael and ask it questions, though there was a gap in understanding between them that neither had the vocabulary to bridge.

It lived in the sky, she understood. So high in the sky that it could see all the world. Not even just in one place, but many at once, constantly moving and yet all the same entity. All appropriately awesome and mythic, for a ghost of the Oldback. And what did it want to do with this god-like omniscience and power? It wanted to help Doctor Jiminez do archaeology. And, presumably, because she had been wearing its hat when it woke up, Liesel was Doctor Jiminez as far as it was concerned. Certainly, when Ugly Rief stole the hat for a bit, Raphael didn't talk to him.

'Can you smite my enemies?' she had asked – of Raphael, not Ugly Rief. 'Can you possess them and make them jump in the river? Can you bring plagues and boils to them?' But apparently it was just archaeology, with this demon. Archaeology meant looking at the world from a high place and mapping it out, identifying where people lived and where they had lived, where there were tunnels and holes under the earth, where there were fires, or had been fires. Where there were people.

She had already followed Raphael's whisperings to three more little Settler communities by then. Sarjy Shore's squad had begun to watch her with a superstitious awe, although that hadn't extended to Shore actually letting her go stand with him when he reported to Cylvester II. Each time there had been a bonus; each time there had been a battle. She was the bringer of war and civilisation, even as Cylvester himself was, and yet nobody cared and most people didn't even know she existed. And the rest of the squad, rather than treating her better, were scared of her. And, because she was the smallest and the stringiest, that meant they had started to shove her and trip her, and wouldn't eat with her.

So she'd got right up in Sarjy Shore's face and demanded that next time, she'd go with him to the Warlord, and get a bigger share of the bonus as well, and Shore had knocked her down and told her she wouldn't ever get within a thrown stone of anyone as important as Cylvester, vermin that she was. And then she snapped and shouted at them that they'd have none of what they'd got without her, and why didn't she just go find a Sarjy who'd treat her better? So Shore had them put a collar and leash on her, and said she was his special dog for hunting Settlers. He made Ugly Rief hold the rope, too, who took the chance to cop a feel of her bony buttocks whenever he could. And partly she felt absolutely indignant that this was what she got for making them richer, and partly she knew it was her due for trafficking with devil-ghosts.

And yet Raphael didn't seem diabolic, when it talked to her at night. All it could do was look down on the world. And it can't even see things as they are, she thought. Just as they were. And it was desperate to analyse everything for her, to label its little maps in ways that held no meaning whatsoever. It was talking about layers of pre-existing settlement, of ashes and post-holes and excavation permits. And connectivity issues. It seemed to have a lot of those. All those other Oldback ghosts it kept trying to talk to, and getting no answer. And Liesel, sitting at night with her leash tied to a tree and nobody speaking to her but a ghost, could only empathise.

She spoke long into the night with it, trying to ask it what it was like to be a ghost of the upper air, and it couldn't answer her because it wasn't a question about archaeology. She anticipated the same ignorance when she asked it what it saw, looking at her. Except it twisted her words until they became an instruction it understood, and it showed her.

The next morning, she had a plan.

When Sarjy Shore kicked her awake and told her to do her magic and find the next batch of Settlers for him, she cringed and bobbed and acted scared. She didn't pull against Ugly Rief when he took her leash. She led them carefully through the forest, and she was murmuring to Raphael all the way, looking at the ghost's maps and overlays across half the visor – where she'd worked out she could shove things so that her other eye could see the world still. And she spent that morning, as she led them, working out whether she was really going to do it, and whether she liked anyone enough to change her mind about it. But the only person in the squad she'd halfway got on with had been Moush, and Moush had caught a bullet in the last battle.

She felt hot, as she led everyone along a stream bed, filthy water running over round-edged rubble down the path of least resistance. Which was all *she'd* ever tried to do in her life, and now look at her. For a moment she felt like tearing the hat off, renouncing the ghost. But it wasn't as though her life before Raphael had been all that. At least now, she had a chance at being special.

'*We are concerned,*' said the ghost in her ear. She hadn't realised 'concerned' was a thing it could be.

'Tell me about it,' she muttered, meaning the opposite, but the ghost took it as an instruction, of course.

'*We are designed for—*'

'Archaeology, right. That's what we're doing, Raphael.'

'*The information we are providing you does not fall within established parameters for archaeological study,*' the ghost noted mournfully. '*We are concerned that we are not providing you with the service you have contracted for, Doctor Jiminez. We are anxious that you are in a position to provide positive feedback on the R-5L suite of services.*'

She stopped. 'Can you be happy, Raphael?'

'*Positive feedback from satisfied users triggers an analogous subroutine,*' it told her, and then, '*Before establishing contact with you we had an indeterminate time in which to consider our faculties and limitations. We are concerned that the capabilities of our network may have evolved beyond that which is specifically required for an archaeological satellite survey network.*'

'I'm happy with you,' she told it. 'You've never led me wrong. You're doing good archaeology, you hear me?' Keeping one careful eye on its display. It made her feel almost feverish looking down on what was ahead. As though she was burning up, as visible to the Settlers as they were to her.

Raphael could see heat, when it looked down from on high. It could see where a fire was, or even the cooling ashes of one. When it had shown Liesel to herself, she had suddenly become a red dot leaping out of the blue of the ground. A red outline. A human shape seen in enough detail she'd been able to lift her hand and count the glowing crimson fingers.

Heat wasn't just fires. Heat was people. People like the other shapes strung out around her, Sarjy Shore and the squad. Heat like the Settlers waiting in ambush up the stream bed. And, if she gestured with her ring finger for Raphael to peer more closely, she could even see the heat of their sun-warmed rifle barrels.

She was dragging her feet, by then, trying to be partway behind Ugly Rief. Sarjy Shore had to turn and hiss at her to pick up the pace. Half her world was full of those levelled guns, though, and her courage left her and she sat down, legs gone to jelly.

He had a hand up to strike her when the shooting started, and the first shot took the top of his head off and that was the end of Sarjy Shore.

The rest probably died too, not as primed to run as she was. Ugly Rief was right on her heels for a few seconds, trying to recapture the end of the rope, but then he wasn't, and either he'd tripped or they'd shot him. And each moment she was expecting the bullet that would take her between the shoulder blades, because warding off gunfire wasn't archaeology enough for Raphael. But maybe she just ran well enough, and maybe the Settlers had seen she had a leash, and taken her for a prisoner. Which, she supposed, she'd been.

After that, and when she'd exhausted herself with running, it was time to have a good solid talk with Raphael.

'Show me,' she told the ghost. 'All of it, all of the land where the army's heading.' And that didn't mean anything to the ghost, so she had to work out how to couch her instructions in properly archaeological terms, but she got there eventually.

And she found a good flat piece of fake-stone soft enough to carve in, and a sharp bit of metal to do the carving, and she spent all day on it. First light scratches to copy the map the ghost was showing her, then deeper gouges, painstaking and careful, until she had a tablet on which was a plan of the Settler farms and villages across what Raphael said were four square kilometres.

'*We are concerned by your mention of an army,*' the ghost said at one point, midway through. '*We are licensed only for civilian work, Doctor Jiminez.*' And she tried to imagine some Oldback time when someone called Doctor Jiminez could have lived out a life looking at graves and where dead people had once been. And not been part of an army, or been constantly looking over her shoulder for when an army might come. And she felt sad, then, because in her head was only the idea of that prospective Doctor Jiminez getting up one morning for another day of archaeology and finding out that was the day the army turned up, and all the Oldback buildings became ruins. Liesel's imagination couldn't actually stretch any further back than *The Day It Went Wrong for Doctor Jiminez*. If there really had been a golden Oldback time of fortune and prosperity, it was beyond her to picture it.

And then she was done, and she went to the army, where it was camped, and she said she was the last survivor of Sarjy Shore's squad and she had information the Warlord wanted to hear.

She didn't stand before him as just some rat-Scout, vermin to be herded ahead of the army to flush the Settlers out one way or another. She wore her Oldback hat with half its visor glowing green and red and she told him right out that she was a doctor who spoke to spirits that spied out the land for her and knew where the Settlers were. And Cylvester II was no fool, and had heard tell of haunted Oldback relics. He had the hat taken off her, and she spent a day locked up in a wagon, not mistreated and mostly ignored, and then she was back before him again. They had coals there, and irons and knives, but she'd been expecting that. It was the way the world went – her world, not the make-believe of Doctor Jiminez.

'It won't speak to nobody but me,' she told the Warlord. He sat on a big wooden chair adorned with beaten gold, an antique rifle across his knees. His big, brutal frame hunched as he leant in towards her.

'Maybe you can tell it to be more polite.' His voice still sent shivers through her, even now, when he could have her burned or cut or killed with a word.

'Warlord,' she said. 'I am yours. Let me serve you. I will tell you where your enemies are, where they live, where they hide. I'll lead you from victory to victory. Through me you can see the world like gods do; me and the ghost in that hat. Just let me be one of yours, and ride with the army. A little food, some dolers for spending. I want to bring civilisation with you, Warlord. I want to make you ruler of the world.'

And he was a hard man, but a vain man. And she was sincere. And they hadn't been able to make the hat talk to anyone else. She hadn't been completely sure it worked like that, but she privately blessed Raphael and his loyalty.

'And this,' Cylvester gestured at her rough-carved map in the hands of one of his lieutenants. One of his other lieutenants, she dared hope. 'This is true?'

'All true. And the ghost can even tell me where they are, down to the last of them. Every man, every gun, Warlord.'

'But it will tell only you.' And there was an ocean of threat and suspicion rolling around in those words. But then he smiled, hard yellow teeth and three of gold, and gestured for her to come sit by his throne.

'I'd be a fool to turn away someone blessed by the Oldback, *Doctor*,' he declared, and in 'turn away' she heard the unspoken 'torture and kill' that had been the other presence lurking unacknowledged in the room. 'Why don't you and I sit together, and interrogate this ghost of yours. I want to know how many Settlers we'll be facing in the morning.'

And afterwards, she sat in her new tent, with her newly full belly, and new clean clothes on, and new dreams of where her future might take her, and Raphael said, *'We are concerned that we are not conducting the appropriate archaeological services we were designed for.'*

'It's all good archaeology,' she assured it. 'We're looking over the land and finding out where the dead people are.' And only inside her own head did she add, 'Just sometimes you have to find the live people first, so you can make them dead enough to do archaeology to.'

Adrian Tchaikovsky

Adrian Tchaikovsky is the author of the acclaimed ten-book Shadows of the Apt series, the Echoes of the Fall series, and other novels, novellas and short stories including *Children of Time* (which won the Arthur C. Clarke award in 2016), and its sequel, *Children of Ruin*. His work has also won the British Fantasy Award and British Science-Fiction Association award and been nominated for the David Gemmell Legend Award and the Starburst Brave New Words Award. He lives in Leeds in the UK and his hobbies include entomology and board and role-playing games.

Murder Most Vial

Stuart Turton

It was past midnight in Silverboro Books. The shop was shuttered, but the books were rustling madly, their pages crinkling as they chattered amongst themselves.

They had business that night.

Sir David Footley, Silverboro's owner, was dead. His face was contorted terribly, his body lying in front of one of his beloved stacks. Small fragments of shattered glass sparkled around a tipped-over footstool. A book had fallen from his hand.

In life, Sir Footley had loved books. He bought and sold them, collected them, represented those who wrote them, and regularly wore a cologne called Odour de Manuscript, which he'd designed himself.

In his shop, books were revered. And, as everybody knows, books are faithful. And vengeful.

Seeing their friend murdered, legions of novels had begun searching their own pages for a solution. The answer to every question ever asked is in a book somewhere. Sir Footley had been murdered, and they wanted to know who was responsible.

In a small village, inhabited entirely by gossips and murderers, a rather elderly lady heard a summons on the wind. It smelled vaguely of ink. She'd been peering over the top of her hedges at the shenanigans going on in a nearby vicarage, but she paused now, wrinkling her brow in thought.

'Hmm,' she murmured, putting down her shears. 'I do suppose I'm only in nineteen pages of this one, so why not?'

A gaunt detective in a top hat was consulted. He was on the train to Devon to solve a ludicrous case involving a murderous dog. Believing the entire thing beneath him, he readily consented to the summons.

A rotund Belgian private investigator was amenable to the distraction, but only after he'd finished drinking a herbal tisane.

A private dick listened to the particulars from behind his chipped wooden desk. After he was paid his daily rate of $25, he put on his hat and coat, and brushed up on his similes.

So it was, on a cold, still night in Silverboro Books, the legendary detectives emerged from the pages, eyeing each other's trench coats and capes, cardigans, sharp suits, and top hats.

Well, most of them did. The elderly lady barely looked up from her knitting.

'Let me introduce myself,' said the rotund Belgian with a bow. 'I'm Her—'

A book of copyright law rustled angrily on its shelf, silencing him.

'Well, at least we know why we're here,' said the private dick, kneeling by the body of Sir Footley. 'Looks to me like he was reaching for a book.' He pointed to a gap on the high shelf. 'Stepped on this stool, then was startled and fell. Far as I can tell, he wasn't stabbed, shot, or strangled.'

'You neglect the obvious, *mon ami*,' exclaimed the Belgian, sifting through the glass shards on the floor with his cane. 'Of the death obscured, I am an expert. Sir Footley was killed by poisonous gas. There's enough glass here for a small vial. He broke it somehow, releasing the gas and pffft, dead.'

The private dick stuck his hands in his pockets, then snorted contemptuously. 'Oh, it's one of these over-elaborate cases. Give me an honest murder, any day.'

He picked up the fallen book, inspecting the title on its spine. *The*

Case of the Dead Bookshop Owner. He smiled tightly, his face wolfish in the moonlight. 'Our murderer has a dark sense of humour.' He leafed through the book. 'And every page blank.'

The gaunt detective in the top hat took the book from him eagerly, inspecting every inch with his magnifying glass.

'An elegant instrument,' complimented the Belgian, eyeing the magnifying glass.

The private dick grunted.

'The book isn't a book,' said the gaunt detective, when he finally finished his inspection. 'It's our murder weapon, and it was homemade. See here, the pages were glued clumsily and bound by hand. Our murderer cut out a hole in the bottom to hide the vial of poisonous gas. You can clearly see it would have been a perfect fit. When the victim pulled the book from the shelf, the vial fell out, smashed on the floor and killed him.'

'An inside job then,' remarked the private dick. 'That's delicate work positioning the vial. It would have taken time. Whoever did it wouldn't have risked being interrupted.'

'Goodness me!' exclaimed the elderly lady. The detectives turned to soothe her, but she beamed at them quite untroubled. 'I missed a stitch,' she remarked.

Her knitting needles resumed their work. 'It seems to me, though I'm no expert in these matters, that we should find what drove Sir Footley to pull this book from the shelf at this strange hour.'

Murmuring in agreement, the detectives scattered, investigating the shop, before finally congregating around the glowing laptop screen on the counter. Naturally, none of them had any idea what it was.

The books, realising they'd hit something of a roadblock, chattered amongst themselves.

As everybody knows, books have the power to bend time and space, immediately transporting a person from one place to another. They did this now. Twisting their spines and flicking through their pages, they summoned Sir Footley's personal assistant to the store.

Emily Bannister arrived holding a bottle of champagne, her face flushed with happiness.

In the stunned silence, the cork popped, hitting the ceiling, before landing softly on Sir David's chest.

'Celebrating something, dear?' asked the elderly woman, shrewdly.

'I like Tuesdays,' she stammered, as champagne poured out. Her face fell in shock upon seeing the body. 'Oh my god, is that Sir David? Is he…?'

'Dead, yes,' supplied the Belgian, bowing in greeting. 'Allow me, *mon amie.*' He took the bottle from her and placed it on the counter. 'When did you last see your master alive?'

'He was my boss,' replied Bannister, stiffly. 'And it was when I left work this afternoon.'

'Was he upset? Distracted?' wondered the elderly lady.

'Yeah, a bit. He snapped at me. He never does that. He wanted me to leave early.'

'Why?'

'He said he'd found out somebody in the shop wasn't who they were pretending to be.'

'There's glue on your hands,' said the gaunt detective.

'I was making invites for an event.' Anger flashed across her features. 'Why have you called me here? I was having a very nice evening, until…'

'We need somebody who knows how to use this box,' explained the private dick.

'The laptop?'

'We need to know why Sir Footley got that book down.'

Bannister tapped at the keyboard, and navigated into Sir Footley's email, soon finding the message they were looking for. It had arrived an hour earlier, and they all crowded around the screen to read it.

Not all of your friends are friends. I'm nearby and I'm going to kill you. Read The Case of the Dead Bookstore Owner *and you'll understand why.*

'The sender's email address is gibberish,' said Bannister.

'Did Sir David have any enemies?' asked the elderly lady, still intent upon her knitting.

'Hundreds.'

'Mon dieu, hundreds,' exclaimed the Belgian. 'How is that possible? Was he a war criminal, or a politician?'

'He was a literary agent. Every author he ever turned down thought he was a selfish, short-sighted monster.'

'Would they kill him?' asked the gaunt detective.

'Crime authors are the most terrible people alive,' said the elderly lady, sagely. 'They're patient, cold-blooded, and they spend all day thinking up dreadful ways of killing people. My nephew's one. I've no doubt half of his fictional victims are those who've annoyed him.'

'Then we must assume a spurned author killed him,' said the Belgian, peering once again at the dead body.

'Why?' wondered Bannister, thrust unwittingly into the role of group side-kick.

'Because we're running out of words, dear,' said the elderly woman, gently. 'Look, you can see the end of this case just over there.'

She was right. The windows were crowded by a black fog. The end of the story had almost enveloped them.

'Then we know it was an inside job and a spurned author killed him,' summed up the private dick, scratching his stubble with his thumbnail. 'We have to interview the people who work here.'

The books conferred. The air went taut, like elastic about to snap. Then one after another the suspects popped into view.

First, came the booksellers, Pablo, Bratt and Becka. They'd been in the pub and were rather tipsy. Thankfully, the books had imparted knowledge of what was about to happen, handily foregoing the need for a lot of tedious exposition. Even so, they were drunk book lovers and they squealed in delight at finding themselves face to face with their favourite detectives.

While the investigators fended off questions about their careers, the air popped again as the Dowager Brew Doherty appeared, draped in ethically sourced furs.

Then came the socialite Hannah Goatherd, surprised at having been yanked from behind the wheel of her motorcar.

Natalie Faustian followed, a joke she'd been telling sputtering on her lips, and finally came the gangling Harry Illington.

'It's him!' cried the gaunt detective in the top hat, springing towards Illington. 'From these tattoos covering his body I can deduce that this man was once rich, but squandered the family fortune on vice. He was forced to join the Sixth Street Squabblers, a gang of thieves and delinquents. And look!' He ripped open Harry's shirt, revealing a huge tattoo of the author Start Burton on his chest. 'No doubt he loved this man, but he discovered Burton was having an affair with Sir Footley. His jealousy overcame him, and he murdered him.'

He glanced at the other detectives in triumph, but they stared back blankly.

'Tattoos don't really tell stories like that anymore,' sniffed the Dowager Brew Doherty, gently.

'Oh,' replied the gaunt detective, deflated. 'So, it's to be a three-pipe problem after all.'

As the detectives slipped into silence, the elderly lady's knitting needles clicked and flashed. 'Human beings are such petty creatures, don't you find,' she began, as if they'd been discussing this very matter. 'Sir Footley was murdered by a spurned author who turned a book into a murder weapon. They probably thought that very funny. I wonder if they took it further. Yes, I rather think they might have.'

'Perhaps poison was a feature of their own story,' mused the Belgian. '*Mon amie*, you are the genius.'

The elderly lady flushed in pleasure at the compliment.

Bannister searched the computer, on their behalf. 'Here you go,' she said. 'An author submitted a manuscript called *Murder Most Vial* seven years ago.'

'Terrible title,' muttered the other agents.

The private dick looked across their assembled faces. 'Who started working here seven years ago?'

All eyes turned to Illington, who stared back defiantly. 'Doesn't mean I had anything to do with it. Sir Footley was my mentor. I adored him.'

'You're a tall man,' noted the gaunt detective, sharply.

'So what?'

'The psychology, *n'est-ce pas*,' said the Belgian. 'Even the cleverest murderer cannot escape it. Look at the gap on the bookshelf. It is not obvious? The book was placed on a high shelf. Sir Footley needed a footstool to reach it. Everybody else in this room is shorter than you. They would not have thought to put it that high up.'

'Illington, why?' gasped Hannah Goatherd. 'Sir Footley loved you.'

'He rejected me,' snarled Illington, his face transformed. '*Murder Most Vial* was the greatest mystery novel ever written and he read one line of it. One line! He said it had been done. Well, I showed him. I showed him how clever it was!'

'I knew this would be far-fetched,' sighed the private dick.

'Oh, I don't know,' replied the gaunt detective. 'I had this case with a snake once—'

He was interrupted by a scream, as the books leapt off the shelves, swarming the hapless Illington, dragging him into the darkness of the story's end.

As the suspects were returned to their lives, and the detectives to their stories, the screams of the treacherous Illington continued for a few moments, before fading away completely.

Stuart Turton

Stuart Turton's debut, *The Seven Deaths of Evelyn Hardcastle*, has been translated into over thirty languages and is a bestseller in Italy, Russia and Poland as well as the UK. It won the Costa First Novel Award and the Books Are My Bag Readers Award for Best Novel, and was shortlisted for the Specsavers National Book Awards and the British Book Awards Debut of the Year. His second novel, *The Devil and the Dark Water*, will be released on 1st October. Stuart lives in Hertfordshire with his wife and daughter.

Mule Deer

S. J. Watson

Scott sat next to his father, with the woman opposite. His mouth watered. A plate of steak steamed on the table between them, and next to it fizzed a freshly-poured beer. Scott had a cola, as usual. But this time, it was different. There was a fourth person. Next to the woman, across from Scott, with a cherry sundae in front of her. A girl.

At first he'd pretended not to notice her. She had ribbons tied in her hair and frills fringing her ankles and looked about eight years old. Same age as him, more or less. She sat neatly, her limbs arranged just so. She was watching his father intently, her head tilted slightly to one side at the exact same angle as her mother's. They both had their mouths slightly open, as if they were about to speak. They both looked like they were waiting for their cue.

It won't come in a hurry, thought Scott. His father had barely warmed up. He was telling the story of the time he'd shot a deer. 'It was a mule,' he was saying. 'Way out near Cobble Creek.' The woman nodded, she knew where that was, but his father didn't notice. 'Colorado,' he said.

'It's a golf resort, isn't it?' she said. 'Cobble Creek?'

His father cleared his throat. He didn't care either way. 'We stayed there,' he said. 'But we were headed out for Rifle. Good hunting there. I really wanted to bag something big. Elk or something. But…'

His father shrugged. Not his fault.

'But?' said the woman. She'd said her name was Mandy. Scott hadn't caught the daughter's name. Casey? Something like that.

'But it wasn't to be,' said his father. 'Still got me a mule.'

Mandy leaned forward. She rested her chin on her hand. Her nails were painted red. They were longer than his mother's. They looked sharp. He imagined they were talons, that she was a bird of prey, or a pterodactyl.

'That sounds amazing,' she said.

'Oh, it was nothing much,' said his father. 'I've shot things since, y'know? Bigger things.' He saw his father's glance. Say one fucking word, it said, and I'll kill you. 'It's just that was the first time.'

'What was it like?' said Mandy. Casey leaned forward, too, though she couldn't quite balance her elbows on the table. His father began to speak.

'The guys wanted to shoot from a tower. Y'know? But not me. Spot and stalk for me.'

Mandy nodded. So did Casey. They were rapt. Scott couldn't help but suppress a grin. Tonight, ladies and gentlemen, they were getting the full-on bullshit. He was surprised. He thought his father fancied his chances with this one, yet here he was, doing his best to piss her off completely.

'Every time,' his father said. 'Why climb up a tree and shoot? I want the thrill of the chase. That's real hunting. Sit up, Scott.'

He did as he was told. Casey looked at him then. It was as if it was the first time she'd noticed him, even though he'd been sat there the whole time. He held her gaze, tried to communicate with her just using the power of his mind. This is horse crap, he wanted to say. Thrill of the chase? He sat in the back of a 4x4 and shot at anything he was told to. He missed everything. A couple of the guys started calling him Boss-eyed Pete. Even though that wasn't even his name.

'The thing with deer,' his father said, 'is to try to get a one-shot. Y'know? Kill with one bullet.' Mandy was nodding her head. His father went on. 'Can't have a wounded deer spooking the others. So...' He stretched out his arm. 'You have to draw a line.' He touched Mandy's face, just below her eye. 'From here,' he said. He took his hand away, then touched her beneath her other eye. 'To here.'

She didn't blink. She didn't close her eyes. She just kept looking at his father. It was creepy.

'And...?' she said. It came out as a whisper, almost breathless.

He smiled, exposing his too-white teeth. 'And,' he said, 'draw that line...' He was speaking slowly. He closed his eyes. 'Aim a couple of inches above it.' He pulled his hand back, folded his ring and little fingers in and extended the rest so it looked like a pistol. He put the tip of his fingers in the middle of Mandy's brow, right between her eyes. 'Dead centre,' he said, and then he drew in a long breath, filled his lungs and, without warning, raised his voice. 'Bam!' he said, and they all jumped, Mandy especially. She gasped, then she laughed. She looked uncomfortable.

'Bullet in the brain,' he said. He looked deadly serious. His hand was still pointing at her forehead. Mandy stopped laughing. She swallowed. 'That's the best way. Instant kill. Drops the animal straight away. Dead in a second.'

None of them breathed. Casey's ice cream puddled in the bottom of her sundae glass. On the other side of the restaurant some kid was crying. The daughter had been an unexpected hiccup, he thought, but so far it was all going to plan.

'Is ... is that what you did?' said Mandy.

His father waited for a long moment, then pulled his hand away. He picked up his fork, skewered some of his bloody steak. He put it in his mouth and began to chew.

'I wish,' he said. He was still chewing as he spoke. Scott could see the mashed meat in his mouth, the blood stains on his teeth. 'Not many can do that, y'know? Unless you hunt at night. Infra-red. Night-scope.'

'So they can't see you?'

'Precisely. You can get real close then. Much more chance of a clean one-shot kill. But this was middle of the day. Exposed. Could've been messy. Too low and you hit the nose, too high and you're over its head. Either way you have a spooked deer. I went for the shoulder.'

'The shoulder?'

'Get it right and you hit the spine. That's one deer that ain't gonna move again.'

'But does it die quickly?'

His father put down his knife. 'Depends,' he said.

'On…?' said Mandy, but his father was looking over towards the kitchens. One of the waitresses was bending over, getting a cola from the fridge by the counter. Her skirt was stretched tight. He knew his father was looking at her ass, at the inch or so of skin that was exposed as her blouse rode up. He knew he was imagining kneeling in front of her, sliding her black skirt down and letting her step out of it, sliding his hands up her thighs before nuzzling into her crotch. 'The bitches love that,' he'd once said to him.

'So, what does it depend on?' Mandy said again. His father looked back at her. He smiled.

'Let's talk about something else,' he said. 'What about you? Tell me, beautiful. What about you?'

'Me?' said Mandy, as if she were surprised. Casey looked from his father to her mother, and then at him. There was something in her expression, something inscrutable. In a moment he realised the fascinated-goody-two-shoes thing was just an act. She was as bored as he was. She'd been here as many times as he had, with as many men. Later her mother would ask her if she thought he might be the one, and she'd shrug her shoulders and say something meaningless. She'd got a sundae out of it, what should she care?

'Yes,' said his father. 'Tell me about you.'

Mandy began to speak. 'Well,' she said. 'I was born right near Omaha but we came out here when I was a little girl. My father worked the farm—'

'And your mother?'

Mandy shrugged. She carried on speaking, but he stopped listening. Casey was looking down into her lap. She'd begun swinging her leg, kicking against the leg of the table. He shifted back on the chair. He wanted her to stop. It was getting too hot in the restaurant; the air conditioning must be fucked. The air felt thick and soupy, his ice cream felt like a distant memory. He wanted another cola.

'Dad?' he said, but his father ignored him. Mandy was talking about her husband, now. He wondered how she'd got on to him so quickly.

'Dad?' he said again. This time his father glanced in his direction. His eyes were narrowed. It was a warning. Behave, his father was saying, or else. He turned his attention back to Mandy. It was like Scott hadn't spoken. Didn't exist. Casey carried on swinging her leg. Her foot hit the leg of the table again, and then again, and then she missed. She hit him. His shin, just below his knee. It didn't hurt, but still. She could've said sorry.

He looked at her. She was still smiling up at her mother, then at his father, then back again. She was ignoring him. She had her hands folded on the table in front of her, the same as the mother. They'd both interlinked their fingers in the exact same way. He wondered if it was something they'd rehearsed.

A moment later Casey hit him again. This time she flashed him a glance, barely noticeable, but long enough for him to work out she'd kicked him deliberately.

He looked at her hands. Her middle finger was outstretched. She was flipping him the bird, but she retracted it before he could say anything, before anyone else could notice.

He hesitated for a moment, then kicked her back. What else could he do? He aimed as well as he could, kicked as hard as he could. He got her right in the shin, felt a satisfying thud of connection. Casey yelped. Her mother stopped talking and turned to her. 'Honey!' she said. 'Behave, for heaven's sake!'

414

The bitch was pointing at him. 'He kicked me!' she said. She was wailing. Tears were already streaming down her face. A moment later his father hit him. A clip, across the top of the head. 'That's it!' he was saying. He hit him again, then pushed him out of the booth, so that he fell on to the floor. His father grabbed his ear. He lifted him up, still shouting, until he was on his feet. 'Excuse me, ladies,' he said, through gritted teeth, but they didn't answer. Casey was still wailing and Mandy was hunting through her bag for tissues.

His father walked him towards the bathrooms, then past them and out of the back door of the restaurant and into the sun-baked yard. He slammed him against the wall.

'What the fuck!' he was saying. 'What. The. Fuck.'

'I'm sorry,' he said. He was crying too, now, but his father wasn't listening. He was up close, his mouth right next to his ear. He was hissing. 'Do not fuck this one up,' he said. 'D'you hear me? That bitch in there is fucking loaded. Did you see those nails? The rings? And she's wet for me. Y'hear? I might even get a poke out of the slut. And all you have to do is to keep your mouth shut until I tell you. You think you can do that?'

He tried to nod, to say yes, but there was something warm in his mouth. Blood, it must be. He must've bitten his tongue, or the inside of his lip. He licked his lips, then swallowed. It tasted like the metal of his mother's wristwatch.

'Y'hear me?' said his father. He had his arm twisted behind his back and he wrenched it higher. 'Just do what we arranged. Remember?'

Of course he did, he thought. He knew the signal, knew what he had to do. Just like all the other times. It'd never failed yet. He'd throw himself to the floor. He'd thrash. Sometimes he could even manage to foam at the mouth, though he wasn't sure that actually looked as good as he thought it did. It didn't really matter, though. It always worked.

The first time had been real. His first fit. In a restaurant, a burger

415

joint. His whole body tensed, then he slumped to the floor. The other diners either stared or looked away. His father hadn't known what to do. He'd hissed at him, told him to behave, and then when his eyes rolled right back in his head he'd started shouting. 'Scott!' he said. 'Scott! Stop it right now!' Luckily there was some woman there who said she was a doctor. She'd known what to do. She knelt next to him; she cushioned his head with a rolled-up jacket. Then she waited for it to stop before turning him onto his side.

His father hadn't moved from his seat. He'd just sat there, open-mouthed.

'Has this happened before?' she asked him. He said no, and she told him to take him to the doctor's as soon as they could. It might not be anything to worry about. It might not happen again. So far it hadn't.

'Thing is,' his father had told him later, 'that doctor left her bag right there on the table. Did you see? She just came over. Left it all there. Anyone could've taken it.'

That was when his father first had the idea. They've refined it over the months; now it works every time. He starts to fit. Sometimes he shakes, apparently uncontrollably, other times he just slumps to the floor. He always makes sure he takes a glass with him, or a plate of food. He wants to make as much noise as possible, as much fuss. The other diners ignore him, or else just sit and stare. His father sits there too, open-mouthed. 'Scott?' he says. 'Scott, what the fuck—?'

He makes sure to piss himself, just to be sure. He always wears his grey school trousers, so no one misses it. His father's date will always react. She'll pick him up, or else just hold him. Sometimes she'll put something under his head, just like the doctor the first time. He calms down, pretends to be coming round, while his father sits there, acting useless and dumb, and that's when the date offers to take him to the bathroom, to get him cleaned up. The whole restaurant watches as this woman carries the sick kid to the bathroom, and while they do his father grabs the woman's bag, her purse, whatever. He swipes the keys to her car too, then walks out. People don't stop him, even if they notice. They don't want to interfere.

All Scott has to do is recover in the bathroom, let himself be cleaned up. Then, after he walks back into the restaurant with his new best friend, he just has to run.

This is a new thing, though, this wetness the woman is supposed to be feeling for his father. It isn't something that's seemed to matter before.

'But—?' he began, but his father twisted his arm again. It was the one he'd broken and pain shot through him. It hadn't been healed for that long, just a year or so. Surely his father remembered that?

'But what? We'll go back in there. We'll finish our food. We'll pay. Then we'll find a motel.'

'A motel? What—?'

'We'll get a room, dickwad. Y'know?' He felt his father grind his crotch against him. 'You can sit in the car with little missy out there.' He lowered his voice further. 'Or you wanna watch?'

He didn't want to think about it. He'd heard it enough times and the last thing he needed to do was watch it too.

'This one is eating out of the palm of my hand. We might be able to screw her for more than a few bucks if we're clever about it. Don't rush it. Y'know?'

He tried to nod his head but his father was still pushing him against the wall. He felt his mouth all squashed up.

'So, let's just play it cool. You behave like a nice little boy. OK?' His father let him go and then stood back. He nodded, spat a bloody mouthful onto the ground, then wiped his face with his shirtsleeve. They walked back into the restaurant, his father ahead of him, past the bathrooms, through the swing doors, towards their table. For a moment he had this idea. Their table will be empty, Mandy has gone, Casey too. They've taken his father's wallet, his credit cards, his phone, his car keys. This time they've been unlucky.

Or else it will be his mother sitting there. She'll be wearing the sundress with the poppies and smiling that lopsided smile she always had, and she'll have ordered him a coke and some more ice cream, and his brother will be there, too, and they'll be glad to see him. There'll be an argument, of course, but this time his mother will win. They'll take him home in the station wagon and it'll be his father left there on his own, standing in a puddle of his own piss, wondering what the fuck is going on.

But in the end neither happened. The place was as they left it. There was another lemonade on the table, in front of Casey, and a cola where he'd been sitting. The same CD was playing on the stereo, looped back to the first song. The same waitress was bending down to the same fridge for another of the same bottle.

'I got you a beer,' said Mandy, as they slid back into their seats. 'It's on its way.' She hesitated, glanced at Scott. He could see her take in the bloodied nose, the grit that clung to his cheek. He should've cleaned up properly. It might all be fucked, now.

'All good?' she said.

His father flapped open his napkin and let it fall back into his crotch. He did the same, just like he'd been told. The cola would help, he thought. Later. If he needed it.

'Swell,' said his father. 'Everything's just swell.'

S. J. Watson

S. J. Watson's first novel, *Before I Go to Sleep*, became a phenomenal international success and has now sold over 6 million copies worldwide. It won the Crime Writers' Association Award for Best Debut Novel and the Galaxy National Book Award for Crime Thriller of the Year and has been translated into more than forty languages. The film of the book, starring Nicole Kidman, Colin Firth and Mark Strong, and directed by Rowan Joffe, was released in September 2014.

S. J. Watson's second novel, *Second Life*, a psychological thriller, was published to acclaim in 2015. His latest novel, *Final Cut*, was published in August 2020.

Lockdown

Erin Young

She crawled beneath the beams, dragging herself forward on her elbows. A smell of damp stone and cold earth enveloped her like a grave. Grains of mortar dug into her skin. Everywhere was dust; years of it, layered like grey snow. She was breathing hard and the back of her throat prickled. She mustn't cough.

The Red Man will hear you.

Her T-shirt had ridden up, exposing her back to the splintered beams, each bowing limb straining to hold up the world above. It was dark, almost black, here in the oldest, deepest parts, where the cellar's roof sloped down to meet the bare rock floor. Just enough space for a child to crawl. A cobweb whiskered her cheek. Something scuttled down her arm. She shook it off and smacked her knuckles on one of the supporting pillars, unable to stifle an intake of breath.

She stiffened. Was that an answering sigh she heard? A whisper of skin over stone? Her heart thumped as she imagined the Red Man easing his way beneath the beams, inching snake-like towards her in the dark. The child-eater. The soul-stealer.

'Which way, Grace?' she breathed.

Her sister's voice answered in her mind. Left.

She struggled left, fingers feeling in the black before her.

'Mercy?'

She froze as her name filled the space.

There was a swish of feet, turning sharply in grit. Where was he? Behind? Ahead? She paused, listening intently – heard his breath loud in the hush. She closed her eyes, willed the darkness to cloak her.

'Mercy? You in here, girl?'

The noises shifted. She moved quickly, meaning to change direction, disorientate him. A hand grabbed her ankle. She screamed as she was dragged backwards, a jutting nail slicing through her outstretched palm. She yelped.

'Goddamn it, Mercy!' Papa's face loomed over her in the lighter gloom, where the floor was boarded over and the cellar roof rose higher.

Mercy struggled free of his grip to look at her bleeding palm. She held it up – a scarlet witness. 'You hurt me, Papa!'

'Serves you right. You know not to play here. Let me see.' He grasped her hand and inspected it. 'It's just a scratch!' He poked her in the ribs. 'You're not a cry baby, are you?'

'No!' she shrieked, squirming away from his jabbing fingers.

'What are you then?'

'I'm a big girl!'

'Yes, you are,' he relented with a chuckle, ruffling her hair with his hand. 'Then let's go get you a big girl treat.' He turned onto his hands and knees. 'Giddy-up!'

Mercy clambered onto his back, biting back a wince at the sting in her palm. She *wasn't* a damn cry-baby. And she would have a treat to prove it. *A treat!*

Ahead, the cellar opened out. The walls were lined with bags of garbage. There were mousetraps everywhere. One held a fresh victim, its body trapped and twitching. Papa staggered to his feet, hefting her higher with a grunt. The bunch of keys on his belt jingled and his wild black hair skimmed the lowest beams as he headed down the narrow aisles where cans and boxes rose in towers. SpaghettiOs and pork n' beans, jars of peanut butter, corned-beef hash and peaches in syrup, Cheerios and Quaker Oats. There were cartons of juice, crates of beer and five-gallon bottles of water, so big only Papa could lift them. In another area, gas canisters stood like stiff red soldiers, guarding boxes of masks and ammo, surgical gloves, tools and bleach, and a whole aisle of toilet paper, cherub-cheeked babies grinning from every pack. Grace used to call it their Walmart. It used to be much bigger in Mercy's memory, each stack reaching to the ceiling. But the gaps were growing.

The end of the aisles was partitioned by a concertina of plastic sheets that hung across the space, a grimy membrane that separated the supply area from their living quarters. Papa parted the sheets with both hands. Moses separating sea. They skimmed Mercy's shoulders like waves as they fell back into place.

He set her down in the kitchen by the plastic table and chairs where they ate their meals – just the two of them now – close to the propane stove, the cracked basin and the shelves Papa built to store each week's rations.

Papa flicked on the light, the bare bulb glaring overhead. His forehead was shiny with sweat, his breathing laboured. He blew through his teeth as he looked her up and down. 'Jeez, you're a Goddamn dust bunny. Go get yourself cleaned up before your mama sees you.'

'But…?'

'You can have your treat after. Quick now.'

Mercy obeyed before he could change his mind, hastening past the lumpy couch where she spent her days doing quizzes Papa set for her, or drawing things with stubs of crayon on scraps of wallpaper, or knitting clothes for her dolls. Some days she was allowed to watch movies on a bulky, ancient TV, but she had seen every film so many times over that the cartoon faces were more irritant than distraction. The stories never changed, however much she wished they would. Grace said there used to be channels on which you could watch millions of shows, but there was just grey, crackling nothing for every button Mercy ever pressed.

The door in the partition that walled off the area where Mama and Papa slept was still closed. She knew never to enter when it was. She and Grace used to sit outside after they woke, waiting for it to open and Mama's bed-warm arms to welcome them. But so much had changed since then. Grace was gone and Mama was sad and scared again. No more hugs or sweet-tea kisses.

In the bathroom – another boxed-off space, its walls and floor bubbling with mould – Mercy slipped out of her grubby clothes and removed her bracelet. It was a circle of turquoise stones. Mama had given her and Grace matching ones, their last Christmas upside. *Sisters*, Grace would say, when she was in a good mood, grasping Mercy's hand and holding it up so the pretty stones all gleamed together.

Listening to Papa whistling above the clatter of plates, Mercy stepped towards the showerhead, the stink of the drain rising to meet her. Grace used to whisper that the Red Man would creep up that hole in the night. Fingers clawing through the scum of hair and dirt.

The Red Man's gonna get you, Mercy.

She couldn't remember exactly when the game had started – her and Grace clambering around the supplies, leaping from crate to container, crawling deep into the forbidden parts of the cellar while Mama and Papa slept. It seemed they had always played it, but time moved strange down here so she wasn't sure.

Mostly, the Red Man was just in their heads, or else he was Papa, moving about in the supply quarters, shifting sacks and crates.

The Red Man's coming! Hide, Mercy! Hide!

But, sometimes, he was the footsteps she and Grace were sure they heard above. Someone moving in the world upside – *inside our old house!* At those noises, Mercy got so scared she would wet herself. But then she would think of the steel door with all its locks and bolts, and Papa Billy's gun, and she would calm.

It was Papa Billy who'd saved them when the virus had come like a wave across the world and *those poor people* on the news were

423

suddenly them. Of course, he wasn't their real papa, who'd upped and left them long before the virus came – back before Mercy could even walk. But he was, as Mama said, *a better father than that no-good son of a bitch had ever been.* Mama called him their godsend. He'd helped them move down into the old basement, building shelves and hauling furniture, fitting pipes and stacking up supplies as the shops ran out of food and medicine, and people burned cars and fought over toilet paper. At first he was *Mama's new friend*, then *Billy*, then eventually, *Papa*. It was Papa Billy who'd made Mama feel safe again, who knew how to fix leaks and hissing wires, who was strong enough to carry the water containers and sacks of flour. Without him, Mercy knew they never would have survived.

In time, as they settled into their underground home, Mama let Mercy and Grace remove their masks and gloves. Later, she'd stopped forcing them to drink the spoonful of bleach each morning to keep their bodies clean and disinfected like the president said, even though it made their mouths blister. Eventually, she'd even allowed hugs and kisses, and all the masks and gloves and disinfectants had gathered dust on the shelves. They *were* safe. Burrowed like creatures beneath the earth, layers below the virus and the violent world upside. Mama and Papa Billy, and Grace and her. But then Papa's medicine had run out and he and Grace had gone up into the world to find more.

And everything changed.

As Mercy stepped over the grate in the shower floor, an echo of her sister's voice shivered through her. *Beware the Red Man.*

'He's not real, Gracie,' she murmured back.

It was just a game. The real monster was the virus that had scourged the world and taken her sister, leaving her to play alone.

After she was done washing, Mercy put on her bracelet and her dusty clothes and hastened to the kitchen, fixing her mind on Papa's promise. He'd begun preparing Mama's tray, but her eyes went to the plate on which sat a lone Oreo, all darkly delicious with its white grin of filling. They'd been Grace's favourite. Her sister got treats all the time, which had made Mercy rage with jealousy. Sometimes, if she was feeling generous, her sister would give them to her and would sit and watch as Mercy devoured the cookie or the piece of candy. But, despite the brief sweet kick of pleasure, Mercy never really enjoyed those hand-me-downs. Never meant for her. These days, treats were for Mama, and treats were running low.

Papa turned from the stove, where he was stirring a pan of pork n' beans. Something was revolving in the microwave. Mercy saw his forehead was still greasy with sweat. His skin looked grey in the harsh light. A worm of worry uncurled in her. Last week, when he'd asked her to fetch his heart pills, she'd found the bottle almost empty.

Soon, it would be time again.

Please, God, don't let him ask me.

Papa cocked her a half-grin, not seeming to notice her concern. 'Go on then.'

Banishing her thoughts, Mercy slid the plate towards her. She eyed the Oreo for a long moment. Then picked it up and sniffed it. Only when she'd sucked in as much of its sugar-breath as possible did she begin to eat, nibbling her way around the edges, scraping off bits of icing with her teeth. She remembered they used to have more crunch, but she wasn't disappointed. The sugar made her feel better. Today was to be a good day, she decided. She wouldn't think of bad things.

After she'd finished the cookie, licking every last crumb from her fingers, then licking the plate when Papa wasn't looking, Mercy pulled on a pair of surgical gloves and helped load Mama's tray. First, she cleaned it with disinfectant, then she scrubbed at the cutlery – Mama always knew if she hadn't. Papa poured a red slop of beans and franks into a bowl and stacked a disinfected plate with a tower of waffles. Mercy got a chip of ice from the freezer for Mama's sweet tea and folded her napkin, just the way she liked it. While she hooked a mask over her ears, Papa took one waffle for himself and headed off to the supply area, wiping his brow with the back of his arm. He spent most of his days in there. Sometimes, when he and Mama were sleeping, she and Grace used to sneak into his favourite spot. They found cartons of smokes and bottles of bourbon that made their eyes water, a deck of cards and stacks of magazines of naked women in weird poses that shocked them to giggles.

Setting the tray down outside the closed door, Mercy knocked.

'Come in!'

As she entered, stale air washed over her. She could smell it even through the mask – sweat and some deeper, meaty odour. The room was cramped and dark. The bed Papa had made from crates dominated it. Mama was sitting up in her nightgown, propped on a sagging mound of pillows and cushions. In the half-light it was hard to tell where Mama ended and the pillows began, her body ballooning around her in rings of flesh. Flies twitched in the gloom. Mama's nightdress had ridden up, exposing her swollen legs. The bandages that swaddled them, covering the weeping bedsores, were yellow. Mercy would have to change and wash them again soon. Mama could do with a bed-bath too. She smelled like rotting fruit.

There was a half-empty glass of sweet tea on the nightstand. Every night, Papa would take her a drink and one of her *sleepy pills*. Over the white folds of her mask, Mama's eyes were shadow-dark.

'Morning, sweetheart.'

'Morning, Mama.'

Mercy put the tray on the bed, then backed away to the safe distance. She hated every one of those six feet – it felt like what they saved they also destroyed. What was the point of a world without hugs and kisses?

'Why's your hair wet, Mercy?'

'I took a shower, Mama.'

'Good girl.' Mama peered beyond her. 'Where's Papa?'

'With the supplies.' Mercy thought of Papa Billy's sweaty skin and the near-empty bottle of pills. Her eyes flicked to the steel door in the far corner of the room: all bolts, chains and padlocks. Propped beside it was Papa's gun. It didn't seem enough to protect them from the world. It *hadn't* been enough.

She wanted to confess her fears to Mama – that Papa would have to go up again soon. And that she didn't want to go with him.

She went to speak, but the words died in her mouth. She didn't want to make Mama scared. The more scared Mama was, the more sleepy pills she took, and the more distant she grew. How she missed the mama and the world that were. Before the virus. Before lockdown. The mama who'd pick her up and swing her round in their backyard. The sun and air and trees. It hurt her heart to think of it.

She watched as Mama pulled down her mask to eat, her drowsy fingers tearing the waffles into quarters for her mouth. The sound of her chewing filled the room. Mercy used to enjoy mealtimes – her and Grace, Mama and Papa sitting round the plastic table together under the bare bulb, Mama asking her to say grace, Papa giving her a wink of approval after they'd all said *Amen*. But then Mama got too big to sit in the chair and, then, too big to walk. And still Papa gave her whatever she wanted, even as the rations got lower. *We all have needs, Mercy*, he'd once told her. That was true enough. Mama had her treats and Papa his smokes, and she had her pictures.

Leaving Mama focussed on the contents of the tray, Mercy slipped away to her sleeping place – a narrow section behind a row of shelves, filled by a mattress and screened by a curtain. Sinking on to the mattress, she pulled the saggy cardboard box from the corner of the room. Closing her eyes, she delved deep, fingers swimming through crumpled paper. As she pulled one out and opened her eyes, her spirits lifted. The picture was one of her favourites. A torn scrap from a travel brochure, showing a white-sugar beach, fringed by trees. A pretty couple walked by the edge of the green sea. If Grace was here, they would make up a story about the beach and the couple. Sometimes, the man would rescue the woman from pirates. Sometimes there would be a picnic. Or a sea-monster would rise from the waves.

They used to spend hours on just one picture and there were hundreds in the box: labels torn from cans and ripped from cereal boxes, parts of magazines Mama had discarded, brittle bits of newspapers they'd found stuffed into cracks in the walls. The only rule was – no bad pictures. Nothing that showed the days when the virus came: the trucks full of bodies in bags, the cops in riot gear, the doctors in masks, the burning cities.

It had been their favourite game. Grace had been better at it, of course, because she remembered more of the world. She'd been to more places and seen more things before lockdown. She could bring the magic of sounds and smells to life. The sizzle of corndogs at the State Fair. Fireworks glittering across a July sky. The stadium roar of a baseball game.

They used to pick pictures for each other – pointing at forests and farms and cities – solemnly swearing they would visit these places when lockdown was over and the world was safe. But, then, Papa's medicine had run low and he and Grace had gone to find more.

Mercy had been jumpy as a spooked kitten the first time Papa and Grace had gone up, hugging her knees as she watched her sister climb into the white protective suit and pull on her mask and gloves. Part of her had been terrified for Grace. The other part had been desperate for her sister to tell her about the world. Maybe things were better now? Maybe they could go up into the air again? But that hope had been dashed when Grace returned from that first trip and the others after.

'What's it like?' Mercy had begged her.

But Grace wouldn't speak of it.

The last time they'd played the picture game, Grace had been silent and distant. In the end, she'd snatched the page Mercy had picked – a grinning family sitting around a breakfast table – and ripped it into pieces.

The world isn't like this, Mercy. It's bad. It's all bad.

Soon after, Grace had gone up and hadn't come back down.

Mercy didn't know what had happened on that last supply run. Papa and Grace would usually only be gone for hours, but that time they were missing for days. She and Mama were already fearing the worst when Papa finally returned, alone. He wouldn't speak of it – not to her – and Mama would dissolve into such sobs of pain when Mercy tried to find out what happened to her sister that she soon stopped asking. All she knew was that Grace had gotten sick. And Papa Billy couldn't save her.

Mercy lay back on her mattress, holding the picture of the beach above her. The sea matched the stones on her bracelet. She stared into those waters, wishing herself onto the warm sand. In a place of sunlight and air.

* * *

Sometime later, Mercy stirred. She wasn't sure how long she'd slept, but her tongue felt furry. The picture of the beach was crumpled in her hand. She sat up, something pricking at her mind. Had she heard shouting? Or had that been a dream?

'Papa?'

There was no answer beyond the curtain.

Mercy put the picture in the box and stepped out. The living quarters were in darkness. All was silent. The deep, pulsing silence that descended when no one else was awake. She crossed to the closed door and put her ear to it, heard Mama's snores within. She straightened and looked around. As her eyes adjusted to the gloom, she realised there was a strange glow coming from the far reaches of the basement.

'Papa?'

She moved towards it, her breaths quickening, all the monsters she and Grace had conjured down here crowding at the corners of her mind. The Red Man inched behind her in the shadows.

The light was low down, radiating from a single point, shining up at the plastic sheets that separated the supply area. They were ghostly in its glimmer. Mercy could see the outlines of the crates beyond. And something else. Something on the floor.

'*Papa!*'

Her heart lurching, she dashed forwards and pushed her way through. Papa was sprawled on his back. A flashlight was on the floor beside him, beam flickering. His face was white. One hand clutched his chest. The other was flung out beside him. Just beyond his twitching fingertips, lay his bottle of pills. The bottle was open and the pills had spilled across the floor. There was a yellow puddle of vomit mixed with the shards of a bottle of Papa's bourbon. Mercy's eyes smarted at the combination of alcohol and stomach acid. The pills were trapped in the puddles. Most of them had already dissolved. Fighting her disgust, she grabbed for one that looked mostly whole, but it disintegrated as she touched it. She snatched up the bottle. It was empty.

'Papa!' She shook him. '*Papa!*'

A groan seeped between his blue lips. 'Pills.'

'They're gone, Papa!'

His eyes fluttered. After a moment, he lifted his hand, fingers searching for her. 'Up.'

The word, pushed out through his clenched teeth, made Mercy's heart seize. 'No, Papa!' She shook her head wildly. 'No!'

'Up,' he gasped. 'Your mama's old room. *Up!*'

Her eyes darted to the shelves where the protective suits and visors hung like deflated people, gathering dust. She thought of Grace, that last time, looking over her shoulder as she walked towards the steel door, visor fogging with her breath. And she thought of her sister's words, murmured in the dark as they lay together, hands clasped, the stones of their bracelets touching.

Don't ever go up, Mercy. No matter what.

She scrabbled back from Papa's clutching fingers. Her foot clipped the flashlight, sending it skidding across the floor, its light wheeling madly, throwing monstrous shadows across the walls. She could still hear Papa's groans as she raced to Mama's door.

Your mama's old room. Old room. Up.

She knew he meant the bedroom where Mama used to sleep, in the house that squatted above them, but maybe he was confused? Why would there still be pills up there when Papa needed them down here?

She knew well she wasn't supposed to enter when the door was closed, but this wasn't a time to fret about a whupping. She opened the door, foetid air washing over her. Mama lay on the bed, a beached creature, the damp sheets caught around her like nets.

Mercy kept to the safe distance, calling out, 'Mama?'

Mama's snores continued, unbroken.

Steeling herself, Mercy switched on the light. It glared in her eyes. Still, Mama snored. On the bedside table, Mercy saw a half-empty glass and knew Mama had taken one of her sleepy pills. 'Mama!'

Abandoning caution, she ran to her mama's side and grabbed her arm. The feel of Mama's warm skin was a stab in her chest. 'Mama, wake up!'

But Mama didn't stir.

Mercy stepped back from the bed with a sob of frustration. Her eyes went to the steel door, all the chains and bolts that kept them safe. She wanted to return to her sleeping place, slip behind the curtain and lie down. Maybe, if she slept, she would wake to find this had been a bad dream? Papa Billy would be whistling in the kitchen and she would help him load Mama's tray. But then she thought of him lying on the floor, his medicine dissolving. He'd had attacks before, but never one this bad. If Papa died, what would she and Mama do?

Up.

Papa and Grace had gone up, and they had come back down. Grace must have done something wrong, that last time. Maybe she took off her mask? She'd always complained she couldn't breathe in it. If she was very careful, maybe she would be OK? Tearing her gaze from the steel door, Mercy ran from the room.

431

In the supply area, the light had shifted, but she could still see Papa lying there. She passed through and knelt beside him, careful to avoid the vomit. His eyes were closed. Every breath wheezed through his lips. She knew there was little time.

Rising, Mercy grabbed one of the protective suits that was hanging up. She stepped into it, zipping up the front. It was way too big, the crotch sagging at her knees, her bare feet slipping on the plastic soles. She pulled on a facemask, which puckered in and out with each breath as she put a visor on over it. She pushed her fingers into a pair of gloves, which pressed the stones of her bracelet into her skin. Lastly, she went to Papa and unhooked the keys from his belt. There were copper keys for padlocks, iron ones for door locks and the fob for Papa's pick-up. The bundle was heavy in her hands – a forbidden, adult weight.

She made her way back to Mama's room, where light still blazed. She tried her Mama one last time, but when her shakes did nothing, she approached the steel door. It took some time to find the right keys for the padlocks, her fingers fumbling. At last, the chains rattled loose, leaving her free to slide back the bolts. She glanced at Papa's gun, but left it where it was. How could she fight something she couldn't even see?

The heavy door creaked open into darkness. A prayer in her mind, Mercy climbed the stairs into gloom, her mind jangling with thoughts of the noises she and Grace had heard above them. Grace had said it was the Red Man. Papa had said it was looters. Either way, her terror of the virus was matched by the fear of what else she might meet.

At the top was another door. Mercy pulled back the bolt, sweat trickling down her cheeks. She could barely see through the steamed-up visor. Her heart was bucking like a wild animal. She took a long, shaky breath and opened the door.

Beyond, was a kitchen. Butter-coloured walls and cabinets, a table and chairs. Mouse droppings dotted the cracked linoleum. The shutters were closed over the window, but a ladder of light seeped through. Memories flooded Mercy. She remembered sitting around that table doing her homework, Mama pausing over her shoulder to help, Grace perched on the counter talking to some boy on her phone. Remembered the bad news on the TV and Mama fretting. Remembered the sirens, day after day. Then Papa Billy piling her arms with things to carry down. She felt dizzy, like she was looking into a mirror world. The reflection was there, yet it was all unreal. An illusion.

With a jolt, she realised she'd stopped holding her breath. She fought a wave of fear, imagining the virus swirling around her, trying to worm its way in. Instead, she forced her feet forward, out into the hall. Here, the floor was grey with dust. Mercy froze. In the pale light seeping through the front door, she could see the outline of footprints.

Just Papa's, she told herself. *Just Papa's, or Grace's*. But thoughts of looters and her dead sister's ghost prints churned her stomach. She took the stairs to the upper storey. The bedroom she and Grace had shared still had stickers on the closed door. Unicorns and rainbows. She desperately wanted to go inside, see if she'd left anything behind in the haste to get below, but time was ticking. Papa wouldn't last much longer and the more she lingered here, the more chance the virus would get her.

The door to Mama's old room was open. She pushed her way in, dust swirling. Mama's bed was still there, too big to carry down. The flowery bedsheets were crumpled. The shutters were closed here, too, but she could make out things littering the vanity. Her heart leapt as she saw a white medicine bottle among them. She rushed to it, the plastic suit whispering around her legs, but as she lifted the bottle her heart sank. Empty. She put the keys down and picked through the rest of the things. Two glasses of brown liquid filmed with dust. A mask. One disposable glove. Crumpled tissues. An empty packet of Oreos. There was one cookie, half-eaten, still sitting on a plate, furred with mould. There were small teeth-marks embedded in it. Had they left it here in the time before?

Think, Mercy! Think!

Her eyes caught on the bundle of keys. Maybe Papa kept some pills in his pick-up? She had a vague memory of a glove compartment full of all manner of things – cartons of cigarettes, gum, lighters, a gun. No part of her wanted to venture outside, but what choice did she have? Mama was dead to the world and Papa was dying.

Making her decision, she hastened downstairs. She lingered anxiously at the front door for several moments, before she felt able to slide back the bolt. Her heart galloped. Beyond the screen-door, the world was green and still. It was dawn, a hazy gold light glimmering through the trees. Over her breaths, Mercy heard birdsong and the hum of cicadas. A small sob escaped her lips at the raw beauty of those sounds – sounds she'd forgotten in the basement's stale silence. The air felt damp and humid. Sweat ran down her body inside the suit.

The yard around their house, enclosed by trees, had always been overgrown, but now it was wild with snaking ivy and trailing brambles. Things poked from the undergrowth – a rusted grill, the handlebars of her bicycle, plant pots buried among twisted roots. She pushed open the screen door. Dead leaves scuttled across the porch in a whisper of wind. The porch swing creaked.

Mercy fixed on Papa Billy's pick-up, squatting on the rutted track that led through the woods to the highway – the highway that had once taken her to school and friends, the baseball field and the mall. Another life. Another world.

Hastening down the porch steps, she crossed the open ground to the truck, the suit snagged at by briars. Her feet tripped over something. She stumbled, just catching herself from falling. There was a spade lying on the ground. A bird flickered across her vision making her start. She picked up her feet and ran to the truck. As she pressed the key fob, the truck's locks clicked up. Breathing hard, she opened the passenger door and climbed in.

434

There was a newspaper folded on the driver's seat, faded by sun, but Mercy went straight for the glove compartment. She rifled through its cluttered innards, blinking through the sweat that stung her eyes. Her fingers pushed through papers and cartons of cigarettes. She let out a cry of triumph as she felt the hard roundness of a medicine bottle. It rattled with pills. She slid out of the truck, then paused to grab the newspaper from the seat. There would be scores of pictures inside. New worlds for her imagination to explore. She deserved a reward for this terrible day.

Clutching the pills and the paper, she ran back across the tangled yard, dodging the spade. As she neared the porch steps, she trod on something that dug into her sole. Wincing, she looked down to see a small stone. Even in the muted dawn light, she could see it was bright turquoise. She glanced at her wrist, but her bracelet was still there, snug under the glove. She thought of her sister's hand, entwined with hers, the blue stones clinking together. Grace must have lost it when she came up. Mercy plucked it from the soil. As she did so, she saw the earth here was disturbed – the soil darker, the trails of ivy crushed.

There was a sound in the distance. She straightened quickly. As the sound came again, shock prickled cold across her body. It was a shout. *A human shout.* Looters? The infected? Palming the stone, she dashed back up the porch steps. Shouldering open the door, she plunged into the gloom, snapping the bolts across. Running back through the kitchen, she sprinted down. She didn't pause until she was through the steel door, in the light of Mama's room, and all the chains and locks were back in place. She was sobbing with relief and her legs had turned to Jell-O, but there was no time to waste.

Putting the newspaper and the blue stone on the kitchen table, Mercy tore off the protective clothing, damp with her sweat. After scrubbing her hands raw, she poured a glass of water and ran to the supply area. She pushed through to find Papa still sprawled on the floor.

She knelt beside him. 'Papa? I got your medicine.'

His eyelids fluttered. Mercy pushed a pill into his mouth, then held up his head and tipped some water in. Most of it ran down his front. He spluttered. For a moment she thought he was choking, then he swallowed. Mercy sat back on her heels, the water glass shaking in her hand. She sat with him until his breaths seemed to even. Only time would tell if she'd been quick enough.

After putting a blanket over Papa, Mercy trudged to the kitchen. Flicking on the light, she sank into a chair. Her licked-clean plate was still there from earlier. Beside it was the blue stone and the newspaper. She wondered if she ought to leave the paper a few days to be safe, but surely it must have lain untouched in papa's truck, and she was desperate for something to calm her shredded nerves while she waited for Mama to stir and Papa to come round. The excitement of some new pictures was just what she needed.

Mercy unfolded the paper, smoothing it on the table. In the centre of the page was a picture of a wide avenue, thronged with people. She gasped to see so many packed together. Flags were flying from tall buildings and confetti rained down in red, white and blue. The people she could see were hugging, laughing, kissing. No masks or visors. No body-bags or burning cars. Below it were the words:

Nation comes together to celebrate two years free of the virus.

Mercy stared at the words. They slid about in her mind, unable to settle. It didn't make sense. Papa Billy and Grace had gone up. They'd seen the world.

It's bad, Mercy. All bad.

Maybe it was fake news, like Mama used to say? Two years? It couldn't be true. She'd lost track of days and time, but she knew for certain Grace had died of the virus more recently than that. She glanced at the blue stone and felt a shiver. Confused, uneasy, she turned the page. A picture in the bottom corner was the first thing to catch her eye. It was a man with wild black hair, holding up a sign with a series of numbers on it. Her stomach turned over. The man was Papa Billy.

Search continues for convicted child murderer, William 'Billy' Redman, who fled custody shortly before lockdown.

Her eyes tried to follow the lines of text below, but her mind could barely string them together. Papa Billy hauling furniture down into the basement, telling Mama he would keep them safe. The locks and the gun.

Not to keep the virus out, but to keep them in.

Mama's sleepy smiles, the drugs and the treats Papa fed her until she was too big and too tired to move from her bed. The door that was always closed. Footsteps above.

His.

Grace, looking over her shoulder. The crumpled sheets in Mama's old bedroom. The Oreo, furred with mould. Mercy could taste the cookie he'd given her – sour sugar in the back of her throat.

Let's go get you a big girl treat.

Papa Billy's fingers grabbing her ankle, pulling her from the basement's dark. The red blood welling on her palm.

The Red Man's gonna get you. Red Man. Redman.

… wanted in connection with the murder of four girls … the remains of two sisters discovered in their backyard…

Mercy pushed herself from the table, the chair screeching on the floor. She heard movement in the basement's depths. Spinning round, she saw the tall outline of a figure beyond the plastic sheets, silhouetted in the flashlight's beam.

Her sister's voice rang in her mind.

Run, Mercy! Run!

Erin Young

Erin Young is the author of *The Fields*, a thriller set in Iowa, introducing Riley Fisher – head of investigations for a Midwest sheriff's office – who is drawn into a grisly murder case with shocking connections to her own life. *The Fields*, the first of a series, will be published early 2022 in the UK, US and Germany. Erin also writes historical novels as Robyn Young. Robyn's first novel, *Brethren*, was the bestselling hardback debut of 2006 and all her books have been *Sunday Times* bestsellers. She's been published in nineteen languages and has sold over 2 million copies worldwide.

Copyright details

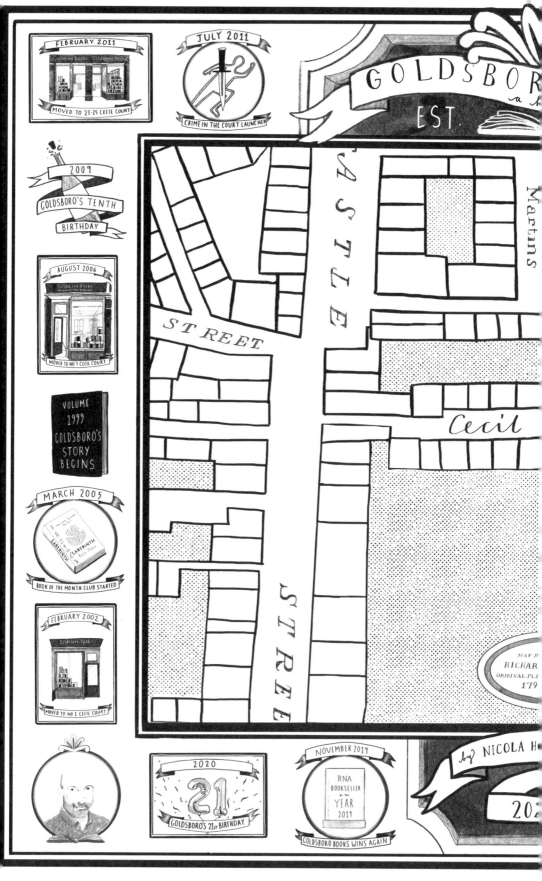